Praise for *The Promise*

"Filled with warmth and emotion . . . *The Promise* is a wonderful book for any lover of historical fiction. . . . Cuddle up in a chair and simply enjoy . . . don't miss it."
—*New York Times* bestselling author Heather Graham

Praise for May McGoldrick's *Highland Treasure Trilogy*

The Dreamer

"An enchanting tale not to be missed."
—*The Philadelphia Inquirer*

"Delightful, fast-paced . . . May McGoldrick has done it again . . . a tantalizing treat." —*Romantic Times*

The Enchantress

"The romance is tender, and the narrative is enhanced by strong characters." —*Publishers Weekly*

"Filled with romance—pure, sheer romance. This is a relationship book that will enchant those of us who just want a wonderful love story and nothing more."
—*Romantic Times*

continued . . .

More praise for May McGoldrick's breathtaking novels

"Fast-paced, emotionally charged . . . rich in historical detail, sizzling with sensuality." —*Romantic Times*

"Impressive . . . A splendid Scottish tale, filled with humor and suspense." —Arnette Lamb

"Brilliant . . . A fast-paced, action-packed historical romance brimming with insight into the 16th century Scottish-English conflict." —*Affaire de Coeur*

The Rebel

May McGoldrick

A SIGNET BOOK

SIGNET
Published by New American Library, a division of
Penguin Putnam Inc., 375 Hudson Street,
New York, New York 10014, U.S.A.
Penguin Books Ltd, 80 Strand,
London WC2R 0RL, England
Penguin Books Australia Ltd, Ringwood,
Victoria, Australia
Penguin Books Canada Ltd, 10 Alcorn Avenue,
Toronto, Ontario, Canada M4V 3B2
Penguin Books (N.Z.) Ltd, 182–190 Wairau Road,
Auckland 10, New Zealand

Penguin Books Ltd, Registered Offices:
Harmondsworth, Middlesex, England

First published by Signet, an imprint of New American Library,
a division of Penguin Putnam Inc.

First Printing, July 2002
10 9 8 7 6 5 4 3 2 1

Ⓢ REGISTERED TRADEMARK—MARCA REGISTRADA

Printed in the United States of America

PUBLISHER'S NOTE
This is a work of fiction. Names, characters, places, and incidents either
are the product of the author's imagination or are used fictitiously,
and any resemblance to actual persons, living or dead, business
establishments, events, or locales is entirely coincidental.

For Carol Palermo
Friend, Motivator, Scheduler, and Promoter
Extraordinaire

Chapter 1

London
December 1770

The snow lay like white icing over the stately plane trees and the walkways of Berkeley Square. Dinner guests, bundled in fine woolen cloaks and mantles of fur, scarcely spared the picturesque scene a look, though, as they hurried from the warmth of Lord and Lady Stanmore's doorway to their waiting carriages. Across the square, a wind swept up from the river, raising crystalline wisps from the barren tree branches, and flakes of snow curled and glistened in the light that poured from the windows of the magnificent town house. Soon, all but one of the carriages had rolled away into the darkness of the city, the sounds of horses and drivers and wheels on paving stones muffled by the fallen snow.

Inside the brightly lit foyer of the house, Sir Nicholas Spencer accepted his gloves and overcoat from a doorman and turned to bid a final farewell to his host and hostess.

"Spending Christmas *alone!*" Rebecca chided gently. "Please, Nicholas, you *must* come with us to Solgrave for the holiday."

"And intrude on your first Christmas together?" Nicholas shook his head with a smile. "This first holiday is for you—for your family. I wouldn't impose on that for the world."

Rebecca left her husband's side and reached for Nicholas's hand. "You are not intruding. My heavens, that's

what friends are for. When I think of all the years that
James and I were alone in Philadelphia! If it weren't for
the hospitality of our friends—especially at the holidays—how lonely we would have been!"

Nicholas brought the young woman's hand to his lips.
"Your kindness is touching, Rebecca, and you know how
hopeless I am about denying you anything. But I've
spent more than my fair share of holidays with that beast
you call your husband. Besides, I understand you have
some rather joyous news that you'll be wanting to share
with young James . . ."

The prettiest of blushes colored Lady Stanmore's
cheeks, and she glanced back at her husband.

"I am slightly better at keeping state secrets, my
love." Stanmore reached out and took her tightly into
his embrace.

Nicholas stood and watched as his friends slipped into
a world that included only the two of them. The bond
that linked their hearts and their souls was so pronounced, so obvious . . . and Nicholas frowned at the
unwanted ambivalence pulling at his own heart. As
happy as he was for them, he could feel something else
squirming about inside of him.

He looked away, forcing the frown from his face. Only
a fool, he told himself, would be envious of a life that
he has been avoiding like the plague.

He already had his overcoat on and was pulling on
his gloves when the two became aware of him again.
Nicholas couldn't help but notice the protective touch of
Stanmore's hand on Rebecca's waist, the intimate en-
twining of her fingers with his.

"Come anyway." Stanmore spoke this time. "Come
after Christmas, if you must wait. You know my family
likes to have you with us . . . though God only knows
why. Seriously, though, I know James will be anxious to
tell you about his term at Eton, and Mrs. Trent will love
to fuss over you."

Nicholas nodded. "I'll do that. That is, if my mother
and sister don't follow through with their threat of coming across from Brussels for a visit. From the tone of
my mother's most recent letter, the brat Frances has become too much for her to handle alone. The latest threat

is to leave her in England so that she can finish her schooling here."

"Well, that is very exciting news," Rebecca chimed in.

"Not for me." Nicholas shook his head and took his wide-brimmed hat of soft felt from the doorman. "I know nothing about how to deal with sixteen-year-old children who talk incessantly, without the least semblance of reason . . . and still think themselves mature beyond measure."

"There is a season for everything," Stanmore countered as he and his wife followed Nicholas toward the door. "It is all part of the great scheme of life. Marriage. Children. Moving the focus of our attention from ourselves to those we love. As Garrick said so eloquently at Drury Lane the other night, 'Now is the winter of our discontent made glorious summer.' "

Any other time and Nicholas might have made some lighthearted retort about humpbacked, wife-murdering kings; but as he looked at Rebecca and Stanmore, the words knotted in his throat. Somehow, even the words "happy and carefree bachelor" seemed difficult to conjure at the moment.

Nicholas leaned down and placed a kiss on Rebecca's cheek. "Merry Christmas."

Outside, the snow was coming down harder, the wind picking up in earnest. Nicholas pressed his hat onto his head and gave a final wave to his friends from the street. As the door closed against the weather, though, he found himself still standing and staring—considering for a moment the events that had brought such happiness to that house. He finally roused himself and turned to his groom.

"Go on home, Jack, and get warm. I believe I'll walk from here."

A gust of wind whipped at the capes of Nicholas's overcoat, and the groom moved on as he was ordered.

The baronet turned up the collar of his overcoat and walked past the fashionable houses lining the square. The handsome windows were still lit in many, in spite of the lateness of the evening. It was the season for entertaining. A solitary leaf danced along the snow-covered street, pressed forward by a gust before being caught in a carriage track. The chill wind burned the skin of his exposed face, reminding him of the warm fire in the Stanmores' library. The image of his friends in the foyer kept pressing into Nicholas's thoughts.

The improvement in Stanmore was so marked. For all the years since his first wife had left him without a word—taking their son James with her and disappearing—he had been a tormented man. And now, since he'd found the lad and had married Rebecca, Stanmore was so obviously happy. "Fulfilled" was perhaps the best word. The change was stunning . . . miraculous.

It was not long before Nicholas's house on Leicester Square came into view, but he was far too restless to settle in for the night. The snow was beginning to let up, so he turned his steps toward St. James's Park.

Since coming back from the colonies more than ten years ago, Nicholas Spencer had worked diligently to keep his life as uncomplicated as possible. He had wanted no ties. He had endeavored to inflict no pain. During his years as a soldier, he'd seen enough suffering in those wounded and killed, and enough anguish in those families that were left to endure the loss, to cure him of ever desiring any kind of attachment. Life was too fleeting, too fragile.

Somewhere over the years, he'd also found that women were more than willing to put themselves in his path for their mutual amusement and enjoyment. Live while we can. Carpe diem. No harm in it for anyone.

Wealth only meant having enough for good clothes, good horses, a little meaningless gambling, and a bit of concealed philanthropy. It mattered little to him that the most polite reaches of society scoffed at his roguish lifestyle. He knew that they perceived him as a gambler and a womanizer, as a sportsman who had chosen to shrug off the responsibilities of his position in society.

And Nicholas Spencer did not dispute this reputation. He was proud of it. He'd earned it. He'd worked hard to establish it. He had never wanted to be answerable to anyone.

So when, he thought, had he become so discontented?

He strolled through an open gate onto the tree-lined walks of St. James's Park. The usual prostitutes and gal-

lants who frequented the park—even this late—
appeared to have searched out warmer haunts, out of
the wind and the weather. He left the paved walk of the
mall, moving into the open field, his boots crunching on
the dry snow.

Indeed, he was as independent as an eagle, but something unexplainable was happening to him. Why, for ex-
ample, had he felt driven to spend so much time over
the past six months with Rebecca and Stanmore? Of
course he cared for them deeply, but spending time in
their company often did nothing to lift his spirits. On
the contrary, it only served to point out how empty and
insignificant his own life was in comparison with theirs.

Fight it as he may, it seemed a desire for belonging,
for permanency, had been edging into Nicholas's heart.
It was an odd sensation, new to him, though he knew it
was a condition as old as time. Nonetheless, he didn't
want to believe it. He was happy with who he was.

Or so he thought . . .

"Spare a ha'penny, sir? Jist a ha'penny fer my sister
an' me?"

Out of the dark shadows of a grove of trees, he saw
the boy's scrawny bare arms extended in his direction.
Nicholas paused to look at him.

"A ha'penny, sir?" Walking on feet wrapped in dirty
rags, the waifish figure came cautiously nearer. The top
of his head barely reached Nicholas's waist. Even in the
darkness, the boy was pale as death, and the baronet
could hear his teeth chattering from the cold.

Nicholas glanced past the thin shoulders of the child
toward the bundle of bare legs and arms curled into a
ball and lying motionless beneath the tree. Hanks of
long dark hair covered the other child's face.

"Is that your sister?"

The boy tugged at Nicholas's sleeve. "A ha'penny,
sir . . ."

He teetered slightly, and the baronet put out a hand
to him. As Nicholas took hold of the boy's arm to support him, he was immediately dismayed by the thin ragged shirt that covered the bony frame. He took his
gloves and his hat off and handed them to the boy.

"A ha'penny, sir?"

It wasn't until Nicholas had taken off his overcoat and was draping it around the boy that he smelt the spirits emanating from the child.

"If you and your sister follow me to a safe house I know, I'll see to it that there are hot food and warm clothes . . . and half a *shilling* in it for you."

Dwarfed by the size of the clothes, the boy stared at him blankly and said nothing.

"No harm will come to you or your sister, lad. You have my word on it."

Nicholas turned his attention to the girl on the ground. She was much smaller than the boy and, as he pushed back the dark tangle of hair, the baronet was stunned by the angelic look of innocence in the sleeping face. Like the brother, she was dressed in nothing more than thin rags that barely covered her. He touched her face. It was deathly cold.

Nicholas immediately gathered the child in his arms, stood up, and turned to the brother. The boy was gone.

The frail bundle of bones and skin in his arm concerned him more, however, so he started across the park in the direction of the house on Angel Court, off King Street. There, he knew, a couple of good souls would look after this child while he searched out the brother.

The loss of his coat and hat was not what concerned him. The boy was welcome to them. What bothered Nicholas was the money he would find in the pockets. There was enough there to keep a man drunk for a fortnight. For a child who would use it for pouring spirits and beer down his throat, there was enough money there to kill him.

The girl weighed no more than a kitten, and Nicholas frowned fiercely at the smell of alcohol that her body reeked of as well. The excessive drinking of both rich and poor was still one of the curses of England. While the rich could afford to take care of themselves and their families, though, the misery of the poor was passed early on to their children.

A face appeared at the window when Nicholas knocked at the house on Angel Court. At the sound of his voice, the door quickly opened. The old woman's face, bright with recognition, immediately darkened when she saw the bundle in Nicholas's arms.

"I found her in the park." He brushed past her. "I think she is unconscious with drink . . . though the cold surely hasn't helped her any."

The old woman hurriedly opened up a door to the right, leading him into a large room where a small fire spread a warm glow over a dozen beds lining the walls. A few children peeked from beneath their blankets, wide-eyed with curiosity.

"Which one, Sadie?"

The old woman pushed a basket of mending off an empty bed, and Nicholas laid the child gently on the clean blanket.

"Go fetch Martha for me, dear," Sadie said to a boy on the nearest cot.

As the child hurried out of the room, Nicholas stood back, watching the older woman's wrinkled hands as they moved over the girl's face and neck.

He was no expert on children's ages, but he guessed this young one couldn't have been more than five. Small curled hands lay on the blanket. Dirty feet stuck out from beneath her rag of a dress. Nicholas's gaze was drawn to the dark hair framing the innocent features of the face. Long eyelashes lay peacefully against cheeks pale beneath the dirt.

Looking at her, Nicholas found his mind racing, planning. The city was a difficult place for a child on her own. Perhaps he could bring this helpless waif to Solgrave when she was a little better. He was certain Stanmore wouldn't mind it, and Rebecca would embrace the idea. After all, they had given shelter to Israel, and he had become a new lad entirely after only six months. She would thrive in the country. She could go to the village school in Knebworth. She could become a child again.

Sadie's sharp glance in his direction stopped him. He went nearer, and the woman stood up.

"The poor thing has already gone to her Maker, sir."

He stared at the woman's mouth as she quietly spoke. A sudden need to deny her words welled up in him, but he restrained the utterance.

He took a step back. With a slight nod, he turned and in a moment was on the street.

Oblivious to the harshness of the winter night or the time, Nicholas Spencer walked the streets. The injustice of such a death was so wrong. And more innocents—helpless and dying—surrounded him. And what he had been doing about it was clearly not enough.

A shelter here and there. A house to offer meals and a safe bed off the street. All well and good, but where did these children go from there? How had his insignificant acts of charity in any way changed their lives? What had he done to keep them from ending up drunk or abused or dead on the streets?

There had to be something more that he could do. A house in the country where they could grow up healthy. A school where they could learn to fend for themselves. They needed something like a permanent home.

Suddenly, he found himself back at Berkeley Square, staring up at the darkened windows of his friends' home. Even the night and winter could not hamper the glow of warmth radiating from inside.

Nicholas was getting old and he was terrified of it. The admission hurt less than he'd imagined. But he'd been battling the emptiness and coldness of his life for so long, that now coming to terms with his ailment was an incredible relief.

An image of the innocent face of the dead child came before his eyes. His life had become a waste and there *was* so much more that he could do. He would need to make a few changes, though. A new life for himself. A real home where he could truly influence the fate of these lost souls.

But such a thing required a wife, and where on earth would he find her?

Chapter 2

Waterford, Ireland
August 1771

Through the stony fields the roaring fire moved, leaping ahead and coiling before jumping forward again, a monstrous living creature greedily devouring all before it. Smoke and ash swirled above, blotting out stars that had filled the night sky not an hour before and replacing them with sparks and cinders that climbed and glowed and quickly died away.

Legions of men armed with clubs swept down into the vale, torching the fields as they approached. The thatched roofs of the first of the clustered hovels flared up, and dozens of panicking men, women, and children ran in confusion into the night. There was no way of fighting such an onslaught. There seemed to be no escape.

From beneath a hide that served as a doorway of one of the hovels, a squalling baby crawled out into the madness.

In the rocky fields around them, crops that had been painstakingly sown and nurtured with toil and sweat flared up as the inferno spread. Barley, potato, cabbage, wheat—gone in moments while the consuming flames licked the smoke-blackened sky.

A screaming mother, dragged away by others, looked back in desperation at the fiery mass that was once her cottage. Carried along by the swarm of cottagers, she was led toward the only place that was not ablaze, the marshy bog to the north of the huts. Beyond the fetid muck and swamp grass lay the safety of higher ground.

A solitary rider tore through the night and met the group as they emerged, their dark shapes silhouetted by the inferno.

The ride overland had been hard, and there had not been time to raise help. The attack here had come without warning, without legal proceedings, without justice, and the same was happening all over Ireland. The rider looked out at the burning village. Tomorrow, these same brutes would be pulling down the walls. In a week, they would be digging ditches to enclose the fields. Next spring, there would be sheep and cattle grazing here, and these tenants would be wandering the byways of a tragically changing countryside.

The desperate cries of a mother rang out across the hills as she ran to the mounted newcomer.

A moment later, the rider was skirting the edges of the marsh, spurring the steed toward the burning hovels. At the center of the cottages, the infant sat in the dirt with her hands raised to the sky, oblivious to the cinders raining around her.

Seeing the child, the rider drove the horse through the hellhole like one possessed. A hut collapsed with a loud crash, silencing the infant's cries for only a moment. The rider dismounted as the marauders approached through the smoke and flames. Gathering the child up, the rescuer climbed back on the restless steed and raced away into the darkness.

On the hill, the mother ran forward to meet them, her face stained with tears and soot, her throat choked with emotion as she received her screaming babe into her arms.

"Bless ye, Egan!"

Chapter 3

Cork, Ireland
One month later

The patchwork of tidy, newly harvested fields north of Cork City had long since given way to a wilder, rockier countryside, and the woman looked out the carriage window with an artist's eye. This land was so different from the relentlessly flat plains around her own native Brussels.

It was certainly no less green than the lowlands of the coastline to the south. Indeed, the darker hues of numerous pines served to set off the silvery greens of the birch trees. Now tinged with autumn yellows, the birches huddled in groves on the rugged hillsides rising abruptly from the valley floor. Looking at the azure sky above, marred by long scrapes of gray, she thought with satisfaction that they had suffered hardly any rain at all since crossing over from the bustling English port of Bristol.

The carriage, wending its way along a surprisingly good road, had been following the bends of the river at a leisurely pace. Occasionally passing a small cluster of cottages—some more rustic than others—Alexandra Spencer had also seen a number of handsome manor houses with fields of pastureland spreading out around them. The scattered forests were beginning to grow thicker now, and she turned her attention back to her two traveling companions with a contented smile.

Her daughter was speaking with all the exuberance

one might expect of a girl of sixteen, and Lady Spencer broke in when she paused to take a breath.

"Really, Frances! Hanging from a castle wall . . . upside down . . . and kissing a stone just to win some dubious gift of eloquence? What nonsense you spout, young woman!"

"But it is true, Mother. They believe the stone is part of the Stone of Scone at Westminster. Not just one but three of the sailors on the ship were telling me about the magic in kissing Blarney Castle's stone."

"Well, I for one have no desire to kiss anything that might have been sat upon by any king . . . English or otherwise."

"Mother!" Frances replied with shocked delight.

"But more at issue . . . what were you doing talking to sailors? How many times do I have to tell you that a young woman should never engage in—?"

"But Nicholas was with me." The younger woman moved to the seat across in the carriage and looped a hand through her brother's arm. "There was a prizefight in the hold. I simply followed Nick down to watch the sport."

"Nicholas Edward . . . !" she started to scold, but changed her mind as her son's sharp gaze moved from the passing countryside to her face.

Running a hand over the fabric of her skirts, Alexandra Spencer searched for the most appropriate way of expressing her disapproval. A difference of eighteen years in the ages of her two children had certainly been harmless when they were younger, but as Frances was now a blossoming young woman, Alexandra needed to find a way of instructing Nicholas on his brotherly responsibilities.

She gazed at her son as his attention drifted back to the window. When Frances had been an infant, Nicholas had been studying at Oxford. A few years later, when Fanny had started attending school, Nicholas had been fighting his way across the Plains of Abraham during the taking of Quebec. And shortly after that, when her husband had passed away, Nicholas had inherited his father's title and estate. It was then that Alexandra had decided it was time to return to her own ancestral home across the channel where she could stay clear of her son's affairs. Of course, she'd hoped he would use the time to start a life . . . and a family . . . of his own.

Well, that hadn't happened yet, and Alexandra was afraid that she had spent too many years away from Nicholas to be able to exert any kind of control over him now—any overt control anyway.

Frances started again, not sounding deterred in the least. "They tell me that one can also lie on one's back now and lean out to do it with a pair of strong arms gripping one's legs." She paused with a frown. "I don't think I should care to rely on anyone else doing that for me but you, Nick."

"I don't believe the world can stand any more eloquence in you, Fanny," Nicholas replied passively. "You are far too perfect just as you are."

The young woman giggled with delight. "You really should save these pretty words for your darling Clara, you know, and not waste them on your sister."

"*Darling* Clara?" Nicholas Spencer asked with emphasis.

Frances darted a hesitant glance at her mother. After receiving an encouraging nod, she turned to her brother again.

"Well, we *are* headed to Woodfield House, are we not? You *have* accepted the invitation of Sir Thomas Purefoy, Clara's father, to stay a fortnight on their estate in this ravishing country, have you not?"

"Frances, I *do* wish you wouldn't use the word 'ravishing' . . ." Lady Spencer put in.

". . . And you *did* escort that extremely attractive young woman to no less than *three* social functions this past spring in London, did you not? Shall I go on?"

"Don't pressure me, Fanny. I can feel the noose tightening without any help from you or our esteemed mother." He ran a finger inside the high collar of his crisp white shirt. He looked meaningfully from the younger woman to the older. "We are making this trip for the benefit of the two of you, not for me. In spite of some contrary opinion, it is important in a young woman's education that she be introduced to members of society outside of the circle of spoiled brats you've been associating with so exclusively at school."

"Liar!" Frances slapped him on his arm.

Nicholas shrugged. "Very well. Have it your way, then. We're here for me . . . because of my love of horses. Sir Thomas is reputed to have one of the finest stables . . ."

"That is so incredibly unmannerly, Nick," Frances scolded, a practiced pout breaking across her young and beautiful face. She withdrew her hand and slid to the farthest end of the seat. "I must tell you that in lying the way you do, you are ruining the very fine image I cherish of my only brother. There is no help for it . . . I shall not speak with you for the rest of this holiday."

Seeing Nicholas's obvious satisfaction with the state of affairs, Alexandra reached out and touched her son's knee. "Pray resolve this right now. If she is not talking to you, then it means she will be complaining endlessly to me. So if you cannot make up with the little vixen, I would just as soon have you let me out at the next coach stop, where I shall find my way back to London without the two of you."

For a longer span of time than his mother liked, Nicholas appeared to be considering the second threat. He finally turned to his sister, and his tone told Lady Spencer that all joking had been put aside.

"I have been very careful not to create any misunderstandings with regard to Clara and my intentions toward her. The girl is nearly half my age."

"She is *not* half your age!" Fanny corrected, sliding over to her brother's side. "Clara Purefoy turned eighteen this past winter. You are thirty-four. At no time since you've known her have you been twice her age."

"By 'sblood, what does one *do* with a child of eighteen?"

Lady Spencer arched a brow. "From the steady stream of rumors reaching me in Brussels, I might have been led to believe that you are quite proficient in managing women of all ages." Alexandra patted her frowning son on the knee. "Your uneasiness, my dear, stems from the thought of marriage and commitment. Clara's age is only an excuse, and you shall quell your fears quickly."

"Truly, Nick . . ." Frances chirped from his side. "She is everything that you could possibly want in a wife."

"And as an only child, Clara brings with her a great fortune."

"Not that you need it," his sister cut in.

"But considering your lifestyle, my dear, it never hurts to have a little more." Lady Spencer gazed out the window, not wanting to pressure him too much at one time. "A matter which I find highly endearing, though, is how smitten with you the whole family appears to be."

"But Mother, everyone knows how advantageous it is when a daughter marries someone with a title. After all, even a baronet with a reputation as bad as Nick's is—"

"It isn't that!" Alexandra waved off her daughter impatiently. "It is your brother's warm personality that has charmed them. His education. His exemplary military service. His respectability—"

"Before the age of twenty."

Lady Spencer directed a severe glare at her daughter. "Frances Marie, you will mind your tongue." The older woman smoothed out the imaginary wrinkles in her skirts again and turned her full attention to her son, who was once again enthralled by the passing scenery. "Where was I?"

"You had just expressed your wish for me to stop this carriage," Nicholas suggested darkly. "So that you *both* can find your way back to London."

The old bishop and his secretary watched in terror as several of the white-shirted rebels whipped the flanks of the horses and sent the driverless carriage down the road. The bishop's half-dozen attendants, who'd been forced from their places when the carriage was stopped, ran off down the country road after the horses.

"You cannot get away with this, you filthy ruffians." The bishop's voice shook with anger. "Your masks and your devilish linen shirts shan't do you a bit of good when they put ropes about your necks and send you off to the Lord's judgment. 'Vengeance is mine, sayeth the Lord.' "

Five men on horseback looked on as twenty on foot encircled the two clerics. The silence of the group was unnerving. Before the bishop could speak again, his secretary—a portly younger man with flushed cheeks—saw one small opening in the ring of attackers. Seizing the opportunity, he dropped the satchel he'd been clutching to his chest and ran. A thick leather binder filled with papers and a very healthy-looking purse of coins spilled out onto the road. No one bothered to stop the terrified secretary.

"I know every one of you behind those masks," the bishop bluffed. "I know your kin and I know the filthy hovels you each live in."

A number of the assailants moved forward menacingly, forcing the old cleric back against a tree at the edge of the road.

"You touch me, you dogs, and I'll call down God's wrath on all of you. I am the servant of righteousness, and you are the spawn of devils. You are . . ." He gasped as a rope looped around his middle from behind, yanking him hard against the tree.

"This is for forcing the payment of the tithe on the tenants north of Kinsale who lost their crops to the tempest last month."

The bishop looked fearfully at the masked man to his right who had spoken the words. Last spring, he'd heard of a *papist* priest who had been left tied to a tree near Kildare. The bugger had gone for two days without any food or water before someone had found him and let him go. There had been another incident involving a curate near Caher Castle not three weeks ago. He didn't care to think of that one. Of course, neither of the clerics had been killed—only badly mistreated and frightened half to death.

Two men grabbed the bishop's hands and tied a rope around his wrists.

"This is for refusing to baptize bairns in Ulster simply because the kin couldn't afford your higher fees."

"That was not I! I have no say what goes on up . . ." The bishop's protest trailed off weakly as his bravado turned to fear. Another member of the group approached with a rope and dropped it deftly over his head. "No! I beg you . . . !"

The clergyman's mind immediately conjured images from the meeting he'd had with the magistrate, Sir Robert Musgrave, not three days earlier. He'd been promised that all priests would be protected against such attacks by the Whiteboys. As a concession, he'd offered to support the landowners around Youghal who were forcing their farm tenants out to make way for pasturing, and in the end, his own safety had been guaranteed. Guaranteed! Where was that bloody magistrate *now*?

"Do you wish to say a final prayer, Your Excellency? Do you wish to ask forgiveness of the Lord for staining His good name? Perhaps for your shameful acts of greed?"

The clergyman's eyes focused on the rope dangling from his neck. The clerics abused before had been simple parish priests. He was a *bishop*. He couldn't help but wonder if these people would actually kill him to send their message loud and clear across the land.

The words that began spilling out were indeed prayers. Prayers asking forgiveness for exactly the things he was being accused of.

As the carriage suddenly slowed, Nicholas put his head out and looked beyond the horses. He'd heard that travelers occasionally encountered highwaymen on the roads— here as at home—but this was the strangest-looking outlaw he'd ever seen.

Beyond a fork just ahead, where one road bent sharply to the right, a fat clergyman was puffing toward them, his arms waving madly in the air, his piteous cries nearly incoherent from his lack of breath.

Nicholas shouted to the driver and stepped out as the carriage rolled to a stop.

"Whiteboys . . . bishop . . . killing . . . there . . . there . . . !" The man appeared nearly out of his mind with terror, grabbing on to him for support. "Save me . . . help . . . bishop . . . !"

Nicholas detached the man from his arm, handing him over to his valet, who'd been riding behind on his master's horse. He motioned to Frances to remain in the carriage as she opened the door to step out. He glanced in the direction from which the clergyman had come.

The wooded slope running up to the west was dark and densely forested. There was nothing to be seen from here.

" 'Twould be safest, sir, for the ladies if we was to keep moving," the driver offered from his perch on the carriage. "Locals call 'em Shanavests. That'd be Irish for Whiteboys. They're a troublesome bunch . . . if ye be asking me."

The cleric, who was slumped against the carriage and trying to catch his breath, suddenly straightened. "But . . . but you cannot simply . . . simply leave him . . . They'll kill him."

"Maybe," the driver agreed. "But these boys'd be armed to the teeth, sir. Rebels through and through, to be sure, and they always travel in fair-sized numbers. 'Twould be dangerous . . . for the ladies, of course . . . not to be going."

"How many?" Nicholas addressed the priest.

"Five on horse . . . I'd say about two dozen on foot . . . I don't know if I saw all of them or not."

Nicholas took the reins of his horse from the valet.

"Can I come with you, Nick?" Frances called excitedly.

He turned in time to see his mother pull the carriage door shut with a bang, squashing Fanny's attempt to step out. As Nicholas directed the driver to go straight to Woodfield House, the valet took a place on the back of the carriage.

He turned to the cleric. "You . . . inside."

Mumbling words of undying gratitude, the bishop's secretary yanked open the carriage door and jumped inside with more nimbleness than his size warranted.

"The new magistrate, Sir Robert Musgrave, has a bounty set on the heads of these boys," the driver said in confidential tones to Nicholas. "Word is, he's planning to hang every Shanavest he catches in the old Butter Market in Cork. Now, if ye be asking me, that's the wrong approach, what with most of the popish farm folk loving those rebels as their own. But I'm just a whip man . . . so what do I know?"

Lady Spencer poked her head out of the window before the carriage pulled away. "You *can* walk away from a fight, Nicholas. I am concerned for you. There are too many of them . . . and this is a strange land."

"No need to be concerned, Mother. I only intend to get near enough to keep a close watch."

"Then why not wait until the following wagon arrives? With the servants to help you . . ."

"I'll be fine." He motioned for the driver to move on. "Just keep a firm hold on that sister of mine."

Nicholas waited until the carriage disappeared around the bend of the road before climbing on his horse. Drawing his sword, he spurred the animal down the road.

The edge of the knife's blade formed a thin white line in the ruddy wrinkled skin of the man's throat.

The terrified bishop had offered everything he could think of in exchange for his life—from having bags of coin delivered wherever they wished . . . to waiving every church fee in the diocese for an entire year. Baptisms, marriages, funerals . . . everything.

They had accomplished what they had come to do, so the leader of the group motioned for the men to withdraw. The quivering cleric remained tied to the tree, his eyes tightly closed, his mouth now moving involuntarily as he mumbled prayers and promises with no particular rhyme or reason. The man's fine clothes were stained with muck. A few scratches on the face were all that he'd suffered outwardly.

"The next time you think of making any deals with the magistrate, just remember this day," a young giant of a man whispered menacingly in the bishop's ear as he sheathed his knife. "We can always find you."

The leader watched the same member of the Shanavests jab a fist into the cleric's side before walking away. The ropes restrained the man from bending over in pain, but the grimace on the old face showed his distress.

The bag of coins was emptied. The loot taken from the bishop's carriage earlier was piled into sacks and carried off. The group dispersed as quietly and unexpectedly as they had come. In a moment, only the masked leader remained, sitting on a handsome horse.

* * *

With his mount tied to the branch of a birch down the road, Nicholas watched from the safety of a grove of pines. It was some time before the bishop lifted his head and looked up at the solitary figure.

"Please don't kill me!" the man pleaded as horse and rider approached in measured steps. Nicholas's fingers immediately tightened around the hilt of his sword, and he moved silently forward. The rebel leader had a single pistol tucked into his belt, but Nicholas knew he might be able to take the man by surprise, before he had a chance to draw and fire.

"I admit my guilt! I offer you every worldly possession I have . . . I . . ." The man's face drained of all color as the rider quickly drew a knife from his belt. "I . . . I . . ."

Nicholas ran forward, but stopped just before reaching the road when he saw the rebel lean down and cut the ropes binding the bishop's hands.

"Teach mercy and compassion to your people, priest. They are virtues that are wanting."

The voice was hoarse and low, and yet something in the tone caused Nicholas to pause. He immediately drew behind a tree again and sheathed his sword as the rider wheeled his horse in his direction. He listened to the sound of hooves starting up the road toward him.

As soon as the head of the horse passed the tree where he was hidden, Nicholas moved forward quickly, taking hold of the rider's shirt and yanking him from the horse. They both tumbled to the ground, the rebel's pistol bouncing into the brush at the side of the road.

Rolling away, the rebel leader picked up a rock, but Nicholas was faster. As the other man hurled it at his head, the Englishman raised a hand and deflected the gray slate away from his skull. Ready to face him again, he was disappointed to see his foe turn and run toward the woods. Without a second thought, Nicholas took off after him.

The man was small but extremely quick and agile, and he moved speedily through the thick undergrowth. Nicholas's long legs, though, enabled him to overtake the rebel not very far from the road. As he was about to tackle him from behind, the outlaw swung around, kicking viciously at his groin. Nicholas sidestepped the blow, and the kick struck him on the hip as he closed on the man.

Falling forward, Nicholas connected with a right hook a moment before leveling the rebel with his body. Sprawled on top of the masked man, he pushed immediately to a sitting position, trapping the slight body beneath him and drawing back his fist to deliver another blow. He froze.

The rebel's hat lay in the dirt, and the scarf that had masked the outlaw had been tugged down. To Nicholas's utter amazement, a woman's face glared up at him. No wonder it had been so easy to pull her from the horse. Her size. Her weight.

By 'sblood, Nicholas thought, staring at her. A woman!

Ringlets of black hair had escaped their confines, framing a most attractive face. Black eyes, dark as night, shot darts of hatred at him. The side of her mouth was already swelling from the blow. Without thinking, he reached down to touch the bloody lip, but she slapped his hand away, spitting out a string of words in Gaelic. From his time spent ringside at dozens of boxing matches that featured Irish fighters, he understood the woman was not extending any complimentary greeting.

"I . . . ? You definitely leave me speechless."

Nicholas raised an eyebrow at the next prolonged curse she hurled at him.

"I should watch what I say if I were you, my little hellcat." He reached inside his coat pocket and took out a handkerchief. "I am willing to forgive you for the names you call *me* . . . but my father? mother? wife *and* horse? That is really going *too* far."

The blood from her mouth had trickled across her cheek. When he reached down to wipe at it, though, she started thrashing beneath him. Nicholas immediately captured her hands, trapping them with one of his own above her head.

"By 'sblood, I am *not* going to hurt you."

As he reached down again to dab at the blood with the cloth, her dark eyes turned on him. It may as well have been an eternity that he gazed into them, for time stopped. The woman was stunning in her beauty, and he saw fires banked in those eyes the likes of which he'd never seen before.

He was still pressing her body into the leaves and ferns with his weight. He could not help but admire the rise and fall of her breasts beneath the white smock. His eyes lingered on the wild pulse beneath the skin of her throat. His gaze took in the dark ringlets in total disarray around her face and stopped at the full sensual bottom lip. The bruising he'd inflicted filled him with a pang of remorse, but then those magical eyes drew him back.

The moment she ceased to struggle against his hold, he was bewitched.

"Who are you?" he asked huskily, gently pressing the handkerchief against her lip. He fought the sudden urge to lower his mouth to her face, to her throat, to stretch his body fully on top of hers and find out if she was afflicted by the same physical desire that had taken hold of him. The attraction was so strong that Nicholas forced himself to release her. He stood up abruptly, struggling to clear his mind of such thoughts. Frowning fiercely, he extended a hand to her, but she didn't take it. Reaching down, he grabbed her by the arm and pulled her roughly to her feet. He didn't release her.

"If I were you, I would start explaining now . . . before the magistrate's men arrive." She said nothing, her dark eyes flashing defiantly. "Do the Whiteboys make a habit of having their women fight for them?"

He was trying so hard to shake off the spell she'd cast that he didn't see her reach for the knife at her waist. She slashed at his arm deeply enough to cause him to yank his hand away in shock and pain. The moment that Nicholas took to look down at the cut was all the time that she needed. Before he could act, she was off and running.

By the time he had reached the edge of the trees, the woman had regained her horse. Quick as a summer breeze, horse and rider disappeared along the road. Nicholas looked down at the pistol lying at his feet and picked it up. He tucked it into his belt. He went back into the woods and fetched her hat as well.

Blood was staining his coat sleeve, and he shrugged

out of the garment. The cut on his forearm was minor, and he used the handkerchief still clutched in his hand to bind it before putting his coat back on. He stared after her.

"A woman," he muttered, walking back down the road to where the cleric was removing the ropes.

"You took him down. Did you see him? Did you get a good look at his face?"

The man stared at the hat that Nicholas was holding.

"The magistrate is offering a great reward for him, you know. *Especially* him!"

"Who is he?"

"The blackguard is one of their leaders. Of all of them, he has the largest price on his head. He goes by the name Egan . . . though 'tis undoubtedly an assumed name!"

"Undoubtedly," Nicholas answered vaguely, looking down at the hat.

Chapter 4

"I definitely did not see *any* man's face well enough to describe him."

Sir Thomas Purefoy frowned and resumed his agitated pacing across the brightly lit Blue Parlor of the Woodfield House. Outside the mullioned windows, the green hills of the Irish landscape rolled downward to a sparkling river.

Nicholas's mother and his sister, Frances, were sitting comfortably on a sofa before the hearth, sipping tea and looking on unconcernedly, while Lady Purefoy and Clara fluttered around their injured guest like butterflies around a flame. Fey, the middle-aged Irish housekeeper, was just finishing up wrapping the wound on his forearm in clean linen. The thick fabric of the jacket and the shirt had served to minimize the depth of the cut, and Nicholas found all this attention a bit overdone. But he remained silent and allowed the red-haired woman to finish.

Sir Thomas came to an abrupt stop before him again. "But you are certain the attacker—the one you came face-to-face with—was the rebel leader. You're *certain* it was Egan."

"Not in the slightest. I had no previous knowledge of the group or its members. I am only repeating what Bishop Russell said afterward."

"He *would* know, by thunder," Sir Thomas muttered before starting his pacing again.

As Fey packed her things into a basket, Nicholas thanked her and rose to his feet.

"If you will forgive me," he said, bowing to Lady Purefoy, "I believe I shall go and change out of these travel clothes."

"Oh! Of course, Sir Nicholas." The blue-eyed, round-faced gentlewoman curtsied pleasantly. Immediately, though, she reached for her daughter's hand. "How foolish of me to be so inattentive. Clara, my dear, why don't you show our guest upstairs to his room. Perhaps as you go, you can also give him a brief history of Woodfield House. It is really quite an interesting history, Sir Nicholas."

The young woman, blushing prettily as ringlets of gold danced around her young face, started to lead the way.

Nicholas made a point of ignoring the mischievous look Fanny was directing his way as he followed Clara from the parlor.

Only a few hours' ride from Cork City, Woodfield House was an impressive ivy-covered stone structure dramatically situated on a high, southern-facing hill. The present manor house had been here for more than a hundred years, Clara informed him, built over what had been the ruins of an earlier house or castle.

"There are four stories in the building . . ." The young woman's soft voice echoed in the halls as they passed along. ". . . though only two of them are used by the family. The ground floor contains the kitchens and the brewery, storage rooms, and a servants' hall. The rooms on the top level are also occupied by the servants. This floor has a number of parlors, my father's study, a fine library, and a hall that we sometimes use for entertaining . . . receptions and things."

Nicholas placed a hand on Clara's elbow as they arrived at the bottom of the stairs. The deepening blush in her cheek, the demure lowering of her gaze, reminded him of the reason why he'd been so fascinated with her since they'd first been introduced in London. Beautiful and unpretentious, she possessed virtues he'd always found attractive in women.

This was the first time they'd been left alone since he'd arrived. Nicholas paused, correcting himself. This was the first time they'd been left alone since meeting in London. Sir Thomas and his wife were becoming too sure of his intentions . . . and that wasn't a particularly comfortable feeling.

His gaze fell on her lips, and he considered whether he should take the liberty of sampling the young woman's other charms. Perhaps—he found himself thinking—if he were to become more attentive on that front, he wouldn't continue to dwell so morosely on the years dividing them.

And then there was another matter entirely that he needed to forget. The face of the woman he'd met on the road—this "Egan"—was an image he couldn't seem to shake from his mind.

The corridor and stairs were deserted, and Nicholas reached out and took hold of Clara's chin, raising it until he was looking into her blue eyes.

"I've heard enough about Woodfield House for the moment. Now I want to hear about you. I wonder if you have missed me at all since we last met."

"I . . . well . . . I have . . . missed you . . . Sir Nicholas."

He saw the tip of her pink tongue unconsciously wet her lips, and Nicholas knew this was his chance to proceed. But a sharp ache from the cut in his arm cleared his mind of the thought. He released her chin and glanced up at the steep stairs.

"I have been looking forward to this visit, too," he said pleasantly, starting up the stairs.

If she was disappointed, he had no way of knowing, for as they proceeded she kept her eyes on the family pictures that adorned the wall.

"What can you tell me about this group of rebels the bishop called the Whiteboys?"

"I hardly . . . well . . . not much. Nothing more than . . . than gossip, anyway."

Her stammer drew his gaze. Her face revealed no emotion, but Nicholas's observant eyes noted the restless fingers fraying the end of the ribbons she wore at her waist.

"While we were trying to catch up to his carriage and servants, I spent a little time in Bishop Russell's company, yet the man had a great deal to say about them. He was quite eloquent in his description of their violent attacks against the clergy and the landowners. He called them thieves and murderers who have no sense of morality, men who do not believe they are accountable to any king or any religious authority, either."

"Naturally, it is in Bishop Russell's own best interests to preach such things. However, in standing up for people who are being steadily bled to death, the Shanavests are arguably better champions of morality than the priests. So of course he should say such things. He'd be a fool not to stain their reputation at every opportunity."

"From the way you talk, one would think you are a supporter of this group, Miss Clara."

The ribbons had become threads in her fingers. "I . . . no . . . Sir Nicholas. I was just expressing an opinion held by . . . by many of our servants and tenants. Many are popish in their beliefs."

She said nothing more and did not look at him again until they arrived at the open door to his room. Nicholas found his valet waiting inside.

"Thank you for the tour, Miss Clara. What time am I expected downstairs?"

Clara glanced uncomfortably down the corridor. "My mother . . . well, she was hoping to have you meet the rest of our family this afternoon . . . before dinner."

"I was under the impression that the rest of your family resides in England."

"They do . . . well, most do. Mother wishes for you to meet my older sister."

"An older sister?" Nicholas smiled. "And I thought you were an only child."

She gave her head a quick shake, making the curls dance around her face. "It is true, though, that I have often felt that way. Sometimes eight years' difference in age can seem like eighty. This is certainly true in the case of Jane and myself."

Nicholas forced back the discomforting thought of how old *he* must seem to such a young woman. He cleared his throat and tried to salvage some of his vanity. "And will your sister's husband and children also be joining us this evening?"

"Oh . . . no!" Clara again shook her head. "Jane . . . well, she has never married."

A moment later, when Nicholas was left to change for dinner, his only thought was, at least he would have another *old* person to talk to. Meeting Jane Purefoy would no doubt be the highlight of dinner.

She couldn't help it. Lady Spencer's curiosity was immediately aroused by the hushed exchange between their host and hostess near the door. She completed her turn around the room and stopped before a rather fine painting hanging to the right of the fireplace.

At a small, round table across the parlor, Nicholas was playing cards with his sister and Clara. The threesome appeared totally unaware of the commotion going on at this end.

". . . you shouldn't force her to come down, Sir Thomas. Not in the condi—"

"I shall *not* hear another word about this, madam. She was told of this engagement far in advance, hang it. Now *send* your servant to fetch her. *This instant!*"

Alexandra hazarded a quick glance at the husband and wife. Sir Thomas's command over his wife was clear, for Catherine Purefoy—though flushed and obviously upset—nodded to the maid who was hovering just outside the door.

As Sir Thomas turned his attention to the room, Alexandra quickly looked back at the painting. In all the years of her own marriage, she couldn't recall a single instance when her husband had spoken to her in such tones. She looked over at Clara and found the young woman watching her parents. There was a definite look of disquiet in her pretty eyes.

Clearly there was more to this family than had been readily apparent when they all had first been introduced at Court in London. And though Alexandra's greatest wish for her son was to have him finally settle and choose a wife, she now hoped that Nicholas would take his time. It was only common sense that they should be sure there was nothing about Clara's upbringing that might have deprived the young woman of what was necessary for a good marriage. Necessary, at least, in Alexandra's opinion.

After all, she thought, self-respect and character counted

for much more than money. And even though she and
Nicholas had spent many of their recent years apart, she
was fairly certain he would need a wife who did not
lack confidence.

A shadow filled the doorway, and Alexandra's gaze
was drawn to the figure entering the parlor.

The woman was dressed completely in black.

The newcomer wore a fine black gown. The tips of
black shoes showed beneath. Black gloves, edged with
Italian lace, were met at the wrist by the long sleeves of
the dress. Her hair, pulled tightly back, matched the
color of the garments, and large dark eyes provided a
stunning highlight to a perfect ivory complexion.

Perfect, of course, except for the nasty bruise on the
side of her swollen mouth.

No one else appeared to have noticed her arrival but
Sir Thomas, and Alexandra arched an eyebrow at the
look of open hostility that she saw pass between father
and daughter as they stood glaring for a moment at
each other.

A chair scraped against the floor in the far end of the
room, and the newcomer's gaze shifted in that direction.
A look of shock immediately etched itself upon the
young woman's face, and Alexandra saw her reach out
a gloved hand to steady herself.

Across the room, Nicholas was standing by the
table . . . looking as if he'd just seen a ghost.

"Come in, Jane," Lady Purefoy said hesitantly. "Sir
Nicholas . . . Lady Spencer . . . Miss Frances. I would
like to present my older daughter."

Chapter 5

Jane only hoped that she looked less surprised than he did at this moment.

She stood straight and tried to gauge what the Englishman would do. If he revealed their earlier encounter, she was a doomed woman. Of course, she could deny everything—but she doubted that either her father or Sir Robert, the new magistrate, would take her word over an English baronet's.

The silence hung like a shroud over the room. Jane averted her eyes, unsure how much more of this she could endure. Then the middle-aged woman who had been standing and looking at one of the paintings approached her.

"Miss Jane . . . or rather, I should say Miss Purefoy, as you are the elder daughter."

Jane stared in surprise at the extended hand of their guest. The Englishwoman appeared to be about the same age as her own mother, but the sharp blue eyes spoke of inner strength that far exceeded Lady Purefoy's.

"Calling me Jane will suffice, m'lady," she replied quietly, taking the hand and dropping a small curtsy. "I have been well beyond such formalities for some time."

"Then you shall call me Alexandra." The woman didn't release Jane's hand immediately, drawing her into the room before taking her by the arm. "You don't know how delighted we are to have finally met you. Your family has been very secretive about you, my dear.

I cannot help but feel quite privileged to have been given a chance to meet Sir Thomas and Lady Purefoy's hidden treasure."

Treasure? Jane would have laughed if her mouth did not hurt when she smiled. She glanced at her father and saw him turn toward the hearth as he raised a tumbler of brandy to his lips.

"This is my daughter, Frances. A more incorrigible young woman you shall never meet."

Slightly taller than her mother and wearing her dark blond curls fashionably styled, Frances was a younger image of Lady Spencer. She also showed a nature that was equally congenial, leaving the card table and approaching the two of them.

"My, but that is a *handsome* cut on your lip, Miss Purefoy . . . if you don't mind my saying so."

"Good heavens, Frances!" the mother remonstrated.

"Honestly, it calls to mind a few that I have seen Nicholas sporting after one of his boxing matches."

"Fanny!"

"Please do not chastise her on my account, m'lady," Jane said to Lady Spencer before turning to greet the bright-faced young woman. "I'm certain that Miss Spencer's comment is exactly correct . . . though I must own that I myself try not to make a habit of boxing."

"Do tell how you got it! Don't take me wrong. I *do* believe it is quite handsome."

Lady Spencer let go of Jane's arm and stepped toward her daughter. "Frances Marie Spencer, you are a most garrulous, undisciplined magpie. I *must* apologize for this creature standing before you. I am certain she must have been changed at birth for my own true ch—"

"I'd be happy to relate the origin of my little bruise . . . though I'm afraid my tale is somewhat mundane." Jane met the friendly blue eyes of the young woman. She hesitantly touched her sore lip and felt another set of eyes closely studying her face. "Just a bit of bad luck, you see. I bent over to pick something up and struck my face on the edge of a dressing table in my bedchamber earlier today. I am generally known to be more careful than that."

Frances opened her mouth to say something else, but a sharp tug on her arm by Lady Spencer curtailed her next question.

Jane shifted her gaze first to the face of her sister. Clara looked pale enough to faint, and Jane saw her sister glance quickly at the Englishman's bandaged arm.

"Sir Nicholas," she managed to get out, turning to the other visitor. "It is an honor having you here at Woodfield House."

She hoped her voice would not betray her. He was still staring at her in a wholly discomforting fashion, and her uneasiness only escalated into the realm of panic when he crossed the room to her. It took great restraint on her part not to take a step back. For nine years she had been actively involved with the Shanavests. Why, after all that time, did her sister's intended husband have to be the first foe to succeed in glimpsing her identity?

"Miss Purefoy." He bowed politely, and when he looked up at her, Jane found herself suddenly arrested by the same intensity emanating from the depths of that gaze as she'd seen before. Allowing this man to look into one's eyes was tantamount to opening the window to one's soul. A feeling of extreme vulnerability washed through her, but Jane could not bring herself to look away.

"You are not the only one injured today, Miss Purefoy." Frances Spencer's words cut through the silence, and she was grateful for the distraction.

"Jane," she said quietly to the younger woman. "Please call me Jane."

"Jane, you should have Nicholas tell you about the great fight he had with the leader of the bandits today. He walked away with a rather dashing wound himself." Frances paused thoughtfully, casting a proud glance at her brother. "Knowing the shrewdness with which Nick fights, I have no doubt the blackguard received far worse in the exchange."

"No doubt," Jane murmured, relieved to see her mother step forward to urge everyone toward the dining room.

Jane retreated into the background and managed to touch Clara's arm in passing.

"I am sorry," she whispered, to which the younger sister nodded with a gentle smile.

Of all the people in this room, her sister Clara was the only one whom Jane cared a rush about. From the day that her own life had become so inextricably entwined with the secret resistance group, her sister had become and had remained the only ally Jane had in the family. Clara was the only person she had ever dared to trust. There were many dangerous and reckless acts Jane Purefoy had committed in her life, but she had always made certain that none of them would ever bring danger or heartache to Clara's door. Until now.

As her mother took Lady Spencer's arm and Sir Thomas escorted the vivacious young Frances into dinner, Jane drifted toward the window . . . as always, forgotten. She didn't mind it, though, as she watched the tall Englishman offer his arm to Clara.

In her mind, he was hardly the kind of nobleman her father would have chosen to bring a good name and restore honor to their family. With his broken nose and his unpowdered blond hair tied back with a ribbon, the blue-eyed giant looked more like a rake and a highwayman than a respectable member of London's *ton*. Handsome in a rugged sort of way, Sir Nicholas Spencer obviously harbored a rebellious quality beneath his refined manners . . . otherwise he would have charged her immediately with crimes against the king.

Looking at him now, she wondered what reason might lie behind the man's silence. More important, she wondered how long that silence would last.

They were the last pair leaving the room.

Nicholas paused by the door and glanced over his shoulder at Jane Purefoy, who appeared forgotten and lost in her own world.

"Will your sister not be joining us for dinner?" His question was addressed to Clara, who was barely allowing her fingers to touch the sleeve of his jacket.

"I . . . I believe she is."

He turned to face the older sister. "Miss Purefoy. Would you give me the honor of accompanying both of Sir Thomas's beautiful daughters in to dinner?"

An instant flash of distaste ran across her fair features, and Nicholas wondered for a moment if he and his offer or the mention of Sir Thomas's name were the cause of it. All the same, though, the dark-appareled woman approached and accepted the offer of his arm. Her hand lay lightly on the bandaged cut hidden beneath his jacket sleeve.

Nicholas couldn't recall when in recent years he'd been so instantly intrigued by a woman. After all, what a curious situation he'd suddenly found himself in. Sir Thomas Purefoy, an ex-magistrate of the king—a man who had been raised to knighthood in the Order of the Thistle after fighting with distinction beside the Duke of Cumberland himself at the battle of Culloden—was harboring under his own roof a noted rebel renegade who just happened to be his daughter. Of course, Nicholas thought, he hadn't ever had a woman cut him with a knife, either.

And this wasn't even half of it. Bishop Russell had told Nicholas all about Sir Thomas's heavy hand when it came to crushing out the Whiteboys' rebellious ways. Apparently the new magistrate, Sir Robert Musgrave, had quite a distance to travel to match Purefoy's severity with the Shanavests and other factions like them.

Life could *not* get more entertaining than this.

He directed a quick glance at the woman who held his right sleeve and was rewarded by the intelligent flash of dark eyes in return. The question was etched in her face, demanding an answer. She no doubt wanted to know what his game was and what he wanted. Nicholas looked straight ahead as they approached the dining table. Well, he had no intention of satisfying her curiosity. At least not while the game was so young.

Dinner itself was a pageant well worth the price of admission. Fanny and Alexandra did most of the talking, while Clara and Lady Purefoy quietly played their roles as the perfect hostesses. Sir Thomas, on the other hand, was clearly a man highly accustomed to his position as lord of the manor. In between drinking large quantities of wine and finding some fault with everything that was served, he managed to talk endlessly about his greatest passion, the breeding of horses.

Normally this was a subject that Nicholas would have found extremely diverting. At present, however, he was far more interested in the family's treatment of Jane Purefoy. Not once during dinner was a single comment directed toward her. For the family, she did not seem to exist, it appeared. The scent of scandal lingered in the air.

"You shall have the pleasure of meeting our dear Reverend Adams after dinner," Lady Purefoy offered quietly, in response to a question by Alexandra about Woodfield House's neighbors. "He is quite a diligent young man, traveling every day through the country-side—"

"He is not coming. He sent his excuses yesterday."

At the abruptness of her husband's words, Catherine's voice took on a placating tone. "You are, of course, correct, Sir Thomas. But he sent a second letter this morning, saying that he shall make a point of stopping here on his way back to Ballyclough. Parson Adams said we could expect him sometime after dinner."

"And when were you planning on telling me all of this?"

"I . . . well, I didn't think it was a—"

"I had a driver take a letter to him this afternoon. Bloody hell! If I knew that he was coming, I would not have wasted the man's time. Once again, you have succeeded in making me look like an ass. By the devil . . . !"

"My apologies, Sir Thomas. I . . . I was in error . . ."

The older woman's stammering discomfort spread a thick layer of embarrassment over the table. All conversation ceased. Even Fanny seemed at a loss for words.

"You see what I am forced to endure, Sir Nicholas?" The older man shook his head and reached for his glass. "Thoughtless, empty-headed women. Do you believe this deficiency is inherent in the species, sir, or is it that I have been cursed with a bad lot?"

Nicholas could see the Englishman was making an attempt at humor to cover his show of temper, but Nicholas was not amused.

"It has been my observation, sir, that thoughtlessness and empty-headedness are no more innate a feature in women than in men. However, considering how delightfully congenial these ladies have been in not reminding us of our own glaringly male deficiencies, perhaps we should not be too hard on them for such a small lack of communication."

"Oh, well . . ." The man made a great show of clearing his throat and reaching for more wine. "We shall just see if you continue to sing such a merry tune, Sir Nicholas, after you've spent some time in these chits' company. I tell you, they are a troublesome bunch, by thunder. You shall come around, sir. You certainly shall."

As another course was served, Nicholas's gaze fell on the profile of Clara, who was seated beside him. The young woman's complexion had turned a shade paler, and she appeared preoccupied with the intricate weave of the tablecloth beneath her plate. One glance at Jane, who was seated to the left of her mother—across from him—and Nicholas knew the pulse of Purefoy women beat the strongest in the older sister. Her face was flushed red, her temper barely contained. Lady Purefoy laid her hand casually on top of Jane's, and the older sister fisted her hand before tucking it beneath the table.

"Miss Purefoy," he asked, "what kinds of activities occupy *your* time out here in this beautiful countryside?"

"I . . . I am . . ." Clara started to answer, but she stopped abruptly, realizing that Nicholas's question was directed at Jane and not at her.

The older sister appeared as surprised to be addressed. As she searched for an answer, Nicholas enjoyed the opportunity of staring openly at her.

Despite the severe hairstyle and the "handsome" bruise by her mouth, there was a vibrancy in her face that shone through brightly. Considering her manner of dress and the injury she'd sustained, Jane's beauty was far different from the kind aspired to by London's fashionable set. But looking past the superficial ornamentation, he saw a vitality there—a natural beauty and spirit—that was impossible to ignore.

"I believe that there is very little difference in the way an Englishwoman is expected to spend her days in Ireland than in England."

"It has been my observation that what is expected of women and what they actually do is not always the same."

"You seem to be quite the observer of human nature, Sir Nicholas," Jane commented.

"You would be amazed at the things one observes when one takes the time to look."

A soft blush crept up her cheeks. "Well, I cannot know anything of that, sir, but I do know that when it comes to satisfying the curiosity of observers, it is a woman's duty to blend what is expected and what must be done. If she is careful enough in her actions, all that one will notice is . . . compliance."

"Do you mean that one should say one thing and do another, Jane?" Fanny asked excitedly.

"I should hope not, Miss Frances," Jane said gently. "Repeated back to me, my own words have a horrifying ring to them. What I am trying to say is that even within the rigid constraints of societal decorum—constraints that are imposed on women practically from birth—there are freedoms that can be exercised, good deeds that can be accomplished. Though silence is imposed upon us—"

Sir Thomas's loud call for one of the servants to bring in more wine made the older daughter pause momentarily.

". . . we have voices, and we can be heard. Being a woman should never be equated with helplessness. We—"

"*Now* do you see what I mean, sir?" The former magistrate glared at his older daughter.

"Jane likes to draw," Lady Purefoy hurriedly interrupted. "She has assembled quite a portfolio of her work."

"Do you?" Alexandra asked with enthusiasm. "May I see them? I have an interest in art, myself."

Lady Purefoy cast a nervous glance in her husband's direction. "Though I am afraid none of them are completely finished. Is that not correct, Jane? Perhaps . . . sometime in the future . . . we shall have some of her work sent to you. Clara, on the other hand, has an excellent hand for needlework, Sir Nicholas. She's done a fine rendering of Woodfield House. After dinner, I shall show you and Miss Spencer . . ."

Nicholas lost interest in the discussion and stopped listening. Once again, the family had effectively shut the older daughter out of the conversation. Jane's face was a picture of tautly controlled anger. He turned his gaze from Lady Purefoy to her husband. Nicholas was beginning to resent the blatant pushing of Clara in his direction. Sir Thomas had all the subtlety of a horse trader. Though he had once been interested, the Purefoys' behavior with regard to both daughters was quickly putting him off.

The host placed his empty glass firmly on the table.

"Now we shall have some time for ourselves, Sir Nicholas." He looked meaningfully at his wife, and she immediately rose to her feet. "You and I shall remain here for a cigar and some brandy I have just received from my man in Cork City. We have a few details to work out that we may put behind us tonight. I'm sure you have a few questions you'd like to put to me regarding the settling of affairs."

The other women followed Lady Purefoy's lead and rose from the table.

"We shall retire to the Blue Parlor, Sir Thomas, and leave you men to your discussions."

Nicholas had no recollection of having yet offered for Clara's hand in marriage, and the confident tone of the knight regarding any possible marital discussions only managed to annoy him further. He had never been one to tolerate being pushed.

"I believe I will excuse myself from accepting your invitation tonight, Sir Thomas." He stood up as soon as the women had left the room. "The ride up from Cork City, combined with this injury, will not make me very agreeable company. Perhaps some other time we shall have an opportunity to discuss *whatever* it is you had in mind."

Nicholas knew from the look on Purefoy's face that the older man was again surprised, though he shouldn't have been. Sir Thomas had been well aware of his reputation as a bachelor and as a rake when they were introduced in London. Despite it all, though, Nicholas's

position and his wealth had obviously made the gamble
of inviting him to Woodfield House a chance worth
taking.

"Very well, sir." The man stood up.

In the hallway outside the dining room, Nicholas spied
Jane Purefoy speaking quietly to a very attentive and
sober-faced stranger he had not seen before. They stood
far too close, their heads bent together in a confidential
gesture. The jagged blade of jealousy that Nicholas felt
running through him at that moment was as unexpected
as it was palpable.

"Reverend Mr. Adams," Sir Thomas called out
loudly, drawing the newcomer's attention. "You've arrived earlier than expected."

"Indeed I have, sir."

Jane murmured something in parting to the parson
and, with a quick look at Nicholas, disappeared toward
the stairs leading to the upper floors. It took a great
effort by him not to go up after her.

The minister turned to the two men. "I hope I'm not
intruding on your company, Sir Thomas."

"Not at all, sir. Not at all. We were just telling Sir
Nicholas about you."

As the introductions were made, Nicholas studied the
cleric. The man had lean, regular features. His gray eyes
were keen, and his face expressed a seriousness appropriate to his calling. His boots and his clothes, though
spattered with mud from his travels, were well made. He
had the look of a man who would have proved an able
soldier, had that been his calling. The intimate appearance of the little tête-à-tête they'd broken up made
Nicholas wonder if the dark-haired young minister might
be the object of Jane Purefoy's affection. The pang of
disappointment that he felt at that very distinct possibility was sudden and sharp.

To the surprise of the ladies, the three men joined
them in the Blue Parlor and, as Lady Purefoy made the
rest of the introductions, Nicholas moved to the younger
daughter's side.

"I can see that we will not have the pleasure of your
sister's company tonight. I saw her retire upstairs."

"Like you, sir," Clara replied after an almost imperceptible hesitation, "my sister has had a tiring day. She asked me to make her excuses to you."

"To me?"

"Of course, Sir Nicholas. She would not wish you to take offense."

"None taken. She is not unwell, though, I hope."

"No. I believe Jane is quite well."

"The bruise on her face appears serious. Has anyone looked after it, do you know?"

"I am certain that Fey has," Clara offered politely.

Nicholas watched the parson conversing comfortably with Alexandra. "Reverend Adams is a close friend of your family?"

"Indeed he is, sir."

"Is he married? Does he have a family of his own?"

"No, he doesn't." With a strained smile, Clara moved a step away from Nicholas, effectively stopping any further questions he might have.

Nicholas casually studied the young woman. With a pretty smile painted on a pleasant face, she stood quietly, not participating in any discussion, but still playing the part of the proper hostess. He found himself suddenly bored beyond measure.

"If you will forgive me, Miss Clara, I believe I, too, shall retire," he said.

She made no objection and expressed no opinion. Nicholas bowed to her politely and made his excuses to the host and hostess as well.

The parson, though, was quick to make a comment. "Sir Nicholas, I was sorry to hear of the attack on you this morning. I hope, however, that you will not judge Ireland as nothing more than a land of barbarians. The trouble you encountered was, after all, an isolated incident. There is a great deal of good that we have to offer here."

"I am quite certain that is true, Parson, though I am hardly one to judge. The little incident this morning was no different than anything one might run into while traveling from London into the surrounding countryside. Besides, it was a trifling thing for us. It was Bishop Russell who was subjected to the greatest fright."

"Tell me, how much truth is there to the rumor I heard in the village this afternoon that you unmasked one of the leaders of these rebellious Whiteboys?"

"No truth whatsoever," Nicholas replied, glancing impatiently toward the door. "We scuffled, that's all."

"But surely you must have some inkling of the man's size. His build or his complexion. Something that could aid in the new magistrate's efforts to arrest the blackguard."

"I can offer nothing," he insisted, no longer trying to keep the impatience out of his voice. "The 'blackguard,' as you call him, could have been anyone. I doubt very much that I would recognize him if I saw him again."

"But you unhorsed him . . ."

"The man I unhorsed could have been *anyone*, for all that I can recall. He could have been *you,* sir."

"I hardly think so, Sir Nicholas," their host replied with a gruff laugh. "What would a respectable Episcopal churchman be doing fighting for a handful of discontented papist peasants?"

"My point exactly," Nicholas offered dryly. "I know nothing at all of the matter. Now, if you will excuse me . . ."

"Indeed, my duties are quite taken up in my living at the parsonage in a little town called Ballyclough, not an hour's ride to the north. In fact, sir, you should see it. It is beautiful country." Henry Adams turned and directed his next words to Lady Spencer. "I would love to have you all come out and visit us sometime soon. Perhaps even tomorrow."

"I fear I shall have to decline, Parson. After such a long day of travel . . ." Lady Spencer shook her head and looked meaningfully at her daughter. "Thank you, but no. Frances and I would never allow ourselves to impose. You would find us dull company, indeed, after our journey. But Nicholas, on the other hand, you will find to be generally ready for whatever challenge is offered to him."

"Aye, a fine idea," Lady Purefoy put in cheerfully. "Clara, dear, why don't you ride over with Sir Nicholas in the morning . . . if he wishes to go. There are a great many things you can point out to him. I'll have the cook prepare a basket for you. You can take your time and stop somewhere for a picnic if the weather permits."

Henry Adams turned to Nicholas. "It would be my great pleasure to have the opportunity of visiting more with you, sir. I promise that you'll not find the day a total waste. And perhaps, Lady Purefoy, you might be able to convince Jane to accompany them."

"Yes, indeed, Parson," Lady Purefoy replied, obviously taken aback by the suggestion. "I shall certainly ask if Jane would care to ride along."

"*I* would also be delighted if Miss Purefoy agrees to go along," Nicholas said, turning to meet the parson's sharp gaze. "I was disappointed to not have the opportunity of becoming more acquainted with her this night."

A deep silence flooded the room. But Nicholas didn't give a damn about the suitability of his claim and continued to size up Henry Adams's reaction. The man's expression appeared impartial.

"Then . . . I shall . . . insist that Jane go . . . along." Lady Purefoy's flushed face reflected her confusion.

Pleased with the results, Nicholas bowed to their hosts and paused by Parson Adams on his way out. "We shall meet again at Ballyclough tomorrow."

The household was still alive with the activities of the night when he left the room. But his mind was totally preoccupied with the decisions that had to be made.

Nicholas refused to be a deuced deceiver if he could help it. Despite his wild reputation regarding women, he found it totally improper to be pursuing these two sisters at the same time. But was this what he was doing? Had his curiosity about Jane already settled into an attraction strong enough to convince him to disregard the younger sister?

As he made his way up the stairs, he tried to examine his feelings toward Clara. She'd appeared to be so charming in London. He'd imagined she would make a proper wife, now that the time had finally come for him to settle down and make a home in the country. But all of that was before he'd seen her here among her own family. She appeared too young—too naïve—too indecisive. The girl lacked will and spirit.

Before he'd reached the top, though, Nicholas admitted the truth to himself. It was meeting Egan . . . or rather, Jane, that was causing him to see so many flaws in Clara.

He heard a door quietly open and close as he neared the top of the stairs. Pausing in the shadows of the landing, he saw the dark figure of a woman glide away from his door. He'd told his valet and his manservant that they were not needed anymore tonight, so his room was unoccupied and unattended. He watched as Jane Purefoy disappeared through the last door on the left.

His curiosity aroused, Nicholas stepped out of the shadows and went to his room. Inside, his belongings were as he remembered his valet leaving them. He checked his pistol and sword. They were untouched as well. His gaze lit on the bedside table where he'd placed the pistol and hat left behind by the fleeing Egan.

Both, of course, were gone.

Chapter 6

On a steep hill facing south, a half-dozen stone huts huddled together against the approaching storm. Small dark windows stared like vacant eyes into the night. Beyond the top of the hill, in a small gorge carved out of the rugged terrain, the solitary wreck of a barn that had long ago been a center of farm life crouched in shadow, its large thatched roof partially collapsed and sagging.

A cloaked figure walking quickly from a grove of scrub pine and birch looked up as a flash of distant lightning accompanied the first drops of rain. It was almost a relief to feel them, for the September air was far warmer than it should have been.

Of the larger group that had gathered inside the dilapidated barn earlier in the evening, only six men and two women remained. They had heard the whinny of a horse, and they sat in silence until a low whistle from the watcher signaled them of Egan's approach. A moment later, everyone stared, their eyes showing their concern and alarm at the bruised face of the woman who came into the light.

She paused just inside the door and met the circle of familiar gazes.

"It is nothing to gape at." She cast aside her cloak and approached the small fire. The silence and the stares continued. "I'm sorry to be late. I'm certain you were saying something, Liam."

She nodded toward the leader and crouched before the fire, where Ronan made room. She kept the bruised side of her face in the shadows and tried to ignore the close scrutiny of the man sitting beside her.

The leader cleared his throat. "Everyone has agreed, Egan, that some of the coin from today's raid should be sent to Seamus's widow and the children. Finding . . ."

Ronan reached over and turned Egan's face around so they all could see the damage. Liam fell silent again.

"I'll cut his throat for this, Egan," Ronan threatened menacingly. "I swear to God I will."

"I know you could shave a sleeping mouse, but don't be a fool," Egan snapped. "You can see it is only a bruise."

Concern was etched on everyone's face. She brushed off Ronan's hand and nodded her head toward the older of the two women.

"Jenny has often enough sewn up many a lad so badly mauled that she could barely pull the flesh together. Look at Patrick here." She touched the man sitting on her left on the arm. "On his best days his face looks hardly less bruised than mine. This is nothing, I tell you."

"He cut your lip open," the hot-tempered young man started again. "He has to—"

"Enough!" Egan stood up abruptly, waving an impatient hand in disgust. "I've been fighting my own battles since you weren't even a wee glint in your father's eyes, boy. I don't need to be taken care of by any *runt* like you."

A low chuckle from Liam broke the ensuing silence. A moment later, everyone else joined in.

Well over six feet tall, with muscles hardened by work quarrying limestone and a temper renowned from Cork to Kerry, Ronan finally joined in as well. They all knew that only Egan could get away with calling him "runt." Anyone else would have been needing new teeth to eat their next meal.

"You were speaking of sending some coins to Seamus's widow," Egan said, not daring to sit down again. She leaned her back against a dark beam. "I can take it to her myself, as I'm to go with my sister and this Englishman to Ballyclough in the morning. While they are visiting with Parson Adams, I'll ride over."

"Warn her to mind how she spends the money," Jenny warned. "With three wee ones at her skirts and a husband dead little more than a fortnight, she has no need to be drawing the suspicion of the magistrate or his men just now."

"I'll speak with her," Egan assured them.

The talk turned to the markets in Cork where some of the local farmers were having trouble getting fair value for their crops. As they spoke, Egan considered yet again the English governance of Ireland and the grinding poverty and injustice that these people lived with because of it. Over the years, she had seen the blood and the pain that resistance cost, but she was not willing to give up entirely the small fights and victories. She knew that this group of fighters, the Shanavests of Cork, had their counterparts in every county and town in Ireland. But deep within, Egan also knew that their daily attempts would ultimately change nothing. It wasn't every day they could get their hands on a bishop. The great landlords were Englishmen, and those with real power were untouchable by those fighting at this level.

On the other hand, here in Ireland there were far too many dead—like Seamus—and too many widows and children left behind to go hungry.

By the time their meeting broke up, the storm was lashing the countryside. Sheets of rain, driven by gusting winds, swept across the sodden fields, while intermittent lightning illuminated the scene. The few who lived in the huts on the hillside trudged off, while others waited for a break in the rain. Ronan fetched Egan's horse from the grove of trees and led the animal back to the ruined barn. Despite the fierceness of the storm, the steed appeared undisturbed by any of it.

Jenny put a hand on Egan's arm as she was donning her cloak. "Everyone was sick with worry at the word of this Englishman seeing your face this morning."

Egan patted the older woman's hand reassuringly. "Some folk worry for nothing. The rogue took my hat, but saw nothing." She thought about the pistol that he had taken—now safely hidden in her bedchamber again—but said nothing of it. "I sat with him tonight at dinner and not a word was said."

"If he suspects, but hasn't said a word yet, it could mean a trap is being laid." Liam's deep voice sounded behind them. Both women turned. "He may already have spoken to Musgrave. They could have followed ye tonight. Maybe they are thinking of laying a net for all of us."

"Say the word, and I'm telling ye I'll cut his throat."

Ronan's low growl raised the gooseflesh on Egan's back. The young man's red hair was soaked by the rain, and the fury of the weather behind him was a perfect reflection of his mood. She saw the exchange of looks between the two men and felt her blood run cold.

"No," she forced out.

Liam's eyes narrowed.

"No," she repeated, taking a step toward Ronan, still holding her horse's bridle. "We are *not* killers of the innocent."

"He's one of them."

"But he hasn't done anything wrong." She turned sharply to Liam. "The Shanavests believe in honor. We fight for justice."

"And justice calls for revenge at times," the older man replied. "If this Englishman is a threat to us, we must do whatever it takes to protect ourselves and those we fight for."

"But he is *not* a threat," she exclaimed a little too passionately and a little too quickly. The three stared at her. "He is here to marry my sister. He is only interested in his future bride and some horses . . . all of which he will take back to England when he goes. From the way he spoke this evening, he cares not a rush for what goes on in this country."

"He saw your face."

"I say he didn't!" she barked at Liam. "He punched me. The hat fell off. I stabbed him in the arm, and before he could look up I was gone. I tell you there is no way he would have made the connection . . . or even have known that Egan was a woman."

"He has the hat . . ."

"I took it back," she said. "Fey is having the man's travel clothes washed. He'll think she took the hat by mistake. I'll have another put back in his bedchamber."

"But he saw the bruise on your face tonight. How—"

Jenny raised a hand and silenced Liam's question. "We *will* trust each other." The woman looked long and hard into the faces of the two men. Her advancing age, the years she'd given to this cause, and the kin she'd lost to it gave her a voice of authority that neither man cared to challenge. "Egan has been fighting for us longer than ye, Ronan, and nearly as long as ye have, Liam. If she believes that 'tis safe to leave this Englishman be, then I say we accept her word for it."

The awkward pause that followed was a test of fortitude for Egan herself. She had been involved with the activities of this group for most of her adult life. As the years passed, however, and as younger, more hot-blooded rebels like Ronan joined in the fight, there wasn't a day that Egan didn't feel her place—never mind her authority—being questioned. She was an English-born Protestant raised in the household of her father, a man who served until recently as the king's magistrate. For those who did not know her history, it naturally took time to learn to trust her.

And now that trust was being tested yet again. With good reason.

Liam spoke finally. "If we kill one of them in cold blood, Musgrave will use the excuse to massacre more Cork folk, young and old, and call it the king's justice." He turned to Egan as she climbed her horse. "Keep an eye on him, though. We'll do what must be done if ye sense your Englishman is about to stir the pot."

She nodded, and as the two men moved back into the darkness of the barn, Jenny's thin fingers reached up and clasped hers for an instant. The woman's green eyes were gentle when they met her own.

"Ye always have been like a daughter to me, my joy, and I know in my heart that ye'll always be. Let's just hope that your sister is grateful to ye for the chances ye take now on her behalf."

Egan squeezed the woman's hand but said nothing.

She had no desire to hear Jenny explain herself further.
Some words were better not said openly. She left the
barn alone.

The rain pelted both horse and rider as she descended
the slippery hill and broke into a gallop along the hedgerows. On the flat, she leaned forward, giving the mare
her head as they made their way home.

Though the old woman's concerns were very real, for
the first time in her life, Jane actually agreed with something that her father was attempting to do. Clara needed
a husband.

She needed a respectable home and a future far away
from the turmoil that continued to rip at the entrails of
this country. For too long, the blood and pain and anguish that had caused such a chasm in Ireland had affected her family as well, festering and contaminating
all.

Clara, however, was young, beautiful, and pliable
enough to forget everything here. There was still time
for her to start a grand new life for herself in England.

The younger sister had come to Jane's room tonight
after everyone had retired, but not to question her about
the incident that had occurred in the afternoon. She'd
come to inform her of the plans to visit Ballyclough tomorrow. She'd asked her to go along, and Jane had reluctantly accepted.

And as Jane now shielded her face against the stinging
rain, she only hoped that her family would complete this
marriage negotiation soon. She didn't care to look upon
Spencer's face for even a moment longer than necessary.
Her first meeting with him was a memory she wished to
bury forever.

The stone arch over the recessed doorway that led out
into the gardens afforded Nicholas a dry place to stand
and smoke his cigar. The teeming rain ran in rivulets
down along the stone-paved paths into the garden. One
of the dogs that wandered about the estate lay curled in
a ball near his feet. Beyond the gardens, he could see
the dark hulk of the ancient stable with its two long
arms of horse stalls reaching out to the stone wall that

completed the paddock enclosure. A newer, more modern horse barn loomed beyond. When the lightning flashed, the slate of the roof looked silvery in the rain.

Despite the excuses he'd used to escape earlier, sleep continued to elude Nicholas long after the inhabitants of Woodfield House had settled in for the night. The sound of the storm and the lash of the rain against his windows had finally driven him from his bed. Restless and dissatisfied with the world, Nicholas stood in the darkness and smoked and watched the falling rain.

A brilliant array of lightning flashes in the distance drew his eye, and he silently counted the delay as he had always done since childhood. Leaning against the stone and mortar of the arched entry, he waited until the thunder reached him, one peal building on the last, impressive in its untamed power. Then, unbidden—even as the air reverberated from the thunder—from somewhere in the back of his mind the image of Jane Purefoy's face formed itself. Ringlets of black hair dancing in the wind. Black eyes, dark as the night, daring him to follow her into the storm.

Nicholas threw the cigar into the dirt and crushed it with his boot, angry for allowing himself to be so easily bewitched. He'd never allowed himself to become consumed with any woman before, and he wasn't starting now.

As he turned to go back into the house, another bolt of lightning lit the fields beyond the stables, and he stopped, fairly certain he had glimpsed a solitary rider skimming across the valley floor.

"Bewitched" was the right word. After all, everyone knew Ireland was the land of ghosts and faerie folk. Of pagan priests and haunted hillocks and storm-riding banshees who carried with them the promise of sudden death.

He stared out into the darkness until another flash illuminated the scene. There it was again—a hooded, dark-caped phantom—and it was covering ground. The rain-slick sides of the black horse gleamed as it tore across the valley. As the blackness enveloped the field again, Nicholas could see in his mind's eye the windswept cape flying behind as this ghostly apparition rode hard out of the heart of the storm.

He waited, listening for the approach of the horse, but the thunder rolling in across the fields and the teeming rain obliterated any further sign. When another bolt of lightning finally lit up the sky, the dark green fields were empty.

He remained still for a long moment, waiting for any telltale sign of what he might have really seen. There was nothing in the pastureland beneath the gardens and the stables, but in a few moments, the sound of a horse drew his attention to one of the stable wings. As he peered through the darkness, he thought he saw a horse being led into the paddock. As if prodded into action, the shaggy gray dog stood up, sniffed the air for a moment, and then trotted off unconcernedly in the direction of the stables.

Nicholas stood for a moment more. There was no sound from the dog. His curiosity finally getting the best of him, he moved out into the rain. By the time he passed by the walled formal gardens that separated the house from the stables, his shirt was soaked through and the rain was dripping from his chin. He approached the stable cautiously, keeping to the shadows.

Looking over the stone wall at the line of stalls opening onto the paddock, he also listened for any sign of the midnight rider.

The rain was pouring off the roof into puddles, but through it he thought he could make out the sound of a horse's hooves shuffling. The soft murmur of a woman's voice. He strained to hear. The words had the quality of one speaking comfortingly to an animal. Nicholas hoisted himself over the wall and moved along the stall doors. The top half of one door was partially open.

"Oidhe maithe agut, mo bourine."

Jane. Whatever it was she said, the words had been whispered in Gaelic, and Nicholas would have wagered that they carried a far gentler meaning than the curses she'd hurled at him this morning. He smiled in the darkness and waited, not wanting to surprise her in the stall. She was quick with a knife, and Nicholas didn't trust his own actions if he were to corner her again. He waited a moment more, expecting her to come through the stall door into the paddock, but there was no other sound.

Finally, he pulled open the top half of the door, clearing his throat as he did.

The smell of the horse and wet leather greeted him, and he could hear the mare shift in the darkness inside, but there was no other sound. A blanket covered the back of the steed.

Speaking in a low voice to the animal, he entered. He caressed the beast's damp mane and glanced over its high back to another door that led into the stables. Pushing past, he made his way through the stall to an alley lit only by small windows. Frowning, he turned and stroked the horse's forelock.

Even in the darkness of the narrow space, he could see that everything was in order—all was where it belonged. Except for the wet face of the horse and the dripping saddle on the door leading to the stables, it was as if Jane Purefoy had never ridden in from a violent storm only moments earlier. The routine was practiced and perfect.

"So fast and so smart," he whispered to the mare before backing out of the stall the way he'd entered.

Retracing his steps toward the house, he moved through the rain with more speed than he'd employed when heading down. He wanted a moment with her. Alone. As he strode quickly up the hill, he realized that he was looking for a reason to put himself again in her path.

The door where he'd been standing before was partially open, as he'd left it. Taking the stairs three at a time, he hurried upward through the house. Whatever secret passageway or hidden stairs she had taken to this floor and her bedchamber, Nicholas was determined to head her off.

He arrived at Jane's chamber too late. A line of candlelight showed beneath the door. Impulsively, he raised a hand to knock, but as he did, the light was extinguished.

Nicholas lowered his hand. His fist relaxed. A smile broke across his face, and he shook his head as he started down the hallway and toward his own room.

He could wait. And tomorrow was certain to be an interesting day.

*   *   *

The bed remained untouched, though the candles had been put out hours ago. A middle-aged man, looking far older than his years, sat on a well-worn, upholstered chair by the window, keeping his solitary vigil. It had been a long night, hang it. Far longer than usual.

The storm outside was easing a little when he heard an ancient hinge creak at the bottom of the secret passageway. As she so often did, she was using the passage that led from the wall between his and the next bedchamber down into the cellars of the original castle and out to the old stables.

Instantly alert, he waited until he had heard the only sounds that brought him comfort these days. He listened closely to Jane coming up the narrow and dusty stairs, to the panel in her room opening and closing, to the click of the latch behind her.

Relieved, Sir Thomas Purefoy flexed his aching joints, pushed his weary body out of the chair, and padded silently across the floor to his bed.

Nine years had passed, but he knew nine hundred more might come and go before she would forgive him.

Jane was so much like him. She never forgot, and she never forgave. But he was still her father. She would never know how much he had already suffered from her rejection of him.

Lying awake, as he had so many endless nights before, Thomas Purefoy stared up into the blackness of the bed canopy above him and tried to recall the days when a black-haired girl had run happily in the green meadows around Woodfield House.

Chapter 7

Her body ached. Her bones creaked from the impact of Spencer's hard body landing on hers. But this wasn't the worst of it. It was morning.

Mornings were not a favorite part of Jane's day—especially not *early* mornings. The housekeeper Fey was accustomed to her failings, though, and despite all of Jane's complaining, the servant simply remained, gently pushing the young woman along until she was up and washed. Supervising with the air of a benign despot, Fey watched with satisfaction as a maid helped her mistress into a black riding dress and black boots.

Looking sleepily into the looking glass, Jane winced at the color of the bruise on her face. Though the swelling on her lip and the side of her mouth had subsided considerably overnight, the sixteen shades of green and yellow seemed to be overtaking the purples and the pinks in the race to dominate. She touched the tender bruise and cursed her negligence for the hundredth time in allowing the Englishman to best her the way he had.

She could only hope the cut on his arm ached like hell.

Another glance at her reflection and she knew there could be no going out in daylight looking like a week-old carcass. Despite her customary nonchalance regarding how she dressed or looked, Jane simply couldn't imagine parading a face so hideously discolored in public. It was one thing to shock her father when he'd demanded that she meet their guests in the parlor, but today was a different matter entirely. And bringing attention to herself was something that Jane Purefoy habitually avoided like the plague.

With a weak smile at Fey, she hobbled out into the hallway and slipped into Clara's bedchamber without knocking. Perhaps her sister would have a solution to her problem. Clara was already up and dressed and greeted her with the usual morning cheerfulness that was so much a part of the younger woman's nature.

Jane thought this might be a perfect time to kill the little cherub, if she only had the energy.

"I can put some powder on your face," Clara suggested, "and tame down the wilder shades of the bruising." She followed Jane to the side of the bed. "But it will still show. And people will be asking questions. And please Jane, for heaven's sake, don't use the same excuse as you did last night."

"I thought it was quite clever."

"Come now. Striking your face on the edge of the dressing table is an excuse far too lame to try to run over any distance."

"You're starting to talk like Father." Jane eyed the smooth bedclothes of the tidily made bed. "I think it is a very good story. Such an accident could happen to anyone."

"Indeed, to anyone who is trying to fib. I don't believe anyone could do this amount of damage only to one's mouth and not the rest of her face . . . or to her brow . . . or . . ."

"I cannot comprehend such analytical reasoning at such an early hour." Jane pulled back the bedclothes and climbed into the bed with her boots and dress on, pulling the coverlet to her chin. "Go without me, shrew, and let me sleep."

"No! We cannot go without you," Clara protested, trying to wrestle the covers off her older sister. "I cannot be left alone with him on such a long ride. Even with a groom to attend us, it would not be . . ."

"Of course you can go. Everyone concerned knows that our dear mother has already seen to it that the finishing touches have been put on your wedding dress. I shouldn't be surprised if the wedding notices didn't go out last evening."

"Don't be horrid. You *must* come!" Clara continued to tug on the blanket that the older sister held tightly to her chest. "Please, Jane. Do this for me. It is not proper for me to be alone with Sir Nicholas, and you know it."

"Proper be dashed. He is here to marry you, and that's all there is to it."

"Jane!" she whined.

The older sister shook her head and held on tightly. "There is nothing that you two can do now that you shan't be doing in a very short while . . . after you are married. What difference should a fortnight make?"

Clara continued pulling. "Please come with us."

"I need sleep." Jane rolled over and pressed her head into the pillows, tucking the blanket around her. "I need rest—peace and quiet. Let me be."

"But I need you. I do not *want* to be left alone with him."

Jane let go of the blanket, and Clara fell back hard on her buttocks onto the floor.

"Why not?" Half rising on the bed, Jane looked down over the edge at her sister.

"That hurt. You intentionally made me fall."

"Why don't you want to be left alone with him?"

"Help me get up." Clara stretched her hands up to her sister.

Jane climbed out of bed, but instead of helping the younger woman, she crossed her arms and towered over her. "Is Father forcing you to marry this man against your will?"

"Don't be silly. He is not forcing me to do anything."

"But you *are* trying, once again, to be the perfect daughter, are you not? You are going along with this whole thing, not because of your own feelings toward the Englishman—as you led me to believe after your return from London—but because you think this would be best for the family. Sacrificing yourself for the . . ."

"I am not doing any such thing." Clara pushed herself to her feet and faced her sister. "You are putting words in my mouth."

Jane studied the younger woman. "Then *do* you like him?"

"Of course I do. How could one not? He is a handsome man, well-to-do; he is a baronet and well-connected in London society. He is every girl's dream. He is the *perfect* catch."

"Then do you *love* him?"

Clara's cheeks immediately flushed, and she turned abruptly and walked toward the mirror. It took a long moment before she answered. "If you want me to tell you that I love him as you loved Conor, the answer is no."

Jane frowned, feeling the old and familiar tightness in her chest as she met her sister's gaze in the mirror.

"I know of no woman who could love a man the way you have loved Conor. I shall probably never come anywhere near having what you have had—your joy when he was still alive, or the suffering you have endured since he was killed. Honestly, Jane, I know of no one else who is as capable of loving a man as you are."

A painful lump in her throat kept Jane from responding. She fought back tears threatening to spill.

"But in my case, you are making a great deal more of things than you should." Clara turned and faced her sister. "The reason why I don't want to be left alone with Sir Nicholas is that he is so much older, so much more experienced. Naturally, I still feel quite shy in his company. I believe, in time, I will learn to trust myself and not be so intimidated by his good looks or his charm."

Jane studied the nervous smile on her sister's face and tried to remember if she'd ever felt this way. She thought of all those times she had run off to meet secretly with Conor by the standing stones on the moor near Knocknakilla. That year, she had turned fifteen and Conor sixteen, but shyness had never been a problem with either of them. But how could it have been? The two had known each other for all of their lives . . . she, the daughter of the magistrate; he, the son of a poor cottager. Just as Jane's mind started to drift off toward those memories of the past, Clara's voice jolted her back to the present.

"You can wear the black hat with the dark veil that Mother wore to the funeral of Parson Adams's mother last winter. That should cover the bruise and more."

Clara reached for Jane's hand and started pulling her toward the door. "Fey tells me that Sir Nicholas has been ready for some time. We should hurry, I suppose. We don't want him to form a poor opinion of us now, do we?"

"Not at all," Jane muttered under her breath as she was dragged from the room. "As his future sister-in-law, I am absolutely desperate with fear that he should form anything but the highest opinion of me."

For the hundredth time, at least, Nicholas watched Jane try to straighten the silly-looking hat perched on top of her head. Thwarting her at every turn, the autumn breeze continued to push the thing this way and that, tugging at the strands of dark hair she must have tucked with such care beneath. The long pins had loosened, though, and the waves of hair threatened to escape, and only the dark veil covering her face kept the foolish thing anchored.

The older sister had not appeared at breakfast with the rest of the family. And even afterward, Nicholas had seen no sign of her until he and Clara had walked to their horses waiting in the paddock. She was waiting for them there amid bustling grooms and stable boys. Arrayed in black, she sat astride her ebony mare, a sight to behold. No sidesaddle delicacy for this one. Jane Purefoy was a "goer" in every way.

Except, of course, for that ridiculous hat.

The breeze stiffened as they rode north across open fields. Though the sun shone brightly overhead, to the northwest clouds lay like a tattered shawl over the round-shouldered peaks of ancient gray mountains. In his mind's eye, he could see so clearly the vision of Jane last night, riding the same animal, carried along on wind and the storm. He'd fervently wished to catch up to her and talk to her before she returned to her room. He'd assumed she'd want to speak to him, too. Nicholas had discovered her secret, but how much he was to reveal—and to whom—had to be a gnawing question. And Jane Purefoy didn't strike him as a very patient person.

The wind continued to buffet them. From his vantage point, riding half a dozen lengths behind Jane, Nicholas could see that she had finally pushed up the dark netting over the narrow brim of the hat.

On impulse, Nicholas spurred his steed forward, suddenly desirous of a glimpse of her face. Upon hearing him approach, though, Jane nudged her mare, keeping the safe distance between them that she'd maintained since leaving Woodfield House. For an insane moment he considered laying his riding crop onto the flanks of his mount and daring her to race with him. But the thought of Clara straggling along behind checked him in time.

He reined in, suppressing a frown as he waited for the younger sister to reach him. Unlike Jane, she sat fashionably sidesaddle and appeared a little flustered. Coming up beside him, she reached up to adjust the delicate feathered hat that she was wearing.

"I'm so sorry. I see I should have chosen a livelier horse this morning." She patted her brow with the back of her gloved hand and tucked some of the golden curls under the hat. "I am not as horrid a rider as you must think. It is just my choice of . . ."

"Not at all. You ride well," he complimented, pulling on the reins of his steed so it would fall in step with hers. He could see that Jane had slowed down ahead and was pulling the veil back over her face. "It is for me to apologize for not keeping to your pace."

"No, sir," she said softly. "No apologies are warranted, I assure you."

Nicholas's attention again was drawn to the tantalizing image of the expert rider ahead and the cruel game that she was playing. She was once again staying just ahead of them. Close enough to torment, but not close enough to be touched.

"I've been wondering, Miss Clara," he said, nodding his head in Jane's direction, "why it is that your sister refuses to ride with us?"

"She . . . I assume . . . I should think she doesn't want to intrude."

"Intrude on what?" His words were tinged with mockery, and he cleared his throat to correct his tone. "What I intended to say is that there could be no intrusion, and this would be a far more comfortable ride if we could

travel together. I had very little time to converse with
your sister last night, and frankly I fail to see why the
three of us shouldn't spend an hour enjoying each other's company."

"I should very much like you to become better acquainted with my sister," Clara responded, and Nicholas
watched Jane again reach up and adjust the abomina-
ble hat.

"Would it help if we both were to approach and tell
her that she would not be *intruding* upon our
conversation?"

"I fear that my sister has a mind of her own." The
blue eyes turned to him. "I hope you believe me when
I say that it wasn't my idea for Jane to be riding so
far ahead."

"I do believe you. But if you would allow me to pry
a little into your family's affairs, I have a question I'd
like to ask you." Nicholas continued after receiving a
cautious nod from Clara. "I've been quite perplexed
since meeting Miss Jane yesterday. Could you tell me
why it was that your sister did not accompany your family to London this past spring?"

"Certainly. That was Jane's choice. She has made a
habit of never traveling with the rest of us."

"Why, then, did your family never mention that there
was an older daughter?" Nicholas directed a piercing
look at her. "Was it Jane's decision, as well, not to be
acknowledged by either parent or sister? Tell me, Clara,
was your sister dropped by gypsies in her infancy at your
parents' door?"

"Hardly, sir!" Clara's gaze fell on the reins looped
tightly around her gloved hands. "Jane is my only sister,
and very dear to me . . . to all of us."

"And yet you have no answer for the secrecy surrounding her existence? Though I am not particularly
opposed to a little mystery . . . or scandal, either . . . I
must say that there is a hint of both in the air at Woodfield House. But perhaps I should take this up with Sir
Thomas."

"I . . . I . . . well, as you see fit, sir. But I can tell
you honestly that my sister never had any desire to be
presented in society, as I have been presented. She had

no balls thrown in her honor. There were no callers courting her. Jane never had any intention of choosing a husband from London's *ton*." She hesitated. "My parents, however, had different plans for me. It is no secret, and there is no shame in admitting to you that my parents took me to London for the purpose of arranging a proper marriage."

And given the right title and qualifications and wealth, Nicholas thought, anyone wearing breeches would have sufficed. Once again the business of marriage reared its mercenary head, and Nicholas found himself repulsed by the idea. To him, the entire process wasn't much different than the owner of a likely mare going to a country fair and choosing a stud. All that was left was to haggle over the price . . . and Sir Thomas was, no doubt, well prepared for that.

As they rode on in silence, thoughts of the marriage of his friend Stanmore to Rebecca Neville last year sprang to his mind. Before leaving for Ireland, he'd made a short trip to Solgrave to meet the new member of their family. Samuel Frederick Wakefield was born at the end of July. With the older boy, James, home for the summer and doting on the new baby, Nicholas could not recall ever knowing a family as content and happy as the Stanmores.

Starting up yet another of the rolling green hills that seemed to go on forever, Nicholas couldn't help but wonder if Rebecca and Stanmore knew how lucky they were that they had so completely avoided the ordeal of bartering for a spouse. Yes, he was certain that they did indeed know.

But, he thought with a pang of guilt, when all was said and done, how different was his own approach to finding a wife than the approach used by the Purefoys? Not very, when one came right down to it.

Up ahead, at the top of the hill, Jane was withdrawing a pin to adjust the hat when a strong gust suddenly tore the thing off her head and sent it—veil and all—swooping past them like some tattered and malevolent raven. In an instant, Nicholas had wheeled his horse and, drawing his sword, leaned down and pinned the thing to the ground. Raising the hat like a trophy on the point of his sword, he did his best to look embarrassed as he turned back to the two women. Gingerly he pulled the hat from the weapon and sheathed his sword as he rode back to the sisters, who were staring at him wide-eyed.

Jane's face, however, was all Nicholas had eyes for as he approached. With her hair now loose around her shoulders and dancing in the wind, her dark eyes were watching his every movement as he approached. Once again, he saw the woman he'd knocked down the day before. As he drew nearer, his gaze took in all of her—from the tips of her black boots to the proud chin and bruised mouth. He could not stop himself from staring at her sensual lips and wondering about their taste.

"Well, sir . . ." Jane said as he reached them. She seemed flushed and breathless, as if she'd been guessing at the direction of his thoughts. "It appears . . . it appears you've not only run it to ground; you've dealt it a death blow!"

"I fear that I have." He inserted a gloved finger where his sword had cut the beaver skin. "And I insist on buying a replacement at the first opportunity."

"No need," Jane responded. "I can wear it as is. When we get back to Woodfield House, I am certain Fey can mend it . . . well, somehow."

She extended a hand for the hat, and Nicholas nudged his horse nearer. But just as Jane's hand was about to close on the brim, he released it. As if shot from his hand, the thing flew off again, carried away on another gust of wind.

Jane watched the hat take flight. Instead of going after it, Nicholas enjoyed the close study of her pretty face. "I see you shall *have* to allow me to find a replacement, now."

"It was actually our mother's," Clara said softly from behind before pulling her horse abreast. "I assure you that she shan't miss it."

Jane watched the hat tumbling across the moor for a moment before turning her attention back to her sister. "Well, as fate would have it, I fear I cannot escort you to Ballyclough, after all. But if you could make my excuses to the Reverend Mr. Adams and Mrs. Br—?"

"No, Jane. You promised to come."

"I know I did. But under the circumstances of my . . . appearance . . ."

"The parson already saw the bruise on your face last night."

"But Mrs. Brown has not."

"It doesn't show so much in the light." Clara leaned over and touched the other woman's arm. "You look fine, Jane. Tell her, Sir Nicholas, that she looks fine."

"I would say that Miss Purefoy looks far better than fine," he offered quietly as his gaze caressed her face. "I should be greatly disappointed if she were to rob us of her charming company on such a pleasant day."

A soft blush actually crept into her cheeks, and Nicholas was happy to know that she was not totally immune to his words.

"Come, Jane. Please? Parson Adams has been after you for some time now to come to Ballyclough, and we are almost there."

A look of frustration crossed the older sister's fair features, and she glanced again in the direction that her hat had flown off. It was still visible far off in the distance, the veil caught on a bramble while the hat itself dangled in the mud of what appeared to be a water-filled ditch.

"*Jane!*" Clara's insistent and pleading tone made it clear that she didn't want to be left alone with him, and this suited Nicholas perfectly.

"I shall escort you to the edge of the village, but no farther. There I shall leave you and ride over to visit a friend near Buttevant. If you insist, though, I shall return in time to have a very short visit with Parson Adams before returning to Woodfield House with you."

Clara was obviously relieved, and the three again turned their horses northward. Before Jane could move ahead of them again, though, Nicholas immediately directed the conversation toward her.

"I must say, Miss Jane, that I am quite surprised that your family would approve of you riding off on your own—to that Buttevant place—without an escort. No fears of the Whiteboys?"

"None, Sir Nicholas." She kept her gaze straight ahead. "They have never been known to remain in the same area after an incident such as the one yesterday. Are *you* concerned, sir?"

"Not at all."

"And how is your arm today?"

"Much better. And your face?"

"I am *very* well, thank you."

Nicholas suppressed a smile, and the three rode along in silence for a moment.

"Those were capital storms last night. Either of you have any difficulty sleeping?"

"Sleep is just about the only thing that Jane holds precious in life," Clara offered. "In fact, part of my sister's crankiness this morning has to do with being awakened too early in the day."

"I sympathize with her completely," he replied casually. "As a creature of the night myself, I had difficulty sleeping last night. So I ended up going outside and watching the storm from the safety of the archway facing the stables. It is amazing how enchanting the night can be when one spends some time in it."

Jane cast a questioning glance at him, and Nicholas held her gaze. Her eyes darkened, sparkling like sapphires, and he reveled in the knowledge that he had again captured her attention.

Clara's voice broke in. "There is the village. Small but quite charming, don't you think, Sir Nicholas?"

Ahead of them, nestled in a valley and surrounded by a patchwork of brown, harvested fields and green pastureland dotted with a few cows and more sheep, lay the cluster of cottages. Up against an ancient castle at one end of the village, the squat gray tower of a chapel could be seen.

"The castle was built by the Desmonds centuries ago," Clara said, following the direction of Nicholas's gaze. "The Purdens live there now, but we don't associate with them. And there is also a limestone quarry at that end . . ."

"I shall be on my way, then." Jane reined in her horse and turned it toward a road heading east. "I shall see you again sometime this afternoon."

Nicholas tried to think of some objection, some excuse

that would keep her with them. "It is too bad we cannot accompany you on your visit to Buttevant. I should very much like to see more of this countryside."

Jane's look told him there was no chance in hell that she would be taking him along.

"That is a fine idea, Sir Nicholas. Why don't you go with Jane to Buttevant?" Clara's remark brought the others' heads around sharply. "It is fine horse country, you know. Why, the valleys along the River Awbeg are famous throughout Ireland. Even the Irish here are riders from childhood. My father often sings the praises of the fine animals he's seen and purchased from the folk who raise them along the river."

"But I am not visiting any horse traders, Clara." Jane's words were spoken through clenched teeth. Her dark eyes flashed.

"I know that, but it would be much safer," Clara assured her pleasantly. "And while you are visiting your friend, I'm certain Sir Nicholas wouldn't mind waiting in the village and enjoying the beautiful scenery. There is even a ruined abbey there, rumored to be as old as any church in Dublin. It's quite lovely, really."

"You don't say," Nicholas responded with interest.

"Excuse us for a moment, will you?" Jane pushed her horse toward her sister. Her whispered words were intended only for Clara, but Nicholas could not help overhearing them.

"*Why* are you doing this?"

"You know why."

"I give you my word that I'll be back. I *shall* go alone!"

Clara shook her head, and Nicholas could see the color rising in the face of the older sister.

"I believe Sir Nicholas is correct about the possibility of the Shanavests still lingering in the area," Clara said out loud, turning to him. "Would you do my sister the honor of accompanying her to her friend's place and then back here, sir?"

He looked from one sister's happy face to the other's tense one. "Are you quite sure Parson Adams would be agreeable to this change in plans?"

"Absolutely."

"But what about you? I shouldn't care to see you slighted."

"Not at all, sir." Clara gave him her brightest smile ever. "I suggested it, did I not? Actually, I am looking forward to spending some time in the parson's company. And with you keeping Jane safe from roving bandits, sir, I shall have the peace of mind that both of you will return shortly. I'll see to it that Mrs. Brown has tea waiting for you."

"If that is your wish . . . ?"

"Then it is settled." Clara smiled and touched her riding whip to her mare's flank. "We shall see you soon."

"What about *me*?" Jane protested, watching her sister descend the hill. A small flock of sheep separated as the younger woman approached them. "No one asked me if I am willing to take *him* along . . ."

Nicholas nudged his horse between Jane and her departing sister. "I'm very sorry, Miss Purefoy, but it appears you are stuck with me for the remainder of the morning. Now, will you try to recall some of your English charm and hospitality and at least pretend to tolerate me?"

"I think not, sir!" She glanced meaningfully at his arm. "You couldn't handle me at your best yesterday. But if you are not careful, today may prove infinitely worse for you."

Chapter 8

"Miss Clara, how lovely to have you here." Mrs. Brown met the guest by the door of the parsonage. "The parson was hoping that you wouldn't mind waiting in the parlor and entertaining your company until he gets back. He was called away unexpectedly and he feared he might be a wee bit late in getting back. But wait, miss, where *is* your company?"

The housekeeper peered out at Clara's solitary horse tied by the gate in front of the parsonage.

Sunlight glinted in the puddles still standing in the rutted road that led through the village. Though the wispy smoke from a dozen cooking fires colored the breezes over the thatched roofs, the village was nearly deserted. Only a few ancient chickens, a goat in a stone enclosure across the way, and a workman carrying a load of sticks on his back at the far end of the hamlet hinted of other inhabitants.

"My sister needed to visit a friend in Buttevant, so I sent our guest Sir Nicholas with her. I wanted to be sure Jane would get back here in time to visit."

"Good for you," Mrs. Brown said encouragingly. She closed the door and led the way down a narrow passage toward the parlor. "We do not see enough of Miss Jane's bright face these days. There's not a day that goes by that someone in the village is not inquiring after her health or asking when her next visit will be. She is greatly missed here, I assure you, and I know for a certainty the parson has been concerned about her absence from Ballyclough."

"Has he?" Clara was surprised by the sharpness of her own tone.

"Indeed. Thinking on it daily, I should say." The housekeeper nodded emphatically and opened the door to the parlor.

The curtains had already been pulled open, and the shutters folded back. Sunshine slanted through the open windows, lighting the spare but comfortable furnishings of the room. A homey, cozy scent of peat and pipe tobacco hung in the air. As she breathed in the smells, a feeling of well-being spread through her, warming her, making her forget the disquiet the housekeeper's words had caused. She loved this house.

Mrs. Brown lowered herself into her chair by the small peat fire and rang a small silver bell that she took from the pocket of her apron. Clara sat down in the settle across from her.

"I hope you don't mind my saying so, Miss Clara, but it would have done your sister a world of good if she'd gone off to England with the rest of you this past spring."

A young servant poked her head into the room, and Mrs. Brown ordered a pot of fresh tea to be brought in.

"Aye. As I was saying to Parson Adams this very morning, if Miss Jane were to find an English husband . . . a good one as you have found . . . why, the child might just shake off the sadness she's been carrying all these years. Aye, what she needs is a good one like yours."

"Really, Mrs. Brown, I haven't found myself a husband, English or otherwise. Sir Nicholas is my father's guest, and he has yet to ask for my hand in marriage. To be honest, I don't care for people going around and presuming things that may not come to pass."

"You are quite right, my dear," Mrs. Brown said, picking up her needlework from a basket beside the chair. "We shouldn't be counting our chickens . . . and all that. But I shouldn't worry. You are so lovely."

"This is the baronet's first visit to Ireland. He might not care for what he sees." Trying to hide her impatience, Clara stood up and went to the window. In the pretty garden beside the house, one of the year's last rosebuds bobbed its head in the breeze. "If I may ask, Mrs. Brown, has Parson Adams expressed a position regarding my sister?"

"Indeed he has. The parson told me, in no uncertain terms, that he does not believe that one English-born nobleman in a hundred—your gentleman excepted—is good enough for your sister."

"Is that so?"

Mrs. Brown continued without looking up. "He thinks most of them are too shallow. And to give him credit, the parson was educated among them, so he should know well enough. And not to bring up a difficult subject, my dear, but he believes once a would-be suitor learns of Jane's younger years, the average English gentleman would cry foul and leave the poor thing standing at the altar. But I say, find a decent one and tell him nothing. She's a fine woman for any man, if you ask me."

"Well, I believe Jane has no intention of accepting suitors." Clara reached up and pulled off her hat. "My belief is that she is perfectly happy at Woodfield House and will remain there for the rest of her life." She put the hat down on the wide windowsill and rejoined the housekeeper by the fire.

"I'm happy to hear that you feel that way, child, but the parson doesn't agree with you. He is a very observant man, and he has been watching Jane closely for some time."

"Really, Mrs. Brown?"

"Aye, and if he says your sister is unhappy at Woodfield House, I believe him."

Clara held her tongue as the young servant entered the room with a tray containing a teapot with cups and several small cakes. Mrs. Brown took the tray from her and placed it on the table beside her. Just as she was preparing to pour the tea, however, the parson could be heard coming in through the back of the house.

"Here he is now." Mrs. Brown finished pouring the tea and pushed herself immediately to her feet. "I'll go and tell him that you are here. Oh my heavens, I also need to tell the cook to wait luncheon until Miss Jane and your Englishman get here."

Clara watched the round figure of the older woman scurry out of the room. She, too, stood up as a wave of unhappiness regarding everything she'd just been told gripped her stomach. She walked to the window, removed her gloves, and placed them next to the hat. She wished for a mirror, but she knew there was none. Absently, she reached up and tried to arrange the curls.

"There is no need for that. Your fiancé is not here yet, Miss Clara."

The young woman jumped and turned quickly to the door. Henry Adams stood on the threshold, filling the doorway. She saw the gray eyes studying her critically, and she felt the heat rise into her face.

"Mrs. Brown tells me that you sent your English baronet off with Jane to Buttevant." He removed his gloves as he entered the room. "You know you are risking your sister's wrath when you start meddling in her activities."

Clara moved to the small table. "May I pour you some tea?"

He nodded. The breeze had ruffled his short black hair, and his probing gaze only added to her unease. "So how did you manage it? Or, a better question, *why* send them off together?"

The cup rattled slightly against the saucer as Clara extended it toward him. "I was hoping for a few moments alone with you . . . so that we could talk."

"What do we have to talk about?" he said coolly.

"About . . . about us."

Their fingers brushed as he accepted the cup from her. "We have nothing more to say to each other—in private, that is."

Her heart sank, and she fought down the tight knot clawing its way up into her throat. "Please give me a chance to explain."

"You have explained, Clara—clearly and utterly. You did so six months ago. I've moved on, and there is no point in revisiting that unpleasantness."

When she lifted her head, his handsome image was blurred, and she blinked back her tears. "I never knew you could be so cruel."

"I? Cruel? Please!" He placed the teacup on the shelf above the hearth and frowned at her. "Shortness of memory has never been one of your failings. But having said that, I must leave you. I find it totally inappropriate to be dallying here with a nearly married woman." He bowed curtly. "I believe I left my . . . my *Daily Meditations* in the chapel. You can have Mrs. Brown send for me when your fiancé and your sister return."

Clara stared for an instant at his broad back as he turned away. Panic seized her, and she ran toward the door, blocking his path. "I beg of you, Henry."

He halted a step away. "Clara, you are making a fool of yourself."

"So what if I am?" She blindly reached for the door behind her and closed it, leaning her weight against it.

"You mustn't jeopardize your reputation this way."

"Reputation means nothing to me now." Fresh tears rolled down her cheeks. "I cannot let you go. Not until you hear me."

"Clara, open the door." He took a step closer, and she could see the sparks of temper burning in his gray eyes.

"I love you, Henry." The words tumbled out. "Please, you must forgive me for what is past . . . for the way I behaved before. Those were empty words I spoke six months ago. I know I offended you . . . hurt you. I was a fool."

"Clara, it is too late for this. You have a suitor who has come all the way from England for the sole purpose . . ."

"I don't care." She threw herself against him, wrapping her arms around him. He stood rigidly as she held him, but she couldn't stop now. She pressed her face against the coarse cloth of his jacket. "Six months ago you asked me to become your wife. You told me that you loved me . . . that you wanted me at your side forever. Please, Henry, ask me again."

"No."

"Please just ask me, and I will be yours."

"I was not good enough for you then"—his fingers grasped her shoulders firmly, and he pushed her back until he was looking into her face—"and nothing has changed. I could never measure up to your expectations for a husband. I am still a second son—a poor clergyman who is happy to labor here, away from the pleasures of society. Six months ago, I was a fool to think I could compete with the advantages you were about to receive in London. Fancy dresses, receptions, and balls awaited you. Wealth and fame awaited you. 'I must marry someone with a title,' you said.''

"Please, Henry," she sobbed. "But you know that wasn't for myself. I was doing it all for my parents. After Jane—after what she had done to disgrace their name— I had to do something to mend the past."

"Jane! Always blaming Jane!" He spat out the words. "I wish you would put aside this pretence of selflessness, Clara. Others might believe you and be fooled, but not I."

His words jolted her, tearing the air from her lungs.

"No," she gasped. "It's true. I was doing it for them . . . and I thought I could go through with it."

"And now?" He towered over her.

"I cannot. Now that Sir Nicholas is here—now that I see that he may truly offer for me—I cannot go through with it. I care nothing for this Englishman. I never will. You are the one who has my heart. You are the only one whom I think of. You are the one I want to spend my life with." She reached up with trembling fingers and touched his lips. "He is too experienced. Too worldly for someone like me. Everything about him intimidates me. But you, Henry . . . my gentle Henry . . ."

She stood on her toes and pressed her lips against his. Softly, tentatively, innocently, she placed small kisses on his firm chin, his clenched cheek, and again on his lips. She kissed him with the same innocence that he had kissed her six months earlier when he'd proposed to her.

"So what is to happen now?" His hand fisted roughly in her hair, and she cried out as he pulled her head back until he was looking into her face. "So what if I yield to your wishes? I only make a fool out of myself before you again. So what if I send away this suitor that frightens you with his . . . with his manliness? I'll tell you. Tomorrow your restless and greedy nature will again assert itself, and another will appear to take this one's place."

"No!"

"Yes! For you know that there are no new wardrobes

of dresses every season for the wife of a country cleric. There are no journeys abroad. No London parties. No dozen or so dashing rogues chasing you about the drawing rooms of Bath. You would be bored to death, Clara. You would curse me for eternity for leading you into the dull drudgery of a clergyman's life."

She shook her head. "I shall be true to my promise. I shall never regret our life together." Tears continued to soak her cheeks. "The love we share will be enough. I ask for nothing more."

"And what of your parents? Of the honor that you presumably wanted to restore to your family name?"

"I . . . I cannot think of any of that now. Not when there is a chance of losing you forever."

"You are so beautiful," he whispered bitterly, his gaze scouring every inch of her face. "So young and naïve and beautiful."

Before Clara could object, Henry's lips crushed down on hers. But this was no kiss of innocence, but an unleashing of repressed desire. His strong fingers delved deeper into her hair and his mouth devoured her lips, forcing her mouth open, his tongue surging inside. She gave a stifled gasp and felt her body mold against him. The sudden awareness of her limbs made her long for something more. Her hands reached up around his neck.

Then, without warning, he abruptly ended the kiss and pushed her away.

"I understand you better now than I ever did before. Like a child, you only want what you cannot have."

She shook her head and tried to move back into his arms, but he kept her away.

"Well, your 'gentle Henry' is gone," he said mockingly. "He was just a fool who treated you like a rare and delicate flower, but found himself stung by those fair petals." He pushed her farther away, his voice hardening. "You chose your way six months ago. Marry your Englishman and finish what you have begun. I wish you all the worldly treasures you were born and brought up to possess, but leave me be."

In an instant, he was gone.

Clara stared in shock for a long moment at the closed door, and then turned to the wall. Standing alone, she wept bitter tears of anguish for the one true love she had so stupidly thrown away.

Her mount was indeed a fine one, and well accustomed to the soft turf and uneven terrain of the Irish countryside. And Jane was the rider to handle her.

For a quarter of an hour, the woman led him on a merry chase. Up hill and down. With her black hair streaming wildly behind her, she leaped streams and ditches and hedgerows with stunning ease and grace.

The pace she set made it impossible for Nicholas to talk to this fiend of a horsewoman. If the ground leveled out into a smooth green meadow, she was sure to cut away to some higher passage where the sharp edges of white rock protruded from the hillside, endangering both horse and rider.

Emerging from a broad, fast-running stream that left him half a field behind her, Nicholas shook his head at her spirit. He had to give her credit. Jane Purefoy had successfully used every racing ploy known to slow him down and create distance between them. She might have been forced to take him along, but that didn't mean that she had to endure his company. At the top of the next hill, Nicholas saw Jane rein in her steed, and he quickly closed the distance between them.

Her cheeks were flushed with health, and she turned slightly in the saddle, black eyes flashing, her chest heaving from the exertion of the ride.

Nicholas didn't think he'd ever seen a more magnificent sight.

She looked away as he rode up to her. The Awbeg came into view. There, along the steep green banks of meandering river, he saw the buildings and broken walls of an abbey and the neat little village just to the north.

"You should be able to find the main thoroughfare through Buttevant with no difficulty," she said, uttering her first words since leaving Clara at Ballyclough.

"What are those two towers?" Nicholas pointed in the direction of the village. He was searching for a way to detain her.

"The ruins of Lombard's Castle."

He noticed the activity beyond it. "And what is being built beyond the town?"

"A barracks to house troops."

"I see." He raised a curious brow. "Well, that should discourage rebellion, I should think."

"With that thought, Sir Nicholas, I take my leave of you."

"I thought you planned to visit a friend here yourself."

"I do, but she doesn't live in the village proper. She lives close by, though." Jane gestured in the vague direction of the abbey. "But the village has an inn and a number of shops and a couple of very fine stables to while away your time. I shall come after you when I've finished my business."

She started along the ridge by the river, but stopped and turned sharply to him when he started to follow.

"That way." She pointed toward the village. "You go that way. That will take you where you want to go."

"Would you at least tell me who it is that you are visiting? Just in case I become lost and in need of your assistance?"

"Come, Sir Nicholas, it is impossible for you to lose your way. Now please be off. Clara and Reverend Adams are expecting us back by noon."

For a moment, he considered being completely disagreeable and trailing after her, but decided against it. With a nod at her, Nicholas nudged his horse down the incline, all the while keeping an eye on Jane as she rode off along the crest of the hill.

He was a man well acquainted with women of all social classes and types. It had long been a leisure activity of his to attempt to understand the many feminine moods and needs. For the most part, women liked him and sought out his company. He'd generally expected the same response here.

Obviously Jane Purefoy was not to be classed with other women.

Nicholas reined in and watched her disappear beyond the crest of the hill. Somehow he had to make her understand that he was not a threat to her or her seditious

pursuits. At the same time, he wanted to let her know
that he no longer had any interest in courting the
younger sister.

He spurred his horse toward the village, knowing that
explanation and extrication could be complicated matters at the best of times.

And these were hardly the best of times.

The path from the rectory to the chapel was empty of
the town's inhabitants, and Henry Adams was glad of it.

His passion had taken control of his reason, and he
was already regretting his behavior. He had given way
too quickly to his anger. His own personal pride, stung
long ago, had possessed his soul far too easily.

The sun was shining down on his bare head, but he
didn't notice it at all, focused as he was on his own
failings. How could a man of the cloth, he thought
harshly, possess a character so fallible and weak?

As he reached the heavy iron-banded door of the
chapel, he hesitated, turning instead to the pathway that
led across the small stream and up the hill toward the
graveyard by the road to Mallow. He would not step into
the house of God with the heat of passion still raging in
his mind and body.

Clara's soft mouth had been so willing. The press of
her firm body offered the fantasy of many tempestuous
dreams. But her words plagued him. They were words
that he longed to believe, but knew not how to trust.

Henry's passion for the younger Purefoy sister had
taken hold of him a year ago, but the fever of it still
raged in his blood.

Although he had known the family for years, it was
Jane whom he'd known best from their youth. The two
of them were about the same age. The two of them had
shared so much of the same outrage over the ill treatment that Ireland endured. When they were younger,
they had both even spoken out—with that indignation
found so often in the naïve—against the English Penal
Laws that afflicted the peasantry and the landowners and
the merchants alike. Indeed, despite the gossip surrounding Jane when they were younger, their own
friendship had remained true throughout their adoles-

cence and his years at the university. To this day, he knew that she considered him a trusted friend, and he considered her the same.

One thing he had not confided in her, though, was his feelings for her sister.

Henry sat on the low stone wall surrounding the crowded graves of peasants, tanners, and quarrymen. Here lay the history of this village, he thought, enclosed by a square of rough gray stone. Our time here is so short. We're born to toil . . . and toil we do. We suffer and then we die. But somewhere between the years of blood and tears, we hope for moments of love.

He looked back across the stony brook at the village and at his rectory. Last summer, the flowers were blooming in his little garden and the fields around Ballyclough green and alive when Henry saw, for the first time, that light in Clara's eyes. No longer a child, she had somehow, without his noticing, grown into a beautiful young woman. There had been other things, as well, that Henry had become aware of then. Her quiet dignity. Her determination to keep peace between the members of her tumultuous family. He also noticed the way that she tried to hide her inclination to hang on every word he said and on his every movement.

It had been easy to fall in love with Clara. It had been even easier to allow himself to dream of someday asking for her hand in marriage. And dream he did. For though he was well born, he was still a country clergyman and she a knighted magistrate's daughter. Nonetheless, whatever her parents might have wanted for her, when he set out to court her privately, she'd been more than willing to receive his attentions.

The rosebuds were full and ready to open when Henry Adams held his heart in his outstretched hands and approached Clara with his offer of marriage. He'd wanted her consent first before broaching the subject with Sir Thomas. His greatest mistake had been in taking that consent for granted.

Anger at the memory drove him to his feet, and Henry walked across the road and into a field that had lain fallow this year. Upon these lands, he knew, cattle and sheep and goats had once grazed freely, their hides supplying the tanners of Ballyclough with the materials of their trade. Now fertile farms surrounded him, the profits of the tenants' labors going into the pockets of the great landowners. The planted lands of the English were far superior to the marshy patches of bog land that the Irish were allowed beyond the next line of hills. And it was the same worship of Mammon that was ruining this country that made Clara refuse him.

Frustrated beyond words, Henry stopped in the middle of the field. He was just not good enough. It simply came down to that. There was no way she could consent to a marriage that didn't improve her family's name—or wealth—or position—or whatever. Clara had been bred to reject him that day. She'd been raised to take that fertile ground . . . and he could offer her only a life in the marshes.

Though he'd been hurt, he had never mentioned any of this to Jane—not out of pride, but because he knew this would be another blow to her. In a family that thrived because of the privilege and superiority that went with being English, Jane had always fought against it, and he knew she believed she'd had some positive influence on her younger sister. How disappointed Jane would be to learn Clara's true feelings. How many sleepless nights had it taken him to come to grips with it!

Henry Adams shook his head. Well, that was behind him now.

He turned his back on the green fields and started toward the decrepit ruins of the tanners' cottages crowding the stream at the lower end of the village. He knew where to go.

Darby O'Connell, with a stubbornness inherited from his father, had remained in Ballyclough, determined to eke out an existence in the tanning trade that his grandfather and his grandfather's grandfather had practiced before him. But his hard life became harder when his wife delivered a dead baby two weeks ago.

She had not once gotten back onto her feet after that—not once stopped losing blood. For nearly a week now the woman had been delirious with fever, and yesterday the husband went for the priest in Mallow. While Darby was on the road, Henry had looked in on her. A

woman from a nearby cottage was doing what she could
to keep the dying woman comfortable. During Henry's
visit, the three little O'Connells had simply looked up at
him with blank expressions from the dirt floor beside
their mother's pallet. He could see at a glance that the
poor woman's time was at hand, and he knew that
Darby would surely go mad when his wife passed away.
He didn't want to think what would happen to the
children.

The tanner's cottage came into view, and Henry
thought for a moment how different this thatched hut
was from the grand buildings of Woodfield House.

No, he needed to clear his mind of the words and
promises Clara had spoken to him today. She was far
too acquiescent to ever withstand the social and family
pressures that would surely pour over her if he were fool
enough to broach the subject of marriage with Sir
Thomas.

Sir Nicholas Spencer had arrived to take his prize, and
there was no competing with him. Title and money
spoke loudly . . . and Henry had neither. She had been
the wise one and he the fool six months ago. Well, he
was wiser now, and it was best for all to keep it that
way.

Darby's youngest, barefoot and only just covered by
his rags, was sitting against the stone wall of the cottage
when Henry came across the stream. As the parson
watched, the child dropped a dirty piece of uncooked
potato that he'd been clutching in a filthy hand into the
mud. The young boy's face was stained with tears and
dirt, and as he got on all fours and crawled after his lost
possession, a small dog darted up and gobbled down the
bit of food, running off again as quickly as he came. The
child immediately began to wail, but stopped suddenly
as he noticed Henry's approach.

The teary eyes and dirt-smeared face turned to the
parson with recognition, and the boy raised his thin arms
into the air to be picked up. Henry leaned down and
lifted the child without a moment's hesitation and
headed toward the cottage door.

As the boy nestled a tired head against his shoulder,
Henry knew that he could waste no more time in snug

parlors, courting young women who had never wanted for anything in their lives.

No, he thought as he ducked his head and stepped into the dark cottage, this was where he belonged.

Chapter 9

Alexandra gaped for a long moment at the dozens upon dozens of paintings stored along the walls and taking up a large area at one end of the attic space. With cloths draped over them, they lined the walls like battalions of soldiers. She was simply stunned by the sight.

The young serving lass had not thought twice about taking Lady Spencer up past the servants' quarters to the large space beneath the roof where Miss Jane often painted and stored her sketches and other work. Lady Spencer was a guest, and when she said that Lady Purefoy had encouraged her to see the older daughter's work, the girl had merely curtsied and led the way.

The last set of stairs, narrow and steep, took them to a large, sparsely furnished open space with sloping roof timbers just overhead. It was the studio of a serious artist—*that* Alexandra could see. And a busy one, she thought, eying the covered rows of canvases.

"Beggin' yer pardon about the smell, m'lady," the servant offered, never coming farther than the top step. "I'm told 'tis the paints. But I know Miss Jane likes spending time here."

"I can understand why," Alexandra murmured as she let her gaze travel to the two large shuttered windows on either end of the space. At this end, a battered stool sat by an empty easel and two worktables, while buckets, rolls of canvas, bags of pigment, and casks of oil were stacked and spread everywhere. "You may leave me. I shan't touch anything that I shouldn't be touching."

The servant returned Alexandra's smile, but didn't retreat. "M'lady, no guest I know of has ever asked to come and see Miss Jane's things."

She liked the protectiveness she saw in the girl. "Maybe that's because none of them know what a talented artist she is. I paint a little as well, and I'm thrilled to look at some of her work."

Alexandra's comment seemed to satisfy her. With a small curtsy, she turned back down the stairs, and a moment later the guest heard the door close at the bottom. Left alone in the room, she felt a prickle of excitement creep along her skin. She hadn't even seen any of Jane's work yet, and still she felt like a child about to open a treasure chest.

She walked down the middle of the attic space, careful not to hit her head on the rough-hewn beams. Moving past the tables and the easel, Alexandra opened the shutters at one end and let the sunshine pour in. The view of the verdant countryside from this far above was breathtaking and the light surprisingly plentiful. Alexandra instantly understood Jane's preference for working here. The single chair and a simple cot she hadn't seen before were tucked back in the shadow beneath the eaves. Jane clearly used this end of the attic space for work and the other end for storage.

She walked about for a few moments, admiring the young woman's organization and leafing through a sketchbook that had been left on one of the worktables. These drawings appeared to be done in haste and were mostly rough sketches of a group of children playing. Her gaze fell on an array of brushes filling a large bucket, and her fingers itched to touch the carefully cleaned bristles. A board, obviously used as a palette for mixing colors, leaned against the bucket. Like a dog trained to pick up a particular scent, Alexandra turned, her eyes fixing on a group of canvases leaning against a beam near the cot.

In general, women were taught to sketch, leaving the work of painting—particularly of painting in oils—in the more "capable" hands of men. Alexandra knew that she and Penelope Cawardine in London were rare exceptions. Of course, she thought, moving toward the group of canvases, it didn't hurt Mrs. Cawardine to have Sir Joshua Reynolds himself as a friend and mentor.

But Alexandra found it entirely pleasant to think of Jane Purefoy, here amid the rustic greenery of Ireland, rebelling against such backward notions.

Pulling off the cloth covering them, she looked quickly at the first two paintings. They were landscape scenes and well executed with a unique style that would have made even the great Gainsborough take note. Alexandra's thoughts of style and structure, of the use of light and color, dissipated into thin air, though, when she uncovered the third landscape. As the older woman gazed at the work, Jane's intention began to dawn on her.

She went back and looked hard at each picture again. They were all done from the same perspective, looking down from an elevation into a rural valley. There was no doubt in Alexandra's mind that they were painted by the same artist and depicted the same location. But the three paintings did not reflect the same scene.

She brought the canvases out into the window's light and stood them next to each other, against the easel and stool. As she studied them more closely, she found herself fascinated by the deft touches that accentuated the passage of seasons in the paintings. The young woman's talent was obvious. Through her use of light, Jane drew the eye to a different object or person in each painting, but she had also created an entirely new perspective on the same scene with only a few adroit brush strokes.

Alexandra crouched before the first one that she had looked at—the painting most recently done—and studied the summer pastoral scene. Cattle grazed in pastureland enclosed by ditches and low hedges. Picturesque ruins of something—perhaps an abandoned abbey that had once stood in the dell—could be partly seen through the tall summer grass.

She looked at the next, a painting that depicted the valley in spring and contained a few men working along the edge of the field. She looked back at the summer painting and then back again. The men were digging the ditches to enclose the pastureland. A man on horseback, his back to the painter, was pointing at something and directing the laborers.

Alexandra moved on to study the third canvas, a winter landscape. An impenetrable mist spread through the lower reaches of the valley, its thick fingers of fog spreading claw-like across a blackened field. The overall effect of the scene was a disturbing one, and Alexandra shivered involuntarily as she stood back for a better look.

The painting contained numerous details that were cleverly hidden in the edges of the mist with mere touches of the artist's brush. The ruins that appeared so picturesque in the summer scene now pushed through the vapor—ghostly and ominous. Alexandra peered intently at the broken stone walls. What were they? She found herself wanting to reach out and brush away the mist with her fingers, as if to discover the secret beneath it. Mist or smoke? She thought for a moment that the stones might even be charred ruins of a building . . . of more than one building.

She looked over at the other two canvases that were still standing against eaves.

Excited, Alexandra crossed over and turned one around. A shocked gasp escaped her lips when her gaze fell on the painting. Leaning it against the worktable, she backed up and sat heavily on the wooden chair.

A great fire consumed the valley. Violently alive with a shocking splatter of color, there were faces and upraised hands, all helpless against the raging inferno. Fear and anger silently screamed out at the viewer. With the subtle touch of oil to canvas, the anguished faces of lost souls became part of the flames that reached upward into the black, midnight sky.

Alexandra felt hot tears well up, a painful knot threatening to choke her. The painting showed an entire village being put to the torch. She stared at the images of people running out into the night and others caught in the raging holocaust. Depicted in the distance, groups of men looking more devilish than human could be seen torching the fields and hunting down the innocents.

It was a nightmarish view of evil incarnate, and Alexandra Spencer believed no one had done it more effectively since the passing of the Flemish genius Hieronymus Bosch.

She looked back again at other paintings. And now she was able to see through the mist. Now she understood that the ruins were the untended gravestones of a terrible tragedy.

The sadness of it all lay heavily on Alexandra's heart. She glanced in the direction of the last canvas still sitting in the shadows. Forcing herself to her feet, she trudged to the painting and turned it to the light.

A cluster of huts. Not quite a village. Neat, well-tended cottages with thatched roofs and kitchen gardens and two old peasant women talking by a well. Children running happily along a sparkling brook. Men and women just beginning the harvest of the fields surrounding the cottages, with older children binding sheaves of golden grain. The painting bespoke the joy of hard-won prosperity, of family, of the pride of heritage.

The sense of serenity that this canvas instilled in Alexandra was fleeting. As soon as she placed this one beside the others, she was struck full force with the power of the sequence. In taking in these scenes, she *felt* rather than simply viewed the destruction of a farming community and its people.

She pressed her fist to her lips to quiet a sob. She'd never been affected by any work of art more than these paintings at this moment. She'd never even glimpsed the ugly reality of what was happening to the people of this land until this instant. It was the kind of work that Hogarth had done in his series of satiric depictions of London . . . but this young woman had taken the work into the ethereal realms of high art.

Jane Purefoy's ability to capture the essence of a people's suffering was a marvelous gift. And her work told of someone who'd experienced this suffering—more than simply the perceptions of an artist who had witnessed a persecution firsthand. But how could she have?

The sound of the door opening at the bottom of the stairs jerked Alexandra out of her chair. As Lady Purefoy called up to her, she quickly replaced the canvases against the eaves and threw a cloth over them. Wiping her hand over her face to compose herself, she turned to see the woman's head appear at the top of the narrow steps.

"Lady Spencer, what on earth are you doing up here?"

Alexandra looked casually at the other woman. "Enjoying myself."

"Here?" She glanced disdainfully around the attic space, but didn't climb the last couple of steps. One might have thought it was a pit of vipers. "I wouldn't even house the servants here. And what is that horrid odor?"

"It is the scent of greatness, Lady Purefoy. Don't you recognize it?"

The mistress of Woodfield House looked sharply at her guest.

"But I couldn't agree with you more heartily about this area. This is a far too wonderful room to be used only for sleeping quarters. For an artist, this attic offers a splendid retreat. And I simply love the way Jane has organized the space. Is it not absolutely grand?"

"Well, I shall defer to your judgment, of course . . ." She cast a doubtful look around.

"And your daughter's paintings!" Alexandra made a sweeping motion over the rows of canvases lining the walls. "There is amazing talent exhibited here! Though I have only seen a few things, her work rivals the greats of our time."

"Jane?" Lady Purefoy replied skeptically.

"Indeed! Who schooled her in the fine arts? I am *most* curious to know what kind of professional training she received. I cannot tell you how impressed I am by all of this."

"Professional?" The woman looked at her guest in bewilderment. "I am sure I don't know what you mean. Jane's education was no different than Clara's."

"Even more impressive. Pray show me where in Woodfield House you have hung her masterpieces. They are surely of a quality that they might adorn any gallery in England."

"Well . . . I . . . We . . . I do not believe we have gotten around to hanging any of Jane's paintings." She stopped, obviously at a loss. "But if you would join me downstairs in the parlor, I can show you some of Clara's needlework that I had framed this past summer. She is

quite competent in her own right, I want you to know.
I myself find it most soothing to look upon her work."

Now it was Alexandra's turn to stare in disbelief at
the waiting woman. Soothing! That is what things had
been reduced to. Clara was soothing and Jane was not.
How disappointing, she thought, knowing deep in her
heart that *soothing* was something that would never do
for her son.

Kathleen stared incredulously at the bag of coins in
her hand.

Seamus's widow and the woman known as Egan were
standing outside the tiny cottage, a growing breeze rif-
fling the young mother's tattered skirts. The rebel leader
closed Kathleen's hand around the bag as the eldest
child ran into the yard, the other two children trailing
behind.

"Let no one see it. Spend it only a little at a time and
never on the same market day," Egan whispered. "Now
that I know how much you are doing without, I shall
bring some clothes for the wee ones and some food for
you and the old woman. If I cannot come myself, I'll
send someone."

The thatched cottage that Kathleen and her three children had taken shelter in was half the size of Jane's
bedroom at Woodfield House. Hardly large enough for
the woman and her brood, the hut was being shared
with an older widow named Bridget, whom disease had
made blind in both eyes this past summer. The arrangement worked well for both women at present, but both
knew better than to get too attached to it. No ground
or shelter was secure. As poor tenant farmers, they knew
they lived at the mercy of their landlords' next whim.
The brutal taking of land by the Royal Dragoons for
their new barracks just north of Buttevant only added
to the increasing number of homeless families.

Kathleen had fled her own burning cottage in the middle of the night, holding under her arm a Bible she could
hardly read and pushing her three young ones ahead of
her. Ignoring his wife's pleas, Seamus had stayed behind
to face the attackers.

Here, as in so many places across Ireland, complete

villages of tenant farmers were being cleared. Once the landowner's crops were taken in, the remaining fields were set ablaze and the cottages pulled down. Land that had been held as common land for generations was now being enclosed. Grassland that had been taken by force and planted by the colonizing English two centuries earlier was now being turned back into pastureland. Cattle now grazed where tenants had been struggling to survive by dint of their hard work and sweat.

Seamus was killed that night, and Kathleen had not yet been given a chance to grieve. The stark reality of poverty that was facing her and her children was a fate far worse than the brutal but sudden death her husband had met.

Now, standing in the sun with the breeze pulling at her skirts, she looked down at Egan's offering of coins. It was clearly too much to comprehend. Though the money represented the desperate woman's first ray of hope since the tragedy, she could not cry.

"God bless ye, Egan. God bless your Shanavests." The woman's gaze lifted from the treasure in her hand. "I . . . I didn't know how I'd be taking care of us."

"This is no replacement for your loss. You take care of yours . . . and Bridget . . . but mind that you keep mum. And don't attract attention by spending it too fast. I'll come back with more when I can."

As Egan turned to go, Kathleen pulled the shawl from around her own shoulders and extended it in her direction.

"For ye, Egan," she whispered shyly. "Ye might be needing this to hide the bruising on yer face."

The coarse wool shawl had more holes in it than a beggar's breeches, but the thoughtfulness of the gift touched Jane deeply. She accepted the offering and poured her emotions into the embrace she gave the woman.

"I shall wear it." And she did, draping it over her shoulders and knotting it in front.

The three children escorted Egan to her waiting horse and even ran after her until she reached the crest of the next hill. Beyond it, she tried not to stare at the growing patchwork of ditch-enclosed fields and remember the lives that had been displaced. Nevertheless, Jane's mood was black as scorched soil by the time she arrived at the bridge leading to Buttevant. She considered for a moment leaving Spencer to his own devices and heading north toward Churchtown, where she'd heard from Kathleen that some of the other families had fled. But she had nothing to offer those families now, and Clara's ploy of sending the Englishman along could not be disregarded without consequences. She had no option but to escort the rogue back.

At one end of the narrow stone bridge across the Awbeg, she waited while a cart pulled by an ancient donkey finished its slow trek across the bridge. A little old man, looking like some gnarled leprechaun, sat on the cart smoking a clay pipe. As she waited, she adjusted the knot of the wrap at her throat and tried to decide on how she could arrange it to hide her chin and mouth, if need be. She gave up finally. The blasted bruise was just too pronounced. She wished now that she hadn't lost her mother's hat.

As the donkey and cart were almost over the bridge, Jane spotted the tall, lean frame of Sir Nicholas leading his horse behind. There was someone else following the cart as well.

Despite her well-founded bias against him, at this moment she had to admire the air of confidence that surrounded the Englishman. Here was a man who was well aware of his advantages in life. But where the other aristocrats wallowed in them, Spencer appeared quite unencumbered. The man maintained no air of hostility to hide his fears of the lower classes. He seemed to feel no need for cloaking himself in displays of haughty indifference. She had seen the way he'd treated the grooms at Woodfield House this morning. She'd also been aware of him on their ride earlier, looking about with keen interest at the landscape and at the people. He had sharp powers of observation—that was obvious—and it was a quality that was sadly lacking in others of his class. Most, Jane thought, preferred to live insulated lives, moving about with blinders on.

He was one who would bear watching.

The cart neared the river's edge, and Jane knew the

moment when Sir Nicholas turned his gaze upon her. Their eyes met for only an instant, and as an already familiar warmth washed through her, she immediately looked away.

This was a future brother-in-law, she sharply reminded herself, totally appalled by the sensations racing through her body. The image in her mind of Clara standing beside Spencer calmed her immediately.

As the loaded cart went over the last bump and cleared the bridge, the old carter raised his battered hat to her, but said nothing. Nodding in return, Jane pushed her horse forward to meet their guest, and noticed with whom Sir Nicholas was walking. Her fingers immediately tightened around the reins. Every nerve in her body became taut, and she fought the desire to ride away.

"Top of the morning, Miss Jane. I cannot believe my good fortune today."

She made no pretence of returning the exuberance of Sir Robert Musgrave's greeting. Instead, she turned her attention to Spencer, trying to imagine how well these two men might be acquainted. She considered once again the possible reason for his silence at Woodfield House about her secret. She frowned, realizing that she simply didn't want to believe that he'd just been biding his time until he could meet with the magistrate. Spencer's expression revealed nothing.

"I must apologize for keeping you waiting, Miss Jane," Nicholas said as the two men finally reached her. "I was intercepted by the magistrate here. It appears that he was planning a visit to Woodfield House for the purpose of interviewing me. I tried to finish our business and save him the ride over."

"Good morning, Sir Robert," she said tersely. "No company of dragoons to accompany you this morning?"

"Not on so fine a morning as this," the man answered, his gaze lingering on the bruise by her mouth. "But to be completely honest, Sir Nicholas, I did have a second reason for calling at Woodfield House . . . and here she is before me."

From the very moment of the magistrate's arrival this past spring, Jane had found herself at odds with the man. The ordeal had begun at a fair in Mallow where, after their initial introduction, Musgrave had been almost belligerent in attempting to make himself her escort. Jane's refusals of him had fallen on deaf ears, unfortunately. And when she finally put her foot down—rejecting his continuing advances in no uncertain terms—others had overheard, and word of it had circulated quickly.

Of course, all of this had occurred before the new magistrate had learned of the scandals of Jane's past.

And that had made the insult cut much deeper.

Jane refused to flinch beneath the man's predatory stare. "What business have you with me, sir?"

"I think you know, Miss Jane."

"I fear that you are mistaken, Sir Robert."

"But you see, I have decided to improve my last offer . . . substantially."

Jane restrained her temper. Having seen Queen Mab in passing at the Buttevant Horse Fair this past July—and having observed Jane's attachment to the horse—the magistrate had suddenly developed a keen desire to acquire the animal. Since then he had been pressing to purchase the horse, claiming he wanted Mab to breed with his own prize stallions. Feeling Jane's resistance to sell, Sir Robert had made an offer to Sir Thomas for the purchase of the mare.

Naturally, Jane had been irate. Though it was her horse, there was no telling what her father might do. Sir Thomas, however, had apparently not been particularly inclined to satisfy the whim of the new magistrate—a man he had openly called a fop before the family—for he had bluntly declined the offer.

"I have learned my lesson, Miss Jane. I now know that it is wiser to talk of purchasing your fine mare with you—the person who obviously has the final say."

Sir Robert's words smacked more of condescension than humility. Even as she considered this, she watched the confident smile steal across his face as he let his gaze travel the length of her before coming to rest again on her bruised mouth.

"I would have been far more comfortable discussing with Sir Thomas such decidedly earthy activities as mounting, coupling, and breeding . . ."

"I shall take you at your word on that, Sir Robert."

His eyes narrowed at her insinuation, but she didn't care. She was tired of the sexual innuendo that the magistrate insisted on weaving lately into his conversations with her. Always—at the edges of his words, in the inflection of his voice, in the look in his eye—she found his sly intimations.

"But before we get to that, miss, I am most curious to know how you came by such a nasty bruise to your lovely face. Indeed, your lips are . . ."

"Accidents happen, sir. This bruise is none of your concern. But if you have any thoughts of making another offer for my horse, the answer is the same. She is *not* for sale."

He nudged his horse a step forward, until his boots brushed against her own. Mab stood firm, and Jane, too, refused to be intimidated. She patted the horse's neck.

"But you haven't even heard the new offer."

"The answer is the same." She drawled each word as if she were speaking to a small child. "And I beg that you not make this the source of any further unpleasantness."

"I let it rest for now. But about the bruise . . ."

"And now, sir, if you will forgive us, Reverend Adams is expecting us."

She wheeled Mab away from the magistrate and found herself looking into the stern face of Spencer. The murderous glare that the man was directing toward Musgrave somehow pleased her.

"I fear that I cannot allow you to go just yet. Accidents *are* my concern," Musgrave called out, turning his horse, as well. "Especially when they happen to a charming damosel that I have sworn to protect."

"Sir, I am no *damosel*, and I have *never* needed your protection."

"Say what you will." The man's dark eyes narrowed—his gaze focusing more on her mouth. "But it is my responsibility to tame all rebelliousness in Cork . . . and that might arguably include solving the mystery of how and why someone like you should sustain such violence to her face."

Clara had been right. The excuse she'd used the day before would only make matters worse and draw the magistrate's suspicions. But her mind was empty of any other explanations.

"I am responsible for the condition of her face."

Jane whirled about to look at Spencer.

Musgrave's attention focused on the visitor. "Is that so, Sir Nicholas?"

"The kind lady is simply trying to protect my reputation, I fear. A clumsy accident in the stables yesterday, and one for which I must bear total blame."

"I don't think that Sir Robert . . ." she started, uncertain of what was to come or what she could say.

"The magistrate"—the Englishman cut her off—"strikes me as an understanding man. Indeed, he knows that accidents *do* happen. The fact is, sir, I pushed open the upper half of one of the stable doors, not knowing Miss Purefoy was approaching on the other side. It was a grievous mistake, but she has been *very* gracious in not embarrassing me before her family."

"Do you mean to tell me that *you*—?"

"I mean exactly what I have told you."

Spencer turned to Jane, who was having some difficulty hiding her surprise. The tingling warmth that spread through her as his blue eyes met hers briefly did nothing to help, either.

The magistrate yanked at his mount's bridle. "It would appear, sir, that you had an *exceedingly* busy day yesterday. Single-handedly rescuing a clergyman from a horde of outlaws, unhorsing their leader, and then this extensive damage . . . I just wonder what are the chances of . . ." The words trailed off, but the suggestion hung in the air.

With deliberate slowness, Spencer removed one of his gloves. "From the tone of your words, sir, it would appear that you have some difficulty accepting statements that are conveyed to you. I *hope* I am mistaken."

The magistrate's stare locked with that of the baronet for a long, tense moment.

"My deepest apologies to you and to Miss Purefoy," Musgrave said finally, bowing with cool courtesy. "One's duty to the Crown can make one jump at shadows sometimes, I'm afraid. My best to your family, Miss Jane."

Chapter 10

"Thank you."

The words were just whispers in the wind, but Nicholas heard them nonetheless.

As they topped the next hill, leaving the river valley—and the magistrate—behind them, he glanced over at Jane but did not respond. His anger still gnawed at him, but he was pleased to have her finally riding with him, rather than leading him all over the countryside in another merry game of fox and hounds.

"Is he always so insolent?"

"Each time I meet him, it seems to get worse." It was obvious that she was still feeling the effects of the exchange. "But I understand that many of the English gentry find him quite accommodating."

"So he is impudent only when he chooses to be."

"And when he has considered the social rank of the person he is dealing with." She gave him a pleased look. "I believe you intimidated him."

Nicholas didn't say it, but he wished he'd done more.

He had felt Sir Robert's eyes on their backs as they rode away from Buttevant. Not that he particularly gave a damn. By 'sblood, he'd come damned close to challenging the unprincipled dog for his treatment of her.

"I admire your restraint," he said. The simply spoken compliment earned him a warm smile. "Despite your agitation, you never lost your temper." Or cursed in Gaelic, he silently finished.

"It might sound like cowardice, but it is not. I prefer

not to draw any undue attention to myself . . . especially from someone like him."

She didn't have to explain more, for Nicholas understood her. Her practiced self-restraint was due to her covert activities with the Shanavests.

She moved in front of him through a narrow passage at the crest of a hill. Talking with Jane was already settling his frame of mind. He hoped that he had the same effect on her.

"I should have insisted on coming along on your visit to your friend."

She half turned in the saddle. "I don't believe she is one whom you might generally find in your circle of acquaintances."

"I shan't correct you on what you do not know. But I will say that anything would have been preferable to hanging about Buttevant and consorting with some bloody government official."

"Better you than I, sir."

He smiled and noticed for the first time the ragged wrap she had around her shoulders. "I see you have found a scarf to replace your long-lost hat."

She touched the wool on her shoulder as he came alongside her. "Very observant. It is a gift, and it came from a woman who, I know, valued it highly. Aside from her children, it may have been her most prized possession."

He watched the way she touched the wool again as if it were made of the finest silk. The simple gesture revealed another layer of this woman whom he was finding most fascinating.

They rode along for a few moments, both lost in their own thoughts. Nicholas broke the silence.

"Despite the little unpleasantness at the bridge, this has been a most enjoyable day. I owe you my sincere thanks for your insistence on having me come along."

When she turned her gaze on him again, Nicholas was amazed at the jolt of awareness that ran through him.

She stared at him for another lengthy moment and then a bubble of laughter escaped her. Delighted by the transformation in her, he joined in. When she laughed,

Jane Purefoy threw off the sadness that hung over her like a cloud. Something else took its place. Something free and full of life. She was attractive to the point of being truly stunning.

"*Insistence* that you come along?" She shook her head. "Sir Nicholas, you speak as if you heard not a word that passed between my sister and me."

"I admit to hearing nothing of what was a private conversation. But you *must* have been agreeable, otherwise I'm sure I would not be riding with you at this moment."

She shook her head good-naturedly. "Sir, you know quite well that I was not given a choice. But now that you mention it, I believe you must have been in on this entire scheme."

"Cut me as you please, Miss Purefoy, but do not wrongfully accuse me." He added as an afterthought, "But tell me, isn't this much more pleasant than our little disagreement in the woods yesterday?"

A flicker of shared knowledge passed between them. Nicholas couldn't help but notice the gentle blush that crept into her face.

"We are late," she finally replied quietly, spurring her horse into a canter.

He fell in beside her and looked at his timepiece. "We have plenty of time. The sun is not yet high, and my watch tells me we have more than enough time to keep our appointment with the good Parson Adams. Do you have some other reason to rush?"

"Sir, you came out today to spend the day with my sister. I have already taken you from her needlessly. It is my responsibility to return you to her as expeditiously as possible."

"Allow me to correct this misunderstanding." He watched her carefully to gauge her reaction. "I came out today with the hope of spending time in *your* company. I have been looking to find an opportunity when we could speak."

Her face immediately sobered. "It was an unfortunate thing that we had to run into each other yesterday as we did. There must be many questions . . . concerns that you have." She gradually slowed her mare to a walk. "I assure you that Clara takes no part in anything inappropriate. She is a perfectly well-bred daughter and subject of the Crown. She is totally innocent of my . . . well, my interests . . . and always has been."

"I don't care to speak about Clara."

"And you should not allow that scene yesterday to affect your marriage plans," Jane insisted. "You should not blame her for what I do . . . or hold my family responsible for *my* actions. Believe me, for years I have lived with the certain knowledge that if my parents ever found me out, they would be the first to hand me over to the magistrate and his executioner."

There was a sadness in her tone, and Nicholas wished he could dispute her words. But based on the little that he'd seen himself of Sir Thomas and his wife, he didn't doubt her in the slightest.

"And now . . . suddenly . . . I find I am at the mercy of a stranger," she added a moment later.

Nicholas knew he should assure her that he had not revealed her secret to anyone and he had no plans of doing it in the future, either. Whatever motivated her to act as she did was her own concern. He didn't give a damn, personally, about the possibility of scandal. And in spite of Bishop Russell's unrelenting condemnation yesterday, Nicholas himself had seen her cut the ropes binding the hands of the clergyman. But he wasn't ready to admit anything that would set her mind at ease. He wasn't ready to have her totally disregard him.

"All I can assure you so far is that my answers to those who have questioned me about yesterday have been—" he searched for the right word—"imprecise."

"And why *is* that?" Her eyes were sharp as she awaited his answer.

"Because I have seen how we Englishmen tend to treat those whom we conquer and colonize." Unconsciously he tightened his grip on the reins. "I make it my business not to judge others based on so little information. I make it a habit not to intervene unless there is a sound reason."

"Although he didn't deserve it, I set that bishop free yesterday. So what was your reason for pulling me off my horse?"

"I was desperate for an introduction. I apologize. I *am* trying to improve my methods of meeting people."

Her laughter this time was full and lingered in his ear like the prettiest of songs. He gazed at her, wondering if she had any idea about her power to charm. Her dark and enchanting eyes turned on him, and he felt the undeniable pull in his gut.

"Then I can assume that you said nothing about our earlier *meeting* to the magistrate?"

"You are perfectly safe in making that assumption."

"How about revealing anything in the future meetings with the man?"

"You are quite persistent," he remarked, enjoying this undivided attention. "As things stand now, Sir Robert and I seem to have developed an immediate aversion toward each other. Unless something changes, I doubt we would have future discussions on the topic, either."

Mischief danced in her eyes as she pressed him further. "Of course, this vague assurance is only good until I stab you in the arm again."

"You shall not have that opportunity very soon, Miss Jane." He gave her a meaningful glance. "I don't believe next time I shall allow you off your back so quickly."

This time the blush was deeper—the awareness between them potent. Nicholas realized the edginess was starting to take charge by the way her hands tightened around the reins of the horse. He was quick to change the subject, as he had no wish to shorten their time together.

"In any case, I assure you that I would not be choosing Musgrave as a confidant. If any questions or misunderstandings arise, my inclination would be to seek explanations and answers from *you*."

She studied him more closely, and Nicholas found himself hoping that she would approve of what she saw.

"You are far more open-minded than I expected—and far more candid. Clearly, we do great wrong in judging a person purely on his station in life."

"You are too hard on yourself."

"I think not," she said matter-of-factly. "Though I can think of no other Englishman I have ever met who would not have seen it as his duty to expose me—an outlaw *and* a woman—if not to the magistrate, then certainly to my father."

"I can see that you do not think too highly of my brethren."

"I fear you are correct in that observation." She gave him a half smile. "But of course, there are always exceptions. Parson Adams is a man who places decency and compassion above greed and class and colonial domination."

Even the mention of the minister's name managed to irk Nicholas. He was enjoying the feeling of ease that was developing with this woman, and the thought of a possible competitor rankled somewhat.

"And may I ask if you have formed any firm plans regarding your marriage to the good Parson Adams?"

The look of incredulity she directed at him was as pleasurable as it was unexpected.

"What in heaven's name should cause you to say something like that? Marriage? Henry Adams and I? That is simply preposterous!"

"Is it?"

"Absolutely. We are no more than old and trusted friends."

"A relationship that most couples can only hope to achieve . . . in the *best* of marriages."

She shook her head adamantly. "I fear you haven't been around a sufficient length of time to understand what things are like here, sir."

"Perhaps you'd be kind enough to enlighten me."

Jane took her time to answer, and he watched with some interest the internal battle that was all too openly reflected in her fair face.

"He . . . Reverend Adams is a respected clergyman. And I . . . well, I have a reputation that I managed to ruin in my youth. And my transgression was such that, no matter how many decades go by, no one shall ever forget." Her cheeks were flushed when she faced him fully, but her eyes were clear and steady. "It is just as well, though, that this topic has come up. And it is best that you should hear the truth from me, for sooner or later you are bound to hear it from someone else. And, frankly, I don't want any embellished version of *my* life to ruin my sister's future happiness."

"So this is 'what things are like' here? You and the good parson are kept apart by gossip and—what I assume to be—some ancient transgression against what are probably vague and outdated standards of respectability?"

"No."

"What did you do, Miss Jane? Participate in this . . . this steeple-chasing race I was just hearing about from the innkeeper in Buttevant? You must have given the bishop's horse and rider a sound thrashing before they found you out. Is that it?"

"Joke if you will, sir, but that is not it, at all. Nothing of the sort keeps Parson Adams and me apart." She gave a firm shake to her head, and more tendrils of her silky hair danced around her face. "As far as my past . . . and reputation . . . the truth and the charges against me are much more severe than what you just mentioned. Let me just put it this way . . . I am *not* considered in any way marriageable by genteel society."

Nicholas could only guess an elopement would be the cause of such ruckus. There was so much that he wanted to know about Jane. But he had to wait until she was ready to confide in him.

"But as I mentioned before, rumors and accusations are *not* what keeps us apart. Henry Adams and I are simply friends."

"Friends?"

"Indeed. We are friends and nothing more. *Nothing* more! Have you never had a woman as a friend? A relationship that is simply built on trust and mutual respect? A friendship that is pure and elevated . . . one that might be considered platonic?"

Nicholas put on a great show of thinking about the question. Inside, though, he was delighted to hear that he wasn't competing with the clergyman for her attentions.

Competing for her attentions.

The admission made him glance at her again. He found her still waiting for an answer.

"Once or twice, I believe I have come close to establishing a friendship such as the kind you describe. But each time it occurred, my *friend* soon became dissatisfied with the boundaries of that relationship. I beg your pardon, but it has been my experience that women always seem to want more."

"Once or twice?" She shook her head disapprovingly. "It has been my experience that generalizations based on limited knowledge are rarely correct and never productive in finding the truth, sir."

"My apologies." He bowed politely. "Women whom *I* have known happen to seek more."

"*Englishwomen.*" She uttered the word as if it were poison on her tongue.

"I find it curious that you do not classify yourself as an Englishwoman, but I see you don't think much of *them*, either."

"I cannot believe you *really* want to hear my opinion on this topic."

"But I do."

There wasn't much silent debate now.

"Many Englishwomen that I have met have simply submitted to traditions that have been impressed upon them. As a result, they have allowed themselves to become blinded by the shallow niceties of being admired for their pleasing looks or for the fashionable cut of their garments or for their silent obedience. And in the process, the things that are important—spirit, independence, intelligence—are viewed by the world, and by many women as well, as highly unfeminine and even *unnatural.*"

"I take it that you find this to be false and limiting to women."

"And to society! Dr. Samuel Johnson, a man who is perhaps the leading light of English letters today, is reported to have said, 'A woman preaching is like a dog walking on its hind legs. It is not done well, but one is surprised to find it done at all.' How very narrow this kind of low humor is when one considers such women as Margaret More Roper and the Duchess of Pembroke and Lady Mary Wroth, to name but a few!"

"Indeed," he replied. "Women of great wit and character."

"And yet," she pressed on, "many Englishwomen—
perhaps even most—are willing to overlook how low
they are ranked in the world. They are trained to lead
their lives in obedience and blissful ignorance, and they
bury their spirit and their will and their deepest passions
before they even cross life's threshold into womanhood.
They allow themselves to be robbed of the essence of
what it is to be a human being."

Jane's cheeks were flushed, her eyes bright with passionate conviction. And Nicholas knew in that moment
that he'd never met a woman as exciting and intelligent
as this one. The fact that she was Egan, a rebel leader,
made perfect sense, for it would be impossible not to
follow her if she carried this same passion into the cause
she fought for.

As they approached the end of a field, she nudged her
horse to the edge of the tall grass, keeping their horses
side by side.

"I didn't mean to sound so complaining . . . so critical.
Certainly your own family is so different from what I
just described."

"Indeed, my mother and sister can easily be considered 'different.' " He smiled. "But there may be something in what you say."

"No." She bent her head under a low branch as they
passed into a grove of trees. The leaves brushed against
her hair. "I *must* apologize. After how civil you've been
to me, and how pleasant Lady Spencer and your sister
were to all of us last night, it is utterly wrong of me to
commit the same error I have just accused you of making. No generalizing. There are many exceptions to the
kind of women I was speaking of. There are so many
exceptions to everything in life."

"And I'm thankful for it, as there is nothing more
tiring than the mundane . . . a charge that could never
be lodged against you."

Their gazes locked again when she turned to him, and
it was impossible to ignore the awareness of desire that
flowed between them. She immediately looked away, but
Nicholas's gaze lingered on the few autumn leaves that
had entangled themselves in her hair. She was part of

nature—part of this land. None of the discontent he felt in the company of Clara existed in these moments with Jane. He was perfectly at ease with her.

He was disappointed to find the village of Ballyclough beneath them when they crested the next hill. Jane reached up and removed the wrap from her shoulder. Handling it carefully, she folded it and held it in her lap. She caught him watching her.

"For Clara's sake, I cannot look too tattered in public. She would be horrified to think you saw me wearing this."

"I'll keep your secret."

She smiled self-consciously. "I find I am in debt to you for keeping so many of them."

They were on the edge of the village, but Nicholas was not ready for their time together to end. A muddy dog trotted out from the first of the village cottages, sniffing at Jane's boot.

"What we were speaking of before . . . of friendships between men and women. You really believe such a thing is feasible?"

"Absolutely. There are many men that I consider friends. A difference in gender has never stopped me from treating another person as an equal. As a woman, however, I can only hope to be treated the same."

Jane answered the wave of an older woman who straightened up from digging in a small kitchen garden beside a cottage.

"And do you think *we* might be friends?"

She turned to him, obviously surprised. "I . . . I cannot see why not. As a future brother and sister, it will certainly be beneficial for all if we were—"

"I have changed my mind. I shall not be asking Clara to become my wife."

Jane yanked at the reins of her horse, halting Mab suddenly. He, too, stopped.

"Why?" she asked. "You told me that you would not let what you know of me—"

"My decision has nothing to do with you," Nicholas lied, knowing full well it had everything to do with her. "Even before my family and I left London, I was not fully persuaded on the notion of marrying. If I had been committed to marrying your sister, I would have at least sent along my lawyers beforehand."

"But my parents. Clara believed . . ."

He let his agitation show. "I misled no one. I served as your sister's escort on a few occasions this past spring, but hardly placed any claims upon her. There were no promises made—no assumptions made—no talks ensuing. And when your parents made the invitation to visit Woodfield House, they understood that I had made no marital overtures."

"But you just told me that you have *changed* your mind. Change indicates that there was a—"

"I was attempting to be completely honest with you. I have always assumed one friend can be honest with another. And since I have never discussed marriage or proposed, Clara should never know the difference."

She leaned toward him, grasping the bridle of his horse. Her eyes showed the temper burning within. "Then, as a *friend*, pray explain to me what caused your change of heart."

"She is not the one . . . and for many reasons. The difference in our ages. Her naïveté and my experience. Her hesitant approach to life and my recklessness." He didn't release Jane's gaze, nor let her speak when she opened her mouth. "It is true that this past year I have been seriously contemplating marriage. I have arrived at a stage in life when it is necessary to have a wife and an heir to fulfill my family obligations. And I . . . I also wish to pursue some other plans that have been ripening in my mind for the past few years. I realize now that I had an impractical, almost hypothetical view of marriage. I had not considered thoroughly enough the qualities of the woman I should be marrying."

"Come, Sir Nicholas. The truth is, now that you've learned about *me*, you find my sister 'impractical.' And you can afford to be more judicious in your choice."

"I told you this has nothing to do with *you*."

"But it does," she spat back at him. "If she was good enough a week ago . . . a month ago . . . last spring. Then she should be now."

"But she wasn't . . ." The look of hurt in Jane's face was immediate.

"May I be so bold as to interrupt?"

Both of them turned simultaneously. There were nearly a dozen people staring from a respectful distance around them. Reverend Adams stood nearby as well, looking up at the two riders expectantly. Nicholas hadn't realized that Jane was still holding the bridle of his horse until she abruptly let go.

"Of course," Nicholas responded belatedly to the clergyman. He realized that they were within walking distance of the parsonage, so he climbed down from his horse. "We were finished with our discussion."

"I hardly think so," Jane corrected, dismounting as well before Nicholas could offer to help her down. "But we shall continue where we left off at a more appropriate time and place."

The comment was addressed to him—her direct look challenging him to contradict her. Nicholas bowed politely. If this meant that Jane was willing to spend more time in his company—even to try to sway his decision about marriage and Clara—then he would be a fool to object. In fact, he was quite pleased with the turn of events and of the prospect of what was to come. His mood darkened, though, when he saw the country parson reach up and remove those loose leaves from Jane's hair.

The touch seemed too intimate, too casual, he thought. And the minister's attentions toward her caused Nicholas to question again if there could not be more between them than she was admitting.

"Are you coming?" she turned and asked after Adams had led her a few steps in the direction of the rectory.

"I am." Nicholas started up the hill after them. "I have no intention of being left behind."

Chapter 11

"*Mother!*"

At the sudden outcry from behind her, Alexandra Spencer jumped and then pressed a hand to her chest. She hadn't heard the door to her daughter's room open. She hadn't been aware of any other noise but the creaking she'd heard inside these walls. She could have sworn something was behind this stretch of painted plaster.

"Did I frighten you?" Frances closed the door of her room behind her.

"Of course not!"

"Then what are you doing listening to the wall?"

"I wasn't listening to the wall, Fanny."

The young woman came closer and peered at the solid wall of the hallway and back again at Alexandra's face. "Then what are you doing standing here? Mother, it was not my imagination that you were pressing your ear against this wall."

"It certainly *was* your imagination." She took a handkerchief out of her sleeve and patted the beads of sweat that had formed on her forehead and upper lip.

"Did you hear a noise?" Apparently unconvinced, Frances mimicked what she had seen her mother doing and pressed an ear to the cold plaster. "Maybe this place is haunted. Or do you think there are secret passages running behind these walls? I love that in the novels, don't you? From what I have learned so far about the history of this place, there was a castle that was previously built on this hill. Now wouldn't it be exciting if . . . ?"

"No, it would *not* be." Lady Spencer placed a hand on the small of her daughter's back and, pressing lightly, started her down the corridor. "Whatever you thought I was doing, it was only your imagination running away with you. My room is extremely warm this afternoon, and I was simply enjoying some of the coolness of this corridor before going downstairs to dinner."

Frances gave an impish grin. "Do you know there are patches of red that climb right up the skin of your neck whenever you try to fib?"

"Frances Marie, this is no way for a young woman to be speaking to her mother." Alexandra paused at the end of the hall and before starting down the stairs. "But on a totally different matter, what were you doing in your room? I thought I heard your and Nicholas's voices coming from the corridor only a few minutes ago. Why are you not with him . . . pestering him . . . doing your sisterly duty?"

"He dismissed me." Fanny pouted in the direction of his door. "He wouldn't say a word about his day. He's horrible. He wouldn't answer a *single* question. And he became quite agitated—snappish even—when I asked him if he'd had the opportunity to propose to Clara yet. He'd better marry soon, Mother. He's becoming positively curmudgeonly."

"You know, dear, I think it might be best if you were to leave that topic alone for now."

"But why?" The young woman crossed her arms over her chest. "Did we not come all the way to Ireland so that Nicholas could propose? It would be so much more pleasant to get to know Clara in the fashion of a sister-to-be than continue in this required hostess-and-guest relationship. We are so close in age, and there is so much we could plan and do together if everyone stopped tiptoeing around the subject. We . . ."

Both of their heads turned as Nicholas emerged from his door. From his shining dark boots to the short, fitted black jacket to the buff-colored buckskin breeches, he was the very image of the country gentleman on his way to dinner. Alexandra noticed, though, the tenseness that had settled around his lips. The look he was directing at Fanny was impatient, if not downright dangerous.

"Am I interrupting something?"

"Why, yes!" The young woman was quick to answer. "You are interrupting my complaints to Mother about . . ."

"Why not be on your way downstairs, young lady." Alexandra turned a sharp look on her daughter.

"But Mother, I think this is a perfectly good opportunity for . . ."

"Downstairs, Frances Marie." This time the mother's tone left no doubt that she meant to be obeyed. "Tell Sir Thomas and Lady Purefoy that Nicholas and I will be down shortly."

Rankled but dutiful, the young woman gathered her skirts in two fists and disappeared down the stairs.

"Thank you." Nicholas closed his door and offered his arm to Alexandra. "I love her dearly, but I have lately acquired so much appreciation for what you have been saving me from these past few years."

"Fanny is a good girl. And she is not always so impatient." She placed a hand in the crook of her son's arm but refused to go downstairs yet. "Is there anything that you want to talk to me about?"

He glanced at her cautiously.

"You know, Nicholas . . . I could be of assistance to you." She paused, gentled her voice even more and looked up into blue eyes that could not hide his distress. "I am still your mother, and there is no reason why you should shoulder all of this pressure alone. I can, with great subtlety, bring up a topic. I can drop a hint regarding your state of mind. Whatever you wish. I can even distract them, if that is what you desire. I want you to know most of all, however, that you have every right to take your time before committing to anything permanent."

His other hand came up and pressed Alexandra's affectionately against his arm.

She looked about the empty hallway and lowered her voice. "I know I should have had this talk with you before we even arrived here. But now is as good a time as any, I suppose." She paused, gathering her thoughts. "We both know that in our society there are certain requirements—*formalities* is perhaps a better word—that must be observed before men and women enter into a marriage partnership. Yes, indeed, partnership is the correct way of stating it, for it has become very much a business relationship. Therefore, a business contract is required of all parties."

"What is your point, Mother?"

"I am getting to it, Nicholas. Knowing you as I do . . . understanding you better than you think . . . I believe you need more than a business partner. You need a woman who can match you in will and in wit. You do not need some ornament who will expect to be put on a pedestal as a wife."

"You are *very* observant."

"And so are you." She patted his arm. "A quality inherited fully from my side of the family."

He gave her a gentle bow of the head and smiled.

"I hope you will not consider my comments as meddlesome, but I have been greatly disturbed by the thought that perhaps my presence here might press you into making a hasty decision ." She let the words drift in the air. This was the most she'd allowed herself to become openly involved in Nicholas's life in many, many years.

"As well, you should be the first one who is told." He placed a hand on the darkly gleaming wood of the banister. "She is *not* for me. I shall not make an offer for Clara's hand."

Alexandra stifled a great sigh of relief. She tried to withhold any sign of jubilation and keep her expression impassive.

"And I am not for her, either. I shall make my intentions known to Sir Thomas tonight, for I do not wish for any misunderstandings or hard feelings to develop. We shall try to avoid any unpleasantness." He glanced down the shadowy stairs before turning his attention back to her. "In fact, if Sir Thomas and Lady Purefoy have no objection, I wish to remain at Woodfield House for the fortnight we had originally planned."

"Splendid!" she managed to squeak, too pleased to say any more.

As they started down the stairs to join their hosts for dinner, Alexandra considered telling Nicholas about her little discovery in the attic that morning. Though he'd never pursued painting himself, she knew he was as much of a connoisseur of the arts as she was. She was certain that he, too, would be much taken by Jane's paintings. She would like to be there to see his face as the power of her message conveyed itself to him. But she refrained from singing the praises of the older sister. Nicholas would have to discover her all on his own.

And staying at Woodfield House for the full fortnight could present the most provocative opportunities.

"And how did you find the new magistrate, Sir Nicholas?"

Clara idly pushed the pheasant about on her plate as they all waited in silence for the baronet to answer her father's question. She dared not peek up at him, though, for she was beginning to suspect that Sir Nicholas had not heard the question at all. Indeed, for most of dinner he'd seemed considerably distracted. His interest appeared to dwell thoughtfully on Jane's empty place across the table.

Earlier, when her sister and the visitor had arrived at the rectory in Ballyclough with Henry, Clara had immediately sensed the tension between the two. The air in the small dining room felt charged, like a summer night before a thunderstorm. Indeed, there had been few words exchanged between the two during the modest luncheon. Thinking about the time there at the rectory, Clara felt the cold lump form again in her stomach. Henry had never once looked at her during the meal.

Then, on the ride back to Woodfield House, Jane had again chosen to ride far ahead of Clara and Sir Nicholas. No one had said anything beyond the necessary courtesies, either on the road or upon reaching Woodfield House.

All of this, however, did little to distract her from her own pain.

Her father pointedly cleared his throat, drawing their brooding guest's attention. "I was hoping to get your opinion on—"

"The new magistrate."

Clara was relieved to hear the baronet finally speak. "Yes."

"I was considering my response, Sir Thomas."

"Measuring it, you mean." Her father let out a burst of laughter, and Clara felt her mood lighten. "You didn't like him, by thunder. I'm sure Musgrave would be distraught to hear that."

Sir Nicholas directed a sharp look toward the head of the table. "I had no idea the magistrate would care about my opinion one way or the other. Perhaps I should have shared it with him before we parted ways this morning."

"Then you do not deny it." Obviously pleased, Sir Thomas shook his head and downed a great swallow of wine. "Please allow me, sir, to pass on your reaction to the man. I would very much enjoy ruining Sir Robert's day with such news."

"You really would waste your energies on such a pointless exercise? Surely there must be more stimulating things for one to do in this country."

The comment, delivered in a slightly mocking tone by Sir Nicholas, caused a ripple of amusement to emanate from all the women at the table. Clara, though, quickly stifled her own mirth as she saw a dark cloud descend immediately over her father's mood.

He cleared his throat in that all too familiar manner that indicated his displeasure. She stared at him, thinking desperately for a way to ease the renewed tension.

"I wonder, though," Sir Nicholas added soberly, "if your enjoyment in 'ruining Sir Robert's mood' might stem from the fact that he has succeeded you in a task that you excelled at for so many years. I believe it is not uncommon to be somewhat critical of the person who has taken on one's own position and responsibilities."

After a long uncomfortable pause, the older man's head nodded once in agreement as he gestured to a servant for more wine. "Indeed, sir. Very observant. And no harm in it, either."

Clara fought back her surprise at the exchange. She had never heard anyone speak to her father quite so bluntly. But Sir Thomas's calm and equally candid re-

sponse nearly bowled her over. Her father emptied another glass of wine before continuing.

"I was the king's magistrate in this region for more
than twenty years. When I took the post here, the violence against the gentry was more vicious than anything
you might have heard in the stories of the Sussex smug-
glers' war of the forties. But I handled them, sir. With
a strong hand, I made the people here know that civil
authority would be respected and obeyed. Those who
would not respect the king's law, however, would learn
to fear it. Because of my work, sir, the landlords finally
found it possible to take charge of their own lands and
control their tenants."

Sir Thomas's hand shook as he lifted his glass again.
"And later . . . when the investment in pasture became
more profitable than tillage, when some of the landlords
decided to lease the land to graziers instead of to tenant
farmers, I was the one who challenged the rebels . . .
the Whiteboys . . . or Shanavests . . . or whatever bloody
hell they call themselves."

Clara's stomach clenched in a knot. Her mother's face
had gone deathly white. Totally unconcerned, Sir
Thomas drank down another glass of wine and continued.

"The Whiteboys only exist because they dare to defy
common decency and threaten their own kind. The
wretches force others of their class to take an oath under
threat of violence. And that, sir, is illegal. Nine years
ago, we caught five of their leaders not far from Waterford. I was one of the judges who ordered the ruffians
hanged. By hanging those five, I was sending a message
to everyone that the administration of oaths in such a
way would be treated as the capital offence it was. In a
single stroke, I curtailed their aggression dramatically."
He pointed a finger at Nicholas. "And this is the root
of the problem with Musgrave. I keep telling him that
instead of wasting so much of his time socializing with
the landed gentry . . . people who for the most part find
him intolerable anyway . . . and instead of going around
the district harassing the papist tenants on insignificant
matters like the nonpayment of rents, he should be going
after these rebel leaders. He needs to be concentrating

his efforts on scum like this Egan that you ran into yesterday . . . or these two others they call Liam and Patrick, a pair of blackguards as bad as the first. And then there is another rogue who goes by the name of Finn. That one doesn't show his face very often, but we know he has his fingers in the activities of at least three of the neighboring counties. Until the day these black-guards' heads are hung on a post in Cork City, Musgrave will garner no respect from the gentry. Thus far he has done nothing to instill fear into the hearts of these rebels."

"I saw a rather large barracks being erected in Buttevant."

"By thunder, talk about a pointless exercise!" Sir Thomas banged his glass on the table. "Those dragoons will do nothing but stir up these rebels. We need strong civil authority in Ireland, not military occupation."

Stealing a glance out of the corner of her eye, Clara could see that Sir Nicholas was staring at the brocade on the silk tablecloth. His face was a mask, but she sensed that he *knew* about Jane. She had not openly questioned her sister about what had taken place yester-day, but when Clara considered the cut on his arm, the blow to her face, the silent message that clearly passed between them when they first met, she was certain. Sir Nicholas *had* to know that Jane and Egan were one and the same.

"I have even made some recommendations to Mus-grave on how he could proceed to set a trap for them."

"A trap . . . ?"

Lady Purefoy practically jumped to her feet. "I . . . I . . . believe it would be best if we women retired to the parlor. This kind of talk is far too shocking, Sir Thomas, and you shall be frightening our guests out of their wits." She looked across the table. "Will you favor us with your company tonight, Sir Nicholas? Or are you staying behind with my husband this evening?"

Clara knew it was not like her mother to take charge such as this, but as her father drained his wineglass yet again, she was grateful for the interruption.

"If you will forgive me this evening, m'lady"—the bar-onet stood and bowed politely as the rest of the women

rose as well—"I should like to stay behind and speak
with Sir Thomas. There are a few topics pressing that I
believe we need to discuss."

Catherine Purefoy practically beamed. "Absolutely,
Sir Nicholas. And please take your time. We shall be
waiting in the parlor for you both."

Clara felt as if a cold stone had lodged itself in her
stomach. She dragged herself toward the door, watching
her parents exchange a look of satisfaction. The momentary air of harmony that hung between them, though,
was a stark reminder of the sacrifice that she had
decided six months ago to make—the sacrifice she'd confessed this very morning that she hadn't the heart to go
through with.

But with Henry's rejection today, Clara was now lost,
set adrift, destined to be swept along on life's currents.

This marriage was to be an emotionless contract between families. Very well. She would suffer through it
and reap the good it would bring her parents. She *was*
selfless—in spite of Henry's condemnation—and she
would prove it.

Egan held back her immediate objections to the idea
and—as she always did—tried to consider what good it
might bring to the people most affected by the English
king's brutality.

"Ye all know that this is not the first time they've
extended an invitation to us," Liam said. "But this gathering in Kildare of the Shanavest leaders will be the
largest ever held. And by having representatives from
all over the south, they know they can plan a campaign
of unrest that will be felt all the way to London. Many
feel it is time to send that message of unity to every
magistrate and high sheriff in Ireland."

"It could be a trap." Jenny, the eldest in the group,
frowned at the circle of faces before turning back to
Liam and Egan.

Liam shrugged. "It could be. But we all live every day
with a noose about our necks."

The leader paused, and Egan watched him focus on
the discussion of those who had gathered inside the ruined abbey. She knew as well as he did that this decision

could not be made without a consensus of those who were here. What they decided would affect the future of all.

Liam shot a look at Egan, but she continued to keep her silence. In the past, she had always spoken against uniting their own efforts with the work of the Shanavests of Carlow, Queen's County, or Kildare. Word traveled quickly in the countryside, and what she had mostly heard of those groups in recent years had to do with their increasing tendency toward violence. Where her own small band would only go so far to scare a land-owner or cleric or to sometimes steal back what had been taken from tenants, these others were known to burn houses, maim cattle, and even commit murder if they saw the need.

While both Liam and Egan tried hard to focus their efforts on helping the displaced, many of the Whiteboys from Dingle to Dundalk seemed only bent on revenge. For now, though, attending this gathering in Kildare seemed to offer benefits too great to ignore.

" 'Tis a good two days to get there . . . and the same to get back," Patrick said, voicing the concern that a few had already expressed quietly. "Most of us cannot just go off and leave our families and our farms. I've still got a harvest to finish . . . and I'm a wee bit surprised that the meeting is to be held now."

"That's the very point of having it now." Liam crouched and picked up an old straw. "Wait until after the harvests are all done, and the English will be watching for us."

Liam's gaze met Egan's. He was looking for her support. She nodded.

"Is Finn going?" Jenny asked next.

"He cannot . . . and well he should not," Liam replied, studying the shredded bit of straw in his hand. Throwing it to the ground, he stood up and faced the rest. "Finn serves as our eyes and ears. We cannot afford to do without him for so long. Besides, outside of Cork, Waterford, or Tipperary, most of our brothers and sisters say he is something we've dreamed up."

"Ye don't have to go that far to hear that." Everyone laughed and turned to look at Ronan, who was standing against a ruined wall, his muscular arms crossed over his massive chest.

"Liam and I should go," Egan said to settle the matter before anyone could get distracted. "And while we are gone, Patrick can keep an eye on the runt here. Everyone else should go on with the harvest as if nothing were amiss."

Egan looked around at the group. She knew them all. Jenny. Liam. Ronan. Patrick. All of them. All of them had lived their entire lives in this little corner of Ireland, and they knew each other like family—celebrating and supporting each other through baptisms and weddings and funerals.

All seemed willing to go along with the suggestion. Jenny, though, was the one who brought up the problem Egan still had to resolve.

"We will all lend a hand and be sure Liam's absence will not mean trouble for his family. His landlord shan't miss him. But ye, Egan . . . to my thinking, ye shall be needing to do some fancy stepping to be away unnoticed for so long."

"That's my specialty." She nodded reassuringly to the group. "Fancy stepping."

"Aye, we have faith in ye, Egan." Patrick asked, "So when must ye be going?"

"Ten days," Liam answered. " 'Tis the latest we can go, if we want to get there in time."

Chapter 12

None of this made any sense. None of it!

The young maidservant held the robe as Catherine Purefoy pushed her arms into it. Her nerves just couldn't take this. She hadn't retired more than half an hour earlier, and now her husband wished her in the dining room?

What a night! Sir Nicholas's comment at dinner had surprised her. Anticipation had then nearly killed her as she'd waited for the men to emerge from the dining room. Minutes had rolled into hours and there had been no news. Hope had finally given way to disappointment, though, and it became clear that she could not wait up any longer for them. Decency dictated that she should go to bed, so she had . . . though reluctantly.

How curious that Lady Spencer did not appear to share in the excitement at all. What a strange woman! And daughter, too! Soon after the women had retired to the parlor after dinner, the young Miss Spencer had simply gone to her room with a book under her arm. Lady Spencer had gone up to bed soon after the daughter without a worry in the world, it seemed. Well, Catherine thought with satisfaction, Lady Spencer would have her time when Frances was ready for the marriage market.

"Are you certain that he did not wish for Miss Clara, as well?" Catherine asked again.

"Aye, quite certain, m'lady," the servant replied.

"And Sir Thomas *said* he wanted me to come alone?"

"Well, m'lady . . . not exactly in those words. The squire just asked for you."

The older woman looked down in search of her slippers. The serving girl immediately produced them. Nothing made sense. *Nothing*, she repeated to herself.

She and Clara had kept their vigil for a while longer, but it wasn't long before Clara had been begging to retire to her room. Catherine remembered thinking that this was a night for celebration, but the dispirited look on her daughter's face had soon put an end to her own happiness.

"And did you say Sir Thomas is still in the dining room?" She pushed her feet into the slippers.

"Aye, m'lady. Waiting to speak with you."

Catherine started for the door, but then thought of what she must look like in her robe and slippers and nightcap. She turned abruptly to the maid. "Is Sir Nicholas still with him?"

"Nay, m'lady. The gentleman left the dining room a while ago." She thought for a moment. "And there was no one in the parlor when we were cleaning up, either. Fey thought he'd retired for the night, as well . . . though I didn't see him, myself, ma'am."

He'd left a while ago, Catherine repeated to herself, hurrying downstairs. The house was quiet. The servants had apparently retired. She hardly knew what to expect, but she knocked quietly on the dining room door before entering.

Her husband was still sitting in his usual chair. A single candle flickered brightly in the center of the table. A half-empty decanter of port and a glass sat before him. He didn't acknowledge her when she came in and closed the door. The passage leading to the kitchen wing was dark and deserted. They were alone.

"You wished to speak to me."

He swirled the dark-colored liquid in his glass and drank it down before looking up.

"Though I should not be surprised, you have failed again, Catherine."

His voice was harsh—the attack wounding her dearly. She stood attentively at the opposite end of the table from her husband, her fingers clutching at the high back of the chair.

"I was under the impression that you had brought this silly chit up right. You assured me that this one would not disgrace me, that this one would know what to say . . . or do . . . or how to act to fetch herself a proper husband."

She shook her head. He was attacking the only bright thing that had come of this marriage. "She does, sir. Clara's manners are impeccable. Her charm—"

"Not enough, by thunder." He slammed a hand on the table, making her jump. She saw his hand shake as he poured more port from the decanter. "She lacks finesse. She acts like a simpleton. Young . . . naïve . . . innocent. The chit appears to the world to have no mind of her own." His words were slurring, and she watched him push the glass away, ignoring it when the liquid sloshed over the rim, staining the tablecloth.

"How else would you have her act?" Catherine could not comprehend him at all. "She is the perfect young woman. Accomplished in the feminine arts. Moral. Deferential. Quiet."

"Well, these things are apparently out of fashion." He leaned back against the chair, glaring at her. "And I do not blame him for not wanting her. I have yet to hear her express an opinion . . . on any subject. The chit has never taken a stand on anything. Defended anything. I never hear her speak without being spoken to first. She is just a pretty face. She has no soul. No substance. No presence. She's a bloody ghost."

Catherine felt hot tears rush to her eyes at this unfair and critical view of their daughter. She knew she could defend her. She could easily remind her husband that Clara was the opposite of *everything* that he hated in Jane. That it was he himself who had required that she be brought up to be exactly as he described.

She fought to be calm, wracking her brain for the real reason that Sir Nicholas had not proposed as they'd expected. There must be another reason, she thought. Well, she was not going to shoulder the responsibility for this. No, indeed.

"There will be other suitors," she said assuredly. "Clara is a noted beauty, and has a fortune to offer, as well. Others who are not as critical or *fashionable* will find no flaws in our child."

"This is it." He leaned forward. "Clara is *not* a child. I do not particularly care to be entertaining other suitors. I want *this* man. He is not like the other fops we saw hanging in the doorway of every party in London. His title and wealth be damned, I tell you. Even without them, I would gladly welcome this one into my family. He is a real man."

Catherine stared, shocked by her husband's words.

"I tell you, he gave me a reprimand after you all left . . . the likes of which I have not seen since the Duke of Cumberland relieved General Hawley of his command in Scotland." Sir Thomas rose to his feet, placing a hand on the table to steady himself. "Hang it, this one is not afraid of me in the least. The valiant rogue looked me right in my eye and said, 'You are wrong.' *'You are wrong,'* he tells me!"

Sir Thomas's shout echoed in the room, and Catherine glanced hesitantly behind her, glad she'd closed the door.

"The . . . *talk* . . . he wanted to have with me this night had little to do with Clara at all." He eyed her critically from across the room. "He had the gall to reprimand me . . . rebuke me . . . for the way I allow *Jane* to be treated."

"Jane?"

"Jane. He does not care at all for how I allow her to be treated by *Musgrave*. By thunder, he went on for a quarter of an hour about the insolence with which the new magistrate addresses her. He complained how *we*"—he pointed a finger at her and then back at himself—"fail to include her properly as a member of this family. He talked unceasingly about Jane. Defending her. Do you hear me? Not Clara . . . he has no interest there. But only defends *Jane* and her bloody impertinence." He laughed shortly and then drew a breath. "Oh, yes. He did say that your prize filly is far too young for him. He cannot possibly consider taking her as a wife."

"What are we to do?" she asked nervously as Sir

Thomas started around the table toward her. "We can't change her age . . . how can we convince him otherwise?"

As he reached her, she could see the look in her husband's eye. She'd seen it more than she cared to admit. He placed a hand on her shoulder, and she tried to hide her distaste.

"Our guest will be staying the fortnight as originally planned. So it is now *your* job, madam, to see to it that while he is here, he . . . he recognizes Clara's other charms."

She swallowed hard as his gaze descended to her bosom.

"I can . . . I can plan a party . . . a ball," she said as he began to move his hands over the silk brocade of her robe. "Girls are always seen in a far better light in such settings. I . . . I shall plan it for this coming week."

"You do whatever you must," he said vaguely, turning her toward the table.

At his urging, Catherine leaned forward onto her elbows. He lifted the layers of her robe and nightgown to her waist. She felt him position himself behind her and stared at the burning candle as he fumbled with his breeches.

"I shall send the invitations out tomorrow and . . ." She winced slightly and braced herself as he took hold of her hips and entered her. "I shall have Fey bring in half a dozen more workers from the farms to help with the serving." Her husband's tempo was increasing, and she felt the heat rising into her face. "I . . . I shall have her . . . have her get more help for . . . for the kitchen, too. And yes, a new . . . a new dress for Clara. Something more sophisticated and . . . and revealing." She was glad to hear his final grunt of release. She frowned and waited as he backed away from her.

"Sir Nicholas was smitten with her in London," Catherine said firmly. "He shall be smitten with her again."

She pushed herself off the table, smoothed the nightgown and robe back over her hips, and turned around. Her husband was already at the door, ready to leave.

"You are ignoring the most critical thing," he said darkly. "Jane."

"Jane?" she repeated simply. "You do not believe he is seriously interested in Jane, do you?"

He shrugged. "Have one of your maids reveal the truth about her past to Lady Spencer or her daughter. That should effectively put an end to any spell Jane might have cast over him."

"But do you . . . do you really think it is wise to let them know? I mean, Jane's past is a shameful reflection on all of us."

"Do it," he ordered. "They will find out sooner or later, in any case. At least this way we can be sure he is chasing the right girl."

Catherine Purefoy watched her husband turn his back and open the door. As he disappeared into the gloom of the corridor, she decided that, for once, she couldn't agree with him more.

Nicholas breathed in the cool night air as he strolled in the direction of the stables. It was difficult to stay calm, but he needed to be patient and keep his wits about him. His talk with Sir Thomas had cleared his conscience and his path. He was free now to be himself and to pursue Jane.

She was a mystery, though. High-strung, impetuous, yet completely lacking in vanity or self-absorption, she was unlike any woman he had ever met. And she was avoiding him.

After inquiring about her when they'd first come down for dinner, he'd been told by Clara that her sister was too tired from the activities of the day. She was resting in her room but might possibly join everyone later.

Dinner had come and gone, but there had been no sign of Jane. Not that any of her family had seemed to care about, or question, or miss her presence among them. No one at the table had been as aware of her absence, or as disturbed by it, as he.

After his blunt and candid chat with his host, Nicholas had thrown caution to the wind. Going up to her bedroom, he had knocked. No answer—no light visible beneath the door. He'd even tried the handle, but it was locked. In spite of it all, though, he had known that she was not inside . . . and he was equally sure that her horse would also be missing from her stall.

A solitary groom stood smoking a pipe and leaning against a post by the entrance to the paddock when Nicholas stepped around the stone wall. Curled up at his feet, two dogs looked like piles of fur, and they lifted their heads with only casual interest as he approached. On the far side of the paddock, a lantern swung gently on its hook beside the main door to the stable. Even in the darkness, Nicholas immediately recognized Paul, the stable master and trainer in charge of Sir Thomas's on-going breeding venture.

When they had come back this afternoon from their ride to Ballyclough, Nicholas had spent a good hour talking to the man about the training of hunters. Breeding horses was not only a gentlemanly pursuit in Ireland, apparently, it was also a profitable one.

"Beautiful night, wouldn't you say, Paul?"

"Aye, that it is, sir." The older man straightened up and took the pipe out of his mouth. "We shan't have too many more of these before the cold settles in."

"I don't mind the cold. That was a wild storm, though, last night. It seemed to fairly race out of the hills." Nicholas stopped beside the burly man and glanced down into the shadowy fields where he'd seen Jane. He could still envision the black cape flying behind her. "It must have bothered the horses some, I should think."

"Most of them were fine, but there is always one or two more high-strung than the others." He put the pipe back in the corner of his mouth. "But I keep my eye open. Always about, I am. So I look in on those that need it. Talk to them. The smell of pipe smoke comforts the horses, too."

The two stood in silence for a moment. "I checked on yer mount last night. He was a brave young gentleman throughout. Picked him up in Cork City, ye said?"

Nicholas nodded. *Always about.* Behind wisps of clouds, a moon was starting to rise in the east. He cast a sidelong glance at the man. Jane no doubt came through here regularly and at all hours of the day and night, so it would just figure that she would need an ally here. "How does Miss Jane's horse fare? She is a pretty stepper over rough ground."

"Aye, that she is. And Queen Mab fears nothing." The man's bearded face wrinkled into a smile. "And Miss Jane knew it the first moment she looked on the poor wee thing as a foal. Now, the rest of us could see plain as day that the filly was lame and unlikely to amount to much of a horse, but not Miss Jane."

"Lame, you say. You couldn't tell to look at her now."

"To be sure, sir."

"Did she name her?"

"Aye. She called her Mab after the queen of faeries. I can tell ye, sir, the good lass spent enough time caring for her and training her and spoiling her till even the mare believed she was Mab herself. 'Tis been four years, now, and I can tell ye that horse *knows* she's a queen." He finished with a chuckle.

Nicholas glanced at the wing containing the row of stalls where he knew Mab was kept. The shadows of the night lay heavily across the line of doors. He wondered if the horse was there now.

"On our ride over to visit Parson Adams, I was watching Miss Jane. She is quite a skilled rider. One might even say she is a bit of a daredevil . . . particularly when she knows someone might be watching."

"Every gray hair I have in this head is there because of Miss Jane, I can tell ye." Paul gave him a knowing nod and a grin. "Ye should see them, sir. There are times when I look down this hill and I see the two of them, horse and rider, moving together like a single creation. Across those fields they go, so fast that ye expect 'em to sprout wings and take to the heavens. Aye, sir, there are times I scratch my head and wonder if what my eyes are seeing is real or only my imagination."

Nicholas had a similar image branded in his mind. One of the dogs stood up and stretched, putting her muzzle in Nicholas's hand and getting a scratch behind the ears for her trouble. He considered his growing fascination. Jane Purefoy was a contradiction to every woman he'd ever known. He knew beyond doubt that the approach he generally used with others would be totally insufficient with her. This was a woman who lived life fully every day. She would accept nothing less than the real Nicholas Spencer.

"But I do not think I'm speaking out of turn to tell ye not everyone approves of the way herself and that horse roam these hills."

Nicholas understood the "everyone" to be her family. He nodded, and they fell silent again for a few moments.

"I heard the new magistrate today leaning on her to sell the mare to him. Your mistress became somewhat riled."

"The devil take the man!" Paul took the pipe out of his mouth and spat on the ground. "Sir Robert will be stoking the fires of hell long before Miss Jane agrees to sell Queen Mab to the likes of him . . . and the cur knows it!"

Watching the groom come alive, Nicholas saw that the man was much more spry than he pretended to be, fiercer than he allowed to be known, and more protective of Jane than Nicholas had initially guessed. Paul stepped impatiently away from the wall.

"For all the years I've worked for this family, I've ne'er known Miss Jane to be asking for one single thing. From the time she was a wee sprite, running barefoot and getting in everyone's way, the lass has not once asked for a bleeding thing. Other first-born lasses get spoilt to their bones, but not herself. I can tell ye, sir, the first time that girl e'er wanted anything for herself was the day she set her sweet eyes on that foal."

Paul drew a leather pouch from the pocket of his battered coat and began packing his pipe again. His eyes seemed almost to gleam, reflecting the rising moon.

"And by the time Mab came into being, 'twas not easy to do any asking of her father." He paused and looked up at the house. "Not after all the muddied water standing between them in recent years. But the lass swallowed her pride and asked."

"And asking for a lame filly was a difficult thing?"

"Aye, sir. More than ye know. But Sir Thomas was planning to put the animal down anyway, so he gave the foal up to Miss Jane." He stuck the pipe back into his mouth. "Four years, she's had her now. For the past four years, Queen Mab has been Miss Jane's horse . . .

the only thing she's ever laid claim to at Woodfield House. And that bleeding magistrate had better turn his covetous eyes toward someone else's property, I'm thinking."

Nicholas felt his own anger rising inside him. "Their exchange had better be the end of it, for Sir Robert heard her response . . . and I can tell you Miss Jane's refusal was clear and direct."

"The magistrate's head is filled with cobwebs, I'm afraid, sir. He hears what he likes."

"Then I may just knock a few of those cobwebs loose. If he ignores Miss Jane's refusal, he shall do so at his peril."

The gruff possessiveness in his comment drew Paul's curiosity immediately, for Nicholas saw the shining eyes turn on him. He didn't know why he'd spoken his thoughts aloud, but it was too late to worry about it now. Hell, he thought, he'd felt protective enough of Jane to give her own father a good tongue-lashing. What did it matter if anyone else at Woodfield House guessed where his interest lay?

Paul continued to study him quietly.

"It's getting late." Nicholas glanced toward the stables. "I think I shall check on my 'brave gentleman' before retiring."

The stable master wished him a pleasant good night, but Nicholas noticed that he kept his vigil in the paddock until he was certain the guest had accomplished his task and was headed back toward the house.

Reaching the stone archway by the main house, Nicholas turned and looked back at the stables. As he watched, Paul finally crossed the paddock and put out the light in the lantern.

The shadowed Woodfield House loomed into view beyond the crest of the hill, and Jane decided how she was going to conceal her journey to Kildare.

Her old tutor, Mrs. Barry, was living with her married daughter in Dublin. Perfect. She'd been invited many a time to visit with the retired teacher. The fact that the older woman would not know anything about the visit was irrelevant. All that mattered was that her parents should be told that she was starting out for Dublin. What happened to keep her from reaching there was something she could work out later.

She thought about the last time Mrs. Barry made a point of inviting her for a visit and an extended stay. Last Easter. Yes, perfect.

Jane had always been a favorite of the Englishwoman. Widowed not long after her husband had brought her and their daughter from the north, Mrs. Barry had been Jane's first teacher and undoubtedly the most patient. She'd been the one to recognize a child's restlessness with traditional subjects, and thought to encourage the young Jane to move beyond sketching and to experiment with paints.

Naturally, there were more than a few Protestant families in search of well-grounded instruction for their girls, so Jane had not been the tutor's only pupil. Despite her popularity, though, Mrs. Barry hadn't stayed around too long when her only daughter had married into a good Dublin family. Jane knew that the woman had been happily overseeing her grandchildren ever since.

Relieved to have a plan, Jane spurred her mount up the hilly fields toward the familiar black shape of the stables. As she drew closer, however, she was surprised to see the glow of Paul's pipe in the shadow of an oak a few yards from the paddock gate. Slowing Mab to a walk, she guided the animal where he stood.

"Is something wrong?"

"Nay, lass. Nothing at all." He put the pipe between his teeth and reached for the horse's bridle as Jane dismounted.

"Why did you wait up?" she asked, walking beside him as they moved toward the paddock.

"Old habit."

Something was bothering him, she thought, as he glanced back at the deserted countryside.

"Ye did not see anyone out and about now, did ye?"

"Not a soul." How many years had he been waiting up for her? She thought of all those early years, and how she would find him sick with worry at the bottom of the hill. Waiting. Scolding. Caring. For too many years than she could count, he'd been more of a father to her

than Sir Thomas. She glanced up at the cap that he wore
low on his head, at the sparkling eyes that continued to
scan the fields she'd crossed only moments ago.

"What's wrong, Paul?" she asked softly.

"I heard about that mealy-mouthed cur Musgrave giving ye a hard time today. That was plenty to get me
going."

"You talked to the Englishman."

"That I did, lass . . . and more than once."

How curious that Spencer refused to limit his time to
socializing only with the gentry. Even at Ballyclough
she'd silently observed him befriending Mrs. Brown and
Henry's cook and even two of the villagers who had just
happened to come by on some business with Reverend
Adams.

They reached the paddock. He pushed open the gate.
"And that's what has me out here thinking, miss."

"Come now, Paul. Out with it."

"Very well. 'Tis just this. I'm thinking everybody's got
it wrong."

Jane turned away, closing the paddock gate behind
them. "Everybody's got *what* wrong?" she asked over
her shoulder.

"He doesn't want Miss Clara, lass. He's set his cap on
ye, sure as I'm standing here."

"Really, Paul! Of all the notions!" Her denial echoed
faintly as the stable master pulled open the door to
Mab's stall. She followed. "You don't have to do that.
I can take care of her."

"I know, my joy. But I don't mind spoiling ye a wee
bit . . . every now and then."

"Thank you."

"Be on yer way to the house now."

She stared after them as they disappeared inside. Jane
shook her head and turned away, not quite understanding what was going on with her old friend.

The house lay dark and quiet on the hill. The moon
lit a bright path through the garden. Though she would
not chance to go that way, Jane also decided against
going through the dank underground passage that had
been in existence since a castle had stood on this hill.

The night was too beautiful, and there was too much

rattling in her mind that she needed to clear. She decided on taking the walk-path, knowing that if the door beneath the great stone arch was barred for the night, she could go in through the kitchen wing. With a sigh, she started for the paddock gate.

"And Miss Jane . . ."

Paul's whisper stopped her. He was peering out from Mab's stall.

"There's far more to that one than meets the eye, I'm thinking."

Chapter 13

Following the path, she climbed the hill toward the sleeping hulk of a house . . . just as he'd hoped she would. As she approached, Nicholas felt his senses sharpen perceptibly at the sight of her. With her came the smell of wind and the tingling promise of darkness. She moved like a cat, her lithe body gliding effortlessly through the night.

By 'sblood, Nicholas thought, he couldn't remember the last time a woman had stirred in him such anticipation.

"A far more pleasant night for riding, I should think."

Startled, Jane whirled and peered into the shadows of the garden entry. Nicholas was almost disappointed when she didn't reach for the dagger he knew she would be carrying. He would have enjoyed getting close enough to have to handle her and the knife.

"What are you doing here?" Her dark eyes flashed like two jewels in the moonlight. "I shouldn't have thought you were one who hides in dark corners and spies on people."

"I'm not . . . usually." He continued to lean a shoulder against the rough stone of the garden wall. His gaze took in the loose-fitting dark breeches, the high boots, the black smock. "I was only enjoying the beautiful view."

She was dressed as a man, and yet Nicholas could not for a moment fathom how anyone who looked at her could be fooled. His eyes lingered on the dark ringlets framing a complexion that rivaled the moon's glow. How could any observer fail to see that she was *all* woman?

Jane cast a glance over her shoulder at the house looming behind her. "If a beautiful view is what you are after, then you are facing the wrong direction."

"I don't believe I am."

The true meaning behind his seemingly matter-of-fact statement was slow to hit her. She was not accustomed to receiving such compliments. He slowly pushed away from the wall and moved through the moonlight toward her. Her objection to his compliment withered on her tongue as a strange, tingling sensation began to spread quickly through her limbs. He had discarded his jacket. Her gaze moved uncontrollably to the open collar of his shirt and the sleeves rolled up to display muscular arms.

"It is very late. I should be going in." But her feet, for some reason, seemed to have taken root.

"Please stay."

If he had made an attempt to use his physical charm in persuading her, she would have escaped easily. But the simple request only managed to unnerve her more. She searched for safe words to say as he came to a stop before her, but could think of nothing.

"Clara!" she blurted out. "Yes, Clara is an early riser. You should go in, too. She will certainly be looking forward to having breakfast with you."

"Well, I intend to sleep until noon tomorrow."

Anger flared within her. "I do wish you would stop treating her so poorly." She couldn't bring herself to look up into his face—not when he was standing so close. "She doesn't deserve to be treated that way."

"She appears to be perfectly happy with the way she is being treated . . . as are your parents and everyone else at Woodfield House. You, Jane, are the only one who complains."

This time, her rising temper forced her to look up, and she was immediately amazed by how tall he was—and how intensely he was studying every flaw in her face. Paul's words came back to her. "But Clara . . ."

"Surrender that cause, Jane. I simply do not care to talk about Clara."

His arm brushed against hers, shocking her with the heat that emanated from the spot. She took an immediate step back. "I . . . I need to go in."

"Stay . . . just for a few minutes." A strong hand reached out and took hold of her wrist. His thumb gently caressed her skin.

"Why?"

"It is a beautiful night. I've been desperate for a tour of the gardens."

"I shall go and awaken Clara for that. She is far more knowledgeable—"

"I lied."

"What?"

"I lied. I do not want a tour. But I recall seeing a stone bench by the wall at the lower end of the garden. I would very much like to sit on that bench and talk."

She tried to ignore the gentle pressure of his fingers—the warmth. "Since you do not wish to talk about my sister, then we have nothing to say to each other."

"But we do." He tugged gently and drew her gaze. "I have questions that I would not want to ask of anyone but you."

She arched a brow. "About Clara?"

He laughed—a deep, hearty laugh that made her smile in spite of herself. "By 'sblood, madam, you are persistent."

"Thank you for the compliment."

"But it was not a compliment," he growled good-naturedly, tugging again on her wrist and unbalancing her slightly. "Trust me, when I give you a compliment, you'll know. Come and sit with me for a few minutes. You might just earn one yet."

Jane pulled her wrist free, and hesitated a moment. There was no denying it. She wanted to go with him. At the same time, she didn't dare even to think why she wanted to. She nodded and tried to make light of the whole situation.

"You are greatly lacking in the power of persuasion." She saw him open his mouth to argue and waved him off, continuing. "*Nonetheless*, I suppose I have let you beg enough. I've decided, therefore, to humor you a little, sir. I shall walk to the garden wall and back."

Another rumble of laughter from the baronet brought a smile to Jane's lips. As far as the rules of propriety were concerned, she knew it was completely improper to be walking at midnight with a gentleman through a dark garden. But then again, she rationalized, she had no reputation to protect. And regarding any potentially dishonorable intentions on his part, she knew she was quite capable of protecting herself. She was a rebel leader, and he knew it. She was not some naïve, starry-eyed virgin hoping to be kissed by some rogue under a trellis of late-blooming roses.

These thoughts set Jane's body and mind more at ease—at least momentarily—as they walked beneath the stone arch. Immediately, though, the fragrant scents of the garden beds surrounded them, and she felt her pulse begin to race again at the sight of the seductive shadows cast by the light of the moon. She felt her sense of security beginning to dissolve, and forced herself to push away such foolish thoughts. She simply needed to treat him in the same way that she treated every other man she knew . . . with blunt honesty and indifference.

"The early hours we keep in the country must be a torment to someone like you."

"The hours *we* keep are perfectly satisfactory. To be candid, I shouldn't care to have anybody else about right now."

Jane found him watching her, and she shook her head. "I was speaking in general terms when I said 'we.' But you might as well put aside your cleverly disguised discourse and charming ways, Sir Nicholas. They have no effect on me."

His arm brushed against hers again, this time intentionally, she thought. "Are you certain I have no effect on you, at all?"

She shook her head and smiled at him. Stepping to the edge of the path, she put some space between them. "I am not one of your London society maidens. I am incapable of being dared or taunted or tempted. Now kindly tell me what it was that you wished to ask me."

The look he gave her told her that he didn't believe her bravado for a moment. But he was clearly enough of a gentleman not to press her. "The topic is a matter of some seriousness."

"I'm glad. I should hate to think of forfeiting needed sleep for anything less."

His hands were now clasped behind his back, his expression grave, as the two of them continued down the path.

"Since our arrival in your part of the world," he continued, "I have had the good fortune of coming face-to-face with a band of well-known rebels and their leader. I also have been questioned about and endured interminable lectures regarding this very same group. Unfortunately, many of those doing the questioning and lecturing I find to be scarcely objective in their presentation of the truth."

Jane frowned in the darkness. She'd been expecting the questions. It would only be natural that he should want to know the reason for her involvement with the Whiteboys. As a member of the English gentry, Spencer would no doubt see it as his absolute duty to ask these things. And after the answers would come the advice that a gentleman *must* provide to insignificant, unintelligent, vulnerable females. She could almost hear him already.

Jane had to give him credit, though. At least he'd been able to delay his meddling for nearly two days.

"So much of what we read and hear in England is based on gross generalization. I know that to be true, for I recall the discussions I heard with regard to the American colonies after I returned from there. What was said often had little to do with the truth or with accuracy. We speak of strife and division here, but ignore the poverty and exploitation that cause it. We discuss the threatened involvement of Spaniards and French against England. We confer the titles of 'hero' and 'villain' on the basis of whether a person is English or not. We only see what it is in our interest to see."

They reached the bottom of the garden, but Jane found herself too captivated by his words to turn back. The two walked beneath a long, trellised arbor of grapevines. Without thinking, she pulled a bunch of the ripe fruit from the vine.

"I saw this kind of ignorance when I fought many years ago against the French on the Plains of Abraham in the taking of Quebec, and later in the campaigns against the Cherokee. I was even carried along by it to some extent. But this time I want to do better. I do not want to make the same mistake. I want to understand the truth." She heard him take a deep breath and let it out slowly. "For the past two nights I have—with your father's permission—spent some time in his library looking through papers he has collected regarding this area's culture and history. But I should not need to tell you that these accounts have been written mostly by Englishmen, and lack any attempt at objectivity and accuracy."

They stopped at a stone bench beneath the trellis, and he placed his boot on it. Leaning on a knee, he turned to her. "So, what I am asking is whether there is someone at Woodfield House . . . or someone who lives in the vicinity . . . who is knowledgeable *and* objective enough to give me a clear understanding of what is happening here."

This hadn't been what she was expecting. She'd been so continually faced for so many years with the flaws of an English system—and the flaws of the aristocracy—that she could not help but wonder about this man's motives. He was not at all like his brethren.

"I must ask you, sir, if this desire for 'understanding' can be traced to our little skirmish yesterday and to your silence about the identity of the rebel. Perhaps you are concerned about your decision not to give me away."

"No." His denial was emphatic. "And I give you my word that as far as the rest of the world will ever know, you and I never met until last night . . . in your parents' parlor."

She paused. "Tell me, then. Why do you care?"

"I told you. I have been questioned about it, lectured about it by people like Sir Thomas, and this morning by Musgrave. I like to know the facts before I form an opinion."

"Facts." She leaned a shoulder against the trellis and met his challenging look. "Facts are all just a matter of perception." She held up the fruit in her hand. "What do you see here?"

"Grapes. Nourishment. The raw materials for wine, I suppose."

"What I see is the substance that holds the seeds of

future growth. The individual grape seed has little hope of growing into a vine. But if I were to bury this entire bunch, in the spring we would find a number of vines sprouting up from the soil. Facts can be interpreted in different ways."

Nicholas pulled a grape from the bunch in her hand and popped it into his mouth. "And sometimes a grape is but a grape." He smiled. "But I accept your point."

"Why do you *need* to form an opinion about us?" She shot him a challenging look. "You are here today, but you will be gone with my sister tomorrow. Why—"

"I shall not be leaving with Clara tomorrow . . . nor anytime thereafter. And stop muddying the discussion."

"Very well." She shrugged. "But my point is that you are here today, but you shall be gone tomorrow. My understanding is that in Quebec, you were sent to fight. It was impossible not to get involved. Here, you are visiting with your family. Why not simply enjoy the beauty of the countryside? Entertain yourself with all this area has to offer? In substance, you will leave here as the same person that you were when you arrived. There is no need for you to know any more about us."

His gaze narrowed. He leaned toward her. "Why are you so set against me learning about your cause?"

Jane shrugged and walked away a step. She looked up at the blanket of stars overhead and tried to keep her tone light. "I am trying to do you a favor . . . save your holiday . . . eliminate undue concerns."

"I did not ask for your charity, but your knowledge."

She felt him move close beside her. She tried to hide the unexpected shiver that coursed through her when their arms brushed.

"Of all the people you have met since arriving, why are you asking me?"

"Because, despite your birth and parentage, you have chosen the more difficult path. And . . . you are the only famous rebel leader that I have had the privilege of becoming acquainted with." Even in the darkness she could feel the weight of his gaze on her face. "It was quite impressive to hear Sir Thomas use Egan's name in the same breath as the others who are such a thorn in the side of the Crown."

"And you thought, 'How sad that he is so blind.' "

"Hardly! I was oddly grateful for his ignorance. There is something impressive . . . and yet disconcerting . . . in the irony that an Englishwoman is a leader in such a movement." There was no mockery in his tone, only quiet admiration. "When you first became involved in all of this, did you ever think that one day you might be considered a hero to those you fight for?"

"Or think that one day I would be hanged as a traitor?" Jane looked down, digging the dirt with the tip of one boot. She was not accustomed to being complimented. "The paths we travel are not always the same ones we started on . . . or would have continued on . . . if we were given the choice."

"Do you regret your involvement?"

"I am content to be the person that I have become. I am resigned to the role I seem destined to play. But I would sacrifice all . . . sacrifice myself . . . if I could change just a few of the tragedies of the past or even one tragedy to come."

Jane dropped the bunch of grapes into the dirt beside the path. A breeze, scented with late-blooming flowers and cool on her face, stirred memories long buried, images of faces long dead.

"I became Egan to close off the pain . . . to forget . . ." A sudden tightness squeezed at Jane's throat. She would never have become Egan if those five young men had not been hanged so unjustly. She would never have lashed out at the viciousness of this country's ruling class if she had not seen her lover's corpse rotting upon the gallows.

If Conor had lived, the extent of Jane's involvement would most likely have consisted of pining for him during his absence. She was no hero. The man she'd loved and his four unfortunate friends were heroes. She was just a survivor.

When Jane felt Nicholas's fingers brush away a tear that she had unknowingly shed, she turned and their gazes locked. She had an uncomfortable, hollow feeling that too much had been revealed.

"Will you someday tell me about your past?"

"My past is an open book . . . up to where the change

was wrought in me. Ask anyone and they will surely tell you all about it."

Too much emotion lay too close to the surface, and Jane recognized her vulnerability at this moment. Her feelings were too raw. The scabs of old wounds were opening up. Jane drew a deep breath, summoned her strength, and turned toward the house.

"Someone like Henry Adams should be able to tell you whatever it is you wish to learn about this country's past."

"How foolish of me to not have guessed. He is a man who seems to be all too familiar with everything and everyone around here."

She was too wrapped up in her own thoughts and ignored the disapproval in his tone.

"Though my life is my own, Sir Nicholas, I know that there are expectations that go along with being a guest. Perhaps we should retire to our respective places. Good night."

She knew the formality of her words sounded forced, but she had to get away.

Jane moved quickly along the garden path, praying that he would not follow. As she walked, she made herself breathe normally and forced herself to be calm.

She couldn't explain the melancholy she found herself suddenly afflicted with. With just a few words, spoken there in that same spot in the garden, the years had melted away and long-buried memories had burned up from within, destroying her insides on their way to the surface. Now she could feel the fiery ache once again in her flesh and in her very skin.

But this was not what she had worked so hard to become. She had never expected time to heal, but to teach her. And she had learned over the years how to survive. She'd struggled and finally succeeded in keeping herself above the molten flood tides of remembrance. But this night, with this man, she had once again become vulnerable and fragile.

Wiping away a sheen of tears, she looked ahead. The sky was clear, the house black and intimidating. The breeze was coming from the east, from Waterford. And Jane remembered.

Nine years ago, she had walked down this same path to meet a man she'd loved. It was the eve of her birthday. She was turning seventeen, and Conor had met her under that same trellis at midnight. A kiss. It was to be a farewell kiss, but neither had known it. They'd only whispered of the future.

How could they know that he would be arrested the next day and executed before a fortnight had passed? How could they know?

"Jane," Spencer called after her.

A painful cry broke free with the next breath, and she quickened her steps.

"Jane!"

As the tears streamed down her face, she hurried through the garden gate, hoping to escape into the house. But his strong hands caught her just as she reached the landing, spinning her around to face him.

"Jane, what's wrong?"

No words would escape her lips. The tears, though, she fought to control. The past was behind . . . why did it still haunt her?

She struggled against the pain, forcing it back, and in a moment or two managed to look up into his face.

"If what I said upset you . . . I . . . I had no idea that your friend meant so much." His fingers squeezed her shoulders. "It was none of my bloody business to—"

"What friend?" Sobriety came instantly as she realized how disconcerted he seemed. She wiped at the wetness of her face with the back of one hand.

"Reverend Adams. I have no right to be critical of him. It is just that you say he is only a friend, but I find myself . . . hell, I find myself competing with the man for your attention at every turn."

"Competing for my attention?" She found herself actually smiling up at him through her tears. "Why? Why would someone like *you* . . . want to compete for *my* attention?"

"You can mock me . . . or continue this stubborn ignorance of my interest in you"—his thumb gently brushed away the wetness under her eyes—"but I ask you to forgive me for the way I spoke of your friend."

The baronet's face was deadly earnest, but Jane was

too consumed by his words and his touch to notice. The need to take comfort from another human being, to feel the unfamiliar warmth of a man's touch almost over-whelmed her with its power. She stared at the glimpse of skin beneath the open collar of his shirt, at the solid pillar of his throat, at his broad and muscular chest. In an instant, she felt a different kind of heat stirring in her middle. A soft glow seemed to flow into every limb, softening the aching there and replacing it with another.

She abruptly tore her gaze away. What was wrong with her? She was clearly losing control of herself. She needed to regain command of her unraveling emotions.

"It is I who . . . who should be sorry," she managed to get out. "This . . . how I acted . . . was totally inappro-priate. My tears have nothing to do with Henry . . . or with whatever it was you said."

He didn't appear convinced. While still holding her shoulders tightly, he looked more closely into her face. "Then why are you so upset?"

The whispered question went straight to her heart, taking her to yet another level of awareness. The caress of his breath against her skin felt so right.

"Ghosts." She searched and found her voice. "From time to time, I have ghosts that haunt me."

"So your tears have nothing to do with Henry Adams?"

"Nothing at all."

Jane shook her head and felt the warmth continue to spread through her as his face relaxed. She had not al-lowed herself to dwell on his striking good looks until this instant. She had not allowed herself to admit that she was wishing that the distance between their bodies might disappear.

Jane immediately tried to make herself push him away, but she couldn't. Nicholas lifted his hand from her shoulder and tenderly touched the bruise by her mouth.

"Now that we are getting around to apologies, I should tell you I am very sorry for this."

Jane had every intention of making some light remark, but the next breath was caught in her chest as she felt his fingers trace the lines of her lips.

"You are so beautiful, Jane. You are so alive . . . and beautiful."

She had to deny this. She had to walk away. But his touch had let loose a flood of sensations, and she found herself fighting just to stay afloat.

"I . . . I don't think this . . . is a good idea."

"You are quite right." The words were drawled as if he meant it. Suddenly, though, she was wrapped tightly in his arms, and his lips were crushing hers.

She forgot to breathe. She could find no reason to complain. All she was conscious of was the consuming fire that was racing through her.

Her hands seemed to move of their own accord, pulling at his shirt, feeling the muscular lines of his back. He groaned his approval. Powerful arms gathered her closer to his body, pressing her to him until there was nothing left between two hearts pounding wildly as one.

Passion had been something she had experienced long ago, but buried away. She'd believed no man could ever conjure in her the need she had once tasted and even become consumed by. But now, wrapped in Nicholas's steely grip, she found herself burning.

As he kissed her, she opened for him, driving them both an inch closer to an edge of oblivion. She felt his tongue searching, tasting. As he pressed her back against the stone arch, his body followed, scorching every inch of her with his heat.

"Jane." He tore his mouth from her lips and pressed it to her throat. His hands glided down over her body— touching, possessing—and all she could do was clutch his hair and drag his mouth back to hers for another searing kiss. "I knew it would be like this between us."

His mouth moved to her ear—teasing, biting, suckling.

. . . *be like this between us . . . between us . . .* The words reverberated in her mind. *Us . . .*

It was almost as if she were floating outside of her own body. As if in a dream, Jane looked down at herself. Nicholas's mouth was tracing a path down her neck while his hands were on her back, sliding over the curve of her buttocks, pressing her to him.

Us . . .

And then, as something clicked in her brain, she was back in her body, conscious and nearly panicked. The moan in her throat became a cry, and the hands that couldn't bring him close enough suddenly pushed to get free.

He stopped instantly and took an immediate step back. "Jane . . ."

Jane still had difficulty catching her breath, but she made sure to speak the words that were screaming within her. "There is no *us*, Nicholas. There can never be an *us*!"

She raised a hand to silence him as he opened his mouth to speak.

"And please . . . please . . ." she begged him as she edged toward the door. "Forget what happened tonight. We both made a mistake. And it can never . . . *will* never . . . happen again."

Jane ran inside, not knowing how she would ever be able to forgive herself for nearly seducing her sister's future husband. Never again, she swore silently, climbing two steps at a time to her workroom beneath the roof. Never again would she allow herself to be alone with Nicholas Spencer.

Not for a second.

From the window of his darkened bedchamber, Sir Thomas watched the baronet walk back into the night. Even from this distance, he sensed the man's frustration as he ran a hand through his hair.

"She is far more of a handful than you thought her to be," he murmured.

As he always did, Sir Thomas had been waiting for Jane's return. Standing by his chair, he'd happened to see her come up the pathway, only to be approached by the visitor. And then he'd watched the two of them walk down into the gardens.

The sight of the two of them had given him a moment's pause, but he had quickly shaken off the thought. There was no chance of anything developing between them. Jane wouldn't allow it. Perhaps he should have advised the young man about it during their private talk after dinner.

He'd been correct—as always. It hadn't been long before he'd seen Jane practically run back toward the house with Spencer hot on her heels. And now he was looking at the frustration of a man rejected.

It was more than the scandal of her past that would keep the baronet and Jane apart. It was more than his own order to hang that presumptuous papist boy nine years ago that kept the wedge solidly between himself and Jane.

There was, indeed, much more.

At first, when he'd become aware of her coming in and going out at all hours, he'd been fool enough to think there was another man involved. Soon after, he'd started studying her paintings and watching her carefully. It had not taken him long to realize that his own daughter had taken up the cause of her dead lover. Jane was now supporting the Shanavests.

Sir Thomas moved away from the window and sank heavily onto the edge of the bed. It was to protect her that he had remained magistrate for so long, hoping that she would tire of the foolishness of the movement. He himself would not move against the rebels again while Jane was involved with them, but she was the reason he continued to harp at Musgrave to take stronger actions now to capture and hang the local leaders. The old man knew that with the ringleaders gone, there would be little fight left in the rest.

Only then, Thomas knew, he'd have a chance of removing the wedge. Only then, he prayed, he might have his daughter back.

Chapter 14

The small workroom Catherine Purefoy used as the center for running her household was abuzz when Jane poked her head in the next morning. There were four servants already standing in a line before her mother and taking a variety of directions from their somewhat hysterical leader. Meanwhile, Clara stood by the single window of the room, staring sullenly out, and totally unaffected by the madness in the room.

A sharp needle of guilt immediately pricked Jane as she saw the gloominess in her sister's face, but just as she'd done a thousand times during the sleepless night, she shut the door firmly on the image of Nicholas and herself standing together beneath the stone arch. Bitterly, she pushed the image deep in the bottomless well of mistakes she had made.

Just as Jane was considering if she should give this lunacy an hour or two to settle down, her mother's victims began to disperse. Two upstairs maids practically tripped over each other in their haste to escape. One of the kitchen servants stormed out muttering a profane curse in Gaelic. Fey, to her great misfortune, was the solitary victim left behind. The mistress's voice rose in excitement as she fired a dozen directions pertaining to a dozen different tasks at the red-haired woman. It was upsetting for Jane to see that even the housekeeper's usually calm demeanor was affected by her mother's ongoing harangue.

As Lady Purefoy paused to take a breath, Jane seized the opportunity and stepped in.

"I need a moment of your time, Mother."

"It shall have to wait, Jane. Not now."

"But it cannot wait." She walked in and sat comfortably in one of the two available chairs. She was relieved to see Clara give her a side glance and a smile before returning her attention to whatever she was so consumed with outside.

Her mother gave her an exasperated glare. "Well then, what is it, Jane? Be quick about it."

"I am planning to visit old Mrs. Barry . . . in Dublin. I shall be taking a coach from Cork and will leave in about nine days."

"And how long will you be gone?"

"A fortnight, perhaps a few days more."

"Very well. I shall tell Sir Thomas about it." Lady Purefoy turned back to the housekeeper.

All as Jane had expected. With very few exceptions, she had not spoken directly with her father for years. Everything he needed to know could be communicated through her mother. And now that she knew of the trip, there really wasn't any reason for Jane to remain. Curiosity, though, held her in her seat.

"Oh, yes. The seamstress we used before our trip to London," Lady Purefoy said, recalling her instructions to Fey. "I want Paul to send a groom with you to Cork City and bring the woman back. Now, I told you what to buy as far as fabrics and colors. Make sure whichever groom Paul chooses to send, he must understand he is not to hurry you."

"I'll not be rushed, m'lady."

"But I want you back immediately. No dallying in the city, mind you. There's much to be done, Fey. *Much* to be done!"

"Preparing for a party, Mother?" Jane asked good-naturedly, trying to gain a moment's respite for the housekeeper.

"A ball," Lady Purefoy corrected immediately. "The grandest we've ever had at Woodfield House."

Catherine leaped out of her chair and scurried behind a writing table, scowling at a neat stack of papers.

"I thought you were planning to help me with these invitations . . . Clara?" She stared at her young daughter's troubled profile for a moment. "You have to start these now so we can have them delivered *today*."

Jane watched her sister, obedient as always, leave her place and sit behind the desk. She was the angel of the household, trained to dutifully follow their parents' orders.

"Is this the engagement party . . . er, ball that has . . . that everyone has been waiting for?" Despite what he'd said to her, Nicholas Spencer was here to marry Clara and everyone knew it. Everyone had accepted it. She had no right . . . no reason . . . to feel this hot iron that had suddenly pierced her chest.

An uncomfortable silence descended over the room. Her mother and Fey were both staring at her. Clara, though, was continuing to scratch the pen across the paper without pausing.

"Miss Jane has just come down," Fey gently reminded Lady Purefoy. "She does not know yet."

"If you were not sleeping half the day away, as you do, then you would know what is happening around here." Jane's mother turned her back and moved the wax and seal closer to Clara on the desk. She picked up a list and started to complain about all that needed to be done.

"Well, does anyone care to tell me what is going on here?"

Clara put down her pen and spoke. "There is no offer of marriage. Sir Nicholas told Father last night that he does not wish to marry me."

"There is no need to state it as if it were final," Catherine protested immediately. She moved behind her daughter, placing her hands protectively on her shoulders and glaring at Jane. The younger sister simply returned to writing the invitations. "He is obviously not ready to make a decision, but his intentions are very clear. He and his family are planning to stay for another fortnight . . . as originally planned."

"So you are giving a party . . . pardon me, a ball?"

"Why not?" Lady Purefoy took an invitation that Clara had finished and carefully folded it. "A young woman's advantages are best displayed on such occasions. There is nothing like good food and drink and dancing to open a baronet's eyes to what he will be missing. I predict he'll be asking for our Clara's hand the day after the ball." She nodded to Fey. "You can go now. And do not forget what I told you about the dallying."

Fey hesitated before leaving. "Now should we not be planning for a dress to be made for Miss Jane, as well, m'lady? If she has no plan of leaving for nine days and the ball is in six . . ." Fey gave Jane a gentle smile. "Do you not think, miss, that 'tis high time you gave up wearing black? 'Tis been—"

"Be on your way, Fey," Lady Purefoy cut in sharply. "Jane is too old to reap any benefit from any of this. And besides, you know as well as I that she does not care for this sort of thing. She never has. Do you, Jane? In fact, what is the difference between nine days . . . six days . . . or two days? Why not plan to leave for Mrs. Barry's right away? You shall be much happier there, anyway, while all this activity is taking place here. I shall tell Sir Thomas to allow you to go immediately."

"No, Mother," Jane protested. She rose to her feet as Fey disappeared out the door. Lady Purefoy had stung her. In spite of the difficult state of affairs at Woodfield House, it was still rare to hear her mother openly assert that Jane wasn't wanted. But that was enough to make her stay. "I shall be leaving in nine days as I told you."

Catherine looked mildly annoyed when Jane stopped at the door and turned to face her. "And Mother, for Clara's sake, please think before you talk. I do not believe you even know how hurtful you can be sometimes."

Jane glanced at Clara, who looked up from beneath hooded eyes only for an instant before silently and diligently going back to work on the invitations.

Patches of thin forests snaked through the worn hills. A solitary trail wove in and out of the wood and disappeared over the crest of the next rise. Alexandra Spencer lifted the charcoal off the paper as a patch of gray cloud moved across the sun. She turned her attention to the east and studied the contrast of shadow and light as the cloud slipped over in the sweeping panorama of foothills, forests, and pastures.

Looking at Jane's work the day before had stimulated that old, familiar thirst in her again. Alexandra needed to draw and paint. She needed to create.

She also needed to talk to Jane and congratulate the young woman on her work. She doubted that Jane got much encouragement, living with the dull rustics who were supposedly her parents. Alexandra couldn't help but wonder if the older sister hadn't been a foundling, after all.

The sun reemerged, but as Lady Spencer readied the charcoal over the paper again, another shadow moved over her. This one belonged to her own daughter, who now stood directly beside the garden bench, effectively blocking her light. The artist's complaint, though, was silenced when she looked up into Frances's tearful face.

"Oh, Fanny. And what is wrong now? Is Nicholas not back yet from his ride with Sir Thomas and the trainer?" She pressed a comforting hand to her daughter's and pulled her down beside her on the stone bench. She had heard Nicholas and Frances exchange a few words this morning at breakfast. She wasn't about to side with anyone over a petty dispute, but all the same she'd thought her son's temper had been shorter than usual. In fact, he'd been quite impatient even to hear what Frances's request was. "He was right about not wanting to take you along. They are looking at horses—talking business—riding through pastures and walking through stables. Why, they're probably knee-deep in manure as we speak. Now, what enjoyment would a young woman like you get out of something so appalling?"

"I am not angry with Nicholas." Frances wiped away the wetness on her face. But fresh tears were soon coursing down her pale cheeks again.

"Then why are you so upset, my dear?" Alexandra put aside her artwork and took out a handkerchief. She handed it to her daughter. "There is no reason to be bored. Lady Purefoy tells me that they are planning a great party for the end of this week. I am certain she could use some help if you were to offer."

The young woman shook her head. "I am not bored, Mother. And I was . . . I was planning to be of some help . . . but when I heard the story . . ." She hiccuped. "Oh, Mother . . . it is *so* sad . . . so sad . . . poor Jane."

Before Alexandra could say a word, Frances had laid her head on her mother's chest and was sobbing wretchedly.

"What happened to Jane? Is she unwell? Did she have an accident?"

It took a few moments before Frances finally began to explain.

"No, she is well now . . . I mean on the surface . . . this happened some time ago . . . but still . . ."

A dull ache had begun to eat away at Lady Spencer. In the short time they had been at Woodfield House, she was already beginning to care for Jane, and all this puzzling talk was too worrying.

"Frances Marie. You start explaining to me what . . ."

"I found out why . . . why the family treats her so . . . so poorly." The young woman straightened on the bench and used the handkerchief to blow her nose. "They . . . are ashamed of her . . . I think."

Instant objections arose in Alexandra, but she bit them back as Fanny turned her watery gaze on her.

"It is true, Mother. These people never told us about Jane . . . until we arrived. And . . . and . . ." She waved an impatient hand toward the house. "They care nothing for her. Last night . . . no one asked where she was. Did you notice? And this morning . . . did anyone inquire after her even once?"

There was a great deal about the Purefoy household that Alexandra didn't understand. "Each family has its own little eccentricities. Just because we have not seen much of Jane, that certainly does not mean—"

"But it does!" Frances clutched her mother's hands. "It does if they believe her reputation is ruined and they consider her a disgrace."

Alexandra kept silent. She knew her daughter. She knew that as distraught as Frances was, everything she must have heard would spill out.

"The problem is that I think Jane is a tragic victim. Mother, I had to question *two* people before I had all of it." Frances's blue eyes narrowed and her voice lowered as she glanced back at the house. "And that's another thing. I think they planned this whole thing out. I mean, letting us know about Jane's past."

"Really, Frances . . ."

"Honestly! Thinking me a simpleton or something, they sent a maid in to tidy my bedchamber. And while she was there, she just *happened* to tell me all the gossip about the older daughter. I hardly think it a coincidence, Mother. I believe, after they saw how Nicholas last night was not happy with Jane's absence, they wanted to make sure that we all think the worst of her." She looked into her mother's eyes. "I might be only sixteen, but I have been brought up to know what is what. As soon as that girl started prattling on about how *horrible* it was for the family when Miss Jane eloped nine years ago with a poor, good-for-nothing papist, I knew something was wrong. Naturally, she went on to tell me that—despite the disgrace—generous Sir Thomas and Lady Purefoy were quick to take her back."

Although Alexandra didn't have all the details, she was still pleased with her daughter for viewing the tittle-tattle with skepticism.

"I knew they weren't going to tell me everything. So after the maid was finished in my room, I went in search of Fey."

"The housekeeper?"

Frances nodded, wiping the last traces of wetness off her face. "It is obvious that she cares for Jane. So I thought the best chance of hearing the truth would be from her."

"And was Fey willing to talk to you about this?"

"She was, after I told her what I'd heard." The young woman lowered her voice again. "Jane's reputation *was* ruined nine years ago. But the thing that the first woman failed to say was that she never got so far as actually running away. She couldn't. Because the boy she'd been in love with for some years was arrested and ordered to be hanged in the same week. Oh, Mother . . . Sir Thomas ordered the boy's hanging . . . and Jane . . . and Jane had to watch him die."

There were fresh tears that the young woman dabbed at.

"That's why she wears black. After all these years . . . she still mourns the young man she loved. That is . . . so sad . . . so sad!"

Alexandra gathered Frances in her arms and let the young woman weep. Such a story, even with the tragedy of the father ordering the death of this young man, was perfectly believable. A reputation lost was a lifetime sentence for a woman. But she didn't want to remind her daughter of any of this now, for what was customary was not necessarily right . . . or fair.

She recalled the paintings she'd seen in the attic room. The power in them bespoke someone who knew suffering. And now Alexandra understood. What greater anguish could a young woman bear than to be sentenced to a lifetime living under the same roof as your beloved's executioner? Especially when that person was your own father!

"I think we . . . we should tell Nicholas about this." Frances once again pulled out of the mother's arms and blew her nose. "I can already tell that . . . that he is interested in Jane . . . but he cannot . . . it would never work."

"We shall tell him nothing, my dear." Alexandra lifted the young woman's chin and looked into her surprised face. "Your brother shall learn what he needs to know on his own. He will then make his own decisions. We shall be here whenever he needs us. But Nicholas can decide on his future without our interference."

Chapter 15

At first, Nicholas didn't know what it was that awakened him. It was still dark outside, and there were no predawn noises coming in the window he'd left open overnight. He listened closer and thought he could hear the soft whisper of voices in the corridor.

He was out of bed and had his door opened a crack in the next instant. The passageway was dark with the exception of a flicker of light coming from down the hall. He recognized the housekeeper's soft voice. He opened the door a bit more and saw Fey standing before Jane's door—speaking hurriedly.

He could hear only snatches of what was being said. ". . . Seamus's widow . . . wee ones . . . Buttevant . . ."

By the time he had retired last night, he had been impatient enough to kick down every locked door and search out every secret passageway in Woodfield House. She had successfully avoided him for two entire days. Most of the day on Saturday, he'd spent with Sir Thomas and Paul. The former magistrate was very proud of showing off his stables and what progress had been made since retiring from service to the Crown. When they'd gotten back to the manor house, though, Jane had continued to be absent throughout the afternoon, not even appearing for dinner. Nicholas had worn a path between the house and the stables, but her horse was missing. Later, he'd found Mab settled for the night, though he had still not seen Jane. And on Sunday, the only other person who'd asked about her had been Parson Adams,

who'd come back with them after the church service to
stay for dinner.

The clergyman's curiosity had only fueled Nicholas's
impatience.

". . . Musgrave . . ."

He frowned at the whisper of the name. The door to
Jane's room closed. As Fey's footsteps started down the
hall, Nicholas shut his own door quietly. He hurriedly
dressed. Though he didn't know the nature of Fey's
early-morning visit, the few words had managed to fill
him with distress. He was almost certain that Jane would
be leaving soon.

The corridor was again immersed in darkness when
Nicholas left his room. Taking a moment and letting his
eyes adjust to the dark, he glanced in the direction of
Jane's closed door. He knew better than to assume that
she would be leaving this way, so instead he started
down the stairs. He would intercept her at the stables.

Soft tinges of dawn were lightening the sky above the
eastern hills when Nicholas arrived at the stables. Going
first to Mab's stall, he found the horse saddled and
ready, though there was no one tending her. He moved
quietly to where his own horse was kept and began
readying it.

Saturday, when he'd been out with Sir Thomas and
Paul, the trainer had continuously sung Jane's praises
whenever the father was out of earshot. If Nicholas had
been fairly certain before of the older man's devotion
to Egan, now he entertained no doubts.

And this morning he'd discovered Fey passing on a
message to her. Nicholas wondered how many others at
Woodfield House were supporters of Egan, despite the
passionate hatred the former magistrate harbored for
the rebel.

He had just finished saddling his horse when he heard
the sound of a horse in the paddock. A moment later,
he heard her riding off. Hurrying, he was coaxing his
steed out of the stall when Paul's tall frame appeared in
the open doorway.

"Sir Nicholas," the man said with a hushed surprise.

"I am going with her, Paul." He started to mount

up, but stopped when the stable master put a hand on his arm.

"Going with who, sir? Everyone is still asleep at the house, to my knowledge."

"I'm going with Jane." Nicholas kept his voice low and turned to face the man. "I don't plan to get in her way. And I won't interfere unless she needs me."

The trainer reached for the horse's bridle. "Nay, sir. I've no doubt Miss Jane is sleeping like the angel that she is. Why—"

"She is going to Buttevant, on business that has to do with the new magistrate." Though Nicholas knew he could overpower Paul if he had to, he was hoping for the man's cooperation and trust. But the stable master had roughly five seconds. "Whatever the trouble is, it could be a trap set by Musgrave."

The man stared at Nicholas.

"I've known who she is from the first day. I've witnessed what she does. She knows her secret is safe with me." He lowered his voice further and brought up the arm that had been knifed by Jane. "I have great respect for her abilities, and I know she is quite capable of defending herself. But I saw Musgrave in Buttevant three days ago, and I believe he is planning something."

Paul's hand dropped from the horse's bridle. "What'll ye do?"

"Just be there," Nicholas answered confidently. "Just by being with Jane, I may be able to distract Musgrave's attention from her."

Paul's grim expression of hesitation gave way to a trace of relief. "If ye ride hard up the valley north and then follow east along the stream, ye should catch up with her."

Nicholas climbed onto his horse. "Make some excuse for me if anyone asks."

"Aye, sir. I've become an expert liar, when it comes down to it," Paul assured him. "But I need to warn ye. Once ye catch up with Miss Jane, there is no saying she'll be taking any comfort in yer company."

"I once thought myself an expert in charming women, but your mistress tells me that my powers of persuasion are wanting when it comes to her."

"Then how are you going to convince her to have ye along?"

"Beg," Nicholas said conspiratorially, putting the spurs to his horse.

Jane rode through the night, her dress and cape flying behind her. She'd considered whether it would be best for her to ride out as Egan or as herself. Until she could be sure of what needed to be done, she had decided it would be best for her to act as herself. Later, if need be, she would get her fellow Shanavests involved.

The message had come from Buttevant. A mother's plea to look after her three children. Kathleen, Seamus's widow, had been dragged by the dragoons to the barracks gates.

The boy who had brought the message to Woodfield House had also told of the soldiers showing up yesterday afternoon at the decrepit cottage and tearing Kathleen from the desperate hands of her screaming children. The little ones had been left behind to fend for themselves in the company of the blind old woman who shared the same roof. The charge lodged against the mother was unknown, but as Jane cut across a shallow stream and onto the Buttevant road, she fretted that it might have had something to do with the bag of coins she'd given the woman three days ago. She spurred Mab along the road, thankful for the first slivers of dawn spreading across the eastern sky and lighting her way.

Jane had another reason for not getting her fellow rebels involved immediately. She knew there was no way they could challenge Musgrave and a barrack full of dragoons without considerable bloodshed. And she was smart enough to know that this may have been exactly what the magistrate was hoping for when he arranged for the arrest of the poor woman.

The first realization that she was *not* the only traveler heading north this early in the day came almost a half hour after she'd left home. On the crest of a hill—as was always her habit—she looked back and spotted the horse and rider racing across the countryside after her.

At first, because of the distance and the dim light of dawn, she didn't recognize him. But as she hesitated a few moments longer, Jane realized that the man pushing the gray stallion at breakneck speed could only be Nicholas Spencer.

Jane's immediate spark of delight quickly turned to annoyance. Forcing the smile from her face, she allowed the anger to well up within her. No one followed her. For all the years she'd been leaving Woodfield House— at all hours of day or night—no one had ever come chasing after her. Until this man.

She had enough confidence to know she could lose him en route if she set her mind to it. But instead she let her temper rise and wheeled Mab around to face the meddling rogue and challenge his presumptuous behavior.

Waiting for him was tough, but Jane endured it by imagining the most wicked punishments she could inflict on him. She even considered riding down into the grove of trees in the next valley and springing on him by surprise. But time was short, Kathleen's children needed her, and she could not allow herself to be distracted, no matter how sweet the reward.

"Good day to you, Jane."

The upbeat greeting as he drew near fueled the fire even more. The smile on his handsome face had a contagious edge to it, so she gave him her fiercest frown.

"You need to be corrected on two counts, sir," she said as horse and rider came to a stop beside her. "I do not consider this hour to be officially day, and I much prefer we retain formal manners of address, Sir Nicholas."

"My apologies, Miss Purefoy."

He didn't appear sorry to her. And she tried to overlook how downright appealing he was with a day's growth of whiskers and blond hair loose and wind-tossed about his shoulders. He was the very image of the rogue, rather than the noble gentleman everyone assumed him to be.

"Sir Nicholas, would you please explain to me, and briefly, what you are doing here?"

"Riding, miss. I happen to enjoy the exercise."

"You might save your wit, sir, for the drawing room. Would you please explain why you are following me?"

"I—"

"And tell me why I shouldn't be suspicious of your motives."

"Well, I—"

"For you have told me repeatedly that you have no intention of exposing me, sir. And yet I find you . . . well, trailing after me."

"Now—"

"And I should tell you I consider lying a dreadful thing . . . in situations such as this." She could see the amused expression etched around his blue eyes. "And this is not the time to think of one of your witty comments."

"Jane—"

"I refuse to be treated as some half-witted, rusticated ass, sir," she blurted out, leaning menacingly in his direction. "The least you can do is to try to think of an answer."

He smiled. "If—"

"But if you cannot, I strongly suggest that you turn your horse around this instant and start back . . ."

He reached over so quickly that Jane was stunned when his large hand slipped around the nape of her neck and his lips crashed down on hers. Everything became still for an insane moment. The urge to fight was suspended in air. And as his other hand drew her still nearer, the temper instantly turned to heat. Her hands clutched desperately at the lapel of his jacket. She was further shocked by the unfamiliar sound of satisfaction that she realized had come from her own throat when he deepened the kiss.

"Now, that's better," Nicholas said in a voice like velvet as he broke off the kiss. His fingers lingered a moment longer, and he traced her lips. "I hope I have not bruised you again. You have the most delicate skin. If anyone were to come upon us, they would know for certain that you have been properly kissed."

A fog hung over Jane for the longest moment. Then clarity suddenly returned, and she straightened in her saddle. How vulnerable she was to his charms, she thought with alarm

"I promise that these bruises will fade much sooner."

He ran a hand over his unshaven face while his blue eyes reflected his smile. "But I will be better prepared the next time."

She wanted to slap the grin off his face, but she thought the punishment too trivial. She had to think of something more painful. To keep her hand off the small dagger at her belt, she lifted the reins, making them look like a noose.

"I had no intention of following you at a distance," he started, watching her hands. "My intention was to accompany you to Buttevant. But you ride with such skill and speed . . ."

"How did you know where I was headed?"

His gaze returned to her face. "I—"

"You *have* been spying on me."

"I—"

"There is no other way that you would know."

As he reached for her again, she made Mab sidestep out of his reach. "Do not dare to kiss me again."

"Oh, I thought you wanted . . . Well, will you give me the opportunity to explain, then?"

Jane opened her mouth, but immediately closed it as the truth dawned on her. She couldn't deny it. Deep within, she wanted to be kissed by him. She coaxed Mab another step back to let her own passions cool.

"Very well, Sir Nicholas. This is your opportunity. Explain."

Nicholas nudged his steed toward Mab until the riders' boots brushed. She felt their knees touch.

"Quite by accident, I overheard snatches of a conversation in the corridor earlier. My intentions were not to spy, but to find an opportunity to spend time with you." He leaned forward on the horse—and let his gaze caress every part of her face. "It has been bloody hell, Jane. You have been running away from me since our talk in the garden."

Jane didn't want to acknowledge the warmth that his words produced instantly in her. She didn't want to admit how much of the past few days she'd spent thinking of him—remembering everything he'd said and then the kiss they'd shared. Her fingers trembled as she pretended to adjust the tie of the cloak. She prayed that, in the dim dawn light, he wouldn't see the blush rising into her cheeks.

"I did warn you, sir . . . pleaded even . . . that we never discuss that night in the garden again. I've already put it out of my mind. I ask the same of you."

He looked stung, but only for a moment. "I do not believe you have forgotten what happened. Our kiss a few moments ago was proof . . ."

"Please. I am having great difficulty understanding my own behavior. I beg of you." She shook her head. "I have important things to do, and I must be on my way."

There was a lengthy silence. "As you wish . . . but I am letting this subject rest only for this morning."

The battle had to be fought in many stages. His concession was a good start. Jane gentled her tone and tried to focus on the more immediate concern on hand. "I have already lost too much time. And I am not taking a ride for exercise or making a social visit this morning. I would greatly appreciate it if you would respect my wishes and stop following me."

"You are not dressed as Egan, so I assume you are not leaving for any secret meeting."

"Nonetheless, sir, this is a private matter and none of your concern."

"Whatever the trouble is, you are going to Buttevant . . . and you might have to deal with Musgrave."

"I resent people who assume that I am incapable. This is not the first time I am making this trip . . . nor is it the first time I have been faced with this type of matter."

"You are quite capable. I admire you for it." His tone was so confident that she couldn't stop herself from looking searchingly into his face. All previous signs of amusement were gone. "I am asking this favor of you for my own peace of mind. I was tremendously irritated when I met the magistrate the last time. Perhaps if I were honest, I would admit that the source of my irritation lay in the fact that each of us was vying, in his own way, for your attention."

"I do not think—"

"Please allow me to finish." He pushed his horse nearer again, and this time Jane didn't retreat. "I outmaneuvered Musgrave in that incident, but I believe the man is contemptible enough to try to hurt you . . . if only to teach me a lesson."

"Sir Robert doesn't need an excuse to be hurtful. And I believe the matters leading to the distressing news reaching me today are totally independent of your meeting with the magistrate."

"Please, Jane," he pressed. "Will you do this for me? Allow me to come along. Only this once."

She should have raised a thousand objections, but said nothing. She felt torn between what she wanted and what she felt she should do. In the end, she couldn't bring herself to refuse him.

"If I . . . if I let you come along, you should understand that you are going only as an observer and nothing more."

"I understand."

"I am planning no meeting with Musgrave. In fact, based on what you've told me, I prefer that you *do* remain with me instead of separating at Buttevant."

"Nothing would please me more."

His quick and obviously heartfelt agreement caused a new flutter of excitement to form in Jane's stomach.

"But in coming," she continued, "you must give me your word that there will be no more talk of . . . of anything that happened between us . . . either in the woods or when we met in the . . . garden."

There was no immediate response. Then he gave her a perceptible nod.

"I agree."

She should have been happy, but deep down she mourned his concession. She turned Mab's head back down the road.

"I can certainly manage this punishment . . ."

Jane glanced over her shoulder and saw that Spencer appeared to be talking to himself . . . or to his horse. She turned her attention back to the road ahead.

"But, of course . . . talk I can do without . . . She didn't say I needed to forfeit anything else."

Jane hid the smile that tugged at her lips. She should have known that he was too much of a rogue to make real concessions without putting up a fight.

Chapter 16

In a shadowy corner of the single-room cottage, a young girl crouched beside her older brother, who continued to sleep fitfully, despite all the noise in the place. The streaks of dirt staining her innocent face indicated tears that had only recently been wiped dry. The child's eyes had turned fearful as soon as Nicholas entered.

He was told by Jane not to speak a word to any Irish whom they might pass. She'd also asked him to remain outside. Nicholas could not let her go in by herself, though, and had stayed directly behind her when she'd passed through the warped wood planking that served as a door. Once inside, however, he had stayed true to her other request and said not a word.

"I do not know where she'd be getting herself those coins," the old blind woman explained, stirring a pot that hung over a small peat fire. The liquid in the pot looked to be nothing more than a thin broth. "Kathleen came back from the village and right away sent Bowie here out to bring word to young Mick to take to ye. She knew trouble was to come and come it did."

The youngest child continued to wail steadily and miserably, but shied away when Jane tried to reach for him.

"She wanted to send word to Egan. Would ye be Egan?"

This was the third time the blind woman had asked this same question. Nicholas wondered if someone else had walked in here and claimed to be Egan, the woman would be revealing as much.

"I am Egan, Bridget," Jane replied softly. "You must remember my voice. I was here not three days ago."

The widow's expression revealed nothing that said she remembered. Meanwhile, Nicholas thought, the lines of age and pain on her face told of one who'd suffered greatly over the years—one who had finally found a way to forget.

"I heard her say it. She wanted a message to be sent to Egan." She lowered her voice despite the loud squalling of the child. "I heard her talking to herself of the coin you gave her, too. She ran to the patch of garden in the back . . . She was still there when the soldiers came."

The baby continued to wail. The young girl in the corner crept cautiously across the dirt floor and picked up her sibling in her arms. The child instantly laid his head on her shoulder and the crying relaxed into a gentle sob. Nicholas thought that she was not much bigger or older than her brother, but the little girl had aged emotionally far beyond her years.

"Did they say anything when they took her? Did they come inside and hurt the children?" Jane moved to the corner and crouched beside the sleeping boy. Nicholas saw her shoulders become rigid as soon as she touched his face.

"They took her in the garden. Only one came in, turned over the table, and left," Bridget said quietly.

"How long has Bowie been sleeping, Maire?" Jane asked of the sister, trying to keep her tone calm. Her hands ran down the boy's neck and pressed against his chest while she waited for an answer.

The young girl didn't seem to have heard the question. She continued to rock the baby in her arms and keep a wary gaze on Nicholas.

"Maire," Jane called softly, but there was still no answer.

She turned her gaze from the sleeping boy to the frightened expression on the girl's face.

"Can you crouch down?" she asked softly of Nicholas. "I believe your size . . . and your clothing might be the distraction here."

He felt like a fool not to have realized that himself.

He immediately removed his jacket and dropped it on the floor beside Jane's cloak. Rolling his sleeves up, he moved to the boy and crouched down beside her. He realized that Jane had intentionally not called him by name.

"That was quite thoughtless of me," he whispered. He could see that Jane had opened the front of the boy's shirt. There were dark bruises on the ribs.

"Who'd be with ye?" Bridget whispered, fear evident in her voice. Frail hands searched the air frantically. "Where are the children? Maire, where is Daniel? Wake up Bowie right away, Maire. Wake him up."

The young girl pressed her young brother tighter against her frail chest and moved farther out of the widow's reach.

"There is nothing to fear, Bridget," Jane assured her. "This man with me is a friend. Like me, he is only here to help."

"Ye must not be Egan," Bridget said accusingly. She tried to push herself up to her feet, but fell back. "She came alone. Ye brought a man with you. Nay . . . Egan would ne'er do that."

Nicholas placed a hand on Bowie's brow. The boy was burning with fever. This close he could also hear the wheezing sound from his chest.

"He is only seven, but has suffered more than someone who is seventy," Jane said quietly. "And there is more wrong with him than the fever. I think he might have broken some bones in his chest."

Jane moved hurriedly to the blind woman as she managed to push herself to her feet. Her hands continued to reach out around her, and she nearly tripped over the steaming pot.

"Bridget, it is I." Jane grasped the thin hands in her own. "Feel this . . . this is the same shawl Kathleen gave me only three days ago." She pressed the woman's hand against the wool and then eased her hold on her, allowing her to feel it on her own.

Nicholas had seen the tattered shawl when Jane had discarded her cloak. His gaze was drawn now to Maire's pale face. The little girl's face had brightened, and she looked alert for the first time. The child moved hesitantly toward Jane. Even little Daniel stopped crying and lifted his head to stare into his sister's face.

"Bowie is ill, Bridget." Jane spoke as the blind woman reached up and lightly touched Jane's face.

Nicholas had no faith in Bridget's state of mind. If this woman were questioned by Musgrave and his men, who could say that she wouldn't describe Egan to them. It was bad enough that she knew Egan was a woman.

"I want to take Bowie away . . . to where I can have a doctor see to him."

"Nay." Bridget shook her head once. "Kathleen is coming back for them."

"I know she is. But Bowie is sick with fever now. He needs help right away. We have to get him help before his mother returns."

At the word "fever," Bridget took a tottery step back.

From the other corner of the small room, Maire crept even closer, fresh tears sprouting in her eyes. Nicholas wasn't certain if Jane was aware of the transformation in the girl since she'd recognized the mother's wrap. He looked for a way to tell her and then he saw Jane's hand stretch out toward the girl.

"I want to take the three of them with me. The children should be kept together."

Nicholas's heart warmed when he saw Maire put her small hand in Jane's. His gaze was uncontrollably drawn to the woman who continually managed to amaze him.

"Nay, miss. I don't want Kathleen be thinking that I . . . that I pushed her wee ones out onto the road."

"She will never think such a thought," Jane assured her. "She knew these three would be too much for you. That was why she sent for me."

Before Bridget could think of an objection, Jane touched the blind woman's arm. "I'll arrange for word to get to Kathleen about the children. I shall make certain she knows where to find them when the authorities release her."

This time when Jane reached for the baby, he moved willingly into her arms, though his gaze remained on his sister's face. For her part, Maire pressed herself into the folds of the black skirts.

Bridget mumbled some words about saints and faerie folk and went back to the cooking pot.

Nicholas took charge of the feverish older boy. As he wrapped his coat around the limp body and lifted him gently, the bitter image of the young girl he'd found in St. James's Park on that night just before Christmas came back to him. Bowie was almost as light and as oblivious as she was. Both of them were dressed in nothing but rags. They each seemed like children abandoned to their suffering, though this boy's situation was very different. A weak cough sounded in Bowie's chest, and Nicholas forced himself to shake off the feeling of doom that was afflicting him. There was still time.

Let there still be time for this one, he prayed.

The bright sunshine outside offered a startling contrast to the gloom inside. The brush of the early fall breeze against Bowie's face made him cough again and bury his face deeper into Nicholas's chest.

The baronet started briskly toward his horse, but he paused for a moment to brand into his memory the gladdening sight before him.

Jane had already climbed onto the back of Queen Mab, and the two children were seated before her. She was speaking softly to Maire and at the same time holding Daniel's hand and encouraging the little one to caress the horse's soft mane. There was softness—affection—love in the actions. It occurred to Nicholas that this might be the most beautiful sight he'd ever been blessed to see.

Jane's gaze turned in his direction, and he saw her anxious look at Bowie. She then looked up to Nicholas's face and, as their gazes locked, he saw in her the woman he'd been searching for.

Silence hung like a pall over the Morning Room. Seated with her two female guests at a small table by the fire, Lady Purefoy sipped her tea and eyed the French-style pastries tastefully arranged on a small platter. Clara sulked in a chair by the window, ignoring the small plate and saucer of tea on the table beside her. The words of greeting this morning had been brief and perfunctory, and the appetite of the Spencer women scarcely matched their hostess's.

Lady Purefoy motioned to one of the servants to pour more tea for Alexandra, and glanced over at her daughter, hoping to get her attention. Clara gazed out the window, ignoring her mother.

Catherine, frustrated with the girl's aloofness, bit into a pastry that she could do without. It had been the same for the past two days—Clara moping about openly before their company. Not once had the young woman followed her directions to ask Sir Nicholas to go out for a walk—or to give him a tour of the gardens—or even to read to him from one of the books she always kept her nose buried in. Why, Clara had not once tried to initiate a conversation.

Giving a ball had been a grand idea, but Catherine knew that one night would hardly be enough to settle her daughter's future. She chose another piece of pastry, but before putting it into her mouth, another idea dawned on her.

"Have you ladies heard of our legendary Blarney Castle?"

Their guest turned to her daughter, seemingly waiting for her to answer. But Frances's surliness had increased daily since they'd arrived. She and Clara made a perfect pair, Catherine thought.

"Yes, we have," Lady Spencer finally replied. "On our drive here from Cork City, Frances was telling us all about the gift of eloquence that is rumored to be connected with kissing some stone in the castle wall."

"Yes . . . indeed. That is exactly the case," Catherine said excitedly. "I was just thinking . . . when Sir Nicholas comes down this morning, perhaps we can convince him that he should take my Clara and Miss Spencer to Blarney Castle. I don't know a young person who would not find it thrilling to . . ."

"I would prefer to stay in today," Frances said quietly. As her mother opened her mouth, Lady Purefoy noticed the sharp look that the sixteen-year-old directed her elder. "I've a headache."

"Clara, I'm certain, would love to go, anyway. Would you not, my dear?" Catherine pressed.

Her daughter's lack of enthusiasm, though unspoken, was very clearly etched in the troubled and pleading blue eyes.

"Then it is settled." Catherine turned to Lady Spencer and gave her a reassuring nod. "This is what these young people need these days. Someone to push them out the door and make them enjoy themselves. Now, when I was younger, we didn't need our mothers to tell us how to court a young man."

The housekeeper entered the room at that moment, surveying the tea and pastries.

"Fey, I was just about to send for you," Lady Purefoy called out jubilantly. "Lady Spencer and I had a wonderful idea that Sir Nicholas and Clara should go out for a picnic today to Blarney Castle. Kindly tell the cook to prepare a basket for them. Oh, and tell Paul it would be best if he were to prepare my open carriage." She smiled at Alexandra's dubious face. "I know your son is fond of horses, and I assure you my Clara is a most talented rider. Call me old-fashioned if you will, but I think a young man and young woman can enjoy their conversations so much more in a carriage rather than on horseback."

She saw the housekeeper still in the room, obviously looking for an opportunity to speak.

"What is it, Fey?" she said curtly.

"Sir Nicholas has already gone out, m'lady."

"Out? Is he out with Sir Thomas?"

"I've no reason to think so. I heard Sir Thomas asking for him when he was taking his own breakfast. When Paul came up, I heard him say that Sir Nicholas had gone out for a ride some time ago."

"Alone?" Catherine turned curiously to her guest, who was delicately sipping her tea. "Do you know where he is gone, Lady Spencer? Or when he is coming back?"

"More years ago than I wish to count, ma'am, I stopped worrying about Nicholas's whereabouts."

"But it is such a beautiful day." Catherine rose to her feet impatiently and walked to the window, glancing outside. "I simply *hate* to see it go to waste. Don't you agree?"

"I do." Something in her guest's voice made Lady

Purefoy turn in time to see the other woman smiling enigmatically over the rim of her cup. "But perhaps Nicholas is not wasting it, after all."

The two women looked with mutual concern at the ailing child lying on the bed between them.

"Where did these bruises come from, miss?"

"On our way here, little Maire told me that Bowie came back just as the soldiers were taking their mother away yesterday. The little fighter picked up a stick and tried to stop them."

Jane squeezed the excess water out of a towel into the washbasin and gently continued bathing the boy's face. Mrs. Brown clucked compassionately and tried to remove his tattered shirts as gently as she could.

"Maire said he was kicked a few times."

Mrs. Brown's ruddy face became even redder as her temper rose. "Sons of devils, they are. Striking down wee ones!"

Jane swallowed her own anger, but promised herself that there would be retaliation for this. Some of the Shanavests, like Ronan and even levelheaded Patrick, had repeatedly suggested that there should be an ambush against the dragoons at the Buttevant barracks for the violence that they were committing more and more freely against the Irish. But Jane had always spoken against it. She did not want to give Musgrave a reason to start searching out the Shanavests. It wasn't any fear of the magistrate's successes that bothered her, but the certain knowledge that many who were innocent would be hurt by the fighting that would surely ensue.

Innocents like Bowie.

"Has Parson Adams sent for the doctor yet?" Jane touched the boy's fevered skin again.

"He went after Dr. Forrest himself. He didn't want the man tarrying because it was only some Irish widow's child that needed tending. Ah, no . . . will you look at that?" Mrs. Brown pointed to more bruises along Bowie's side.

"Will he come, though?"

"The parson will make sure he does," the housekeeper replied with certainty.

"The boy's sister also said that Bowie had been sick for a few days before the soldiers came. Coughing and shivering." Jane watched the other woman's capable hands gently open their patient's mouth and feed him a few drops of water. "The sickness . . . and then the upset of the mother being taken away . . . and then the beating. Far too much for one as young as this."

The young boy's throat worked painfully, but he seemed to swallow the liquid.

"Aye," the older woman said, straightening her back. "If you don't mind, Miss Jane, would you go and look in on the wee ones? Cook was trying to feed them, but the lass . . ."

"Maire."

Mrs. Brown nodded. "I don't think she'll take a bite unless you comfort her yourself. She is a worrier, I can tell."

The housekeeper raised Bowie's head on some pillows and pulled a clean sheet over the boy's chest.

Jane reluctantly stood up. She knew Mrs. Brown was far more capable than she was in seeing to the needs of this sick child. But she also knew how fragile Maire, in particular, was.

"Is Sir Nicholas still downstairs, or did he go with Parson Adams?"

"Neither." The housekeeper looked up in surprise. "I don't know where he disappeared to. He carried the lad up here and put him on the bed, and then went down those stairs and out the door."

Not surprising, Jane thought. This was surely much more than he'd bargained for. Much more than he'd been ready to commit to.

But she had no time to think of any of this now. She cast a final glance at the child's still form and quietly slipped out of the room.

This was what she was meant to do with her life. And she wouldn't let herself take a step off this path, no matter what the temptation.

She told herself she should be glad Spencer had come to his senses.

Chapter 17

Praying that she wouldn't be seen, Clara tucked the worn copy of *The Castle of Otranto* under the blanket she carried over her arm, and scurried past the small grove of fruit trees where she'd accidentally come upon Lady Spencer busily sketching.

More than anything else, she just wanted a few moments of relief. A few moments alone. One more careless word by her mother, one more vulgar mention of how she could more effectively flaunt herself in front of Sir Nicholas, and Clara knew she would surely go mad.

Out of the corner of her eye, she saw Lady Spencer put down her sketch board, stand up, and stretch. Looking away, Clara moved deeper into the meadow. Though their guests—both mother and daughter—were nice enough people, she simply couldn't bear to be engaged in conversation right now.

After breakfast, Lady Purefoy had insisted on having a long chat with her daughter in her workroom. The *chat* had consisted of a long lecture on how disappointed both her parents were with the way Clara had been conducting herself with their esteemed company. And the scolding had ended with direct instructions about just how Clara should behave in order to win the distinguished gentleman's attention, affection, and proposal of marriage.

Clara felt sick at the recollection of some of the things her mother had said. How different now from the instructions she'd received en route to London! She shook her head, realizing how shockingly ruined she would be if she attempted to put into practice most of what her mother had told her. She might as well walk to Cork City and join the streetwalkers along the waterfront.

And to think that Catherine was quick to object to Clara reading mere books like the one under her arm! And here, when it came to real life . . . !

She soon arrived at a favorite spot—a corner of the meadow, close to the paddock but protected by a hedge behind her. Here, with the valley spreading out beneath her, the sun was warm and she could hear the goings-on in the paddock and stable without being seen herself.

Spreading her blanket, she sat down and opened the book on her lap. As she paged through it, Clara recalled the exciting part where she'd left the story last. *Isabella had just vanished from the monastery.*

As she searched for the place, she paused for a moment, thinking of the seed of an idea that had occurred to her while she was enduring her mother's lecture.

Henry had been invited to the party given this Friday, and Clara knew that he would be here. Now, her mother had made certain that absolutely no one outside of the immediate family and Fey had been told of Sir Nicholas's rejection.

How interesting it would be if Henry were somehow to be told . . . perhaps through a letter. Henry had loved her once. The thought that he might conceivably see it his duty to console her regarding the loss made her tingle with anticipation. And how absolutely delightful it would be to use some of her mother's suggested methods—not to try to trap the worldly Sir Nicholas—but to seduce the infinitely more kindhearted Henry Adams.

The very thought sent an excited shiver down Clara's arms. Without having read a single word, she closed the book and rose impatiently to her feet.

This was it. She had the way. She'd had a taste of his passion three days ago. He still loved her, despite his hard words. He would succumb if she pursued. And he was far too honorable not to marry her if they were . . . to somehow . . . find themselves in a compromising situation. All she had to do was send him the letter to start her plan in motion.

Almost giddy now, she was gathering up her blanket

when she heard a horse come up the road. The rider called out to someone in the paddock, and Clara immediately recognized the man's heavy brogue. The voice belonged to a groom who worked for Henry. She would send her letter to Parson Adams with him. Surely, she thought, this is Providence itself at work.

She stepped through the hedge and walked toward the paddock gate. She would make the letter very short. Perhaps, she wouldn't even explain anything, but say it was critical that Henry meet with her somewhere . . . in private.

Yes. In person and in private. Face-to-face, she had the greatest chance of success.

Clara intentionally slowed her steps. She couldn't look too eager. The man had dismounted and was talking with one of the Woodfield House stable boys.

"Roger," she called.

Henry's groom immediately turned and, recognizing Clara, doffed his cap.

"Why, Miss Clara! A fine good day to ye. I was just coming up to the house to deliver a letter from the parson."

"Perhaps I can take it . . . since I am here . . . and I am going that way."

The other groom nodded politely to her and walked away with Roger's horse. The messenger took a letter out of his pocket and offered it to Clara.

"Thank ye, miss."

"Is it for my father?"

"Nay, miss . . . I mean aye, miss. Now that I think of it, Parson Adams didn't say which one of your parents to deliver it to. I just thought to give it to Fey, though I believe there is a name on the outside, is there not, miss?"

Clara looked at it. "Indeed, there is."

"Does it say Lady Purefoy, miss?"

"I didn't know you can read, Roger." Clara tucked it into her pocket. "That's exactly what it says."

"Reading is something I've ne'er had time for, miss. But I thought, 'tis about Miss Jane, so it must be meant for your mother."

"I shall take it up to her directly."

"Thank ye, miss."

"Would you mind waiting a few moments before you return, Roger? My mother might wish to send a message back. Also . . . I have a letter that I would like you to take to Ballyclough for me."

"As ye wish, Miss Clara." He nodded politely again. "I need to be seeing to the parson's horse, anyway. The old devil threw a shoe at the bottom of the hill, just now."

Clara started up the hill, but instead of thinking about what she was to write, her attention focused on the message in her pocket. Roger had said that the news was about Jane. For too many days now, Jane had been flitting in and out of Woodfield House. For the past two days, Clara had not even thought to worry about her when she hadn't shown up for meals. She knew, though, that their parents hadn't bothered to notice any of Jane's comings and goings, either.

As soon as she left the paddock, she crossed over and took the path through the gardens. When she was safely out of sight, Clara took the envelope out and stared at Henry's seal. Lady Purefoy always asked her to read and respond to correspondence anyway. So her curiosity of what was inside—her worry about Jane, Clara corrected herself—pushed her to break the seal.

Leaning against a tree, the young woman let her gaze wander over Henry's graceful handwriting before the actual words began to register.

Jane was in Ballyclough today. Henry was letting Lady Purefoy and Sir Thomas know that their daughter was visiting some of the families in the parish. And since she was also determined to spend some time at the bedside of an ailing child in the village, the parson's recommendation was for her to stay at the parsonage overnight rather than risk traveling home late at night.

It took a moment for the words to sink in. When they did, though, a jealousy she had never before experienced clawed sharply at Clara's entrails. Tears hot and sudden stung her eyes.

Henry no longer cared for her. He was smitten with

Jane, and Clara should have known. She crumpled the letter and stuffed it in her pocket before running for the house.

She should have seen it, she thought bitterly. For all these years, Clara had secretly admired him, watched him, had been in love with him, but his attention had always been on Jane.

Clara blindly climbed the stairs to her room.

She had rejected his offer six months ago, not only because of her parents' plans, but partly because of that continuous measuring with Jane. The day before his proposal, Henry had spent the entire afternoon with Jane. The week before that—and a dozen times since—it had been Jane's opinion that he'd come seeking at Woodfield House. Time and time again, he would ask after Jane's health . . . or her art. Indeed, he was the only one who Jane would invite to her workroom in the attic.

Clara seethed to think how much time the two of them spent up there together. Alone. Now she knew the *real* reason Jane had not made any fuss about not going to London.

She banged open the door to her bedchamber and slammed it shut behind her. The tears had stopped somewhere along the way, and a cold fury had taken their place.

"How blind!? How blind could I have been?"

She started pacing the large room. Even Mrs. Brown had hinted at Henry's concerns and interests last week, but Clara—too blind to recognize the obvious—had thrown herself at him.

And he'd rejected her. He had *rejected* her, not because of the reasons he'd listed, but because he wanted her ruined sister.

Hurt . . . anger . . . revenge . . . Emotions so long suppressed churned within her. She felt ready to burst when a persistent knocking finally drew her attention. She stormed to the door and yanked it open.

The young servant took a step back when she saw the wrath blazing in Clara's face.

"What?"

"Beggin' yer pardon, miss. Someone saw ye coming

up to the house. Yer mother wants to know what the message was about—"

"Take her this." Clara tore the crumpled letter from her pocket and threw it at the girl. She was ready to slam the door shut again, when the girl put out a hand plaintively.

"Pardon, miss. She was asking if ye have something to go to . . . to Parson Adams, as his man is waiting."

"No! Nothing." Clara's hand gripped the edge of the door. "But there is something you can do for me."

The servant nodded worriedly and waited.

"Find out if the baronet is back. If he is, then have the cook prepare a picnic basket and ask Paul to get an open carriage ready. He and I are going for a ride."

"And if he is not?" she asked nervously.

"Then come and get me as soon as he is."

Clara continued to hold the door even after the serving girl disappeared down the hall. Her parents were right—her mother especially. She was too fine a creature for a place so coarse as Ireland. She was too beautiful and well-bred not to be able to make an advantageous match for herself.

Nicholas Spencer hadn't asked for her hand in marriage, that was true. But it was only because, since leaving London, she had worked on hiding her charms, her pleasing attitude, her intelligence, and her wit.

Now that she was resolved that he would do for a husband, the handsome baronet didn't have a chance. They would be married in a fortnight.

Her mother was always right, she thought with bitter clarity.

Slumber was finally taking the children into her soft golden arms. Daniel's eyes drifted shut for a long moment, and then immediately opened wide. He clearly didn't want to miss any of the story. Maire's two small hands were clutching one of Jane's, and the young girl's green eyes became huge when Jane reached a particularly exciting moment in the tale.

Despite the significance of the news he had to share, Henry Adams couldn't bring himself to intrude on this serene scene. The two children shared the bed. Jane sat beside them, telling an Irish tale in Gaelic. He watched her reach over and caress the little one's hair.

A new awareness washed over Henry, taking him by surprise, as his gaze was drawn to Jane's face. He didn't remember ever being so taken by her beauty. She seemed to shine from within. A softness, a maternal side of her that he'd never known, made his heart ache and recall how cruel her own society had been to her.

This was her right—to be a woman, a mother. She had loved once and had suffered greatly in losing her lover. But people never forgot. They never looked at the person beyond the gossip and scandal.

She ended the story happily, with peace and harmony prevailing for the good folk who triumphed over evil. Daniel's eyes were already closed, but Maire's pale face was smiling. Henry watched Jane lean over the child and brush a kiss over her brow. The young girl's hands were reluctant, but finally released her hand as Jane stood up.

Jane blew out the candle on the table near the bed. When she straightened up from the children, she noticed him for the first time. "How long have you been here?"

She smiled and Henry felt another tug of warmth in his heart. She had been his friend for so long.

"Long enough to be lulled and even enchanted by the magic of your tongue."

"After all these years, I cannot believe you have never learned to speak Gaelic, Henry," she whispered, giving a final glance over her shoulder before following him out of the room.

"How do you know I don't speak it?"

She gave him a suspicious look. "Because I have never heard you."

In the narrow passage, she partially closed the door to the children's room.

"You'd be amazed what you might learn about me if you came around more often." He took her hand and lifted it to his lips. "Why is it that you always smell so good?"

She paused and this time gave him an odd stare. "What are you about tonight, Henry Adams?"

He laughed and, letting go of her hand, placed an

arm affectionately around her shoulder. Together, they started down the corridor. "You always see through me, do you not, Miss Purefoy?"

"I should . . . considering all the years I've known you." She stopped at the closed door of Bowie's room. "How is he?"

"Still running a fever. But he was awake when I looked in on him."

Excited about this change, she had her hand on the door latch when Henry stopped her.

"Be prepared for a surprise."

His expression revealed nothing, but Jane remembered his relaxed attitude standing in the other doorway.

"This can only be good." She pushed the door open and immediately gasped with delight. "Kathleen! You are here!"

Bowie was awake and was holding his mother's hand tightly. Still, the young woman came to her feet and smiled tearfully at Jane. "I just arrived . . . a scant minute or so ago."

Jane walked in and hugged her fiercely.

"Thank you E . . . Miss Jane," the young mother whispered and cried quietly. "I knew you'd be coming after them. I knew you would never fail us."

Behind them, Mrs. Brown entered the room with a tray carrying a bowl of soup and a loaf of bread. Jane finally let go of the young woman.

"Maire might be still awake next door, Kathleen. Daniel is with her."

Bowie reached for his mother, and Kathleen sat down again beside her feverish but happy son.

"Aye, miss. I'll go to them in a minute."

Too happy for words, Jane turned around and saw Henry leaving the room. She followed and caught up to him at the top of the stairs. When he heard her footsteps and turned around, Jane—overwhelmed by the magnitude of his efforts—threw her arms around him.

"Thank you, Henry. You are a good man. Thank you for managing this."

The arms that had wrapped around her in return gently caressed her back. "I wish I deserved your sentiments. But 'twas not I who brought Kathleen back, but Clara's fiancé . . . Sir Nicholas."

Jane's head immediately jerked off his shoulder. Her arms released him, and she looked up to his solemn face. "But I thought he left . . ."

"He left for Buttevant this morning. He told me he intended to find Musgrave. He mentioned something about some donation of coins he'd made with your help to some of the needy families in the area. He told me he was going to ask the magistrate about the reason for Kathleen's arrest. If it had anything to do with that money, he was determined to demand her release."

"You didn't tell me any of this!"

"I didn't think he had much chance of succeeding." He turned to descend the stairs.

She tugged at his sleeve to stop him. "What do you have against him, Henry?"

"Why ask such a question?" he said evasively, his face devoid of emotion.

"It is obvious that you two do not like each other. Why is that?"

"If you insist on knowing, I can name a number of reasons why I find him objectionable for Clara, but you will have to ask *him* the reason for his surly behavior toward me."

Jane blamed herself for Spencer's attitude. She should not have praised one before the other. She might as well have given a bone to one fighting dog while the other stood watching.

"Where is he now?"

"I believe he was returning to Woodfield House."

"You didn't invite him to stay for something to eat? Or asked him if he wished to see me?"

He shrugged. "No! I thought he would be anxious to return to your sister."

"Oh, Henry! Sometimes you can be so thickheaded." She slipped past him on the stairs, and he followed her down. "How long ago did he leave?"

"I didn't slam the door in his face, Jane. And he didn't ask to see you, in any case."

Jane gave him a sharp look. "*When* did he leave?"

"Not very long ago. But you are not going after him now, are you?"

"I am going back to Woodfield House," Jane stated

when they reached the front entrance hall. She threw her cloak around her shoulders.

"How about Kathleen and her children?"

"Tell them I'll be back tomorrow."

"But I sent a message to your mother, telling her that you would be staying here tonight."

"She won't know the difference," Jane assured him, giving him a light kiss on the cheek. "Good night, Henry."

Lighting a wick from a candle in the front entryway, she walked out toward the stable where her horse had been settled for the night. Working quickly, she saddled Mab, blew out the tiny flame, and led her out.

Nicholas had done this for *her*, she thought as she tossed the reins up over the horse's head. He had gone back to the barracks at Buttevant . . . and most likely saved the young mother's life in doing so. She couldn't wait to find him and thank him.

Jane was about to mount up when she saw Henry's long frame leaning against a tree next to the parsonage, watching her silently. And this was another man that had to hear her appreciation. With a guilty smile, she walked back toward him.

"I am sorry . . . I had no right to be so critical."

"You are forgiven." He spoke solemnly, but she detected the trace of a smile tugging at the corner of his mouth.

"And I never thanked you for what you are doing for Kathleen and her children. I take so much for granted in you, Henry, and—"

"Just go, Jane," he said with a knowing nod. "Go and catch up to him."

Chapter 18

"Perhaps we should get Sir Thomas to send out a search party for him. Your son has been gone *all* day!"

Alexandra patted Lady Purefoy's arm. "I am quite certain that is completely unnecessary. Knowing my son, he is probably developing a fond friendship at this very moment with a number of your neighbors at some village inn. As we speak, they are probably drinking and rolling up their sleeves and trying to outdo the next with war stories. And in a few hours, they will be wagering on a brawl taking place outside . . . that is, if Nicholas is not one of the combatants."

The horrified expression on their hostess's face was precious, but soon the woman let out an uneasy laugh.

"I am not always prepared for your quick wit, Lady Spencer. So many times I just cannot separate truth from jest."

Alexandra arched a questioning eyebrow. "Do you think I was speaking in jest?"

She was pleased to see the cloud of confusion settle heavily on the other woman's face. Casually, but before she was asked again about Nicholas's whereabouts, Alexandra walked to where Fanny and Lady Purefoy's daughter were engaged in a card game of some kind. Clara's stylish and revealing dress tonight was far different from anything she'd worn before. But there was something else different about the young woman tonight. Alexandra used her artist's eye to try to discover what it might be.

Clara certainly appeared as quiet as ever. But the air

of dreaminess that had pervaded her manner seemed to have evaporated. She appeared alert—even intelligent.

Alexandra sat in a chair near them. "So what do *you* think of a wellborn Englishman who becomes deathly bored with spending too much time with the people of his own rank?"

"I find him charming. Where could I meet such a man?"

"Frances!" Alexandra scolded lightly. "I was speaking to Clara."

"But Mother, you need to be clearer in your description. I, for one, would be curious to know if this noble gentleman happens to be young and incredibly handsome and desperately in search of the love of his life." Frances's blue eyes danced with mischief when they met her mother's. "After all, I am not too young. Sixteen is the perfect age to start the search for—"

"*This* discussion doesn't concern you, young woman." Alexandra spoke the words quietly and sweetly, but she made sure that daggers laced her tone.

"Oh! Now I understand. You were referring to *Nicholas.*"

Lady Spencer glared at her daughter as the young woman hid a smile. Knowing any further reproach would be completely useless with the little troublemaker, she turned toward Clara.

"And what is your opinion?"

She was greatly surprised to see this young woman was trying to stifle a smile, as well, hiding her face behind the cards.

"Well, Miss Clara, this is a side to you we haven't seen."

Clara lowered her cards and looked Alexandra in the eye.

"My apologies, Lady Spencer. But I find your daughter's gift of honesty and candor delightful."

"What a curious way to describe a curse."

As the two of them giggled like conspirators who had just snitched the church wine, Alexandra considered with some amazement the transformation that had taken place in the relationship between the two of them, as well.

"The incorrigible and the corrupted," she said breezily, walking away with an arch smile.

In her heart, though, a heavy weight was settling. It was difficult to admit, but she had been much happier *not* liking Clara. Whom this young woman was trying to imitate, or had suddenly become again, was a woman who had a much greater chance of success. She was no doubt once again the woman Nicholas had, at some point, considered marrying.

Walking to the window, Alexandra stared out into the darkness and thought of Jane. She had made a decision not to interfere. She'd thought it would be best to allow Fortune's wheel to turn as it will. But now she wasn't sure if that was such a good idea. With Clara obviously setting her mind to compete for Nicholas's attention, the older sister didn't have a chance to succeed. And though Jane had not shown any hint of even being interested in Nicholas, Alexandra had been watching her own son. He was wrestling with feelings that were leaving him unsettled. For every meal the older Purefoy sister had been absent, Nicholas's attitude had worsened tenfold. He was not one to allow himself to become so affected by a woman—unless there was something more between them than anybody knew.

Sir Thomas's brooding figure appeared in the doorway, and he cast a look around the parlor before settling a frowning glance on his wife. "Sir Nicholas is not back yet, I take it."

Catherine Purefoy laid down her needlework and rushed to her husband. "I've had Cook wait dinner, but it is getting late and"—she lowered her voice—"Lady Spencer believes we shouldn't wait at all."

The man gave a curt nod. "Have a tray sent to me in the library."

Alexandra watched her host's rude behavior with disgust as he walked abruptly away. A glance at Clara showed the young woman's cheerful demeanor return as soon as the conversation between her parents had ended. But Jane. Where was Jane?

Armed with new purpose, Lady Spencer knew that she had to help the older sister. Fortune's wheel sometimes did not turn quickly enough, she decided. It was up to her to meddle.

The rising moon cast long stretches of shadows and made the mountains in the distance appear to loom large over the land.

Nicholas tried to restrain his anger and frustration and instead focus on the moonlit countryside. So much of the land was already familiar. The Blackwater River lined by rolling farms and pastures. Farther south, the higher moorland cut by deep valleys of marsh and woodland. The sight and the names of mountains and pagan stones and villages nestled into the hills were becoming inscribed in his memory. Boggeragh, Banteer, Drommahane, Nad. Tonight though, wherever he looked, Jane's face was all he saw.

He wanted her. This fierce yearning for a particular woman was a new sensation. It was one he'd never experienced before. And frankly, he found it as maddening as it was magical.

He wanted to spend endless hours with her. He wanted to see her. He wanted to touch her. He wanted to lose himself in her taste and softness. He wanted to see her smile and watch her turn to him as she had done this morning when they'd left Kathleen's cottage.

But he couldn't have her. By 'sblood, he'd be damned if he would compete for her affection if she were already in love with another man. Nicholas refused to play the part of any second. He wanted her body, heart, and soul all for himself. He wasn't about to share her with anyone.

Jane had said that there was nothing between Henry Adams and herself, but he believed she wasn't being honest with herself. It had been to the parson's house that she had wanted to take the three children. It had been the parson's help that she'd sought.

There was trust, friendship . . . and something much more, he suspected, between them.

A sound coming from somewhere to his left caused Nicholas to rein in his horse and peer into the darkness. He was the only one abroad as far as he could see. He could see no one on foot. No light shone from any cottage or villages nearby. He put his hand on the hilt of his sword and tested the convenience of the knife in his boot.

Confident that he could handle whatever trouble might be lurking in the moon's shadows, he turned his gaze on the appearance of a horse and rider coming over the crest of a hill to the east. They were still quite a few yards away, but the drumming of his heart in his chest—more than the strength of his vision—told him who the rider was.

The moon was over her shoulder. Woman and horse presented a magnificent sight, and Nicholas found himself swallowing hard. With her loose dark hair dancing in the wind and her graceful body moving in harmony with the animal, she was surely an apparition from his dreams. As she drew near, she slowed Mab to a walk. With each step, Nicholas's tongue knotted tighter in his head, and his heart hammered louder in his chest. Her beautiful eyes, shining in the darkness of night, studied him, appraised him—and a different kind of tightness formed in his gut when she reined Mab to a halt right beside him.

"You give an incredibly good chase, Sir Nicholas."

"You have the eyes of a cat." His voice was hoarse and low. "Have you been following me, Miss Jane?"

Her gaze studied his face with a longing that scorched him—then it fell on his mouth. Nicholas's hands tightened around the horse's reins, but he didn't move.

"I have."

"What do you want from me?"

She leaned toward him, her hand reaching behind his neck. Drawing him to her, she stretched herself upward until their lips met. Her mouth was soft and her tongue playful as she teased and tasted him. Nicholas savored the pleasure of the kiss, but his restraint was short-lived. Starved for her taste and her touch, his arms reached for her as their mouths engaged in a duel of passion. But just as he was about to pull her from her horse and onto his lap, she ended the kiss. Mab took a couple of steps back.

He eyed her across the short span between them. "This is a dangerous game you are playing."

"I know." She sounded breathless and it took great effort on Nicholas's part not to reach for her again.

"What was the kiss for?"

"To thank you . . . for what you did for Kathleen . . . and for her children."

Gratitude? That was no kiss of gratitude. Suddenly, he wanted her to admit that the kiss was more about her desire . . . passion . . . about the way she felt about him.

"Were you equally grateful to Reverend Adams? He helped . . . he is helping that family, as well."

"Do I hear a hint of suspicion, even *jealousy*, in your tone?" She smiled.

"I am just a simple person asking a simple question."

"There is nothing simple about you, Sir Nicholas Spencer." Her softly spoken words caressed and soothed. "You have amazed me and surprised me and charmed me from the first moment that we met."

"Was that before or after I knocked you down?"

"Very amusing."

"Do you mean you didn't kiss Parson Adams?"

She laughed, and Nicholas found his mood improving. "No . . . I did not. Not the way I kissed *you*, in any case."

Before he could ask the question about how was it exactly that she had kissed the minister, Jane reined Mab around and pointed at the hills to the south and west.

"If you are in no great hurry to get back to Woodfield House, then I can properly thank you by showing you one of the most interesting sights in Munster. And before you ask"—she smiled at him—"I've never taken Parson Adams to the stones at Knocknakilla."

"I should not have dreamed of asking." Nicholas brought his horse alongside hers as they started off. "And, to be frank with you, Jane, if you are not at Woodfield House, I haven't any particular care *ever* to go back."

Even in the darkness of the night he could see the way the words affected her. She looked at him and, for a moment, he thought she was about to reach her hand out to him. An owl hooted somewhere in the distance, though, breaking the spell. She smiled and turned her gaze to the western hills.

"Try to keep up, Spencer," she said, spurring Mab on. " 'Tis a good ride we have ahead of us, and I do need to return you to my family at some reasonable hour."

While their horses grazed on the windswept moor, they walked together toward the ancient circle of stones. The stillness of the night, so perfect and complete, could not have been more at odds with the turmoil going on within her.

The agitation Jane was feeling had nothing to do with the man walking beside her. It had everything to do, rather, with coming back to this place.

There had been certain things that had remained sacred to her during the past nine years. She continued to wear black. She had never allowed herself to become emotionally or physically attracted to another man. She had foregone passion. And she had never come back here.

There were other things that had remained constant, too, for a rebel's life is often cut short. She never allowed herself to plan or dream of a future. She never wished for things that she could never have. Love, family, children—none of them had any place in Egan's life.

And yet, being here now, surrounded by night and the magic of the land . . .

For the first time in so many years, Jane felt the growing ache of what might have been.

She placed a hand on one of the stones and found it warm. Within it, she sensed the pulse of life.

"Is it not beautiful?" She filled her lungs and, looking up at the blanket of stars, turned her back to the breeze that came up at that moment.

"Stunning."

Jane turned her head and found Nicholas looking only at her.

"*You* are stunning," he repeated, coming closer. With each step Jane's heart pounded faster. Every limb in her body tingled with awareness as his gaze swept over her.

He stopped only a breath away. His large hand cov-

ered hers on top of the stone. An unfamiliar rhythm of
need began to pound within her. It was as terrifying as
it was exciting.

Jane tried to focus on the beauty of the land and not
on the man. The moon had risen high in the sky. Not
far from the circle of stones, a deserted cottage stood
half-hidden in the high meadow grass. In spite of the
brilliance of the moon, a million stars lit up the velvet
cloth of heaven.

"I had forgotten how this place made me believe I could
touch the sky . . . become part of the wind." She met his
gaze. "Too many years I have been away from here."

"Wearing black—staying away from here—playing the
hermit—being frightened of any attachments. They are
all related, are they not?"

"I am not frightened of attachments," she immediately
protested, not entirely certain that she was ready to pour
out her heart . . . and her past.

"But you are, Jane." Nicholas's fingers brushed the
windblown hair away from her face. His warm touch
lingered on her skin. "You are frightened of me. I am
not talking about my physical size, or if I can handle
you or not when you are pointing a knife at me. And I
am not referring to whatever knowledge I might have
of your secret activities, either." He gave her a knowing
smile. "You are afraid of the man, of our mutual attraction, and what is happening between us."

"There is nothing between us." She tried to pull away
from the stone, but the pressure of his hand held her in
place. She still wasn't ready to give up the fight. "If you
believe that because I kissed you, I am attracted to
you . . . I told you that was an expression of gratitude . . .
I was moved by what you did . . . and . . ."

"You appear flustered, Jane." He brushed his mouth
against hers, and pulled back before she could either
push him away or melt against him. "You want to ignore
'us.' But you do not know what to do with everything
you are feeling here." He pressed a finger at her heart.
"And here." He gently touched her temple. "I could
gladly show you where else you are confused, but I
would not take such liberties until you readily admit you
are as attracted to me as I am to you."

"This is foolishness." She turned her face away, not wanting him to know how accurate his words were.

"Why did you bring me here?" Nicholas cupped her chin and turned her face to him. "There is something here that you want to show me . . . or perhaps tell me."

"I only brought you here for the excellent view."

"At night?" he asked softly.

She asked the same question of herself. The impulsiveness of riding after him, and then kissing him, and then wanting to share . . . this particular place. What had she been thinking? These pagan stones at Knocknakilla held a special place in her life. They had belonged for so many years only to two young people in love.

Looking up at him, she wondered with a moment's panic if it was just because of this man that she was willing to open this door to her past. How could so much change so quickly?

"I have seen you in action, Jane. You have no fear in risking your life for these people—for your beliefs. And yet, right now you are afraid."

Of course she was afraid. She knew the pain a wound to the heart inflicts. She knew the rending ache that comes in the night, tearing at you until you pray you will die before the dawn comes. She knew what it was like to lie curled in the corner of a room and watch the evening light fade, and have no more tears to cry.

Yes, she was afraid. She was afraid of how he would act—how he would feel—if he knew the whole truth.

But she was also afraid that she cared for Nicholas Spencer much more than she could ever put into words.

The stars seemed to disappear in the sky. Everything around them became still. The birds. The breezes. Nature itself appeared to be waiting for Jane to speak.

"It is inevitable that you should hear scandalous rumors of my past while you are staying at Woodfield House." She spoke quickly before losing her courage. "I myself have hinted more than a few times of my ruined reputation. I brought you here because . . . because I thought instead of rumor, you deserve to hear the truth . . . from me." She took a deep breath and met his gaze. "Once you hear what I am all about, then we can rethink this business about your . . . your attraction to me."

He entwined his fingers with hers on top of the stone. "Tell me this thing that is so horrible about your past."

It would have been much easier to talk of her past if she were not faced with the reality of the present. Nicholas Spencer was all around her.

"Right here, in this very place, I gave my maidenhead to a man I loved." She hoped to shock him with the bluntness of the truth. "We played together as children, fell in love quite by accident, and—on many nights just like this—stood where we are standing and planned our future together."

Jane looked around her and saw all the images of long ago imprinted on the grass and stone.

"Conor was everything to me. He was my past, my present, my future. He was my life and my dreams. He was my hero and my hope. He offered the sanctuary I had never found within my own family." She looked up into Nicholas's face. "I have no regret for what I did, and I feel no shame in talking about him . . . to you or anyone . . . ever."

"Nor should you." His touch stayed—his eyes dark and shining and never once wavering from hers.

"But he was a poor farmer. A commoner. A Catholic. Even worse, Conor was a Shanavest who had a heart generous enough to love me despite the sins of my father and my country against his people." She didn't want the tears to come. By God, she didn't! But they burned her eyes, and she turned away from him, this time pulling her hand free.

The wind began to pick up again. Jane pulled the cloak tighter around her shoulders and walked to the center of the circle of stones.

"Unlike my own people," she said bitterly, "who spend their entire lives judging others by narrow, hypocritical standards and acting in ways that breed hatred, Conor treated me as a living, breathing person . . . and not as some straw figure representing his English oppressors. He refused to judge me based on the past. He

refused to be intimidated by our differences in station—
or my so-called education. We would all be judged as
equals in God's eyes, he would say."

She looked up at the stars through a sheen of tears.
The hurt still cut so deep. The memories, though hazy,
continued to stab at her heart.

"Where is he now? Where did he go?"

"He was hanged." The salty taste of tears reached
Jane's lips. She tried to take a deep breath to steady her
voice. "Conor was hanged on the orders of my own father. He was killed not because of any horrible crime.
He was always the most peace-loving of the Shanavests.
The magistrate"—she stabbed at the tears—"my
father . . . issued his death warrant because of his
involvement with . . . *me*."

The tears choked the words in her throat. Jane let out
a broken breath and tried to fight the sob rising in her
chest. She walked out of the circle and stared at the
valley beyond. In her mind's eye, she could see Conor's
dead body swaying heavily. In the wind, she could almost hear her own cries echoing through the town.

Nicholas's arms reached around her and captured her
hands, and Jane welcomed his strength when he drew
her gently back against his chest.

"This is a hard world, Jane." His chin brushed against
her hair. "And I am sorry for the injustice we bring
to it."

She leaned against him. Nicholas's strength gave her
courage to find her voice again.

"We were to elope the next day. But somehow—
through one of the servants, I think—my father found
out about our plan. I was locked in . . . but I managed
to send Conor a message. Still, though, he showed up . . .
hoping, I suppose, that I'd be able to get away." She
closed her eyes to lessen the pain, but it could not be
shut out. It was inside of her. "Four other Shanavests—
Conor's friends all—were arrested that night, as well,
not far from Waterford. None of them, though, had any
idea how quick their end would come."

Jane tried to pull a hand free to wipe her face, but
Nicholas turned her gently in his arms and carefully
brushed her tears away himself.

"They . . . my family . . . were planning to keep me locked up. They wanted to hide what I had done . . . what Conor and I were going to do. As far as they were concerned, no one outside of the household would ever know about their daughter's shame. But they couldn't hold me. I ran away." She stared at the lapel of Nicholas's jacket, but all she saw were five bodies dangling in the wind. "When I found him . . . them . . . I made sure everyone knew. I was mad, I suppose. I forced my way through and cut those bodies down. I knelt on that gallows and cursed my father and the others who were responsible. I told the crowds that gathered that Conor was my lover. I . . . I even claimed that I was carrying his child."

"Were you?"

"I thought I was. I prayed that day that I was. But it was just not to be."

Nicholas lifted her chin. The brush of his callused thumb against her skin caused her to shiver involuntarily. In her mind's eye she saw another man, barely more than a boy—a work-roughened thumb brushing away her tears. How many times had she cried in Conor's arms, fearing for their future?

"The only vengeance I could wreak that day . . . on my father . . . on my family . . . was in ruining their name. I never thought for an instant that their peers would sympathize with them over the incomprehensible wickedness of a daughter. Indeed, the world . . . and my father . . . would cut me out of the light. From that day on, I would become the daughter who they never had."

He simply pulled her tightly against his chest and held her. Jane let her sorrow pour out, her tears falling on his jacket. She didn't know how long they stood there. No words passed between them, but with an occasional brush of his lips against her hair, the press of his hands on her back, a change began to occur within her.

For too long she had lived for vengeance she could not exact. Deep inside, she knew that killing one man— her father—would never bring back those five men or ease her pain. But joining the Whiteboy movement had helped.

Sometime later, Jane realized she had stopped crying.

As if just awakened herself from a deep sleep, she found her gaze focusing on the dark shapes of the standing stones. There were five.

Five stones standing for longer than anyone knew. Five stones carried here and erected for some mysterious purpose by people long gone. Five of them standing against the elements. Standing against wind and rain. Against sun and ice. Five of them.

Perhaps, she thought, the descendants of those people still lived here. Still worked this land and claimed it as their own. Despite the invasions of marauding Vikings and Romans and Englishmen, these people—these stones—still stood defiantly on the moor. Five that would stand forever.

Jane breathed in the clean smell of the fresh night air. She looked at the stones and felt the endless hours of loneliness and anguish quietly slip away. She would no longer allow herself to be crushed by grief.

"I see tragedy and sorrow in your past—but no shame," Nicholas whispered. His fingers threaded gently into her hair, and he pulled her head back until she was looking up into his face. "I admire your courage. I admire the woman you have become despite the adversity in your life."

There was understanding and compassion in his face . . . but fire, as well. Something within Jane thrilled to find that, despite hearing the truth of her past, he still wanted her.

"The present and the future belong to those who seize it, Jane. Seize it with me."

"Genteel society shuns me. It will be scandalous for you to have anything to do with me."

"Genteel society can go to hell," he growled. "I know the hypocrisy of the world. And I know what is good and decent when I see it, too."

His mouth descended, brushing over hers, before coaxing her lips apart. Jane's hands moved up his chest as he kissed her thoroughly. Realizing she was falling too deep and too fast, her fingers fisted on the lapels of his jacket, and she tore her mouth away.

"Wait! There is Clara . . . We cannot."

"I have said this before, Jane. There is *nothing* be-

tween Clara and me, and there never will be. I have
already spoken to your father." Nicholas's large hands
framed her face, and he looked steadily into her eyes.
"How must I say it for you to understand? Who else
should I tell? What will it take to convince you that
you are the one who fascinates me. *You* are the one I
am pursuing."

Jane rose up on her toes and kissed him again. This
time, she tried to convey all of her frustration—all of
the longing that tore at her—into the heated press of
lips, the chafe and dance of tongues. Nicholas's reaction
was immediate. His arms wrapped around her, his mouth
as greedy as her own as he gave as much as he took.
Jane clung to him, trying to keep her balance and retain
a shred of sanity.

Too many years had passed. It had been so long that
she'd forgotten what it was like to lose herself in a haze
of passion. But as Nicholas's hands caressed and molded
the cloak and dress against her body, and as every inch
of Jane's body came alive with a sensual awareness, images of young love no longer danced before her eyes,
but the hard, hot reality of this man and her own admission of what all of this meant.

There could no longer be any denial. Nicholas already
had become much more to Jane than she would have
thought possible. Still, though, she had gone this route
once before and had suffered. And what was worse, this
time around she saw the journey would be even rougher
and more painful.

She pushed at his chest, and he immediately let her
go. Jane took a step back, but couldn't bring herself to
look into his face.

"We . . . we should go . . . 'Tis late. They shall be
worrying about you." She took a few steps toward their
horses, but turned around when she realized Nicholas
was not coming.

He hadn't moved. He stood there among the stones,
the moon behind him, his face in shadow, watching her.
Her own heart was hammering in her chest, her tingling
body crying out for his touch. It took all of her strength
not to run back to him.

"Nicholas, I . . . I am planning to go back to Ballyclough

tomorrow. I will be going from there and making other visits, too. If you . . . if you wish to come with me . . ."

"I do."

She tried not to be distracted by the relief washing through her.

"Then . . . I shall let you know tomorrow morning."

"I'll be waiting."

Patrick placed a firm hand on Ronan's arm, stopping him from moving out of the ruined cottage.

"Nay, ye have no business going out there. Let's get back to the horses."

"I've business enough."

"Ye'll not lay a hand on her."

"I've nothing against Egan. That filthy English bastard is another thing entirely."

"He's done nothing to rile ye." Patrick watched the two begin to mount their horses.

"The dog has made a pact with Musgrave, hasn't he?"

"We don't know if he has or if he hasn't. We only know that he went into the barracks at Buttevant alone and came out with Seamus's widow. We don't know what went on there, but I'm thinking we have as much reason to be thankful as we do to suspect him. Maybe more. We don't know what that magistrate will do for someone like him."

The two men, keeping an eye on the barracks since news of Kathleen's arrest, had followed Spencer and the widow to Ballyclough, and from there they'd kept a discreet watch on him . . . until Egan had caught up to the man halfway to Woodfield House.

"I still want to break the bastard's neck."

Ronan's menacing tone made Patrick put a hand on the fighter's muscular arm. "Ye want to break his neck, sure, but is it because he was kissing Egan, maybe?"

"The man is taking advantage of her," Ronan growled.

"Ye seem to be forgetting that she's the one that came after him," Patrick retorted. "When are ye going to get it in yer thick head that Egan is a grown woman? She doesn't need the likes of ye to be pining and drooling after her like some lovesick whelp."

"What do you mean, the likes of *me*?" The young

man turned fiercely toward his companion. "The likes of *him* is what she's been running away from all these years. She . . . she's fond of me. She's just waiting for me to do the asking . . . and she'll be taking me in the place of Conor . . . bless him."

Patrick shook his head disbelievingly. "I'm thinking when she calls you 'runt,' she must be talking about the size of your brain."

"Ye may be my mate, Paddy, but ye are about to feel my knuckles on yer head."

Patrick met Ronan's glare without flinching. Age and experience gave him an upper hand that he knew Ronan would not test.

"Ye can do yer worst with me anytime, Ronan, but get it in yer thick head right now that ye'll never do for her. Ye'll never be a Conor. And ye have a better chance of becoming Lord Lieutenant of Ireland than ye do of making her take ye as her man. I've known Egan since she was a wee spit of a lass, and I'm telling ye *she* is one that'll be doing her own choosing."

Patrick looked over his shoulder and found Egan and the Englishman had disappeared. Thank the saints.

"I say Liam should know about all of this."

The older man returned Ronan's hostile glare. "And Liam will. But remember, not a word about this kissing business, or I'll tell Egan myself about your stupid notions of becoming her man."

Ronan waved off the threat and started out of the cottage with Patrick on his heels.

"And God help you then, runt."

Chapter 19

The moment he heard the light tap on the door, Nicholas yanked open the latch and grabbed Jane's arm. Her gasp of surprise was silenced the next instant when he closed the door again and pressed her back against it. The next moment his mouth was ravenously devouring hers.

It was some time before he drew back and let both of them catch their breath.

"I . . . I do not recall . . . ever being so delighted with a morning greeting." She smiled up at him.

"That's because I had all night to plan it."

"You have quite a way with words, Sir Nicholas."

His body was still pressing hers against the door. The mold of her soft curves against his hard edges was perfect. "I didn't care much for your insistence on arriving at Woodfield House at different times last night. I had no chance to kiss you good n—to say good night."

Jane's dark eyes danced with mischief, and her arms tightened around his waist. "Are you telling me that the want of a single kiss last night is responsible for your greeting this morning?"

"Very well. It wasn't only the kiss . . . but everything about you that is responsible."

His mouth descended. This time with patience, he coaxed and parted her lips again, his tongue darting inside to sample and tease and unleash her passion. Jane's body arched against his. Her hands rubbed the shirt's fabric against his back, and her hips answered the slight but seductive movement of his own.

Nicholas dragged his mouth to her ear and bit the lobe. "All night I dreamed that I was making love to you."

His hand pressed against her breast through the dress, and he felt the peak of the nipple harden as his thumb brushed over it. Jane laid her head back against the door and closed her eyes, and he tasted the skin of her neck.

"You were here. We locked the door." His hand moved down the front of the dress. "I slowly peeled away each layer of your clothing until my mouth tasted and feasted on every inch of your sweet flesh."

A low moan escaped her lips when Nicholas's hand cupped her mound through the layers of cloth.

"We made love on that bed . . . and then on the floor . . . and once there on the chair, with you mounted upon me . . . and once more against this door."

Her face was flushed. Her eyes, incredibly dark and large, opened and stared at him when he pulled up the heavy fabric of her skirts and pressed his fingers against her moist folds.

"What do you say to that, Jane?" He brushed his lips against hers while his fingers stroked her below. "What do you think of my dream?"

He didn't wait for an answer and slipped his tongue between the parted lips. He felt the moan of pleasure as his fingers copied the motion of his tongue.

The time for questions or answers was past now, and he pleasured in her body's responses as his gentle ministration of her flesh set her on fire. Slowly, expertly, he manipulated the center of pleasure and sweet torment, lifting her ever higher, reveling in her cries of release as she finally came apart in his arms.

Fighting to ignore his own raw need, Nicholas cherished the feel of her in his arms. He loved the softness and the strength—the struggle and the surrender—the beauty and the intelligence. He held her tight while the waves of release continued to ripple through her, and kissed her tenderly.

The sound of two women's voices in the corridor outside his door jerked Nicholas back to reality. Jane descended like a stone from her place of bliss, and he couldn't help but smile at her efforts to focus on the present. He dropped her skirts and pushed her behind him as the knock came. Nicholas chuckled inwardly, thinking it was a good thing he hadn't dragged her directly to his bed for he hadn't even latched the door. With a reassuring look at Jane, he opened it a little.

The surprised faces of two young servants greeted him.

"Oh, sir . . . begging yer pardon, sir. We saw yer valet and . . . we . . ."

"We thought . . . ye were already . . . down . . . taking your breakfast . . . downstairs . . ."

"We were making up the bedchambers and . . . and . . ."

"Come back in half an hour," he told them. "Then you can do with the room what you will."

Both curtsied hurriedly and disappeared down the hallway. Nicholas waited a moment and then cast a quick glance up and down the now empty corridor before closing the door.

"I . . . I cannot tell you how shocked I am . . . by my own behavior," Jane whispered from the wall. A trembling hand pushed loose tendrils of hair behind an ear. "Acting the way I did . . . falling so wantonly into your arms . . . allowing you to . . ."

"Yes, such a moment can leave you shockingly satisfied." Nicholas pulled her away from the wall and into his arms. "If it were not for those two coming back, I would show you the meaning of wantonness."

He brushed his lips against hers, and he felt her body melt again into his embrace.

"Tell me, my love. Where are you taking me?"

It took her a moment to focus on his words, but he watched her eyes clear as she placed her hands on his chest.

"As it turns out, only to Ballyclough to check on Kathleen and her children, and back again."

"Nothing after that? No bishops to rob? No kingdoms to overthrow?"

"On the days that I spend at Woodfield House . . . of which there are many . . . I use the afternoons for painting."

"And where do you paint?"

"In my work area, in the attics."

"Will you take me there?"

Jane fixed a wry look on him. "Are you always so demanding?"

"Only when I can get away with it."

"Why do I have this feeling that there is a great deal that you get away with?"

She smiled up at him, and Nicholas held her tightly, cherishing the wild beat of their hearts.

"I will take you there, sometime. But we do have more important duties to attend to first."

Nicholas couldn't bring himself to let this moment go. "Tell me, are you going to force me to wait for five minutes after you have left before I can face the household? I will not be required to go to breakfast by way of Cork City, will I?"

"As a matter of fact, I am going to insist that you go and have breakfast with my family without me." She did manage to break free of him. "Apparently, my mother was complaining incessantly yesterday about not seeing you. You can meet me at the stables when you are finished."

He caught her arm as she reached for the door. "I will only go down into that den of lions if you come with me."

"Are you serious?" she scolded over her shoulder before peeking out into the corridor. "Do you want the pyramids to crumble? The oceans to run dry? No, sir. If I join them, they will think the Second Coming is surely at hand."

"Jane, I will *not* go down if you will not join me. We can leave for Ballyclough now."

"But we cannot just go," she insisted, her expression growing serious. "In spite of anything you say . . . about your plans not to marry Clara . . . they have high expectations of you down there, and it is—"

"Then come with me."

"Heavens, you are stubborn, sir."

"Come, Jane. We shall go down separately and behave as perfect strangers."

As she stared at the door, considering momentarily, Nicholas had to stop himself from bending down and placing a kiss on her long and graceful neck.

"I just want to look across the room and see your beautiful face before me."

"Well, that is too much to ask." She sent him a cross look.

"What? Sitting across the room from me?"

"Nay! Making my face beautiful."

He laughed and placed that kiss on her neck to show her exactly how beautiful he already thought she was. Jane sighed contentedly but then placed a hand on his chest.

"Very well. But I shall make my entrance before you. And not one look . . . nor touch, either . . . "

"I give you my word." He stole another kiss before she quietly slipped out of the room.

Nicholas buttoned up his shirt, tied his cravat, and reached for his jacket. Glancing once in the mirror, he was amazed at the starry-eyed face staring back at him. He'd seen other men wearing this look, he realized.

Men in love.

"What do you mean, she's disappeared?" Sir Robert Musgrave planted his hands on the desk and pushed himself to his feet. "Yesterday you told me the woman is old and blind. How far can a blind old woman go?"

"We have turned the cottage inside out."

The captain of the dragoons was sitting bolt upright in his chair. He was an idiot, of course, Musgrave thought, but he was also the youngest brother of the earl of Kildare's wife.

"I had my men scour the countryside around the place. I even had them drag out a few of the farmers in the area and question them about her. Naturally, no one knows anything of her whereabouts. She was there last night, Sir Robert, but she is gone this morning."

Musgrave strode angrily to the window. He should have followed his intuition and had the older woman brought in yesterday, right after the baronet had left with the other one. All that slop Spencer had fed him about wanting to help the poor still sat ill in his craw.

He'd had Kathleen arrested because she was the widow of the miserable cur who'd been killed last month. He knew how the Whiteboys worked—and he knew they took care of their women and children. So he'd had his spies keeping an eye on the widow. And just as he'd expected, the woman had shown up with money to spend in the market.

"Spencer be damned!" Musgrave muttered to himself. There must have been someone else . . . someone from that damnable gang of thugs . . . who had been in touch with her. He was determined to find out who.

Kathleen, though, had been as stubborn as a mule in answering any of his questions. But he'd thought time was his ally. A few days in the hole with his lonely dragoons to keep her company, and the woman would be singing like a lark.

How he was beginning to hate Sir Nicholas Spencer! The arrogant bastard had shown up, threatening him with the serious displeasure of the lord lieutenant, who just *happened* to be a dear family friend of the blackguard.

As he'd lain abed last night, the situation had run through his head over and over. He knew he had released the widow too hastily, but one couldn't be too careful with the influence of *dear family friends*. But something else kept nagging at him. So many times in his mind's eye, he had kept seeing the tattered shawl Jane had been wearing around her neck the day before. She always dressed in black—but never in rags. But why would she even have such a thing in her possession, unless it were a gift from some papist woman? It must have come from the widow. Sir Nicholas had not mentioned it, but who else but Kathleen would have given it to her? And why did Kathleen give it to Jane, rather than to Sir Nicholas himself, unless she was extremely grateful for something other than a few coins?

He turned on Wallis, who was studying his thumbs closely.

"Did you learn anything else, Captain?"

"Aye, Sir Robert. We did confirm that Sir Nicholas and Miss Purefoy were the ones who took the widow's children yesterday."

The magistrate turned sharply to his captain. "And where did they take them?"

"We . . . er, we have not ascertained that as yet, sir."

"Are you telling me that you did not have someone follow Spencer and the widow yesterday? I am certain he would have taken the woman to where her children are."

A dark shade of red crept up the officer's thick neck. "I beg your pardon, Sir Robert, it never occurred to me that you . . ."

"Must I do *all* of your thinking for you, Captain Wallis?" Musgrave clamped his hands with disgust behind his back and walked toward the embarrassed officer. "Is it absolutely necessary for me to give you minute-by-minute orders? Your leadership, Captain, is a reflection not just on you, but on me as well. And it is a reflection on your family, sir. Do I make myself clear?"

"My apologies, sir," the man said quickly. "I assumed . . . mistakenly, it appears . . . that you were satisfied with your meeting with the baronet and . . . and I clearly erred in not having them followed. But I was quite wrong, Sir Robert. I shall never make such an assumption again."

Musgrave's pique called for more haranguing of his subordinate, but his common sense reminded him that there was always more to be considered than just the immediate situation.

"There is another matter—a related matter—that I want you to attend to, Captain."

"Indeed, Sir Robert," the officer replied, standing up. "I shall not fail you."

"I'm sure," Musgrave said, nodding solemnly. "This matter is of the utmost importance, and I want you to be certain your men do not miss anything. And I want *you* to conduct the questioning personally."

The dragoon captain waited attentively.

"Yes . . . questioning. I want everyone who has *ever* come in contact with the rebel Egan to be brought here and questioned. By everyone, I mean your own dragoons, as well, who might have caught a glimpse of him. I mean the area clergy. The landlords and their tenants. Even Sir Thomas's guest."

"What about the bishop, Sir Robert?"

"I shall handle the bishop . . . but I want you to talk to that fat clerk of his." Musgrave stared down his subordinate. "The questioning, this time, will be different. Instead of what happened and how many and all those other useless things we usually try to find out, I want your full attention to be given to this Egan. I want his description. His build. The color of his hair. The color of his eyes. His weight and height. I want to know everything we can learn about him. I also want to know details about the horse he rides. Is it always the same one or does he ride a number of different steeds? Does he ever travel on foot? What language does he speak normally? Does he speak English with an accent? Do you understand what I am after, Captain?"

"Perfectly, Sir Robert. You want to learn the identity of the cur."

"I want that blackguard's head, Captain."

"Aye, sir."

"Then get your men moving. I want results . . . and I want them now."

To Jane's great disappointment, all the members of her family were still at breakfast when she walked into the Morning Room. She uttered a quiet greeting to Lady Spencer and Frances, ignored Sir Thomas's suspicious glare, and sat in a chair by her surprised mother.

"What a delightful surprise to see you this morning, Jane," the young Miss Spencer blurted out excitedly. "We were just told by Lady Purefoy that you were visiting some people in Ballyclough, and no one knew when you would return."

"I see. Well, I decided I would return last night . . . late." Jane nodded gratefully to the young serving girl who poured her some tea. "There was no way for anyone to know."

"And how was good Parson Adams?" Lady Spencer asked interestedly.

"Very well, I think. Both Mrs. Brown and Parson Adams send their regards." She hid her face behind the cup and let her gaze drift to Clara, who was sitting by the visitors. A distinctly petulant thinning of her sister's lips made Jane wonder what had Clara so riled this morning.

"I hope you do not mind my persistence, Jane," Lady Spencer continued, "but I was hoping to steal a little of your time for the selfish reason of the two of us just chatting about . . ."

"Clara *loves* to chat," Lady Purefoy interrupted.

"Indeed, Lady Purefoy," the guest replied breezily. "However, I find that Jane and I have quite a few interests in common, and I was hoping to spend some time in *her* company."

Their guest's emphasis on the word "her" immediately silenced Catherine. But Jane actually felt sorry for her mother momentarily. If she only knew how much damage she inflicted on Clara's chances each time she pushed her forward so brazenly.

"Thank you, Lady Spencer. I . . . I should love to spend some time with you," she responded quietly. "But I promised to return to Ballyclough this morning to check on a sick friend. Perhaps . . . perhaps this afternoon when I get back."

"As you wish, dear. I . . ."

The appearance of Nicholas in the doorway threw the entire room into chaos. Lady Purefoy immediately sprang to her feet, ordering the servants back to the kitchen for hot platters of everything. Clara, too, was on her feet. Frances made some teasing remarks about her older brother sleeping the morning away, and if it weren't for Lady Spencer's interference, the young woman would have relayed a story about her brother that was obviously not too flattering. Sir Thomas even made some casual remark about Nicholas's solitary excursion yesterday being a sure sign that he must be feeling quite at home in Ireland.

Her sister's reaction, however, was the most disturbing one for Jane. Unlike the first night, this morning Clara's attention was focused completely on Spencer. And her mood of a minute earlier had altered considerably.

Jane watched her sister bring him a cup and saucer, taking the tea from the servant and pouring it herself before sitting down near him. Amazed, she looked on as Clara made some private comment that brought a smile to his lips. When her sister reached out, however, and touched his sleeve, laughing in a charming way at his vague answer about what he'd had for dinner last night, Jane sat back, stunned.

Clara was interested.

The resentment that cut sharply through Jane appalled her. She refused the offer of food by one of the servants and tried to hide her flushed face behind a cup of tea while lively conversations ensued around her. As she regained control of her feelings of anger, though, she wondered with horror if perhaps she had guessed wrong about Clara's true interest. The realization that she herself might be having an illicit affair with her sister's future husband only compounded her dismay.

Watching them, Jane knew that she could live with shame, but she didn't think she could endure the ripping pain in her heart that jealousy was causing at this moment.

"You have been here less than a week," Sir Thomas asserted, "and you are already better acquainted with the countryside than most who have been here for years."

"Only with the inns, sir," Nicholas said in a humorous tone. "I believe that to know the land, you need to get to know its inhabitants. Now, what better place to meet them than where they gather to eat, drink, and . . . the rest of it."

"But that is one of the reasons that we are having the ball on Friday, Sir Nicholas," Lady Purefoy offered enthusiastically. "This will be a perfect opportunity for you to meet everyone who is anyone."

"But they will hardly be the ones who are one with this land, madam."

Jane didn't have to look up to know that Nicholas's gaze was on her with every sentence that he uttered.

"Why should I leave London if my interests lay only with the gentry?"

"Well said," Clara spoke softly from her chair. Jane looked up and found her sister's admiring gaze on Nicholas's face. "But as important as it is for someone like you to get a feel for the people and their lives, it is critical that you also get a proper view of the land. There are some very fine views that surround Woodfield House. And now that I know the depth of your interest, I am assigning myself to be your guide. We can take a carriage or we can ride, whichever you prefer. And—starting this morning—I guarantee that you shall be totally enchanted by everything that I show you."

"You are very kind, Miss Clara, but I regret that I must refuse your offer."

Nicholas's words stunned those listening into a shocked silence. Jane felt her own hand trembling as she put down her saucer of tea and hid her hands on her lap.

"I fear I have a previous engagement for today. But perhaps some other time."

"When?" Lady Purefoy chimed in immediately. "When? Outings such as this should certainly be planned in advance."

"If you will excuse me," Jane murmured as she rose to her feet. "As I mentioned before, I am expected at Ballyclough this morning."

Avoiding the looks of everyone in the room, she started for the door. She didn't wait. She didn't even pause. Positive that the lump in her throat would surely choke her, she rushed from the house and ran blindly toward the stable.

Chapter 20

His excuses about the day slipping by sounded about as hollow as an ale cask after May Day. His responses to the queries about his "previous engagement" were vague and brusque. Nicholas had only one thing in his mind, though, and that was going after Jane. And he didn't give a damn about what everyone thought of his hurried exit.

If it was too obvious that he was going after her, then so be it.

"Where is Miss Jane, Paul?" Nicholas asked, catching sight of the trainer in the paddock. One of the grooms was just leading Queen Mab out into the pasture in the back. Her black coat was gleaming in the sunlight. "I was to ride with her to Ballyclough this morning. Has she left?"

The stable master shook his head and nodded toward a building beyond the stables. "Ye'll find herself in the carriage house, sir. Miss Jane has a load of clothes and blankets and things that Fey packed for the widow and her wee ones. Ye might go right through the stable there."

As Nicholas started past the man, Paul laid a hand on his arm.

"A word of warning, sir. 'Twas no happy lass what passed through here a few moments ago. So don't ye be telling her I sent you that way, for she told me in no uncertain terms that she wishes to go on to Ballyclough alone today. No groom for the carriage . . . and no Sir Nicholas, either."

"I shan't get you in trouble with her, Paul," Nicholas assured him before striding quickly in that direction.

With high ceilings and partitioned stalls for ten carriages of various types, the carriage house was obviously a new addition to the stables of Woodfield House. One carriage was missing, and Nicholas found it on the drive beside the building. The two-horse phaeton, modern and handsome with its oversized wheels and shock-absorbing springs, was already loaded and ready for Jane.

One of the stable boys stood holding the horses' heads.

"The kitchens, sir," he replied to Nicholas's question of Miss Purefoy's whereabouts.

Starting quickly toward the house, he found her coming out of the kitchen door with a large basket of food in her hands. He had the advantage of studying her for the moment before she saw him, so he saw the red-rimmed eyes and the sadness that showed so clearly in the set of her shoulders. He immediately moved to her and reached for the basket.

"Can I help you with this?"

She seemed startled for an instant before jerking the basket away. "I can handle it myself. Thank you."

Her tone wasn't sharp or angry, just tired and defeated. He fell in beside her. "Would you like me to ride my horse and pretend I am heading south? I could catch up to you on the road to Ballyclough later."

"I wish to go alone today."

"But you told me—"

"A change of plans. Sorry . . ."

Frowning, Nicholas cast a side glance at her. There were unshed tears shining in her dark eyes. He brushed the back of his hand gently against hers. She recoiled from his touch and stepped aside.

"What's wrong?" he asked quietly.

"Nothing is wrong." She shook her head and turned her face away.

With the exception of the lad waiting by the carriage, no one else could be seen around the carriage house. The fellow took the basket from Jane and placed it securely on the seat. She asked him to lead the vehicle to the drive beyond the paddock, and Nicholas placed a hand on her arm as the carriage rolled away. "Can we talk?"

"I fear I haven't the time right now."

"This won't take long."

"I said I haven't the time." She tried to shake off his touch, but he only tightened his hold. Temper flashed in her eyes. *"Let me go."*

"Not until you give me a moment of your time."

"I shall see you in hell before I allow you or anyone else to bully me."

He'd have been ready if she pulled her dagger on him again, but he wasn't prepared for the solid punch that she delivered to his midriff. Hiding his momentary inability to breathe, he flashed a broad smile at Jane, who was flexing her fist in obvious discomfort.

"Is that the best you can do?"

"It is not."

He saw the next barrage coming. As her temper exploded, a flurry of kicks and punches erupted. Knowing his best chance of avoiding injury was to attack, Nicholas moved quickly forward, managing to pin her arms to her sides and lift her off the ground. He moved briskly into the carriage house.

"You let me go, you . . . you boor . . . you black-guard." Writhing like a snake, she fought him every step. "I am going to cut you into a thousand pieces. I'm going to gut you like a hare and feed your heart to my dogs."

"This is such an improvement over the first time we met, Jane." Nicholas smiled, holding her tightly against one of the stalls to minimize the damage she could be inflicting on him. "But perhaps not, considering I could only understand about half of the curses you were hurling at me in Gaelic that day."

"No one gets away with what you—"

His mouth captured hers, and he felt the vibrations of her next complaint fade to a murmur as he deepened the kiss. Her halfhearted struggles against him lasted only a moment longer, and Nicholas tried to control his own body's urge to make love to her here . . . now. The moment she melted against him, he felt his surging desires flare up, nearly overwhelming him. Images flashed through his mind of her soft flesh this morning, moist and alive, welcoming him. He pressed into her, relishing the feel of her mouth and body eager to receive him.

His body held hers tightly against the wall, his hands feeling beneath the cloak. Her breasts were firm through the dress, and her hands were pulling at him with growing ardor, drawing him close. And then she stopped.

The salty taste of her tears mixed with the kiss, and he tore his mouth away. Through the haze of his passion, he saw her closed eyes and the crystal droplets rolling down her cheeks.

"Jane," he whispered against her lips. "Jane, talk to me. What happened before I came to the Morning Room?"

She turned her face away, but he took hold of her chin and drew it back. She opened her eyes, and he found himself drowning in the sadness he could see there.

"You should have . . . accepted Clara's offer . . ." she managed to get out. "You should be . . . be spending time . . . with her and not . . . not with me."

He paused for a moment, stunned by his own blindness. Of course she would be upset at the constant thrusting of her sister upon him. But nothing had changed.

"There is nothing between Clara and me, Jane. *Nothing.*"

"She invited you and—"

"Must I accept every invitation extended to me? Do *you* acquiesce to every request for your time?"

She shook her head. "But this is different. You see . . . I . . . I let myself become . . . become interested . . . because I thought Clara was not."

"Did I never have any say in this?" He tried to keep his tone light. "I have told you before. I never pursued her. My interest has only been in *you* since arriving here."

" 'Tis not that. My own reaction is what appalls me now." Fresh tears escaped. "No matter . . . whom you might have been interested in . . . I would never have allowed myself . . . to become . . . entangled with you if I knew my sister had the slightest interest . . . or hope.

It was . . . is wrong of me . . . to be near you . . . to spend time with you . . . to become tempted."

Thousands of arguments formed in Nicholas's head, though expressions such as "*Who cares* if Clara is interested!" were burning on his tongue. He felt his frustration and anger growing. The younger sister had everything that she could possibly wish for in life—parents who doted on her, wealth enough to guarantee an excellent marriage, beauty, and a well-hidden intellect that wouldn't intimidate many potential husbands among the gentility. Nicholas wanted to shake Jane and wake her up. Her concern for her sister was needless. Instead, she needed to look inside and see what *she* wanted from life. But Nicholas already knew this kind of talk would only push her farther away from him.

He looked deeply into her eyes. "I have been involved with enough women to know that Clara's apparent interest this morning was all a show. There is no substance in this sudden attraction to me."

As Jane shook her head and turned her face away, he again captured her chin and forced her to look up at him. "Can you not see she was acting for the benefit of your parents? She is trying to be a good daughter and show them . . . especially your father, I think . . . that she is doing her part to win me over. I know what the purpose of this ball is this Friday night. I'm not blind to the expense and trouble they are going through. And it is all for the sole purpose of getting my head spinning enough to change my mind and ask for Clara's hand in marriage."

"She seems to want it now, too."

"She does *not*," he corrected harshly. "If no one else were about this morning, she would never have even stayed behind to keep me company. In so many words, she has already told me that I am too old for her. She appears intimidated by me. Frightened, even, at times. What kind of marriage would this be?"

"A genteel English marriage?"

Angry, he pushed himself away from her. "I am *not* willing to waste my life with the likes of Clara. I know of dozens upon dozens like her in England. Why should

I have her when I have already met someone else who suits me so much better? Someone who has a heart and a soul that I already hold dear." He took a few steps away, but then whirled around. "True, a few months ago I stood in the snow in London and thought that almost anyone with a pleasing look and reasonable fortune would do . . . but no longer do I think in so limited a way. No, Jane. I will not accept just anyone . . . and I refuse to be manipulated by your parents."

Nicholas stormed toward the door of the carriage house. By 'sblood, he loved the damn woman! But admitting it . . . but saying those words to her . . . would accomplish nothing until she could shed her blinders and begin to see *him*.

"I would . . ." The brush of her fingers against his brought him to an abrupt halt by the doorway. Her voice was soft and tentative. "I would very much like you . . . to come with me this morning."

"Do we ride separately or together?"

He saw the struggle play out on her face as she looked out the door. When her gaze came back to his face, her eyes were decided.

"Together."

It was midmorning before Alexandra caught Fey alone, lacking the troop of servants who were always swarming around her. The visitor immediately seized the opportunity and walked into the Blue Parlor, closing the door partially behind her. The housekeeper glanced up from her inspection of the fireplace.

"Lady Spencer, may I help ye with anything?"

"Yes, you may." Alexandra smiled encouragingly and moved closer to the redheaded woman so their voices would not be inadvertently overheard by someone passing in the hallway. "Was it my imagination, Fey, or has Lady Purefoy arranged for a dressmaker to be staying at Woodfield House this week?"

"Indeed she has, m'lady. The woman has been brought in from Cork City. She is a very capable seamstress, too, I must say."

Alexandra moved closer. "How attentive of Lady

Purefoy always to be thinking of her daughters. I assume she is here to make ball dresses for Clara and Jane?"

"Only Miss Clara," Fey put in shortly, turning to brush an invisible speck of dust from a clock on the mantle.

"But why not Jane, as well? I can see that she favors the color black, but surely for something as grand as what is planned, Lady Purefoy would want her elder daughter to be dressed in the height of fashion."

"I do not believe Miss Jane has a place in the mistress's plans for the evening."

"Her plans or her hopes?"

Alexandra's whispered question drew the housekeeper's intelligent gaze. A moment of silence preceded the woman's answer. " 'Tis not my place to suppose I could know the mistress's thinking. 'Tis not my job to meddle, either, m'lady. However, if there is something I can do for ye . . . ?"

Lady Spencer idly picked up a book lying on a table by Clara's customary seat. *Sternwood's Sermons*. Dreadful, she thought, laying it back down. She could understand Fey's answer perfectly. She could also sense the frustration just beneath the surface of her words. She looked up to see Fey waiting with an expression of subdued hope on her face.

"Indeed there is, Fey. You must have a good idea of how much work Lady Purefoy has given this woman—this dressmaker—for this week. Now, do you think if I wished to have something made . . . say, a dress . . . could the woman manage it?"

"Would this be for . . . someone we both know, m'lady?"

"It would, indeed."

"I should have to ask her, m'lady," Fey replied excitedly. "But I think she could do it. But there is a matter of fabric and accessories that would need to be attended to . . ."

"I believe my daughter, Frances, and I will be making a quick trip to Cork City this afternoon to shop for exactly those same things." Alexandra moved closer to the housekeeper again and lowered her voice "Now, do you think this dressmaker might be clever enough if I were to work with her . . . and tell her exactly what it is that I am looking for?"

"Aye, ma'am. I think she might."

"Of course, this dress I have in mind would not be able to be tried on for size until it is done."

"I've a lass working in the kitchens who might suit ye for size, m'lady."

"Excellent. And of course, I'll make it worthwhile for the dressmaker . . . beyond whatever Lady Purefoy is paying her."

"She is a working woman. I believe she will do as ye tell her."

"Very well." Alexandra beamed, turning to go. "You have a talk with her, and I shall return this evening with all she shall need."

"Is there something, m'lady . . . ?" Fey's question stopped her. "Is there anything more you might be needing from me?"

"In fact, there is." She gauged the woman's expression for a long moment. "I was hoping you would keep this little discussion just between us."

Fey nodded, the trace of a smile on the housekeeper's lips. "If you insist, m'lady."

"Perfect." Lady Spencer smiled broadly and started for the door. There was nothing like a little surprise to brighten up a grand ball, and she was determined to make this surprise—and this ball—the brightest and the grandest these people had ever seen.

Kathleen waited until Mrs. Brown, following a serving girl carrying an empty tray, had left the room before she clasped one of Jane's hands to her lips.

"God bless ye, miss," she whispered, sinking to her knees. "Lord knows, I cannot think of any words good enough to use in thanking ye."

Jane pulled the young woman to her feet. She led her to the two chairs by the window and sat the widow beside her. "You deserve far more, Kathleen, after the hardship you have all been through." She glanced at Bowie, pale and weak. There was reason enough to be happy. His fever had broken, and he now looked down

at his siblings playing on the floor beside the bed. "And
I am hoping things will improve a little from here on.
Parson Adams told me this morning that he has offered
you a cottage that is vacant in the village here."

"Aye, that he has." Fresh tears rolled down the mother's cheeks. " 'Twill be a blessing to have a roof over
our head again. And with everything ye brought us this
morning, we'll be living grander than when my Seamus
was with us."

"I am sorry, Kathleen. I know nothing will replace
him. But the way you all had to run from your own
place, I thought you might be needing these things."

The young woman nodded and wiped at her tears.
"Ye have a generous heart, Egan." Her voice was
hushed. "And a brave one."

Jane held on to Kathleen's fingers.

"Ye know, long before I met ye, I would hear these
wild tales of Egan. The little fire, the elders called ye."
She gave her a teary smile. "Egan could fly over the
mountains, they'd say. Egan could walk through fire . . .
ye could vanish in the bright of noonday. But Egan always arrived in time when a mother cried out in the
dead of night." She blushed slightly. "To be truthful, I
never paid much heed to what was being said, for I know
the way of us Irish. We need wondrous tales to help us
get through the suffering of our daily lives."

"But those *were* tales. You were right not to believe
them." Jane patted the woman's hands gently and
looked at them. The palms were hard and callused, with
dirt so deeply engrained in them that St. Peter would
surely know her for a worker when she arrived at heav-
en's gates. "Kathleen, the folk around here have always
made much more of me than I deserve. I am just a
woman . . . like you."

The widow shook her head. "But that's it, don't you
know? Ye're *not* like the rest of us. And knowing now
who ye really be . . . knowing the sacrifice ye've
made . . . the love you carry here"—she touched her
heart—"for poor folk like us . . . makes me believe in
ye more than all the legends and stories of angels and
saints. Ye be *our* joy, Egan. Our own angel sent by the
Lord himself to watch over us."

Jane fought back the tears burning her eyes. "I . . . I am not worthy . . . of all that you say, Kathleen. I was not chosen . . . or sent . . . by the Lord. I am just a simple woman. That's all."

The young mother again cupped Jane's hand in her own. "This is a land of believers, Egan. And no matter how unworthy ye might think ye be, I believe in ye. We believe in ye."

Jane wished she had the strength to argue with her. She wished she had the courage to be everything that these people wanted her to be.

"But 'tis not what ye do for us in the future that matters so much, as what ye've done already," Kathleen started again. "Ye've given us courage . . . a hero to call our own. And we must protect ye, as well. And this is the reason I'm telling all this now . . ." She lowered her voice. "They are after ye, Egan. The magistrate and his dragoons are becoming more brutal in questioning everyone about you. But we cannot let them discover ye."

"They shan't discover me." Even to her own ears, her tone lacked conviction. She needed time to think—to refocus on her purpose.

"Do not put yerself at risk, miss. If they take ye, we'll all feel the lash here, inside," she said softly, pressing Jane's hand to her heart.

"I will not let them take me."

"I'm glad of it, miss. For mark me, 'twould be better for Egan to disappear unbeaten than to see her hanging from the gibbet in Cork City." Kathleen's eyes shone with her belief. "Our memories keep us strong, but to lose her to these brutes would surely break our backs."

Though Nicholas walked the width and length of the village of Ballyclough, he saw nothing of what he passed. Finding himself sitting on a low stone wall encircling a graveyard situated on a hill overlooking the village, he shook off his haze and looked at the small, crumbling castle and the chapel near it. Following the brook with his eyes, he considered the humble cottages at the lower end. Abandoned wooden vats and stretching racks in various conditions of disrepair indicated that the village had obviously thrived at one time on the tanning industry. But no longer.

Things change, he thought.

He pulled up a tuft of green from his feet. Green three-leaved plants that looked much like tiny clovers were interwoven with the grass. Looking at the roots, he wondered if one could separate the two plants, once joined like this, and have them both survive. He was beginning to have his doubts.

The attraction between Jane and him was undeniable. Nicholas had already admitted to himself that he was in love with her. Once the awareness had set in, the admission was not difficult.

But so many complications lay in their path.

She was an active member of this Whiteboys movement. By the devil, she was one of their leaders.

Nicholas didn't give a damn about the reputation she'd destroyed years ago, but it obviously made a difference to her, and so would affect any future decision she made about the two of them.

Plus, she was worried about Clara's future.

And as much as she tried to put on an air of indifference, Jane was deeply hurt by her parents' rejection of her.

There might have been even more issues that he could think of if he set his mind to it. Jane's earlier rejection of him and the silence that had settled between them en route here this morning had indicated her own difficulties. But Nicholas was not one to be so easily deterred. He loved her, and he was determined to resolve every problem.

But he needed her help.

Pressing the tuft of green back into the earth, he stood and followed the path back toward the village and the parsonage.

A young servant led Nicholas to the parsonage's parlor. As he removed his hat and gloves, Henry Adams appeared in the doorway.

Ah, yes! And then there was the matter of the good parson.

"Did you have a pleasant walk, Sir Nicholas?"

"Yes, I did."

"I am afraid Miss Jane has not concluded her visit this morning," the parson announced, remaining in the doorway. "I realize you shared a carriage coming down. If you wish to get back to Woodfield House, I can arrange for one of my grooms to ready a horse for you."

Nicholas bristled. "I am in no hurry to get back, Parson, but I thank you for your concern."

"But I was under the impression that you are spending the afternoon with Miss Clara."

"Were you?" Nicholas moved to the center of the room. "Do you know something, Reverend Adams, that I do not?"

"Perhaps I do." With his hands clasped behind him, Henry entered the parlor, a disapproving glare painted clearly on his features as he studied Nicholas. Adams was easily as tall and broad as the baronet, and the room suddenly became much smaller. "Perhaps I find your behavior . . . odd. Spending the mornings in the company of one sister and the afternoons in the company of the other. I find it improper, sir, to see you charming these two young women at the same time. I wonder if you are considering the implications . . . and the possible consequences for one of them?"

"You are treading a dangerous path, sir," Nicholas growled.

"Am I?" The minister took another step toward him.

Regardless of the man's profession, Nicholas realized he was about to call the man out. He didn't like his insinuations. He didn't like his tone. And frankly, he was beginning to dislike the man's looks.

But for Jane's sake, he reined in his temper for the moment. "And I wonder if you are asking these questions in your capacity as these young women's *spiritual* advisor."

"Now it is you who is treading dangerously."

"Am I?" Nicholas crossed his arms and turned only slightly, measuring the man. "I don't know if it is any of your business, but I spoke with Sir Thomas the day after my arrival to correct any confusion regarding my supposed interest in Miss Clara. There is not going to be a proposal. There have never been any marriage plans, and I have no wish to marry the younger daughter. And, having clarified that point with the parents, I do *not* spend any time in her company."

"And how does Clara feel about that? About being led on, I mean?"

The man's accusing question pricked the visitor's restraint. His glare menacing, Nicholas took a step toward the parson. "Miss Clara was never led on by me, and I am warning you now that I am finding your insinuations an intolerable affront to my honor."

"If your intentions have been as honorable as you claim, sir, then there is nothing to be offended by. Which, in turn, brings me to your intentions regarding Jane." They stood an arm's length apart, Adams's fierce glare matching Nicholas's. "I have known and valued her for too many years to allow a stranger to walk in today and leave tomorrow, and cause her pain. I refuse to allow . . ."

"What is between Jane and me is none of your concern, and I . . ."

"I am making it my concern—"

"Am I interrupting something?"

Jane's softly spoken question from the doorway stopped the two men. But like two bulls ready for combat, neither moved nor averted his killing stare until she repeated her question.

Henry Adams was the first one to turn and face her. A look of tenderness passed between the two, and something in Nicholas's belly curdled when the parson took her hand and raised it to his lips.

"And here is Jane. Interrupting? Nay, I was practicing my . . . my hospitality."

Her brilliant smile as she brushed a kiss against his cheek was another blow to Nicholas's midriff. He was roughly five seconds away from breaking the good parson's jaw, and he found himself taking a step toward the two.

"Are you ready, Sir Nicholas?" She turned her magical gaze on him, and he felt the room warm around him. "To avoid giving our host any temptation to poison you . . . with his hospitality . . . I am refusing Parson Adams's insistence on our staying to dine with him."

Adams hadn't asked them to stay, and Nicholas wished he could smile at her attempt to lighten the tension between the two men. But his jaws were clamped too tightly shut to move.

"Indeed, I think we will be leaving immediately," she said, blessing Adams with another smile as she looped her arm through Nicholas's. "I'm quite sure this house can handle only so many guests at one time."

Chapter 21

For the hundredth time, Jane glanced over at Nicholas's brooding face and contemplated her best approach. The man clearly needed to bleed off some of his anger. What she'd seen in the parlor of the parsonage had been no illusion. Whether they would have resorted to fists or swords or pistols, Nicholas and Henry had clearly been ready to do battle. And considering her involvement and friendship with each of these two men, Jane was deeply disturbed to think *she* might have been the reason for their obvious hostility.

"Are you trying to give me a taste of my own medicine?"

She might as well have asked the question of the blue jay that darted from the hedge as they passed. Nicholas continued to glare straight ahead as he drove the horse and carriage. He gave no indication that he'd even heard what she'd asked, other than flicking the reins at the pair.

"I know I was not very talkative on our drive to Ballyclough. But I needed time to think and consider everything . . . between us. I needed to think through all that you told me before we left." A bump in the road jounced Jane against Spencer's side. She moved away only a little. "I have come to accept that nothing between you and me can be simple. Our pasts, our lives, even the people whom we care for seem to be doing their best to wedge themselves between us."

She stared at the familiar countryside. "Though it might appear reckless to someone looking from the outside—this life I have chosen for myself among the Whiteboys and the locals—it fills some need in me. It is a deep-seated need . . . for justice . . . and for adventure, I suppose. There is security in what you come to be comfortable with . . . even this. Despite the danger, I consider the ground I walk upon solid . . . and good."

He cast a sharp glance her way. "Are you telling me that you do not want what is happening between us?"

She looped her arm through his and looked into his eyes. "It would be much simpler if I could say that I do not want it, but I cannot say that." A layer of darkness lifted from his expression. She brushed her cheek against the wool of his jacket when his gaze shifted back to the road. "I wish I knew how long this thing might last between us, but I have no such gift for seeing into the future. The way I feel about you, though . . . the way you've thrown my emotions and my life into such total disarray . . . I cannot simply turn my back to it."

She moved closer to him, trying to take strength from his presence. "Most people search all their lives and never find even once what I have been fortunate enough to come across twice in my life. I am willing to take the chance."

"How about Adams?"

He hadn't even looked at her to ask the question, and Jane understood his frustration. After all, she, too, had been plagued with the same uncertainty this morning . . . about Clara.

"He is a dear and trusted friend. Nothing more."

"Perhaps to your thinking. But there is a great deal more at his end."

Jane searched for the right words to explain what it was that made the friendship she shared with Henry so different and special. "We've known each other all of our lives. We've been as close as a brother and sister who are about the same age can be. We've shared the same interests and beliefs. And for many years, since Conor's death, Henry has taken it on himself to fill the emptiness that my parents' treatment of me has created in my life. He is always there if I need him. And he is as protective of me as you would be of Frances."

"I would not face someone who was waiting for Frances the way he faced me today."

"I believe you would," Jane challenged. "Put yourself in his position. What exactly does he know of you? He believes, as we all did, that you came to Ireland to marry Clara. Now he finds that you are spending many hours in my company."

"I explained that to him today. But there was no change in his hostility."

"That is because Henry is a man of reason and logic. He knows the scandal of my past. He knows that such a past allows no possibility of a future in your society. Therefore, he concludes you and I have no chance of finding a future together . . . not an honorable one, at any rate." As he opened his mouth to speak, she shook her head and continued. "He is also aware of how I feel about you . . . how much I care for you . . . and this disturbs him. He is determined to intervene, for he does not wish to see me hurt again. You cannot tell me that you would not do the same for Frances . . . or for any friend who might have suffered in their lives. I believe you would intervene if you thought that ill-conceived choices were about to be made."

Jane stared at his rugged, handsome profile. He looked away and murmured a name under his breath. She drew his chin back to her.

"Would you care to repeat that?" she said, brushing a kiss against his cheek.

"Stanmore." He spoke more clearly this time, giving her a grudging half smile. "He is my oldest friend. And I did poke my nose in his private life last year when I had my doubts about the woman he was set to marry."

"I see. And what happened?"

"The woman turned out to be innocent of all suspicions. They've since married. And now, I'm happy to say, Rebecca and I are the greatest of friends."

Jane wrapped her arms around him and hugged him fiercely. "You see . . . given time, you and Henry could end up friends, too."

"I doubt it."

"Oh, you foul-tempered, bull-headed . . ." She gave

up on the words, drew his face down to her, and put all her frustrations and passion into a kiss.

As she kissed him, Jane felt the carriage come to an abrupt halt, and she found herself pulled onto Nicholas's lap. His mouth slanted over hers with a kiss deep and hot enough to set her entire body on fire.

"I . . . I want you," she whispered raggedly when his mouth left hers.

His lips touched and teased the fevered skin of her throat, and his hands were already beneath the cloak, caressing her breasts.

"I want to make love to you, Jane."

She thought for a moment that the meadow they were crossing would serve them as well as any bed, and then an idea dawned on her.

"How long can you be patient?" she asked with a smile, scrambling off his lap and taking up the reins of the carriage herself.

"Where are you taking me?"

"You shall find out."

"Very well. Then you be sure to pay complete attention to your driving, for I shall be otherwise engaged."

As the phaeton raced across the countryside at breakneck speed, Nicholas's mouth and hands continued their teasing play. Jane thrilled to the feel of his attentions until the pressure in her body was so overwhelming that she thought she would lose her mind if they didn't arrive at their destination soon.

The ruined stone castle, deserted by people and time, sat high on a ledge looking over the Blackwater River. Jane—as Egan—had many times taken shelter there against the weather.

"I thought we'd never get here," Nicholas said, reluctantly withdrawing his attentions as the edifice came into view. "Where are we?"

"Just a little place I keep in the country," she joked, urging the horses up a slope toward the castle wall. "They call it Cuchulainn's Seat."

Nicholas gazed up at the impressive rise of the walls and then at the rolling valley. The two ducked their heads as she maneuvered the carriage through the narrow, ancient gate and brought the horses to a halt.

"Are you coming?" she asked, stepping down from the carriage and taking the basket of food Mrs. Brown had sent along with her. She backed toward the door of a square tower that formed most of the western wall.

The intensity of Nicholas's blue gaze on her made Jane shiver with anticipation. She saw him take a blanket from the seat and start across the courtyard after her. It was dark in the spiral stairs leading up to the upper story of rooms that had surely been inhabited at one time by the lord of this castle and his family. Near the top, she stumbled once, nearly losing the basket of food, but Nicholas was beside her in an instant. As he set her back on her feet, he claimed a kiss for his efforts.

She led him to the only room on the upper floor that still had a part of a roof and three standing walls. The wall facing the valley, though, had long ago crumbled to the riverbank.

"This is one of Egan's secret hiding places," she said quietly, watching the room fill with Nicholas's presence as he walked in. "You mention it to anyone, and there will be a price to pay."

His silence only made her skin burn hotter. When he dropped the blanket to the ground and approached her, she realized that this was to be nothing like the experience she'd shared so many years ago with Conor. That was simply the discovery of passion's fires by two innocent youths. What she was facing now was a man. And Nicholas Spencer was a man who'd spent his life in the company of worldly women. She was certain there was little he did not know about the ways of love. Fears and insecurities cast a shadow across her mood, but he was quick to hold her close.

"Stay with me," he growled against her lips as his hands undid the tie of her cloak. The garment pooled at her feet. He turned her in his arms and had her lean against a wall while his hands started undoing the buttons on the back of her dress.

"I am frightened," she whispered, pressing her forehead against the cold stone.

"I am, too."

She felt the air, so cool on her skin, as he spread the back of the dress.

"I want so badly for this . . . to be right. For me to be able to show you . . . how much I love you."

Stunned by his words, Jane turned in his arms, only to be overwhelmed by the depth of emotion she found in his blue eyes.

"Nicholas . . ." The words caught in her throat. Tears burned her eyes.

"It is true. I love you, Jane." He kissed her deeply, thoroughly, while his hands peeled the dress to her waist. The feel of his large hands holding her breasts through the thinness of the chemise made her arch her back for more. Her breathing stopped altogether when he slipped the straps of the chemise, as well, down her arms. When he drew back, she saw his eyes darken as he gazed at her breasts before returning to her face.

"You are so beautiful."

She gasped out loud as his mouth lowered and he took her flesh into his mouth. There was no longer a doubt, but only need in her soul. She felt herself melt, become moist. Her arms wrapped around him. Her body was ready, eager to accept him. Drawing her down onto the blanket, he pushed her clothing down over her hips, helping her to extricate her legs.

He quickly shed his own clothing, and a moment later the walls rang with her cry of ecstasy at the joining of their bodies. She felt the sky wrap around them, lifting them both up on a cloud of infinite blue.

I love you.

His whisper echoed in her mind again and again, but Jane tried to blot it out, trying for once to lose herself in this one miraculous moment.

All rational thoughts soon fled and only the throbbing pulse of the love dance was left. Even time hung suspended, counted only by the beat of their bodies pounding together as two souls rose up to that joyous moment of release.

Later, as she lay in his arms, Jane thought again of the declaration she could not make. No matter what she was feeling, "love" was a word she could not say.

Love, she thought, dashing a tear away, was something their world would never allow.

*   *   *

Patrick found his man in Cork City's old Butter Market. The young fellow, organizing the goods on his cart before the ride back to Woodfield House, spied him and dropped a crate of tea onto the cobbled ground.

Under the pretence of helping him lift the crate back onto the cart, Patrick whispered the message that had to be delivered to Egan before nightfall. ". . . to meet at the same time and place as the last. Liam says Egan should come early. Finn is to be there. Be sure to tell her."

Casually rising to his feet, Patrick picked up his youngest son. The lad had lagged behind a little to stare at a brilliantly painted gypsy wagon. He lifted the boy onto his shoulders, pleased that the message had been delivered without any trouble.

As father and son started off toward the river, though, Patrick failed to notice the two dragoons watching carefully even as they followed at a safe distance behind.

Clara shifted a little, forcing herself to sit straighter in the chair. The sharp end of one of the French stays was digging mercilessly into her flesh. It had taken two maids, working under her mother's supervision, to squeeze her into the undergarment. Surely, some cruel woman-hater must have devised the insidious thing.

Frustrated, she glanced down at her breasts propped up like pillows by the stays. Her nipples were barely concealed by the dreadfully low neckline of the dress. She was certain that if she were to reach forward even a little, or allow anything to tug even faintly at the dress, she would be spilling out of her gown like springwater over the dam.

And for what? she thought, the warmth rising in her cheeks. The baronet had not spared her a glance.

Clara wasn't blind. Since sitting down to dinner, Nicholas's attention had been focused on Jane. Jane and her high-collared black dress, so conservative that it didn't reveal even an inch of skin. Jane, who had managed to show up for the second time today to a meal. Jane, who actually participated in the conversations at table and even seemed not to take offence at anything their parents said. Jane, who actually smiled at an attempt at humor on the part of Sir Thomas.

Clara found herself disliking this Jane a great deal.

"Lady Spencer, you have been very mysterious today, spiriting your daughter to Cork City and back."

Clara shifted again, trying to ignore the pressure on her ribs. This was the second time her mother had asked this question tonight.

"Not at all," their guest replied cheerfully. "I just thought it would be good for Frances to see what your shops had to offer. Of course, we couldn't help picking up a little of this and a little of that while we were there. Fanny picked out a lovely bonnet."

"Well, if you would like to go again, I should love to accompany you. I know of the dearest little milliner's shop, not far from the new Butter Exchange."

"That would be lovely."

"But how about you, Sir Nicholas?" Lady Purefoy turned her attention to the baronet. "Tell us which little corner of our countryside you were exploring today."

"I went to Ballyclough with Miss Jane."

His blunt response drew every eye in the dining room. Lady Spencer and Frances exchanged a quick look. Sir Thomas, his glass halfway to his lips, grunted and downed the wine before sitting back in his chair. Catherine gaped for a moment before recovering herself. Clara thought that it might be the first time in her life that her mother had been struck speechless. The color had risen in Jane's face, and her gaze was now fixed on her plate.

Clara began to seethe, and she shot darts with her eyes at her sister. For most of the day, she'd been brooding on the fact that Jane was going more and more to Ballyclough. She didn't like it, not one bit.

Henry had never wanted Clara herself to come and visit him every day. Henry had never asked *her* to join him on his visits to the parishioners. Henry never shared his thoughts or his plans with her. Clearly, it just came down to this—Henry was infatuated with Jane.

And so was Sir Nicholas.

Obviously having a tarnished reputation was what a woman needed to attract attention these days.

Her own malicious thoughts shocked and hurt the young woman, and her chin sank to her chest.

But the bitterness continued to eat away at her. The thoughtlessness of her sister to want to take away *both* men was appalling . . . unfathomable. For all her talk of having loved only *one* man in her life—of her devotion to Conor, of the grief she still carried—all of it was nothing more than a lie. Jane was just looking for sympathy. And attention. And obviously, Clara thought, she had succeeded.

"I . . . suppose . . . we should leave the men . . . to their port and their cigars," Lady Purefoy finally managed to get out. She rose to her feet, and everyone else followed suit.

Clara's eyes remained on Jane. There were silent messages passing between the baronet and her older sister. Even as an observer, she could feel the heat in the air between them. When Jane left the room ahead of the rest of the women, Clara saw the scarcely concealed desire in the man's eyes.

She was quick to follow her sister out. She was riled and resentful enough to say something while the women crossed to the Blue Parlor. But as she made her way along, Clara saw Jane disappear up the stairs.

Her brutish Shanavests must be calling, the young woman thought. Going into the parlor with their guests, Clara began planning her talk with her sister. It was time someone advised Jane about the futility of her attempts.

It was time someone told Jane that she didn't have a chance . . . with either of these men.

Though Sir Thomas had wanted to toast everyone in London society individually, Nicholas had excused himself before the second bottle of port appeared.

She hadn't said anything to him, but Nicholas knew that she'd be gone. A trip to the stables had confirmed it. Queen Mab was not in her stall.

Strolling back up the hill toward the house, Nicholas could think of nothing more tiring than joining everyone in the parlor. It seemed he could think of nothing else but Jane. Hell, he didn't *care* to think of anything else but Jane.

Visions of their lovemaking this afternoon played again and again before his eyes. The haunted look in Jane's eyes when he'd confessed his love was an image he would never be able to scratch from his memory.

Nicholas glanced up at the dark lines of the house and tried to guess where her workroom might be. He wanted to be surrounded by nothing but her.

"I thought I might find you out here." His mother's voice drifted out of the shadows of the arched entryway. "I am disappointed, though, to find you alone."

"No more than I." He'd made a pact with himself today. There would be no denying of his feelings for Jane . . . publicly or privately. "What are *you* doing out here, m'lady?"

"I tire of drinking wine with our hostess, I'm afraid. And though Clara is ostensibly playing at cards with your sister, she looks like she might cut someone's head off."

Lady Spencer took a couple of steps into the night and looked up at the star-filled sky. "So, with Jane shunning our company and Sir Thomas retiring to his study a few minutes ago, I decided that whatever excitement Woodfield offers, it must be out here."

"And pray, what were you planning to do if Jane and I were out here alone?" he asked, amused as always by his mother's way of thinking. "Not planning to spy on us, I should hope."

"Heavens no! Only keep watch on your behalf." She smiled tenderly. "I know you do not need my approval. But still, I want you to know that I think very highly of Jane. She is a very special young woman."

"I know," he agreed quietly.

She walked past him and stopped by the edge of the garden—her eyes scanning the dark valley beyond. "Perfection does not exist, Nick. Beauty is only a passing illusion. Happiness is not a beginning or an end, but a lifetime of commitment. It is a journey." She turned to him. "To love is to give."

This was not the first time Nicholas had heard these

same words. They represented the principles he'd been raised to believe in, to live by. He'd heard them many times in his youth, though he wondered where it was that he'd begun to feel unworthy of happiness. Somewhere on the Plains of Abraham, he supposed.

"I haven't forgotten."

"That's good." She nodded, satisfied. "You'll need to remember them. Jane deserves it."

Nicholas said nothing as his mother walked back toward him.

"However, seeing that you obviously have nothing to do this evening, would you care to see the greatest treasures Woodfield House holds?" At his wry smile, she shook her head and patted him on the arm. "No, you can find your own way to Jane's bedchamber, my dear. I am speaking of her workroom. The studio where she paints."

"Your vast knowledge and wisdom continue to amaze me, m'lady." He offered her his arm.

Chapter 22

"I spoke with Finn earlier today, Egan," Liam said as the two waited for the others to arrive. "He said that John Stack's and Denis Cahill's tenant farms were paid a visit this morning by the dragoons. And this afternoon, they were over to Kilcorney, putting their noses in at the Connell place, at Jock Dineen's, and at Ned Ryan's, as well. They were questioning everyone about ye."

She tried to make light of her friend's worry. "Unless they're dividing and passing out bits of heaven, I do not think these folks will say anything different about me than they did the last time . . . or any of the times before."

The farmers Liam had mentioned would cut off their right arms before informing on her. The families mentioned all knew perfectly well who Egan was. Each of them had aided the Shanavests or, at one time or another, provided shelter for displaced families over the years.

"But Finn thinks this is only the start," Liam warned. "There are many others out there who shan't be as loyal . . . or as brave . . . or as smart to know what to say or not to say. He's worried about ye."

"About me? In all this time, the man has made a point of not making himself known to me!"

"Aye . . . well, I cannot answer for him on that. But, sure as I'm standing here, the man is concerned. He even had us move the blind woman, Bridget, to Charleville last night because ye had talked to her. And don't ye know, this morning at dawn there were dragoons searching all over Buttevant for her."

"You and I have been involved with this fight too long to become frightened so easily," Egan said confidently. "This is not the first time they have searched through the straw for us."

Liam shook his head. "There has always been safety in numbers, and in knowing that when they come after us, we can spread in a dozen different directions and give them the slip. But this time, they appear to be after ye alone, my joy, and none of us like it."

Egan glanced at the group that was now gathering. She looked past Ronan's deep frown across the fire and searched the faces in the crowd until she found Patrick. Her friend's gentle and loyal face was a reminder that she needed to push aside her own disregard and really listen to what she was being told. These people *did* care for her, and she for them.

"What does Finn recommend?"

"He wants ye to stay in the shadows for a while. With a wee period of calm and easy going . . . with no sign of Egan . . . he thinks the searching and the questioning will soon die down."

"How about the gathering at Kildare?"

"Finn thinks we should decide on someone else to go for ye." Liam studied the gathered crowd. " 'Twill be good if we can tell the people about the change in plans tonight."

Very well, she thought. So she would not go on the trip. As everything stood now—and especially after today—she was afraid that she would be distracted by her feelings for Nicholas. Her friends needed better representation from their group than what Egan could offer now.

"So who do ye think should go for ye?" Liam pressed the question again.

"Patrick," Egan answered. "He would be perfect for it."

At the sight of the empty stall, Sir Thomas's hopes dropped like stones into a chamber pot. At the same time, frustration fueled his temper.

All along tonight, he'd assumed Jane was with the baronet. Seeing both of them disappear after dinner, he'd thought—nay, he'd hoped—that the two would be sneaking off together to some dark and private corner of the night.

He had not been mistaken. Subtle as they were, the signs and gestures had been all too apparent. Spencer was smitten with Jane . . . much to the blackguard's credit. And, by thunder, if the scoundrel was man enough to go after her even after learning of her scandalous past, then, hang it, who was he to get in the way? Aye, something good might turn up after all. Despite his roguish reputation, the baronet looked to him to be the type to act honorably when it came to Jane. He had the look in his eyes. This had all the makings of a love match—if such a thing existed in this world of hard hearts and itching palms. But Sir Thomas had known straight away that Spencer was cut from a different cloth.

He glanced again around the empty stall.

Damn Jane for trying to ruin it!

Sir Thomas stormed out of the stables and up the hill toward the house. The cursed Whiteboys needed to be set back on their heels soon. They needed to see their leaders dancing in the Cork breeze. They needed a goodly taste of fear. Scare the buggers off, and Jane might just be discouraged enough to give up the cause while there was hope of something with Spencer.

Enough was enough, hang it. He had left Musgrave to do his job too long. Sir Thomas needed to get involved once again and show the dandy how an old dog goes for the throat.

The flickering light of a dozen candles brought to life the images on the canvases. Nicholas stood back and stared at the paintings he'd uncovered and stood up in every available space.

After bringing him up into the attic studio, Alexandra had gone without a word, leaving Nicholas alone to peer through this window into Jane's mind. To view on his own a young woman's burning talent. To sense the life that had produced such work.

He had pored over her paintings with the fervor of a

treasure seeker who had just found the long-hidden riches of Croesus himself. And as he went from canvas to canvas, he'd felt an unexpected rush of emotion that had forced him simply to sit and gaze from time to time. He had been touched, impressed, and his eyes had opened to the battles and the grief that had played such an important part in her life.

But the most disturbing revelation had been the magnitude of Jane's love for Conor. For a woman to forgo *so much* of her life, to become so consumed with a cause that she wasn't born to, bespoke great devotion to this man. It was daunting to think that she would ever be able to love another . . . that he would ever be able to win her.

But hell, he thought fiercely, the taking of Quebec had not come easily, either. And this was far, far more important.

He strode to her worktable and opened a leather case of sketches there. A charcoal drawing of himself was on top of a number of other sketches. He gazed at it carefully. It was quickly drawn, but unmistakable in its intent and its power. It was a depiction of him looking at someone he was holding captive beneath him.

It was a representation of the first day they'd met. She'd captured the mixture of surprise and heat in his face. The rest of the picture, however, confused Nicholas until it occurred to him that it was the work of her imagination. In the sketch, he was wearing a loose flowing shirt, unbuttoned and showing the muscles of his chest beneath. His hair was loose and wild around his face. His hand was reaching out of the sketch, reaching toward the artist.

What he was looking at was an erotic evocation of what might have been . . . of what was yet to come! She had been drawn to him from the beginning.

The creak of the door opening at the bottom of the stairs jolted Nicholas into the present. He peered down the steps and saw Jane looking up at him.

"So you found this place," she whispered. Her face was hidden by shadows, and he did not know immediately if she was pleased or angry.

Nicholas watched her come through the door and

latch it. Desire rushed through him as he watched her slowly ascend the steps. She was wearing the black breeches and shirt—her white smock had been discarded—and the image from the sketch came to life in his mind.

"I took the garden path back from the stables . . . but when you were not outside, I thought you might already be . . . asleep." Nicholas saw her eyes take in the jacket and cravat he had tossed aside. Her gaze lingered on his rolled-up sleeves and bare arms.

"Our time together this afternoon was too brief." He extended a hand to her, and she took it. He drew her up onto the top step and into his arms. "I must warn you that you have created an insatiable appetite in me for what I sampled today."

Her lips opened under his and Nicholas tasted the sweetness and smiled even as he kissed her.

"And I thought I was the only one who was suffering," she murmured.

Her fingers worked the buttons of his shirt. The feel of her cold hands touching his warm skin sent another surge of desire through him.

Nicholas led her to the middle of the attic studio. She frowned slightly as her gaze took in the paintings he'd uncovered and displayed around the room. The look of uncertainty in her eyes pulled at his heart.

"There are so few who know that I use this place as my studio . . . and even fewer who have seen any of my work. I am not . . . traditional in what I do. Perhaps, what I lack in . . ."

"I would account myself only a fairly knowledgeable critic of the fine arts, but I have seen enough of the acclaimed works to say your work places you easily among the greatest of those artists painting today."

"These are . . ." Jane shook her head and spoke softly. "You mock me."

"Hardly." He cupped her face and looked steadily into her eyes. "I want to make love to you, Jane. Here . . . with these works of genius . . . with these windows to your past around us."

He kissed her until she was leaning into his touch and

her hands began to move down over his chest. He caught her wrist as it reached his waist.

"We should not rush through this. Not this time."

Jane's eyes rounded as he pulled the narrow cot to the middle of the room. Around them flickering candles and glistening paintings provided both light and color, and he drew her down onto the cot. Once again, his mouth feasted on hers. She shivered with anticipation and leaned back on her arms as he started unfastening her shirt. With a deliberateness that he hoped would not prove his own undoing, he caressed each inch of exposed skin . . . until he reached the top of her chemise. There he found not only the linen undergarment, but also a specially made inner shirt, one doubled in thickness and tight to bind and conceal her breasts. He smiled at the dozen tiny hooks that appeared as he finished opening the outer shirt.

"Do you remember the first day we met in the woods?" he asked softly.

"Yes," she replied.

Laying her down on the cot, he carefully undid hook after hook. When the task was done and the inner shirt lay open, he looked at the buttons of the chemise.

"Just to torment me," he murmured. "Well, two can play . . ."

As he unfastened each button, he pressed his lips to the newly revealed expanse of skin, causing her to draw in her breath sharply and grip the sides of the cot as he reached the soft curves of her belly. He lifted his head and slipped the shirts and the straps of the chemise over her shoulders. Sliding his hands lightly over the smooth lines of her collarbone, he drew a line with his index finger down into the valley between her breasts. Freed of the constraining clothing, the perfect ivory flesh and the hard, extended tips rose and fell. She arched her back as he cupped one breast and ran his thumb across her nipple.

"So beautiful . . . and ready to be tasted."

One of Jane's hands slipped over his hip and touched the burgeoning manhood trapped in his breeches. He slid down along her body, moving himself beyond the reach of her hand.

"No, my sweet. You cannot move, and you are mine to torment." He gave her a look of mock warning before lowering his mouth to her waiting breast. She moaned and he felt her fingers thread their way into his hair when he started to tease and suckle.

This afternoon they had not had time for discovering each other's bodies. Their lovemaking had been passionate, powerful, and direct. It had not been a time for seduction and exploration. But Nicholas was determined to give her just that now.

He let his mouth trail to the other breast where he feasted until her breaths became ragged. He slid still lower, and his lips kissed their way down her soft, smooth stomach. His fingers were deliberately slow as they undid her breeches and began pushing them over her hips.

"Nicholas . . ."

Jane's hands reached for him as he moved down on the cot and removed her boots and stockings and peeled the breeches from her legs.

"Come to me," she whispered hoarsely. "I need you now."

"Yes . . . and I need you."

Her naked limbs were a glimpse of eternal beauty glowing before his eyes. They were unmatched in art. Not Michelangelo or Botticelli or Titian—or any of the modern masters, either—had ever captured the curve of this foot where it bowed gently from toe to heel. He lifted it and placed his lips there. He slipped his fingers over the tapered lines of the ankle to the softly muscled calf and the perfect machinery of this knee. He kissed the dimpled skin and smiled at the little panting sounds of her breathing. With her foot now resting in his lap, his hands caressed with the lightest touch the firm flesh of her thigh until they reached the apex of their journey, that tantalizing triangle of hair and the moist folds beneath.

He saw her breathing heavily, her breasts rising and falling with no discernible regularity. But her dark eyes were watching every move he made.

"Nicholas . . . I never . . . I . . ."

This was the response he'd been waiting for, so he pressed his mouth to her moist flesh. He heard her moan as he entered and stroked her with fingers and lips and tongue, suckling the very center of her womanhood until he knew she had entered a paradise of bliss.

When she cried out softly, clutching at the cot as her body arched and shuddered, he knew that no artistic joy could ever rival the natural joys that lovers share.

Slowly he relented in his ministrations as her waves of ecstasy subsided—for the moment.

"Nicholas," she whispered, reaching for him.

He sat up just out of her reach and discarded his shirt. "Not yet, my love."

Her eyes were smoky pools of ebony as she watched him stand and remove the rest of his clothes. When he tossed his breeches aside, her gaze narrowed as it fell upon his erect manhood.

A soft blush colored her cheeks and spread down her neck and breasts. "Is it possible that you . . . and I . . . ."

"Let me show you the possibilities."

Moving back between her legs, he pressed her down against the cot and kissed her as the head of his staff entered the slick folds. She drew a sharp breath as he drove into her, and he silenced her cries with his mouth.

Passion that he'd never known overwhelmed him when her tight sheath closed around him. When her hands clutched at his buttocks, he felt her drawing him even deeper, demanding that he drive into her again and again, filling her sweet depths with his own pulsating flesh. Together they found the rhythm of the dance, and together they rose to what he was sure must be the very heights of Elysium.

When her release came, it came with the sweet abandon of the innocent, triggering a matching explosion in his head and in his loins. He muffled his cries against her throat as he continued to drive into her, pouring his seed into her body. As he came, she wrapped her legs around his hips and kept him locked in her arms and in her body.

A long time passed before either could speak or even catch their ragged breaths.

"How long can we stay up here without being discovered?" he managed to ask finally. He lifted his head and looked into her beautiful flushed face.

"A long, long time. Months probably. No one ever comes up here, but me."

"Good." With their bodies still joined, he felt himself hardening again inside of her. He rolled Jane on the cot, until she was on top. He took hold of her buttocks and drew her tightly against him, eliciting a surprised gasp. He gazed at her full breasts pressed against him—the cascading ringlets of hair framing her smiling face. He was once again fully erect.

"You want to make love again?"

"Actually, I was hoping for a tour of this magnificent gallery of art. But, of course, I shall need little entice-ments between the works, to keep my attention and sus-tain my self-esteem. I am very limited in my talents, you know."

"I fear I cannot agree on that score at the moment," she said, raising an eyebrow and then smiling. "But what kind of enticement did you have in mind, sir?"

He let his gaze travel around the large space. "Let me see . . . after we have finished with this cot, we would need to make love with you on my lap in that chair. And perhaps once against the wall . . . and once again with you facing the wall. We definitely need to try the strength of your worktable. And then that beam cer-tainly has an interesting angle to it, I should say . . ."

Laughing, she pounded her fist lightly on his chest. "You are not planning to take advantage of a poor artist now, are you?"

"Of course I am." He pulled her knees until she was upright and straddling him. Lifting her bottom, he low-ered her again, driving deep inside of her. "Indeed, I am planning to make love to you many times, in many ways, until you beg me to stop. And then I shall set a condition for stopping . . . temporarily . . . and you shall be forced to agree."

"What . . . what is the condition?" she asked vaguely, rotating her hips slowly on top of him.

"That you marry me, Jane."

*   *   *

The dawn had barely broken in the eastern sky when Jane cast a last wistful eye over her work area and started down the steps. She had sent Nicholas away about an hour ago, after convincing him that she would definitely make an appearance downstairs in a couple of hours.

It had taken longer than she'd expected to put her attic workplace back in order, she thought, fighting back a smile.

Marry me, Jane. Marry me, Jane.

Her smile disappeared. Like some liturgical chant, Nicholas's words kept repeating over and over in her head. She had avoided answering him, but she could not prevent the warming power of it over her heart and her mind. Even to dream of spending the rest of her life with him was far beyond anything she'd ever allowed herself to hope.

She loved him. She knew that. And indeed, she had found the most passionate and fulfilling moments of her life in his arms. This, she had thought, would be the extent of it. It was all she could have hoped for. A moment and a memory.

But to *marry* him . . .

Jane still had a smile on her face when she opened the door of her bedchamber and stepped into the half-darkness of the room.

"Late night for you. Or should I say 'early morning'?"

Startled, Jane turned around and found Clara sitting on her bed. The young woman's back was against the headboard, her face hidden in the shadows. Her slippered feet were stretched out on the undisturbed bedclothes.

"Early would be correct," Jane answered brightly. She had an impulse to run over and hug her sister, but fought it. This foolish giddiness was a sensation so new, but she didn't want to frighten anyone. "Good morning, Clara. Why are you up so early?"

Without waiting for an answer, she laid out underclothes and a dress. The water in the basin was cold, but she didn't care. She dipped a washcloth in it, and started to undress.

"I have been up all night."

"Are you feeling unwell?" Jane asked over her shoulder, thankful for the darkness of the room for it occurred to her that her fair skin might show the marks of Nicholas's attentions.

"You might say that."

"Then why are you here? You should have stayed in bed. I shall go and ask Fey to bring up . . . "

"*Nothing* that Fey could bring up would make me feel better." Clara's feet swung over the bed and made contact with the floor.

Jane heard the touch of sadness and temper in Clara's voice, and she paused in her washing and wrapped herself in a linen wrap.

"What is wrong?" she asked softly, moving toward the younger woman.

"*You* are what is wrong."

Jane came to an abrupt stop. "I . . . ?"

"Yes . . . you and your thoughtlessness." Clara stood up. "You and your lack of consideration for anyone else in this family."

Jane bristled at the charge. "What is Sir Thomas accusing me of now?"

"This is not about Father." Clara moved out of the shadows. The tearstains and swollen eyelids were a shock to Jane. "And this is not about Mother. This is about me, Jane—your only sister—the one in this family that you have always claimed you cared for."

Jane opened her mouth to ask more questions, but immediately shut it as a sickening feeling gripped her middle.

"What do you have against me?" Fresh tears rolled down Clara's cheeks as she came within a step. "Why is it that you . . . are so set against . . . seeing me happy?"

"I . . . I do not . . ."

"It is jealousy, is it not?" Clara attacked before Jane had a chance to find her words. "You have managed to ruin your own life. Now you cannot accept the fact that I might have a chance . . . a chance to get away from the disgrace you brought upon our family. You are jealous of me ever being happy."

"That is not true."

"You are lying," the younger woman snapped. "Why

else would you intentionally keep him away from me? Sir Nicholas came to Ireland for *me*! He wanted *me*! But you could not stop yourself from hurting me. You had to take the happiness that should have been *mine*."

"*You* were the one who pushed him away." Jane was able to find her voice as the arguments roiled inside her. "You . . . you were the one who forced me to come with you . . . and then pushed him at me."

"So it was right for you to take advantage of my shyness? You could not let him be . . . or give me time to . . . to find myself. To become accustomed to him. It was right for you to take him away to Ballyclough yesterday . . . and the day before that? Do not deny any of it, Jane. I am no fool. I know he was with you that day, as well."

The thought ripping through Jane's mind at that instant was that Clara didn't know about last night. She had no way of knowing the two of them had been making love all night only two floors above where they now stood.

"What do you hope to accomplish by any of this, Jane?" The younger sister seethed. "Do you believe you are good enough to become his wife? Are you so selfish that you will not hesitate to bring shame to another family's honor? And what about your dear Shanavests? How will you manage to keep him while you are riding about the countryside until dawn . . . like this . . . with groups of ruffians and marauders and *traitors*?"

Tears sprang to Jane's eyes. She sat heavily on the edge of a chair. She tried to swallow the painful knot in her throat and speak.

"But there was no marriage proposal. I . . . I was told that he . . . did not ask . . . for . . ."

"He did not ask . . . *yet*!" Clara snapped. "But given the time, he would . . . he still will . . . if you *let* him be."

Jane turned her face away as tears slid down her cheeks. She felt Clara's hand on her knee as the younger woman crouched beside her.

"I have never asked anything of you, Jane, but I ask you this. Please do not ruin this chance for me." Her voice was no more than a soft whisper. "If you ever loved me as a sister . . . if you care even a little for me . . . then please give me a chance to win his affection." Clara clutched Jane's hand. "I need this chance. I need him to take me away from this place . . . from this godforsaken land. I promise to make him happy, Jane. I will be as good for him as he is for me."

Jane turned around and looked into her sister's face through a sheen of tears. "I cannot tell him whom to marry . . . or whom to love. That is not the kind of man he is."

"Then go away, Jane. Leave Woodfield House and stay with one of the dozens of friends you have around here. Let *me* convince him." Clara squeezed Jane's hand hard. "Please."

Chapter 23

The doors of the study were closed and locked. On direct orders from Sir Thomas, the arrival of their visitor was not announced to the mistress of the house or to anyone else. This meeting was highly private.

The message delivered to Sir Robert Musgrave not long after dawn had explained Sir Thomas's genuine interest and willingness to help in whatever way he could to arrest the leaders of the local rebel faction. In addition, the former magistrate had hinted at methods and even informants that he was willing to share in order to guarantee success.

By midmorning Musgrave was at Woodfield House, and whatever differences of opinion the two men had harbored before meant nothing now. They were both keen on achieving the same results.

Sir Thomas listened intently to the new developments in Buttevant. And he was careful not to show any signs of surprise when the magistrate informed him that Jane and Sir Nicholas were the ones who had relocated the papist widow's children. He was also told about the baronet coming back after the mother.

"An act of charity, I have no doubt," Sir Thomas explained with a dismissive wave. "But tell me . . . this woman . . . where is she now?"

"My understanding is that she was taken to the village of Ballyclough."

"Ballyclough?" the older man growled. "How do you know that?"

"It appears Dr. Forrest was sent for by Parson Adams

to see to an ailing Irish boy. The doctor has indicated that the mother . . . this woman Kathleen . . . now does indeed reside in the parsonage."

"And you truly believe this woman can identify Egan?"

"I do, sir," the magistrate asserted. "The issue of who exactly gave the money to the woman is insignificant compared with the fact that the two *must* have met. Otherwise the Shanavests would not go to the trouble of removing the other woman . . . the blind widow . . . from the cottage."

"Very astute, sir. But you have been unsuccessful in gaining Kathleen's cooperation before. What changes now?"

"I plan to be more . . . persuasive. We shall arrange for her children to be brought in as well when we arrest her." A grim smirk thinned the man's lips. "I have heard she has a small daughter. If need be, we shall give the little chit over to one of our jailers and let the mother watch. The woman will be telling us more than what we need to know."

"I insist that you leave the children out of it," Sir Thomas snapped, rising to his feet. Wrestling with his temper, he turned and walked to the window. "You err in arresting the mother while she is staying at the parsonage, as well. Henry Adams will not take kindly to having people dragged out from beneath his own roof, and we do not want our own people rising against us."

"As magistrate, sir, I have the right to—"

"Keep peace!" the older man roared. "Your job is to maintain at least the appearance of peace and justice in the king's name. You let that woman go once. You cannot take her out of the care of Reverend Adams without having a damned good reason."

"She is my strongest connection with Egan right now."

"That does not say much for your efforts, does it, Sir Robert?"

Musgrave was red in the face when he bolted to his feet. "If your purpose in inviting me here today was to insult me, sir, then—"

"Blast your thin skin, Sir Robert, and get hold of yourself."

"I say . . . !"

"Focus, man! Put aside all this wasted effort that will surely come to naught." Sir Thomas clasped his hands behind his back and walked toward Musgrave. "To catch these foxes, we must make bigger plans. My suggestion is this . . ." He stopped, frowning at the man. "But perhaps you are not interested in succeeding."

"Of course I wish to succeed!" Musgrave sputtered.

"Then this is our plan. Carry out a punitive raid on one of the larger villages. You have the authority to do so. But before the attack, make certain . . . in a discreet way . . . that word of the raid leaks out. Meanwhile, have your men keep watch. Lay a trap. The Shanavests *will* show up."

"But there is no guarantee that any of their leaders will be there."

"There is no guarantee that you won't be buggered in your sleep tonight by the man in the moon, either!" Sir Thomas glared disapprovingly at the magistrate. "I will tell you the secret to succeeding here. You must plan carefully and then execute those plans quickly. Today is Wednesday. Plan the raid for tomorrow night. The word should get out no sooner than tomorrow at noon and only after some of your own people have been placed in strategic places in and around the village. This will not give the Whiteboys much time to react. One of their leaders . . . if not more . . . *will* show up to assist with the villagers."

"As far as these people that you say I should place in the village." Musgrave tugged on an ear. "I have no one whom I could put there . . . without raising suspicions."

"That is why I wanted us to plan this together." Sir Thomas smiled. "I can be of help."

The night air was heavy with the feel of an upcoming storm. The two men standing in the paddock were the only ones outside.

"I was in the forge with the smith when she left. I didn't even see the lass go." The trainer leaned a wide shoulder against a post and made a great show of poking at the tobacco in his pipe.

Nicholas was receiving the same answers from Paul

that he'd heard from everyone else. He was being thwarted everywhere he'd turned with his questions. Each person seemed to have been prepared. Each said the same thing. They didn't know where Jane had gone.

Nicholas wasn't convinced, though, and the way they all spoke to him triggered a feeling of anxiety in him that he could not shake off.

When he'd seen no sign of her by midmorning, he'd stormed down to the stables and found Queen Mab gone. Deciding that she must be at Ballyclough, he had saddled his horse and raced across the Irish countryside after her. Though Parson Adams was not at home, the housekeeper had assured him that Miss Jane had not come visiting the parsonage that morning. But, of course, he was welcome to stay and speak with Reverend Adams when he returned. Nicholas had not bothered, and had rushed back to Woodfield House instead, thinking she might be back.

In any other family or household, he would have had some success in questioning the parents as to their daughter's whereabouts. But Lady Purefoy's breezy response, "I long ago gave up keeping account of Jane's coming and going," had been a dark reminder of how *little* she was cared for by this family. Sir Thomas appeared to have even less interest than his wife, and questioning Clara had only managed to sharpen his ongoing suspicion that something had gone terribly wrong. Rather than answering him, the young woman had simply extended her previous invitation of acting as his guide, if Jane was unavailable. When he had declined, she'd done her best to try to engage him in a conversation regarding horses and racing.

He had struggled, but somehow managed not to be rude.

And Paul was being equally unhelpful. " 'Tis hardly amiss, sir, for herself to be off like this for a day or so."

Nicholas forced away the dark thoughts in his mind and watched the wreath of smoke around Paul's head. He tried to remind himself that it was completely within reason that she may have received a message after he'd left her this morning. But the anxiety wouldn't ease up . . . for he was certain she would have left him some word. "How long does her family wait before they grow curious about where she is?"

The arching of the stable master's bristled eyebrow gave Nicholas his answer.

"How long before *you* become concerned?"

Paul turned his attention to his pipe again, giving Nicholas his answer to that as well. The man knew where Jane was, and he wasn't concerned.

"I've spent the better part of that lassie's life worrying about her," he said evasively.

"At least tell me that she is in no danger," Nicholas pressed doggedly.

"I wisht that I could, sir. But the truth of the matter is, Sir Nicholas, ye might just resign yerself to what ye be feeling today. Miss Jane is not like any other lass. For a long while now, she's answered to no man—nor woman, neither. She's been given her own head for so long that I don't think she even remembers the feel of the bit between her teeth or the lash about the flanks, either. She's fierce in her independence, and that's all there is to it. So if ye be set to care for her, ye might also set yerself that you'll be having no peace of mind this side of the grave. 'Tis good for ye to be facing this now."

Paul's gaze was thoughtful when it met Nicholas's.

"Now, sir . . . if ye be looking for something . . . someone safe, then ye should be looking up that hill, for it appears as Miss Clara's giving up waiting on ye."

Nicholas glanced in the direction of the house, annoyed at the sight of Clara, candle in hand, making her way down the hill. As he turned back to Paul, he found the man already halfway to the stable door, doffing his cap to the young woman as he went.

"I should have known that your love of horses would draw you here. My guess is you could probably spend endless hours with my father's trainer. He is quite knowledgeable on the topic." Clara smiled brightly as she reached him. "But after everything I have heard of your own involvement and interest, Sir Nicholas, you cannot possibly be lacking anything."

He found the false adoring tone repellent, but he kept his views to himself. "Were you looking for someone down here, Miss Clara? If it was Paul with whom you wished to speak, I can still call him before he gets away."

"No. I had no wish to speak to Paul." She ran her free hand up and down her bare arm. "I should have brought a wrap. The night is far colder than I thought."

But then again, he thought grimly, a wrap would have defeated the purpose behind the fashionably revealing dresses Clara was beginning to wear. Be fair, he chided himself. All his frustration over Jane's absence was getting the best of him. He knew he had to get away.

"If you will excuse me, miss, I was just on my way back to the house."

He did not wait for a response from her before starting toward the paddock gate.

"Do you mind if I walk with you?" she asked a bit breathlessly, catching up to him. "We haven't had much time alone together since you've arrived, and I have been missing . . ."

"Do not do this, Clara," Nicholas barked, stopping abruptly and turning to face her. "I find this to be a very deceitful game . . . and entirely unworthy of you."

"But what do you mean?"

"Do not pretend that there is something romantic between us—or that there ever could be." Her eyes were large and innocent-looking, and they glistened in the lamplight. But Nicholas felt no pity. "I have no doubt that your father has already passed on the gist of our conversation. And regardless of what your mother may be planning, I am *not* interested in you, Clara, and I cannot express my feelings more clearly than that."

Her chin trembled, but she held her head high. "But that is now, sir. If you gave us a chance . . ."

"No." Impatient, he took a step away, but then turned around again, facing her. "I know you are young, but you must try to understand that giving 'a chance' to two people as different as we are will not change things. I do not want you for my wife. And in spite of whatever foolishness is going through your head at this moment, I know that you don't want me, either. But this does not mean that my rejection should be the end of it all for you. You are a beautiful and intelligent young woman.

You have great promise. And you should be doing your own choosing, rather than allowing yourself to be guided by the whims of your parents."

Tears stood out in her blue eyes, and Nicholas gentled his voice.

"There are many men out there, far more deserving than I. In time, you will meet someone who will be your perfect match. Until then, do not throw away your pride by settling for someone whom you can never love."

"There are many kinds of love, Sir Nicholas."

"There is only one kind of love fit for a husband and wife," he responded roughly. "And I, for one, intend to have it."

Clara turned away, and Nicholas frowned at his harsh tone.

"You deserve better, Clara," he said as gently as he could. "Do not settle for anything less than the right man."

Without another word, Nicholas strode up the path. When he reached the house, he turned to look at her. She had blown out the light in her lamp, and he could just make out the hooped expanse of her skirts' light material where she stood motionless in the dark.

What he could not see were the uncontrollable sobs that were wracking her body as she wept.

Two full days had passed, and Jane still was not back.

Alexandra sat on the bed and ran her fingers over the delicate cloth of the gown that Fey had carried into her room only minutes earlier. The workmanship was excellent. The design was exactly as she'd desired. But what good would this garment be if the one it had been made for was nowhere to be found?

Ah, but where could she be?

Tomorrow night was the ball, and still no one seemed to care where the older Purefoy sister had gone . . . or when she was to return. And if that were not distressing enough, Alexandra had been faced with having to find excuses for Nicholas's empty chair at dinner.

Oh, she knew he was at Woodfield House . . . when he wasn't out combing the countryside. He, too, was looking for Jane. She was sure of it. His features had been set in an expressionless mask, showing nothing of what she knew he must be feeling inside. His words gave away even less.

In recent years, when she'd thought about Nicholas settling down and marrying, she'd never considered the situation might also entail any of this pain that he was going through now. Women, in general, had been plentiful in Nicholas's life. Foolishly, she'd assumed that taking the next step would be as simple as picking one from the flock of eligible heiresses. She had been so wrong.

Alexandra left her bedroom and went directly to Jane's attic studio. When she'd run into Nicholas before dinner, she had seen him going in that direction.

The quiet of the upper floors pressed on her ears like January cold. Every servant in the household was apparently downstairs, bustling about under the sharp eye of Lady Purefoy as the house was prepared for tomorrow night's ball.

She knocked on the door before opening it. Nicholas appeared at the top of the stairs, his face hopeful for a moment before seeing who it was. He was wearing no jacket or tie. His sleeves were rolled up to his elbows and the white shirt lacked the crispness with which he always presented himself.

"May I come up?" she asked softly.

"I assume she has not returned."

She shook her head and climbed the stairs. Alexandra wished she could be the bearer of good news, but other than just wanting to be here with him, she was at a loss as to how she could help.

At the top of the stairs, she paused, not trying to hide her awe at the display of Jane's work. Unlike the first time that she'd been here, when everything had been hidden beneath covers, nearly every painting was now arranged for viewing, and the space was ablaze with the light of dozens of candles. If she overlooked the rough and inadequate finish of the room, she could easily imagine that she was in one of the finest galleries in Europe.

"So much talent," she murmured. "I am so glad she has decided at least to display her work up here."

Nicholas had moved to the opposite end of the room

and did not respond, if he heard her. She watched him uncovering another canvas and looking carefully at it, before placing it against a wall with others that were similar in color and theme. Alexandra realized he was the one who'd taken it on himself to uncover her incredible gift. She picked up a candle from one of the tables.

"She is so prolific a painter." She admired the sheer amount of work. There was much here that she hadn't seen on that first day. "I never had a chance to speak to Jane about coming here and looking at more of her work. I hope she doesn't mind . . ."

The words died in Alexandra's throat as she heard a low curse. Nicholas was crouched down before a canvas he'd just uncovered. She wanted to go to him and see for herself what had affected him so. She held back, though, silent as death while her son sat for what seemed like eternity.

Alexandra remembered her own reaction to the canvases Jane had painted of the seasons' passage and the destruction of an Irish village. Finally, she could wait no longer and broke the silence.

"If someone were to convince Jane . . . to tell her about the genius so apparent in her work. If someone were to convey to her the powerful sense of reality she depicts in every painting. The balance, the structure, the coloring, the use of light and shadow. All of these things. Perhaps these paintings could provide a new beginning for her somewhere beyond the walls of Woodfield House."

He remained engrossed in the work.

"This family does not deserve her. They have no appreciation for the person and the artist she is." She whispered her feelings. "These paintings must be shown at the Royal Academy in London. Or, if not, then on the Continent."

Alexandra didn't know how far the relationship between Nicholas and Jane had progressed. Though she was sure the beginnings were there, she had no way of knowing their level of commitment to each other. Understanding her own son's independent and rebellious nature, she could not pressure him or ask his intentions, but at the same time she decided to explain the plans that had gradually been developing in her mind for most of this week.

"I should like to invite Jane to come back to England with us. From there, if she wants, she can come back with me to Brussels." There was no reaction to her words, and Alexandra slowly approached Nicholas. "I think she should be introduced into the top artistic circles at Court. I am certain that Sir Joshua Reynolds, your neighbor in Leicester Square, would love to take her under his wing. He is a powerful force at the Royal Academy. He is also tremendously jealous of other portraitists, of course, but I have great confidence in her work and know that he and others will see her genius. After a lifetime of receiving no encouragement here, she could use some genuine praise . . ."

A gasp escaped her as she glanced over Nicholas's shoulder at the canvas in his hand. Her candle flickered, and she dashed a tear from her face.

The small canvas portrayed five bodies hanging from gibbets in a town square. The background of faces in the crowd and the buildings framing the scene were only muted brushstrokes—an effect that highlighted the shocking reality of those who'd been executed. Their condition cried out from the canvas. It was obvious this was a work that had been completed much earlier than anything else that Alexandra had seen, but still Jane had managed to capture the tragic emotion of the scene with power and style.

"I have asked her to marry me."

Nicholas's voice drew her gaze to his solemn profile.

"I believe she was frightened by the offer—and perhaps by my persistence. I should have given her time to become accustomed to the idea before pressuring her. Now I have driven her away." His fingers touched the three-quarter view of the man's body hanging in the foreground. "He has been dead for nine years, and she is still in love with him."

"Devoted to him," Alexandra gently corrected. "And she will always have a sense of loss when she thinks of him. But I am certain she thinks of him less now than she did then. And that does not mean she is incapable of loving again."

He rose to his feet, and she saw the doubt clouding his features.

"We must remember that life has not been kind to her," she continued. "She has been alone—held responsible for a scandalous act from such an early age. Regardless of how she feels for you, she undoubtedly sees so many obstacles that stand between the two of you."

"Damn her reputation and everyone else here."

"You can afford to ignore society's view of your life and future. You are a man, first of all, and you have intentionally worked at establishing a reputation for recklessness. As far as the *ton* is concerned, once you do settle, they will recall your roguish ways only as youthful wildness. But Jane knows nothing of how your society works. All she knows is that you were reputable enough to be considered the ideal husband for her sister, but now you are interested in her." She followed him when he moved away. "If she were any other woman, she would have jumped at your offer. Clara would have jumped at it. But not Jane."

"She might at least tell me how she feels . . . then I will know what is to be done."

"But she is." She placed a hand on Nicholas's arm. "Nick, you have all the blind stubbornness of your sex. Can you not see? In her own way, she *is* showing you her love by running away. She doesn't want to ruin your reputation by linking you with her . . ."

"Ha!" he laughed bitterly. "I have thought about what she should have to bear because of *me*!"

"But don't you see? She values you more than she does her own future and happiness." Her hand made a sweeping motion over the paintings in the room. "Look at this place—at all of this work. These paintings are a window to this woman's soul. The compassion with which she paints these canvases is the heart of the woman herself. And yet what does she do with this talent? She hides it in an attic. She covers it with cloth. She brings no attention to herself or her gifts." She met her son's burning gaze. "You have a great challenge ahead of you, Nick, but you are the man to handle it."

"How?"

His question tugged at her heart. It had been a long while since he'd asked her advice on anything.

"You must be here for her. You cannot give up. You must try to understand the motives behind each of her actions . . . the same way that you try to understand the message behind each of these paintings." She placed the candle on the worktable. "It will all work out. You two were made for each other. Just make her see it. Prove it to her."

As Alexandra descended the stairs and made her way back to her room, she knew the biggest challenge still lay with her. If these two were to have any chance of finding a future, she had to locate Jane now and bring her back.

The village, peacefully perched on a curl of the Blackwater River, erupted not an hour after sunset in an explosion of activity. They were coming.

The western sky still glowed with the last shreds of orange and red when a half-dozen masked Whiteboys came silently out of the darkness on foot, led by a single rider dressed all in black—but for the white smock of the Shanavests. The news swept through the village like the wind, and each cottage sprang to life as the inhabitants roused themselves.

The entire village was to feel the blade of the King's justice for their history of helping the Shanavests. Indeed, the dragoons were coming.

Disbelief quickly faded as panic chilled their souls. The villagers knew what their fate would be if they didn't escape. They'd heard of the barbarism that had been inflicted on other towns larger than their own. The horrors were nearly unspeakable.

Now was not the time for packing the treasures of a lifetime. Now was not the time to tarry at all. They were coming, and the shock of the news quickly gave way to action.

The poorer villagers—those with less to part with— were the first to start down the river road to the place where the bog land offered the best protection. They could all hide there for weeks, if need be, deep in the marshes that flooded each spring with the rising of the river. If the dragoons decided to leave their horses at the edges of the murky swamps and follow, then the villagers would push beyond, leaving the bogs in the dead of a moonless night, climbing into the hills, and making their way to the south.

But where would they go then? they wondered as they gathered their children and the few belongings that they could carry. Where?

The torches of a hundred mounted men lit up the road on the far side of the river. As the leader of the Shanavests ushered the last and more resistant of the fugitives along, the raiders closed to within a league or two of the deserted village. Looking back, the mounted Shanavests saw the advance riders reach the village bridge, and it was only a moment later that the screams began to cut through the night.

"Old Rohane's cottage," someone from the group gasped.

"I went to their door, but there was no one inside," another man explained.

"They are not with us," a voice from the dark called out.

"My wee Kevin is with them, too," a woman cried.

Egan touched another member of the Shanavests on the shoulder. "Move them on. I'll go back for those missing."

Without paying any heed to the man's immediate objection, Egan spurred Mab back toward the village. The main body of dragoons was still minutes away, and the screams that now were recognizable to be those of a woman were continuing. They seemed to be coming from the livery stable sitting on the riverbank by the bridge itself. Drawing her pistol from her belt, Egan dismounted in the shadows and ran toward the building.

When she pulled open the heavy door, the acrid smell of smoke greeted her. Panicky livestock pressed to escape through the same opening. Egan pushed her way through them and stepped into the smoky darkness.

The first cold flash of fear clawed at her when she realized the cries of the woman actually were retreating from her. She felt her way quickly across the stable floor and saw two people slip out the door leading to the smith's forge. She reached the door in seconds, only to find it already barred from the outside.

She could no longer hear a cry for help, and a sickening chill crept up her spine. She sensed the presence of others in the stable. It was a trap.

Egan whirled around and saw soldiers coming out of every corner of the darkened stable. Pistols and swords glinted dully in the dim light. She could hear more outside, and she knew that the dragoons across the river would be here in a moment. Once they surrounded the building completely . . .

Someone doused a burning blanket in a corner near the door that she had used to enter. Another one shouted to others outside.

"We have him. We have Egan."

She pressed her back against the barred door and looked frantically about for any means of escape. Someone with a torch came in at the door to her left.

Pointing her pistol at one and then another of the steadily closing circle, she realized her only route of escape lay in shooting one and then trying to run through the dozen drawn weapons. Not a very good plan, she thought, considering that there were probably quite a few more waiting outside.

Egan drew her dagger with the other hand. She would kill first before they took her down. She took a step toward the approaching group.

"The magistrate's order," someone shouted, coming in the far end of the stable with another lantern. "Take him alive. He must be taken alive."

The distraction was all Egan needed, and she leaped into action. As she charged the two men farthest to her left, she spotted a rope hanging from the high rafters and leading to a loft. Perhaps if she could just get from there to . . . to where?

Screaming Gaelic curses as she attacked, she delivered a sharp kick to the first one's groin, whirling and slashing at the hand of the man holding the torch. He cried out in anger and shock, but the torch fell to the ground, and Egan leaped past him as the dry straw immediately crackled and caught fire beneath her feet.

Tucking the pistol into her belt, she jumped at the rope and climbed a couple of feet. The shouts were echoing around her and she felt a soldier's hand grab her boot. Before he could drag her down, she managed to draw her pistol and fire. The man screamed and fell back as the bullet struck his foot. Someone else already had a grip on her neck, but she swung the pistol hard, striking him across the face and knocking him into several soldiers behind him.

The flames were spreading fast around their feet now, and the soldiers were in total disarray. Seizing her chance, Egan climbed the rope as quickly as she could, expecting a bullet to end her escape at any moment. Her mask and hat were dangling down her back, but she didn't pause or look back. Instead, she pulled herself hand over hand until she could clamber into the loft.

The smoke was thick and she could hear the shouts of the dragoons. Working her way through the mounds of hay, she found a shuttered window that she kicked open. In a moment she was out on the sloping thatch of the roof.

Egan climbed quickly, trying not to think of what would happen if a section of the roof gave way. The smoke was billowing up through gaps in the thatch. She stood up and glanced at the mayhem surrounding the stable below. Dragoons—afoot and on horse—were running here and there, clearly in disorder because the village was empty.

Or because Egan had eluded them . . . so far.

She knew it would not be long before the soldiers made their way to the loft and then to the roof.

Somewhere below, she heard the neigh of Queen Mab. Scurrying to the end of the roof, she peered over and saw her horse rising on her back legs and pawing furiously at the air and at the soldiers who were trying to capture her.

Flames appeared through the smoke, licking the dry thatch and sending sparks crackling into the air. Egan climbed to the peak. There was a lower slate-roofed building across a narrow alley, but she also saw three dragoons already waiting by that building.

"Jump, Egan! Jump!"

She recognized Patrick's shout, and a thrill of hope lifted her spirits. Crossing a patch of open ground at the edge of the village, a dozen Shanavests on horseback raced toward her.

The encroaching flames were beginning to light up the roof like an inferno, and she realized she had no choice but to jump across. Backing up, Egan ran a couple of steps and leaped for the slate roof of the next building. She landed hard on her ankle, but this was no time to be delicate. As she was scrambling to the edge, she heard an exchange of pistol fire. Peering over the side of the building, she saw the mounted Shanavests swarming the soldiers and Mab. While a dozen of them fought fiercely with the dragoons, two of them pulled her horse away.

She jumped again without hesitation, again feeling her ankle when she hit the ground. The pain burned through, nearly overwhelming her, but she limped to the horse and pulled herself onto Mab's back.

There were whistles and shouts. Surrounded by the masked group, Egan and the rest withdrew as speedily as they'd arrived, galloping across the fields away from the village. After passing through the first line of hedges, though, they wordlessly split into groups of twos and threes and headed off in different directions.

Egan found herself in the company of two masked Shanavests, Patrick and another on a horse she didn't recognize. She frowned at the man's back. He was a stranger, but one adept at the use of a sword . . . that she knew. Though he spoke in Gaelic, his accent was unfamiliar. There was, however, something distinctly familiar about his voice.

What perplexed her most, though, was that he was giving orders.

"After crossing the river, Patrick, I want you to take her east. I'll draw anyone coming after us to the north. You have a place to hide your horses."

"Aye, the same places we're always hiding them."

"Finn!" she whispered. She tried to get a better look, peering through the dark. The large, tricornered hat and the mask thwarted her efforts.

"Are you Finn?" she asked finally.

"Ye see, Egan, our Finn is not a ghost of Liam's making, after all," Patrick answered, riding to her right.

Before she could ask another question, they splashed into the shallows of the river and then continued to ford it. There was no sign of any followers. Her ankle was throbbing badly.

She stared at him again. For several years, she had known of Finn. Liam had used his name often in conveying key information to their group. He appeared to have many contacts in the English regiments as well as the volunteer militias. He had at times even seemed to know things that had to come from someone close to Ireland's Lord Lieutenant himself. In spite of his participation in the fighting tonight, she had never known him to step out of his usual role.

Indeed, she had never met him—or seen him—until now.

"Act as if nothing has happened," Finn told her as they prepared to separate on the far shore. "Resume your other life. Pretend you know nothing of tonight. They are bent on capturing you, and you must not allow them to succeed."

He turned and she watched him disappear quickly into the darkness. Patrick urged her to move, and she proceeded. But Egan's mind was racing with Finn's words.

Resume your other life . . . Resume your other life . . .

What other life? She no longer had any other life. Just as the hard slate roof of the stable had hurt her ankle, Clara's words had destroyed the already unsteady footing she was feeling at Woodfield House.

Though the pain shooting up her leg from her ankle hurt tremendously, the ache in her heart was hurting far worse.

Between the two wounds, Jane knew she had nothing to stand on.

Chapter 24

The housekeeper saw the curious glances of the cooks and servants and grooms—some working, some taking their breakfast—when she entered the servants' hall with the persistent guest on her heels. She simply had to put a stop to this. She turned and left the room with the woman still dogging her.

In the narrow corridor, still dark in the morning light, she whirled around. "Ye just cannot follow me about like this, m'lady. Certainly not on a morning such as this . . . with so much left to do before the rest of the house is up. I told ye once, and I'll tell ye a hundred times, if I must, but I cannot help ye find Miss Jane."

"But you *know* where she is," Alexandra persisted. "And by God, I am not giving up until you tell me where she is . . . or at least have someone take me to her. It is absolutely urgent that I should bring her back here for the ball this evening."

"But clearly she doesn't care to come back, m'lady. She wouldn't give a beggar's boot for any of this fanciness. I'm telling ye, mum, she doesn't care to hear their sniggering behind her back."

"This will be different, Fey." Alexandra lowered her voice and looked into the other woman's face. "I shall make the whole lot of them eat their words. We did not go to all our trouble to have them laugh at her. After tonight, your gentry will think twice before they ridicule her."

"A fine dress is nary enough, m'lady." Sadness shone in the gentle woman's eyes. "She has been hurt too much before. I do not think she wants to face such things again."

"But she must! She must come out of hiding and face them." She placed a hand on Fey's arm. "Do you think she is truly happy where she is, or how she is treated by . . . well, by certain people close to her? Does she not deserve better than what she is getting?"

"What I think and what will happen are hardly the same, m'lady."

"But they *can* be . . . with our interference," Lady Spencer quickly interjected. "I know them. They are like parrots . . . waiting for one to say something so they can all repeat it. And that is what will work to our advantage. That is what Jane needs. Someone to begin talking about her in a way that points out the noble qualities in her."

Fey stared at the floor, unconvinced.

"There is something else I am planning to do as well, but I need Jane's permission to do it."

Fey's eyebrows arched with interest.

"Without revealing very much to Lady Purefoy, I have received her permission to remake one of the parlors to a theme of my choosing." Alexandra lowered her voice. "I wish to make it into a gallery, but I need Jane's permission to use her paintings."

"Her paintings, m'lady?"

"Indeed. I wish to bring some of the canvases down from that attic work area of hers and display them about the room."

"But she . . . Miss Jane never . . . never shows her work to anyone." Fey wrung her apron in her hands.

"But Jane has tremendous talent. Unless they are complete boors, all of them will be impressed by her paintings far more than by anything else we can do." Lady Spencer nodded with conviction. "I am speaking the absolute truth, Fey, when I tell you Jane's work is equal to some of the greatest masterpieces of our time."

"But some of what . . . she paints . . ." The housekeeper frowned and shook her head. "I am no expert, mum, but some of it is a wee bit revealing of her . . . her private life."

"That is exactly why I need her . . . why you must

help me find her. Only Jane can decide what to show and what not." Alexandra took hold of the servant's hand. "If my praise of her as a person has no weight with these people, I know her talent will turn the tide. This is a perfect opportunity for Jane to come out before her peers. There could never be another chance like this anytime soon." She gentled her tone and met the woman's thoughtful gaze. "If nothing else, please take me to her so I can explain these things to her. The decision will be hers—but she has to be told, while there is still a little time left."

After a moment, a look of resolve replaced the indecision in the housekeeper's face. "No one else can be going with ye."

Alexandra nodded.

"And ye shall need to wait until midday, when I can find someone to spare for a few hours."

"Just tell me when, and I'll be ready."

With a book tucked under her arm, Clara once again took refuge in the gardens. The entire household continued to be in an uproar over the ordeal tonight, and the young woman had even found the privacy of her bedroom invaded by the dressmakers and seamstresses and servants who were ready to bathe her and do her hair and whatever else Lady Purefoy had ordered them to do.

And she was ashamed of all of it.

Clara couldn't forgive herself for the lunacy—for assuming that she was capable of seducing Sir Nicholas and getting him to change his earlier decision about asking for her hand. The cutting remarks he had delivered to her two nights ago had been as mortifying as they were sobering. Instead of learning from Henry's rejection earlier and trying to make a change in her life, more so than ever before she was trying to be her parents' puppet.

Clara moved deeper through the garden and thought of the injustice she had done to her older sister. Jane had gone away without a word to her of where she was going and how long she was staying away. Her older sister had done just as she had asked her to. And for what?

Henry was right. She was selfish. It was Jane who behaved selflessly . . . and deserved better.

Tears were running down her face by the time Clara
neared her favorite spot by the paddock. As she approached the hedge, the voices of two men engaged in a
tense conversation on the other side cut into her misery.

"I do not understand this at all, Captain," her father
was saying in an angry but hushed tone. "I have been
generous enough to offer him a plan for capturing these
leaders of the Whiteboys. It is not too much, I should
think, to expect Musgrave to be frank about what happened last night."

"As I said before, sir, he sends his regards and says
he intends to give you a full report tonight." The other
man's voice was apologetic. "I have been ordered to say
nothing more."

"But I am entertaining tonight." Sir Thomas seethed.
"My wife has a blasted ball planned that I must attend.
Come, Captain . . . you served me well when I was
magistrate. What did he find or whom did he arrest that
requires such secrecy?"

"I fear, Sir Thomas, that the present magistrate must
make his own explanations, sir."

"Out with it, Wallis. You were there. What happened?"

Clara cringed at her father's menacing tone now. She
could only imagine the man facing Sir Thomas must be
even more affected by his growing fury.

"I . . ."

"The devil take you. Did we succeed or not, man?"

There was a long pause.

"This . . . this must remain just between us, Sir
Thomas."

"As you wish," the older man growled impatiently.

"I only tell you this out of respect for our efforts
together."

"Indeed, Captain. We made a good team, you and I."

"Last night, we made no arrests, but we were able to
unmask the rebel Egan. That is all I can say. Our trou-
bles are far from being over, but the magistrate—as he
plans to explain to you tonight—is confident that we are
close to capturing the . . . the rebel."

Clara's hand was tightly clamped over her mouth as all she'd just heard continued to whirl in her mind. *They'd unmasked Egan.*

"I see." Sir Thomas's voice was far more subdued when he spoke again. "So, other than coming here and keeping anything of import from me, why do you want to search my stables? Does Sir Robert think I am hiding rebels in the hayloft?"

"The magistrate wishes to know if any horses were missing from the stables of any of the landowners last night. We are looking, in particular, for a large black horse . . . one similar to the mare that is often ridden by your daughter, Miss Jane."

Clara could wait not a minute longer. Clutching her stomach in an effort to ward off the queasiness rising into her throat, she ran frantically toward the house. She needed to get her cloak. She needed to find Jane . . . to warn her of what the dragoons already knew about her. If they had unmasked her, that meant they already knew her identity. They would be coming after her . . . here . . . possibly tonight!

She couldn't let this happen to Jane. Seeing a gardener on the path, she brushed away the tears and ordered him to go to ask Paul to ready a *good* horse for her. She had to find her sister . . . somehow.

Conor's blood was already on her hands. She could not bear to go through life with her sister's blood on them, too.

Jenny's cottage consisted of three rooms. In size and in its furnishings, it was far more comfortable than many a tenant's hovel. But still, for someone of Lady Spencer's quality, it would normally be considered hardly suitable for entertaining.

Jane, however, was relieved to see that the visitor was so comfortable in the cottage. She made no hint of finding anything offensive in Jenny's home. In fact, as Jane watched the two women chatting amiably before the small peat fire, she was extremely pleased with Alexandra's affability and natural charm in her manner toward Conor's aunt.

Jane waited, impatient to learn the reason for this unexpected visit. Nothing could have been wrong with Nicholas, or Lady Spencer would not be so calm, she decided. But there had to be a good reason. Fey and Paul would not, under normal circumstances, reveal Jane's whereabouts to anyone. Nonetheless, Alexandra had been brought here by their direction.

Jenny soon excused herself and left the two of them alone. Lady Spencer turned her sparkling eyes on Jane.

"I have seen your paintings."

"You have?" she replied, surprised.

"Yes. Jane, you have tremendous talent. I cannot tell you how impressed I was in seeing them. Your work is . . . inspiring!"

"I don't know if—"

"But I have a favor to ask of you," Alexandra said, going on to explain her elaborate plan of displaying some of Jane's paintings during the ball for the purpose of regaining the local English gentry's respect. Jane tried patiently to listen to everything the good lady said.

"But none of this I care one whit about," she interrupted finally, not wishing to give Lady Spencer any false hope by her continued silence.

"It is an artist's natural inclination to fear sharing her work with others. We all fear the rejection of an audience. None of us wishes to be embarrassed by criticism or even by some offhand remark. I believe it is quite normal to want to keep our work and ourselves safely in seclusion. Most of us claim that we only like to paint for ourselves."

"I do not *claim* that, Alexandra. I *do* paint for myself. To me, taking a brush to the canvas or charcoal to paper is not for the sake of creating a piece of art. I do it to let out the emotions that are trapped inside of me." Jane spoke passionately. She followed the other woman's gaze to the drawing tablet on the windowsill beside her. Jane had been sketching when Lady Spencer had arrived. "I hope you will forgive my bluntness, m'lady, but even if I had the slightest desire to share my work with others, these people would be among the last I would choose. Gaining the respect of my father's friends is not high on my list of what I wish to do with my life."

Jane wished she could get up and walk about the

room. She was feeling frustrated, crowded. But her bruised ankle stopped her.

"But, my dear, people need something to talk about. Rather than prattling on about the past over and over again, would it not be far more pleasant if they had something as thrillingly powerful as your art to discuss?"

"I care nothing for their pleasantries." Jane shook her head in disagreement. "I have never cared about what they think of me, but I refuse to put myself in a position of having to endure their criticism in any public arena. I do not need them, and they have no use for me. I am quite resigned to things as they are."

"I understand your bitterness." Alexandra leaned forward in her chair, lowered her voice, and touched Jane gently on the knee. "But can you not see that what I am trying to do has a purpose far grander than allowing you to make peace with a few provincial snobs who cling to the outdated prejudices of yesterday?"

Jane's heart started beating faster in her chest. She had feared that Lady Spencer's true purpose today had nothing to do with the paintings.

"My purpose is far more selfish. I am trying to do this for Nicholas . . . and for you," the older woman continued. "I have watched what your absence over the past few days has done to my son. For the first time in his life, Nicholas appears . . . well . . . lost. His spirit, his joie de vivre . . . it all seems to have lessened dramatically since you have been away from Woodfield House. And now, here I am . . . and I find the same kind of melancholy afflicting you."

Jane blinked back the tears suddenly burning her eyes.

"You two simply *must* resolve your differences." She clutched Jane's hand. "And though I know that nothing of your past matters at all to Nick, I also know that *you* would be far better resolved to a future together if you were able to walk away from some of the darkness of your past."

Jane had made love to Nicholas. She had given her body and her heart to him. But looking down now at her own black apparel, she knew she still had far to go to leave her past behind.

"My dear, I am here to help you in whatever way I

can. I have connections in England, you know, and there is always a way to improve on matters of the past." The intense blue eyes were pleading when they met Jane's. "Please allow me to make a difference."

The young woman looked down at her own fingers clutching at Alexandra's hand like a sailor gripping a lifeline. A desperateness was wracking her body and soul. By all the saints in heaven, she needed help in more ways than she could name. Jane believed her only chance of ever finding happiness again lay with Nicholas . . . and her love for him. Despite the endless tears she'd shed since arriving at Jenny's cottage, though, she didn't need to remind herself that she was still there because of her sister's request. She could not ruin Clara's chances when her own future was so uncertain.

"No one can make a difference." Jane shook her head, avoiding the older woman's gaze. "And I truly appreciate your belief in me. But there is just too much scandal in my past . . . in my life now . . ."

She let go of Alexandra's hand and stared at the fire.

"Nicholas and I have no chance of happiness. I should have stopped it before anything began. It is my fault. I am to blame for his situation. I am sorry."

Despite the pain in her ankle, Jane pushed herself to her feet and stood by the window. The view before her was a blur, but she held back her tears, refusing to allow herself to fall apart before this woman. Not after everything that she'd just said.

Lady Spencer said not a word more, but Jane heard her rise from her chair and walk out of the room. Only after the door had closed behind the visitor did Jane allow the tears to come. They were bitter tears, helpless tears, angry tears . . . for she knew there would never be another chance for her. She was now a captive to her own past and family for life. There could never be an escape for her.

Jane quickly wiped the tears from her face when she heard Jenny enter shortly after.

"I . . . I am sorry, Jenny, that you were forced to entertain this afternoon. I never thought . . . I never imagined anyone would be coming here . . . like this."

"Never ye mind, lass. I don't mind that one. In fact,

I should say I liked yer Lady Spencer a great deal. In many a way, she reminded me of ye, my joy. Aye, she's the kind of woman I'd like to be seeing ye become when ye reach her age."

Jane looked over her shoulder at the older woman and tried to smile. But the small boulder lodged in her throat would not allow it.

"Why are ye doing this to yerself, child?" Jenny scolded. Seeing Jane's stricken face, she hurried to her side and wrapped her arms around her. "When are ye going to stop punishing yerself?"

"I don't know what you mean."

"Stop the mourning. Let him go, my dove. Nine years is far more than enough. Conor is dead, and ye must be living. Do ye hear me? Ye must be living!" Jenny's voice was becoming increasingly urgent, impatient. She drew back and looked into Jane's face. " 'Twas not yer fault that he was hanged. The lad knew what he was doing. He understood the dangers and the risks, both with the Shanavests . . . and with wanting ye. He lived every day of his life as he pleased. I was his kin. I raised him as my own. And I tell ye now that my Conor would not be having anything to do with ye if he saw how ye're fading away with him gone."

"I am not fading away." Jane stepped to the hearth. The peat threw very little heat, but she could feel her face burning. "I picked up where he left off. I have kept our band of Shanavests to the course . . ."

"Nay, my joy. You have lost the spirit of Egan. I think ye are no longer Conor's 'wee fire.' " Jenny moved beside her. "Egan would know how to let that boy's memory rest. Ye talk about guilt. How would ye feel if yer situations were changed about? What if, after these many years, ye were looking down from St. Brigid's right hand, only to see such sadness afflicting *him*? Do ye think 'twould make him happy to see ye throwing away a chance like the one ye just sent packing with Lady Spencer? Do ye truly believe our Conor would be one to hold a grudge if ye were to settle with this woman's son and finally begin living?"

Of course, she thought, considering the size of the

cottage, it would only be natural for Jenny to hear everything that had been said. "I . . . Sir Nicholas . . ."

"I have ears, child." Jenny placed a gentle hand on Jane's shoulder again. "With Ronan's big mouth yapping, everyone from Cork to Limerick knows the baronet is sweet on ye. And everyone knows that ye have feelings for him, too."

Before Jane could say a word, Jenny continued. "And that's the way it should be. Finally, someone has come to call who is deserving of my Egan." The older woman smiled. "Just knowing that he didn't give you away that first day! And later, hearing what he did for Kathleen—old fool that I am—sure ye can't blame me for hoping something might happen between the two of ye. And today, after meeting himself's own mother . . . well, darling, I can only ask what ye could possibly be waiting for?"

"I cannot." Jane shook her head adamantly. "There is more dividing us than Conor and the Shanavests and . . ." She drew a deep breath. "It is no use, Jenny. He and I . . . we just cannot."

The older woman frowned at her for a long moment before speaking.

"This has something to do with yer sister, does it not?" she asked, her disapproval evident in her tone. "Everything, no doubt."

"Leave Clara out of this." Jane ran her hands up and down her arms. "Please just accept what I say and let me be."

A lengthy silence fell over the room while Jane once again found herself struggling in her own thoughts. Jenny's tone was much softer when she spoke again.

"Ye still must go back for the doings at Woodfield House tonight."

Jane looked with surprise into the woman's face. "But I—"

"Liam sent me a message. Finn wants you to go back—ye must make yerself visible, he says. Ye must attend yer mother's ball. Ye must pretend that there is nothing wrong and that ye know nothing of what happened last night."

After her years with the Shanavests, Jane had mastered

the ability to block the dangers of raids and their aftermath from her mind. With the exception of tending her swollen ankle, she hadn't given much thought this morning to the trap and to her unmasking last night. It had been dark, though, and she had never really come face-to-face with anyone after the mask had been torn off.

She frowned. Queen Mab, though, had been seen close up by a number of soldiers. And it was possible that someone might have guessed that Egan was a woman. "Has there been any significant news? I am certain no one saw me."

"All I know is the message that he sent."

Finn had said the same thing to her last night—about resuming her other life.

"But the complications of going back . . . I cannot just walk in with that ball tonight . . ." Not to mention that she would need to face Nicholas again. Perhaps it had been a cowardly path, but she hadn't thought she could face him. She knew she could not explain things to him after her meeting with Clara.

"This is not for ye that I am speaking, now. You must do this for the rest," Jenny insisted. "Even the smallest of suspicion falling upon ye, and more than a few of us would be tied to the band through you. That includes those at Woodfield House. Jane, ye have no choice."

Jane sat down in the nearest chair. The pounding in her head was now a hundred times worse than the ache in her ankle. She couldn't argue against what Jenny was saying. With Musgrave's sharp claws poised over her, it was very well possible that he would make the connections. "I . . . I wish I had thought of this . . . while Lady Spencer was still here."

"She *is* still here." Jenny shrugged at Jane's immediately suspicious glare. "I asked her to wait in her carriage and give me a chance to talk to ye. I knew ye had to go. And as I listened, I thought, 'What better ruse than this . . .'"

The older woman continued to explain, but Jane had an uncomfortable feeling that she had been duped.

Chapter 25

There was no time to be wasted.

Jane was not at the parsonage at Ballyclough, and Mrs. Brown said she had not seen her sister in the past few days. Clara asked about the whereabouts of Parson Adams, but then refused the housekeeper's offer that she wait for him there. Setting off on foot and in the direction she was pointed, she walked as fast as her legs could take her toward the lower village until she saw him coming along the knoll, beyond the Mallow road.

Her customary reaction to seeing him—the inability to breathe, the hammering of her heart in her chest, the images of them together in her mind—all of this quickly came and went as the pressing nature of her search washed them away. Clara ran toward him for a few steps, slowed to a fast walk, and then ran again until she reached him breathlessly.

"Henry! You must help me. I am looking for Jane, but . . . but . . . I have no idea . . . idea . . . where else . . . to look . . . It is so urgent!"

Placing a hand on her chest to calm her breath and find her voice, she looked into his face for the first time and was surprised by the sadness she saw there. Her heart sank. She placed a desperate hand on his arm.

"No! Please do not tell me something has happened. Please . . . no!" The tears fell fast and furious, and denial twisted her throat into a knot. "Not Jane . . ."

Clara felt him take her by the arm and lead her away from the road and the curious eyes of the villagers. She was vaguely conscious of moving down a path across the stony brook and then up through green fields. The tears, though, continued to fall.

"It is all . . . my fault," she hiccuped. "If I had not . . ."

"Nothing has happened to Jane," he assured her calmly.

Clara stared unbelievingly into his red-rimmed eyes. "But . . . you . . . you look like . . . you have been . . . that you are upset!"

"I have just left a funeral." The gray eyes looked back at the lower end of the village. "The tanner Darby O'Connell's wife, may she rest in peace. God knows she never knew any until now."

"Oh. I am so sorry," she whispered, wiping away at her face. "Was she young?"

"Very."

"And she left children?"

"One died during the childbirth that killed her. There are three more young ones left behind."

Clara wiped away more tears. "And . . . the . . . husband?"

"Nearly mad with grief, poor devil."

Her tears would not stop, and she dashed at them incessantly. She couldn't seem to get hold of her emotions. In a moment, Henry placed an arm gently around her shoulders. It only made things worse as she melted against him.

"I am . . . so sorry," she sobbed. "Here, I did not even know the woman. But it is so sad and I am so worried about Jane. But I cannot . . . find her . . . and I know she is angry with me. She might not even believe what I have to tell . . . her. But I overheard . . . Captain Wallis talking to Father . . . and . . . I have to find Jane . . . to warn her."

Clara hadn't even realized that she was babbling until Henry turned her around in his arms. She stopped abruptly. Her face flushed with heat when his hand lifted her chin until she was looking into his intense gray eyes.

"Start from the beginning. What was it exactly that you overheard?"

Clara took a deep breath and blurted out word for word everything she'd heard by the paddock.

"Captain Wallis did not say that they think Jane is

the rebel Egan, but if they are looking for a horse like Jane's . . . and if they come tonight and arrest her, I . . ." Clara broke down under the weight of her own misery. She could not even try to control the sobbing that was robbing her of her breath. The tears continued to fall even when Henry pulled her against him. His strong hands caressed her back. Her head nestled beneath his chin.

"You cannot allow yourself to fall apart like this. We cannot give them confirmation of something they may only suspect."

"Please, Henry! I have to find her." She clutched at the lapel of his coat and looked up into his stern face again. "We cannot let them catch her. Please . . . !"

"We shan't let them take her away," the parson assured her solemnly. "I want you to get back and prepare for the ball as if everything is as it should be. Pretend nothing has happened."

"But I cannot. I must find her . . ."

"This is all nothing more than an opening gambit. Musgrave is beating the drums of rumor, and then waiting to see who runs. If he had proof that Jane is the rebel, he would have already had Captain Wallis and his dragoons turning Woodfield House inside out."

"But you do not know that for certain. Henry, I cannot chance that she might . . ."

"You must trust me, Clara." He took hold of her shoulders. The gray eyes bore into her. "I shall be there tonight . . . and I will try until then to find Jane. She must be present as well. Musgrave is a coward, and he must be faced down."

Twinges of doubt still raked at Clara's insides. "But what do we do if he decides to arrest her tonight?"

"Out of respect for your father, Sir Robert would not risk making a scene during the ball. But I give you my word, I shall come up with a way to thwart him if he is so foolish as to act. Nothing will happen to your sister, Clara. Nothing."

Henry's assurances worked to calm Clara's worries. But the growing awareness of the touch of his hands and the gaze on his face revived another deeper ache. It might have been entirely the fault of her hopeful imagination. Or the pressure of his fingers still on her arm. The closeness of their bodies. The feel of his warm breath so close. And then she saw his gaze fall on her lips.

She prayed to God that he would kiss her.

"Go," Henry whispered hoarsely. His hands dropped from her shoulders. "We must be at our best tonight."

Clara didn't give a rush about the appropriateness of any of it. She wrapped her arms around his neck and planted her lips firmly on his for an endless moment . . . before turning and walking away. He hadn't responded to the kiss, she thought, glancing back as she reached the edge of the village. He was still standing where she left him, staring off into the green fields.

But he hadn't pushed her away, either.

"She *is* here, Nicholas. Really she is." Frances nodded emphatically at him from her horse. "I saw Jane with my very own eyes. She came back with Mother not half an hour ago."

Nicholas dismounted, handed the reins of his steed to a groom, and started quickly toward the manor house.

"But you cannot go to her," the young woman warned, urging her mare up the path alongside the garden. "The guests will begin arriving in less than three hours. Mother and Jane are in the middle of some little scheme having to do with some of her paintings. And just before I came down from the house, I heard Fey ordering a bath brought up for Jane. And after that, she still needs to dress and do her hair and all the other things to get ready. And you have a lot to do to get ready yourself, as well, Nick!" Frances glanced from the tip of his muddy boots to the stained shirt and unshaven face. "You look absolutely hideous. By the way, your valet is already waiting in your room and . . ."

He started toward the archway. Frances reined her horse to a halt.

"And Mother told me to warn you not to scare her off again," she called after him.

He stopped at the door and turned to frown fiercely at her. "Do you mean to say that Jane was staying away because of me?"

Frances carefully weighed her words before speaking

again. "No. I do not know that exactly. But I did hear Jane tell Fey that if you asked to see her . . . well, to say that she was not available."

Without another word, Nicholas turned on his heel and yanked open the door.

Every member of the gentry within fifteen miles appeared to have ridden over for the ball. The noise of the throng, mixed with the harmonic rhythms of the music, drifted up the stairs and into her bedchamber.

The invited guests had arrived. The rest of the Purefoy family was already down playing their parts as hosts. But Jane continued to sit rigidly on the edge of her bed, dubious and fretful as she returned the gaze of the stranger reflected in her mirror.

She had thwarted the hairdressers' insistence on using plumes of feathers and whole gardens' worth of flowers in her hair. She'd then refused to wear the tall, powdered wig that Lady Spencer had brought in. As a compromise to everyone, though, she'd allowed them to gather and arrange her own dark hair, without powder, so that a few ringlets framed her pale face while the rest was piled up safely behind.

The hair she could live with, but the elegant dress that appeared was an ordeal that she hadn't been prepared for.

At the same time, she had not been able to fight wearing it. She could not bring herself to hurt Lady Spencer's feelings . . . not after everything she had already done for her. From the embroidery on the soft yellow and white silk to the fitted bodice with its lace and ruching, to the quilted petticoats with their lace and fringe hem, this was perhaps the most graceful and beautiful dress Jane had seen, never mind worn. But this high style hardly helped to ease the tension that coiled inside of her.

There were people down in the Hall and in the parlors whom she had loathed for all of her life. There were others whom she had hoped might once again respect her, but who had never been able to overlook her transgressions. And her family? As far as any of them knew, Jane wasn't attending the ball tonight.

And then there was Nicholas. Her hand unconsciously traveled to her exposed throat. As she sat and looked at the ample skin showing above her breasts, Jane realized what she feared most was his reaction.

There was a soft knock on the door and Jane rose immediately to her feet. She cast a final glance at the mirror. She only wished she could feel some of the reflected woman's apparent confidence. It was amazing what some clothes and powder could hide.

Alexandra's encouraging smile helped a little.

"Lovely," the older woman whispered confidentially. "It is late, my dear. I do not want you to miss a moment more of the admiration pouring forth in the Blue Parlor. Almost everyone has come through at least once already. And some of the guests have decided not to move an inch until I reveal the artist's name. It is most exciting."

Until they find out it is me. Jane didn't voice her concern and instead quietly accompanied Alexandra downstairs. Her ankle still hurt dreadfully whenever she put weight on it, so she tried to take her time. Without asking any questions about the nature of the injury, Lady Spencer had been very considerate earlier in the afternoon and she continued to be so now.

The stairs were agonizing, but as Jane descended— and as the curious gazes of a few guests who were mingling in the entrance hall fell on her—she found herself growing totally numb. When she and Alexandra finally reached the bottom, Jane was certain that no one had even recognized her, for the faces continued to be friendly, even admiring.

"The worst is over," Lady Spencer whispered softly, touching her on the elbow and nodding toward the parlor and where a small crowd of people were blocking the doorway, waiting to enter. "Shall we go in there and stir the pot a little?"

As the two women started past the front door, though, Jane cringed as a late-arriving guest entered and stepped into their path. Sir Robert Musgrave had no difficulty recognizing her.

"Miss Jane, I cannot believe my eyes."

The hush that fell over the bystanders was immediately followed by urgent whispers. She could almost feel the news rippling through the parlors and the Hall.

"Sir Robert." She nodded politely, trying to mask all traces of hostility in her voice and hide, as well, the unnerving sense that every eye was now on her.

"Miss Jane, I must say you look absolutely stunning." He stepped so near her that his presence encroached upon the very air she needed to breathe. He lifted her hand to his lips, but his smile was cold. "I truly approve of your choice of hairstyle . . . and this dress! You are a marvel, I must say. The style is elegant and the fit is fashionably provocative . . . within the bounds of propriety, of course." He lowered his voice. "So very much like yourself."

Jane tried to show nothing under his predatory gaze.

"I have to admit, though, I find myself speechless at seeing you attired in something other than that dreaded black."

"I find you are not *completely* speechless, sir," Jane replied matter-of-factly. "Now if you will forgive us, Lady Spencer and I need to speak with her daughter."

"But I cannot let you simply disappear, Miss Jane. Not until you promise me the pleasure of a dance."

"I fear, sir, that I cannot promise any such thing." She looked impatiently past him. "Please forgive us, but I believe I just saw Miss Spencer pass by the parlor door."

Stepping around him, Jane nodded politely to her companion, and the two made their way toward the parlor.

"You have wonderful poise," Alexandra whispered a moment later, as Jane sailed past the open stares of the guests with her head held high. "I am very proud to know you."

These last words almost pierced Jane's emotional armor, but she fought it off. The throng of people by the door to the parlor parted, and she followed Alexandra into the crowded but now silent room.

The canvases she and Lady Spencer had chosen earlier had been arranged on temporary wooden easels in various places around the room. Now, however, all gazes were fixed on her and not on the paintings that had drawn them into the parlor initially. Jane searched the expressions of the strangers and those she knew. She saw Henry standing beside Clara by the window. Her sister's gaze fell to the carpeted floor, but the minister sent Jane an encouraging nod. She couldn't worry about Clara's reaction to her arrival now. Frances beamed at her enthusiastically from across the parlor. Next to her, Jane found the one she'd been looking for all along. Her heart pounded, and her stomach danced at the sight of him.

"I cannot be more pleased with this warm reception . . ." Lady Spencer began, speaking in a clear voice to everyone in the room. Jane found she had some difficulty focusing on her friend's words, for only Nicholas existed now.

He was impeccably dressed, but Jane thought he looked tired. He held a glass of port in one hand while he casually leaned a shoulder against the mantel of the hearth. Even from this distance, Jane could see the way his eyes studied every inch of her body from the tip of her shoes to her hair. His attention was the warmth she'd lacked. She waited until his eyes finally met hers, but she started at the hurt she saw in them. Hurt she knew she herself had caused.

" . . . and so the treasure lies among you." Lady Spencer took Jane's hand. "Miss Purefoy . . . yes, indeed . . . Miss Jane Purefoy is the artist of these splendid works which we have all been viewing so appreciatively."

There was a very brief moment of silence, and then someone started clapping from somewhere to her left. That one person's applause quickly spread, and Jane watched with utter astonishment as every person in the room and around the door joined in. As she turned to look at Alexandra, a loud conversational buzz erupted around her.

Jane had no idea what to say or how to act. This positive reception of her work was totally unexpected. But what was even more astounding was the way the guests immediately approached her with congratulatory comments and questions about her style and her subject matter.

Trying to answer whatever she could to the best of her abilities, Jane searched for Alexandra at her side and found the older woman wearing a proud smile and standing away from her by a series of paintings she particularly liked. She glanced again in Nicholas's direction and found him raising his glass in a toast to her.

"And what is this all about?" Lady Purefoy's cheerfully complaining tone rang out from the hallway. "What kind of a ball is this where everyone deserts the dance floor and crowds into parlors? Is there card playing going on in here? Come now . . ."

A few guests shifted around and others followed the hostess in.

"Oh yes," she said. "Lady Spencer's special arrangement. I'd almost forgotten. What have we here?"

Catherine waved the fan she was holding and peered about in surprise.

"Oh, my! Lady Spencer, are you in here?"

"I'm here."

The crowd around Jane parted and Catherine Purefoy became slightly paler when she saw her older daughter standing at the center of the crowd.

"Why, Jane! Whatever are you . . . ?" She quickly tried to recover her composure and looked at her houseguest. "Lady Spencer . . . I thought when you said you wanted to use this room . . . I never imagined that you meant . . ."

The hostess waved her hand vaguely at the paintings and failed miserably at hiding her confusion. She shook her head and tried to begin again.

"Ah, but Jane . . . dear . . . I did not know you had returned!" she finally managed to get out.

Jane took a step toward her mother to explain, but the magistrate's voice by the door raised the hair on her neck.

"Were you away, Miss Jane?"

There was no reason for this loud and public question, and she so wished to tell Musgrave exactly that, but her mother's answer cut off the opportunity.

"Indeed, Sir Robert. Jane has been away for three days." Catherine smiled in embarrassment at the group. "This was the reason for my surprise . . . my *delight* in seeing her. I had no idea she was planning to return in time for the ball. I mean, it is always a joy for a mother to see her children, but since I did not know where she'd gone, and I received no message about her time of return . . ."

A murmur of disapproval rolled through the room, though Jane had no clear idea whom it was aimed at. She reached for her mother's hand and looked beseechingly at Clara, hoping for her sister's assistance with taking control of this situation. But Clara's flushed face was turned toward Henry Adams, and she was whispering something into his ear.

"And I notice that you have sustained an injury, Miss Jane." Musgrave was cutting through people and coming closer. "Tell us, is it your knee or your ankle?"

"You were not unwell when you left, Jane," Lady Purefoy asserted pointedly.

"And you are such a fine rider that I doubt you would have fallen from your horse. Now, you wouldn't have sustained such an injury jumping from the roof of a building, would you?"

He was now standing before her. His gray eyes watched her every move.

"I have been long accustomed to taking the stairs, sir," she put in acidly, hoping to cut short this very public inquiry.

"And the cause and nature of the injury?"

"That is none of your concern, sir," she answered curtly. "I should think someone with your responsibilities would hardly have the time to concern himself in such an ongoing fashion with my foolish mishaps."

The magistrate opened his mouth to respond, but Jane saw his eyes narrow and focus on someone behind her.

"If you will forgive us, Sir Robert, Lady Purefoy mentioned that this is, after all, a ball. And I have been waiting too long already for this dance that Miss Jane promised me earlier."

The heat that rushed through her when she heard Nicholas's voice buoyed her immediately. Her cheeks burned and her eyes misted over with affection when she turned and met his intense blue gaze. The tongues were wagging again, but Jane didn't care as she slipped her hand through his proffered arm.

"Are you ready?" he whispered softly as they started toward the door.

"More than you know. More than I ever was." He cupped her hand on his arm, and she moved closer. He was trying to give her support for her ankle, but she wanted to melt against him, kiss him, explain to him everything that had happened, and tell him what a lost soul she was without him.

Jane was surprised to see her father standing just inside the doorway as they approached. She immediately bristled, expecting to see his disapproval. But his look was reflective, mysterious.

"If you have just a few moments, Miss Jane, there are a few questions that I still need to ask."

From the steely frown on Nicholas's face, she could tell that Musgrave's persistence angered him as much as it did her. He pressed her hand reassuringly, though, and turned without letting her go.

"Really, Musgrave. Can this not wait?" Nicholas asked impatiently.

"I am afraid not, Sir Nicholas. My duty as magistrate, acting on behalf of the Cr—"

"Are you here as a guest or as a government official?" Nicholas's sharp tone and question silenced the crowd and a path opened between the two men.

"I fear my duty must always supercede—"

"That is too bad for you, sir. However, the rest of us are not afflicted with the same burden. Would you mind allowing us to enjoy our host's amusements and hospitality?"

"I would if I could, sir." The magistrate stepped toward them. "I assure you that there is no need for a private conversation . . . unless you need the opportunity to think of an excuse for this good lady's injury."

The baronet's words were cold and measured. "This is not the time, sir. But I assure you, you and I will have a private discussion in the *very* near future."

"What was it the last time?" Musgrave asked, ignoring Nicholas's threat. "You struck her face with the stable door, was it not?" He laughed without mirth. "Perhaps this time we should just say you pushed her from her horse, thereby causing the pronounced limp she suffers from tonight."

"Sir Robert," Lady Purefoy gasped. "What are you saying?"

Nicholas's hands dropped to his side, his tone icy. "Be clear, sir. Are you accusing me?"

"No, of course not!" He laughed again, though no one else seemed amused by the confrontation. "Surrounded by all this magnificent art, I am simply trying to be creative."

Jane could not take any more of this. She understood the threat in Musgrave's words, and she had no wish for Nicholas to fall victim to it. She pressed a hand on his arm and faced her foe.

"I believe this unpleasantness is entirely unnecessary." She looked around at the room full of people. "If you have *official* questions to ask me, sir, why not proceed in private. Surely there is no reason to deprive my parents' guests of their evening of enjoyment."

"But is this not as much entertainment as any promenade or dinner or bottle of port, for that matter?"

"For you, perhaps," she replied. "But not for anyone else."

"Have you been drinking heavily, Sir Robert?" Lady Purefoy asked hopefully.

"No, madam." He turned his back on the hostess. "And I happen to disagree, Miss Jane. How often will these good people have an opportunity to witness the King's magistrate acting to solve a crime?"

"Very well, sir," she responded coldly. "Ask your questions and be done with it."

"As you wish." He bowed with a mocking flourish. "Would you enlighten us as to where you have been for the past three days?"

"I was visiting a friend."

"Did you take a carriage or ride your fine horse?"

"As is my custom, I rode my horse."

"And does this friend live anywhere near the village of Banteer?"

She paused, considering her answer. "I believe it would be safe to say my friend lives in that general direction."

"What did you do while you were staying there?"

She shrugged. "Nothing unusual. We visited."

"And what were you doing last night?"

"This is becoming quite tedious, Sir Robert."

"Did you go to Banteer last night?" He walked toward her.

"I cannot think of any reason why I would be in Banteer, sir . . ."

"But you were seen there, last night, Miss Jane."

"Was I?" She met the man's accusatory gaze at the same time that she felt the brush of Nicholas's arm against her own. His strength flowed into her, and she found comfort in his presence beside her. "I am certain whoever *imagined* seeing me must be mistaken."

"Do you have anyone who could confirm your claim?"

She hesitated, unwilling to use Jenny's name. As far as the magistrate was concerned, there could be no connection between the two women. Even if Jane were to escape this time, Conor's aunt would know no peace for as long as the magistrate held power.

"Yes."

Henry Adams's voice drew everyone's attention to him. A murmur again rippled though the crowd.

"I was with Miss Jane last evening."

Jane felt Nicholas stiffen beside her.

"Parson," Musgrave started, surprise evident in his voice. "Are you saying you visited Miss Jane at her unnamed friend's house last evening?"

"No." The minister moved to Jane's side, and she felt suddenly dwarfed between Nicholas and Henry. "No. What I am saying is that Miss Jane has been a guest at the parsonage in Ballyclough for the past three days. This unnamed friend she speaks of is I, Henry Adams."

Chapter 26

"I do not know what all this secrecy is about. But I know she wasn't there, Nicholas. I went after her," Lady Spencer whispered anxiously. "I know she wasn't staying with Parson Adams."

Nicholas had managed to stand by Jane as notes of scandal mingled with those of Purcell and Handel. He'd stayed beside her as Adams had responded to Musgrave's question about the whereabouts of Jane's horse last night, and listened with appreciation as the parson had verbally attacked the magistrate about the lack of order in the district . . . evidenced by the fact that horses routinely disappear from stables at night, with only some of them reappearing a few days later. If the horse that was seen was indeed Jane's—though it was doubtful, he asserted—this was obviously what had occurred.

Musgrave had clearly been thrown off stride by the parson's shocking claim, and his complaint—seconded by several landowners looking on—further disoriented the man.

Nicholas continued to stand with Jane and Adams until the magistrate had said something about the ineptness of the dragoons assigned to him and grudgingly mumbled an apology for creating such an inopportune disturbance. Once Musgrave had withdrawn, Nicholas had also taken his leave.

He could not remain beside her and pretend he was unaffected by the parson's announcement. He knew that Jane was not at Ballyclough. He himself had gone there looking for her. What bothered him greatly, though, was that Adams seemed to know more than he did.

Nicholas had left the house and was standing in the field beneath the paddock wall, staring out into the blackness covering the valley, when his mother had caught up to him. Behind him, the stables were bustling with activity as carriages continued to be sent up for guests who'd had their fill of food, drink, dancing . . . with a bit of scandal thrown in.

"Well, this is a party no one will soon forget," she said. "Everyone is gobbling down the supper our hostess prepared and is heading for the hills. And to think that in London one would have no chance of *pushing* anyone out the door. The wolves would be waiting around, hoping for a bloody finish!"

"There may be blood, yet."

"I shouldn't think so," she replied. "Parson Adams and Sir Thomas have locked themselves away in our host's study. But I am quite uneasy about any solution that those two might come up with."

Nicholas said nothing, and Alexandra waited a moment or two before pressing him.

"Jane needs you, Nick. She is trying to be as brave as she can, but I know she will fall apart if you do not go back to her soon."

"Henry Adams has been doing an excellent job helping her. I would hate to interfere."

"You cannot mean what you are saying." She touched him on the arm. "Nothing that Musgrave said to her, no look of severity from anyone in attendance, upset her as much as when you walked out of that room. It is as plain as those stars in this sky. She needs *you*, Nicholas. You."

"And tell me. Did she say that? Did she send you after me?"

"Jane would have if she thought it at all possible. But how could she?" Alexandra stepped in front of him. "Every movement she makes, every word she says, is being carefully scrutinized by a dozen people at any given moment. Those who have not left yet are watching her closely, waiting for something noteworthy to carry to the club, or the card party, or whatever it is they do out here to socialize. She is bearing it well, for the moment, but I do not know for how long."

Surely, it would be easier just to ride away and forget he'd ever met this woman, he thought. But he couldn't. The old Nicholas could have done just that and never looked back. But the new Nicholas Spencer—the one already far too consumed with Miss Jane Purefoy—could not.

"Where is she now?"

"In the library. The musicians have packed their instruments and trotted off for their supper in the servants' hall. I should think the house will be empty in another hour. Lady Purefoy is still bustling about, of course, trying to put a good face on everything and looking foolish for her efforts. But the girls and Jane are waiting in the library for Sir Thomas and the parson to end their discussion."

Clara was consumed by the darkness outside the window. Frances was pretending that she was deeply involved in a book she had open on her lap, though she hadn't turned the page for quite some time. Lady Purefoy barked more orders at the servants and returned to sit heavily on the sofa. Her agitated fingers opened and closed the delicate fan she was holding.

Jane immediately stood up when she saw Nicholas enter with Lady Spencer. Without any regard for her mother's disapproving glare, she had managed to get halfway to him when Henry Adams and Sir Thomas appeared in the doorway.

Everyone stared at the two men.

Henry's expression was guarded as he cast a brief glance at Jane before focusing his gaze on Clara. Sir Thomas headed directly to a side cabinet holding a bottle of port and glasses. He poured himself a full glass and gestured an offer to the other men. Both declined. He downed the wine and poured himself another before turning to Jane and addressing the group.

"The Reverend Henry Adams has asked for Jane's hand in marriage."

The very breath was caught in Jane's chest at the announcement. She turned in confusion toward Nicholas, still standing by the door, and saw the flash of anger, hurt, betrayal even as he returned her gaze. Tears pooled in Jane's eyes, and she shook her head helplessly. Henry was still staring at Clara. The younger sister's face had fully turned toward the window.

"What *wonderful* news!" Lady Purefoy piped up, breaking the heavy silence. "Reverend Adams and Jane . . . who would have thought it? But considering what was said tonight . . . and Parson Adams's excellent reputation . . . it makes perfect sense." The fan opened with a snap of her fingers, and she waved it before her face. "Actually, it will be seen as a most loyal and generous act. Absolutely the thing to do . . . saving our Jane from her shocking past."

"From the warm reception your daughter received tonight—before the good parson *saved* her—I would have hoped that you'd realize that Jane is a prize in her own right."

Alexandra's sharp retort in her defense made the tears fall for the first time onto Jane's cheeks. Nicholas was glaring at Henry fiercely enough to cut him to pieces.

"Oh, we knew all along Jane had some talent." Catherine waved her fan dismissively in the air. "But a good brushstroke does not arrange a good marriage or hide the scandal of one's past."

"Naturally, we disagree there, too, Lady Purefoy," Alexandra persisted. "It is generally the support of one's family toward its members—or the lack of it—that sets the limits to how others in their set behave openly in most situations."

"Not that this concerns you, given your son's lack of interest in Clara, but *I* did not push Jane into the arms of any papist cur. She did the damage. She can bear its consequences."

"None of us, I am sure, is completely without some youthful indiscretion in our personal history," Lady Spencer said mockingly. "And I wonder what would have happened to *us* if we all were blessed with such righteous and unforgiving parents as she."

"There is no point in this." Catherine closed her fan with a snap. "The announcements will be sent to the papers tomorrow. We shall set a date for no later than a month, though if we could arrange it sooner, so much the better. If you have no objections, Parson, we shall simply send notices of the wedding to our family from England and your older brother and . . ."

"What do *you* think of this, Jane?"

Sir Thomas's gruff question was so abrupt and out of character for him that Catherine continued to speak a few more words before realizing her husband had asked the question. Jane was fairly astonished, too. She could not remember the last time her father had directly addressed her.

"I . . . I believe we all are jumping at shadows." Jane quickly found her voice. She turned to Henry first. "I am honored and touched by your offer. But I am greatly distressed, as you and I both know there has never been anything that might be construed as improper between us. *Ever.* You spoke before the magistrate tonight to protect me from certain accusations. However, there is no reason for us to act rashly . . . and thereby encourage any wrongheaded notions by those who were here tonight."

Jane turned to her mother. "Henry and I have spent many days together since childhood. In the recent years—and since his installation at the parsonage—I have spent many nights, as well, at Ballyclough as a guest of his and Mrs. Brown's. As we speak, these good people are assisting a widowed friend and her children. There are justifiable reasons for me to be staying at the parsonage. If you were to take the time and explain the situation that way, there should be no reason for Henry's reputation to be tainted or linked in any way with mine."

"But Jane, that is an excellent offer! No matter *how* everything might be explained."

"An excellent offer for *whom*?" Jane lashed out at her mother. "Shall we punish Henry for being noble and wanting to do the honorable thing for me? Shall I marry him against my will and, in so doing, rob him of any chance of future happiness with a woman who could be deserving of him? I believe the only one who will benefit from this *excellent* offer of marriage is *you*, Mother . . . for you shall finally be rid of me."

"Sir Thomas." Catherine turned pleading eyes on her husband. "Tell her she must marry."

The ex-magistrate did not say a word, but his dark gaze locked on his daughter's face. Jane was surprised to find herself capable of looking into the man's eyes without the hostility of a lifetime clouding her vision. She found him different from the man she knew him to be. Something unexplainable had penetrated the layers of harshness and arrogance. She answered his unspoken question.

"I should like to wait and let the rumors fade." Jane turned to Henry and smiled gratefully at him. "You understand."

He nodded.

Before anyone could move or say anything more, Alexandra spoke out. "Perhaps distance, as well as time, can be of assistance in this situation."

She paused and then turned her attention to Catherine. "What would you say, Lady Purefoy, if I were to take your two daughters with me to England on a holiday for a few weeks or so. Perhaps, during their absence, explanations can be circulated and rumor will die a natural death. More importantly, however, they will get a chance to become better acquainted with my family."

"Oh . . . !" The suggestion clearly startled the hostess. "Do you mean Sir Nicholas would be accompanying you back to England, as well?"

Alexandra received a nod from her son. "Of course. Nicholas and Frances will both come back with us. And I shall even arrange that we all escort them back to Ireland in a month or so."

The suggestion brought immediate life to Lady Purefoy's demeanor. Jane and everyone else could plainly see that the woman's delight centered on the prospect of Clara and Nicholas spending time together. But Jane was too drained to worry about any of this now. She had avoided one disaster with Henry; now she had a short holiday left to convince Nicholas that—even though she loved him—he had to accept that there could never be a chance of a future between them.

"Sir Thomas," Catherine called jubilantly to her husband. "What do you think of Lady Spencer's brilliant idea?"

The ex-magistrate gave a curt nod. "I agree. Jane needs to be away from this blasted Ireland."

Chapter 27

⌒

Seated in the spacious library of his Berkeley Square townhouse, the Earl of Stanmore watched with a great deal of interest and curiosity as his best friend paced back and forth across the room. He had never seen Nicholas as enraged as this.

Very interesting, indeed, he thought, hiding a smile.

Stanmore had already pieced together that his friend had sailed from Cork City on Sunday, arrived in Broad Quay in Bristol the same night, and had ridden all day yesterday to arrive in London late last night. And already this morning, Nicholas had tracked down the Lord Lieutenant of Ireland, who happened to be in London en route to a shooting party in Yorkshire.

Stanmore glanced at his pocket watch. It was barely ten o'clock in the morning, and Nicholas seemed to have the rest of the day filled with meetings with Crown officials and who knew what else! By the devil, he'd never known Nicholas to rise before noon, unless it was for some sporting reason.

"Stanmore, you know I have never been in the habit of asking favors of my friends. But this time I am making an exception." Nicholas came to an abrupt stop before the earl's desk. "Meet with him at noon. Stress everything I have told you. It is essential that something be done about Musgrave before he does some irrevocable damage."

"But you have already told me that the man was very sympathetic to your concerns and promised to look into it."

"Perhaps he will, but I cannot afford the matter to be put off. It is crucial for him to act immediately. In hearing it from you, one of the distinguished members of the House of Lords, in addition to hearing it from the Surveyor of the Navy . . ."

"Blast, Nicholas! Have you already been to Nathaniel Yorke's house, as well, this morning?"

"Of course not! I went there last night." He planted his hands on the earl's desk. "This is very important to me, Stanmore. More so than you can ever imagine!"

The chiseled features of the earl reflected his genuine interest as he leaned back in the chair.

"Who is she?"

Clara had not weathered the rough journey from Ireland very well, and as a result of staying beside her sister, Jane had seen very little of Nicholas during their trip. Even those few glimpses, however, had been better than his disappearance soon after their ship tied up in Bristol. Nonetheless, she could not bring herself to ask his mother or sister about his whereabouts or his expected return.

Curiously, after spending the night in an inn at quayside in the port town, Lady Spencer had developed a keen interest in visiting an "ancient" friend in Bath. As they breakfasted, she'd mentioned that a visit to the nearby resort city would also have its advantages for Clara, who could spend a couple of days recovering there before they hired a carriage for London.

And then, for some inexplicable reason or other, Frances was extremely impatient to get back to London. So after a short discussion, it was agreed that Jane would accompany the younger woman to London and Lady Spencer would follow in a few days with Clara.

During the trip, which had been broken up into comfortable stages over two days, Frances had spoken ceaselessly, telling Jane everything about the school she had been attending in Brussels to her excitement over settling into a girls school in England. She'd also made certain to drop Nicholas's name in at least every other sentence, singing his praises in a way that Jane knew only a sister trying her hand at matchmaking for her brother could do. Jane had been touched by the attempt, knowing all the while that there was not a thing she could say or do to make Frances understand how unlikely such a union could be.

That would be a conversation for Jane and Nicholas alone, and until then, she would keep her sorrows to herself.

In the afternoon of the second day, Frances stirred from the nap she'd been taking as the escalating city noises announced the arrival of her coach in London. She gave Jane a sleepy-eyed smile and stretched. Once again, Jane was overwhelmed by the young woman's beauty and innocence . . . and her strong resemblance to Nicholas. She had been trying so hard not to dwell on the talk that the two of them *had* to have. There had not been an opportunity to explain anything to him since the day she'd fled Woodfield House in the early hours of morning. Their last moments alone together had been spent making love on the small cot in her work area.

Not a bad memory, Jane thought, quickly blinking back tears and lifting the shade to look out onto the busy streets.

"I cannot believe what good time we made," Frances said excitedly, moving to the seat facing Jane and looking out, as well. "Perhaps after dinner, if you don't mind, I can invite my friend Elizabeth to come over for a little while. Her family has a house on Leicester Square—quite near Nicholas's—and although she is younger than I by a year, we really enjoy each other's company. She is quite lovely."

"No, I don't mind at all."

Frances placed her hand on top of Jane's. "And thank you for staying with me . . . with us. I remember, from Clara's last visit to London, that you have some family here. But I am so glad that you have decided to stay with us instead."

Jane smiled warmly. "I would have never left Ireland if I had to spend my time here with my parents' family. I am afraid my father's sisters have never recovered from the scandal of my youth. And on my mother's side . . . well, perhaps we should just not mention them."

"When was the last time you were here?"

Jane thought back. "Three years ago. I was here when one of my aunts, the youngest sister to my mother, was marrying. We arrived a week before the wedding, and I left for Ireland two days later."

"They asked you to leave before the wedding?"

Jane smiled gently at Frances's shocked expression. "It was a mutual decision. I was not going to wear anything but black to the ceremony, and this did not agree with the flower bouquet the bride was carrying."

Frances blinked once and then burst into laughter. Jane couldn't stop herself from joining her.

"I must say, Jane, you have become my ideal," the young woman said a moment later, her beaming smile lighting up the carriage. "I so admire your courage . . . your intelligence . . . your independence . . . your forthrightness. I strive to become like you someday."

"Oh, Fanny." Jane grasped the younger woman's hand tightly in her own. "Contrary to what you think . . . I am someone to avoid. Nothing good will come out of becoming as ill tempered as I have become."

"I beg to disagree with that." She leaned forward and smiled meaningfully. "You have not only managed to capture Nicholas's interest, you have redirected his life entirely. I should say—remembering the impossible bachelor rogue that he was before—you have accomplished a most astonishing feat."

"There are much easier ways of capturing a man's interest than the route I have taken."

"But I doubt there are many that are more exciting."

Before Jane could argue further, Frances pointed to an approaching street. "And here we are! That is Elizabeth's house. And right there . . . on that side of the square . . . is Nicholas's."

Jane looked out the window at the line of fashionable houses surrounding a large fenced area of greensward and walks with a garden and statue in the center.

"The gilded statue of the man on the horse—" Frances pointed again. "That is the first King George."

Jane's attention was still on the house. She did not know if Nicholas was in London or elsewhere.

The carriage rounded the square and came to a stop in front of the house. Instantly, footmen and servants were lining up before the steps as Jane followed Frances out onto the street. They had obviously been expected, for more servants rushed out to carry up the baggage.

It was the smell of London that struck a chord in her memory. So different from the clear farm air and the smell of peat, here the crisp autumn air carried with it the not unpleasant scent of coal fires.

Inside, she was introduced to the house steward, a rather formidable-looking rough named Charles, who appeared to be blind in his left eye from some horrible injuries he'd sustained on that side of his face. The housekeeper, Mrs. Hannagan, was a surprise to Jane, for the woman was from Dublin and as cheerful as she was apparently efficient. Their reception was warm, and, to her delight, the housekeeper answered the question that had been burning on Jane's tongue since yesterday.

"Sir Nicholas has been out all day, miss. But he did send a message around noon that if you were to arrive early enough, that you should rest and be ready for a late dinner at the home of the Earl of Stanmore's house tonight. Lady Stanmore insisted, miss."

Jane remembered Nicholas mentioning the name and referring to them as his best friends.

"Oh, they are in London?" Frances asked in obvious delight.

"Only for a few more days, Miss Fanny. They'll soon be leaving for Solgrave—that is their estate in Hertfordshire, Miss Purefoy—but Lady Stanmore has insisted on meeting Miss Purefoy and visiting with you both."

As they were ushered upstairs to their rooms, Jane spoke up. "I think it would be best if I were to stay behind. I am a stranger and . . ."

"Do not even think it!" Frances gave her a bright smile. "Knowing my brother's friends, the main purpose of this dinner tonight is to meet *you*." She shook her head before Jane could speak. "You heard what Mrs. Hannagan said. They want to meet *Miss Purefoy*."

"But that is surely Clara and not I."

"They met Clara last spring." Frances patted Jane's hand. "Accept it! You will have to spend another evening under the lens. But this time I believe you will not mind it."

"And why is that?" Jane asked suspiciously as Mrs. Hannagan directed a serving maid to open the door to a spacious and beautifully appointed bedchamber.

"Because Stanmore is dashingly handsome. Because Rebecca is about your age and is as untraditional as any countess in England. And because they are the happiest married couple I have ever encountered in my life. Is that not so, Mrs. Hannagan?"

The housekeeper smiled in agreement.

"Trust me, you shall love them." Frances nodded with all the conviction of a true woman of the world. "And *they* shall love you."

No stone had been left unturned. Of that he was certain.

As a result, Nicholas was late in arriving at his friends' Berkeley Square town house for dinner. Philip, Stanmore's ancient steward, greeted him with uncharacteristic warmth, however, just inside the front door.

"And how was your day today, Sir Nicholas?"

Nicholas studied him with suspicion as he handed his hat and gloves to a doorman. In light of the rigidly unresponsive manner with which the steward customarily addressed anyone, the simple query constituted a fortnight's allowance of pleasantries. Perhaps a month's worth.

"Very well, thank you. And how was yours, Philip?"

"Despite it being a little cold for September, I was able to accompany Lady Stanmore and the young masters to St. James's Park this afternoon. Master James is starting his session at Eton this fall a month late, you see, on account of the excitement of having a new brother. Of course, Daniel . . . you remember my brother Daniel, sir? The steward at Solgrave? Of course, sir. Well, Daniel has already arranged for the lad's tutor, Mr. Clarke, to meet with us at Solgrave. As was the case last year, we already know that Master James will be far ahead of the other pupils when he arrives at school next month."

Very well, Nicholas thought. That constituted roughly a year's measure of chitchat for Philip. He bit back his smile at the change in the steward. Rebecca's positive

influence during the past year on Stanmore and on everyone else around them had been the most amazing
thing to observe. But this drastic change in Philip since
Nicholas's last visit was inexplicable. He was a hard old
nut, but something had managed to soften his shell.

"And where is everyone, Philip?"

"His lordship and your sister and Master James are
in the East Room, sir. Her ladyship and Miss Purefoy,
however, went upstairs to put Master Samuel to bed, as
he was becoming quite . . . assertive, sir."

Nicholas paused by the upward sweep of stairs in the
hope of catching a glimpse of Jane. All of the arrangements he'd made with his mother to send Jane and Frances ahead while she took Clara to Bath had worked out
perfectly. Now he had to capitalize on his efforts.

He was certain that Jane's change of heart and disappearance from Woodfield House had been the result of
some discussion with Clara. Whatever words had been
exchanged between the sisters had once again planted
in Jane's mind the idea that Nicholas was destined to be
married to the younger sister.

The ship out of Cork City had not even passed Knock-
adoon Head before he realized his only opportunity lay
in separating the two. That way he would at least have
a chance to talk some sense into Jane.

"May I be bold enough to congratulate you, sir?"

Nicholas turned in surprise and found Philip standing
beside him. There was no reason for denial. The man's
meaning was very clear.

"She hasn't agreed to marry me yet."

"Fear not, sir. I believe you are second only to his
lordship himself in persuasiveness. If he was happy
enough to succeed, then I shall place my wager on you."

Nicholas smiled and fell in with the steward as he
started toward the East Room. "I know it has taken me
a long time to admit this, Philip, but I am actually starting to like you."

"Your secret is safe with me, sir."

Everything Fanny had said about this family was true.
In spite of the fact that Jane was quite prepared to

dislike the Earl of Stanmore, a well-regarded member of the House of Lords, after only a few hours in his company she could not stop herself from liking and respecting him. Quiet and direct in speech, Stanmore was a dashingly handsome man as well as quite obviously intelligent and surprisingly broad-minded.

And the countess was a rare gem. Unpretentious in a manner unlike any of the aristocracy Jane knew, Lady Stanmore had a beauty that radiated from within. Rebecca, as she insisted on being called, had welcomed her as if the two of them had been lifelong friends. By the end of the evening, Jane had fallen under her charm so much that she found herself wishing that a long-term friendship between them could be possible.

Why, even these couple's children were exceptional. Their older boy, James, who had turned eleven this past summer, appeared slightly hard of hearing in one ear and only had two fingers in his deformed right hand. But neither of the problems affected either the lad's spirit or his attachment to his infant brother.

The young Samuel Fredrick Wakefield, only two months old, demonstrated his strong personality at regular intervals. Holding the round-faced baby had made Jane's heart swell with unexpected emotion. And later on, when she'd watched Rebecca nurse the child herself and put him in his crib, Jane had found a startling maternal yearning clutching at her breast.

The only thing that had exceeded those feelings had been the fluttering heat that had erupted within her upon coming downstairs and finding Nicholas standing in the East Room. His eyes smiled warmly when he saw her enter.

Other than some cordial and public pleasantries, not much more had been said between them. But he rarely ever took his eyes off her for the remainder of the evening.

As the farewells were said and they prepared to leave, Rebecca pulled Jane aside for a private word.

"Jane, I have already done my best to impress it on Nicholas, but now I am petitioning you. Do please come and stay a few days with us at Solgrave. Our short visit tonight has only managed to whet my appetite for getting to know you better, and I am so eager to have a longer visit with you."

Jane was pleased with the invitation and said so. "My sister and Lady Spencer should be arriving in London tomorrow or the next day, I should think. I should tell you I am very much under their direction for the length of our short stay in England."

"Very well." Rebecca smiled and looped her arm through Jane's. Together, they walked toward the open front door. "Then I shall send a letter to Lady Spencer about it and make sure you all come to Solgrave."

"I, for one, would be delighted." She returned the warm smile of the countess and said goodbye to Stanmore before following Frances out into the pleasantly cool night. A carriage and a groom were waiting for them on the street, as well as several of the Stanmores' footmen.

"I had the best of times." Frances's happy smile turned into a yawn that she hardly tried to hide. "But I believe I should spend most of the day tomorrow in bed."

She was handed into the carriage first, but just as Jane started to climb in after her, Nicholas's firm grip on her elbow held her back. "You go on to the house, Fanny. Jane and I will walk the few blocks home."

Jane's stomach leaped pleasantly and her heart began pounding hard in her chest, but she was not so blinded not to notice the glint of Fanny's mischievous smile as the young woman sank back into the carriage seat. "I hope you won't think me impolite, Jane, but I am not waiting up."

After the carriage had pulled away, Nicholas's hand tightened on her arm. "I hope you have no fear of walking with me."

She shook her head, but couldn't bring herself to look into his face. His touch, his voice, the promise of the two of them alone together again set the tingling feelings racing along her skin. He dropped his hand, but they fell in step as they strolled down the street.

"How careless of me not to ask! How is your ankle?"

"Perfectly well, thank you." She looked about contentedly. "They are a lovely family."

"It is hard to believe that they have already been married over a year." He cast a parting glance back toward the house. "Time passes by so quickly."

"Lady Stanmore told me how she and James had been living in the American colonies for nearly ten years before coming back to England and meeting the earl."

"She does not share the story of her life with many people. She obviously likes you."

"The feeling is mutual. I believe I am quite fortunate to have had the opportunity of meeting them. Thank you."

"Well, after the relentless questioning that Stanmore subjected me to this morning—during which time he forced me to talk about nothing but the mysterious and beautiful Miss Jane whom I was so absorbed in—there was no getting away with it."

Surprised, she glanced up at him, only to be staggered by the look of tenderness in his blue gaze.

"I have missed you, Jane."

The force of the simply spoken words caused her heart to lodge immediately in her throat. She couldn't say the words, but her hand moved on its own accord and slipped through his arm. The streets on the next block were darker, with only a single lamp hanging from a house near either end. He tightened her hold against his side.

"Though I knew the horrible chaos of war in my army years and even sought out the pleasures of confusion later in my unpredictable, unprincipled rogue's life, I had never truly understood the painful joy of turmoil until I fell in love with you." They halted in the darkness. "No one could have described it to me. No matter what my past experiences were with women, I was unprepared for the ups and downs of what we have gone through."

"I am sorry, Nicholas," she whispered guiltily. "I know I've done a great deal that needs explaining, but nothing about me has ever been simple. I should have done a better job of protecting you . . ."

"No." Nicholas's hand pressed hers on his arm. "Perhaps it sounds foolish, but I am trying to become a better man—a more worthy human being—because of you. And finally I find I am able to feel . . . to love . . . to plan . . . to want a future for us. And all because of you. I have no regret for any of this. My only problem is I am impatient to begin having you beside me for the rest of my life."

She turned her head away abruptly to hide sudden tears. A carriage rolled by them on the street, the driver eying them suspiciously as he passed. They continued along the sidewalk in measured steps, but Jane was too numb to feel the ground.

"I had promised myself that I would not rush you again. And here we are, our first moments alone together in days, and I am doing just that." He pulled her closer to his side until their arms and hips brushed and their bodies moved in unison. They turned onto Leicester Square. "I shall try to be better. Can you forgive me?"

She laughed through the tears and brushed away the wetness with her free hand. "Yes, I think so."

"Then it is settled," he said more cheerfully. "Being the paragon of courtesy that I am and knowing that you must be quite tired from the day of traveling, I shall allow you to get a good night's sleep tonight."

"That is *very* generous of you, sir."

"But tomorrow is a different matter," he warned.

"And how is that?"

His voice dropped, his tone low and confidential. "Because tomorrow I need you to arise early. I plan to take you around London and show you some of the unsavory elements of Sir Nicholas Spencer's life."

"Are you telling me you are not *perfect*?"

"Far from it, my love." He walked her up the stairs to the front door of his town house. After a rather weary-looking doorman opened the door and greeted them, Nicholas walked her as far as the bottom of the stairs. "Now you go up and latch your door before another unsavory part of me comes out."

Jane smiled, but before she could turn away he brushed his lips across hers. It was a chaste kiss. Curiously enough, it was entirely different from everything they had previously shared. But it was also a reminder of the passion that flared between them whenever they touched, and of the love that lurked just beyond the mist.

Chapter 28

Jane stood over the trunk, staring at the layers of clothing separated by delicate papers. How Fey had managed it, Jane wasn't quite sure, but there was not a single black dress in the thing.

She smiled. How could she be angry? Fey had just known intuitively that Jane's few days in London should be unrelated to anything in her past. This was a time for color and silk and lace.

Frances had not yet stirred when Jane came down around seven, but to her delight Nicholas was already up and ready to start the day. His weariness had disappeared, and he looked refreshed and buoyant.

"I am very happy that you awakened so early. I have much to show you."

"How about your sister?"

"I would suppose she shall be sleeping for most of the morning. After that, she will want to visit some of the slew of friends that Charles tells me have been beating a daily path to my door since we left for Ireland."

She couldn't think of any reason to object, considering she was so looking forward to spending this day in his company.

Once they had breakfasted, her host escorted her to his waiting phaeton and helped her in.

"For two night owls like us," he remarked with a smile as he took up his whip, "to set out so early in the day is rather an accomplishment."

"Where are you taking me this morning?"

"You ask too many questions. Patience, my love." He

touched her affectionately on the knee. "You shall find out soon enough."

With a groom mounted behind them, Jane found herself rolling through narrow side streets. Skirting Covent Garden, they were very soon cutting into the heavy traffic of the Strand and heading for the Temple Bar and the City of London. Carriages and carts vied for space and pedestrians risked their lives on the crowded thoroughfare, and very shortly Nicholas turned off onto a lane so narrow she wondered how he even saw it. It was soon obvious that he knew it well, as he drove on with confidence through a rabbit warren of twisting alleys and lanes.

As her host maneuvered around carts and an overturned sedan chair that had been stripped of its essentials, Jane realized that this was not the fashionable London that she remembered. The neighborhoods quickly grew poorer. The light and air here became dark and heavy with dampness and the smells of poverty. Many of the houses—mere skeletons lacking windows and doors—seemed to lean upon one another for support. Some had simply collapsed into themselves from neglect.

And everywhere she looked, it seemed, Jane saw people who equaled the houses in obvious need.

"You are still not telling me where we are going!"

"You shall see in just a few moments."

True to his word, at the shadowy twist in the alley, they came upon a squalid river or canal. Jane was unsure what it was, for it was filled with slow-moving liquid of some unnatural color, and Nicholas reined in his team. The waterway, lined with dilapidated houses that hung out over it at rakish angles, contained the moss-covered remains of indeterminate objects and reeked of sewage. A rickety bridge led across, and dozens of the neighborhood's inhabitants stopped to look with surprise at the carriage . . . until they recognized the driver.

Cries of "Halloo, Sir Nicholas!" or "If it ain't our own Sir Nicholas!" or "Oy, Nick, we've not seen ye much o' late," rang out, and he waved back as he carefully urged his team across the bridge.

"These people know you," she whispered with amazement. More people waved at them as he arrived on the other end.

"I have a bad habit of getting around." He brought the phaeton to a stop beside a deserted warehouse of crumbling brick, and climbed down. Ragged folk passed going in either direction, but only the legions of street urchins stopped to cast more than a curious glance at them. Along the buildings lining the thoroughfare, men and women stood or crouched in the idleness that poverty breeds.

Even as he turned to smile encouragingly at her, it occurred to Jane that she didn't know of anyone in his class who would dare to set foot in neighborhoods like this, but Nicholas showed no hint of either fear or disgust. When he reached for Jane and motioned for her to climb down, she didn't hesitate.

"Despite its rather unpleasant appearance," he said, seeming to read her thoughts, "so long as you are in my company, you can walk in this quarter in complete safety."

"I am not worried." She gave him a confident smile.

"I know . . . I know. Nothing is too threatening for the celebrated Egan. Nonetheless, hold on tightly to your handkerchief and purse." He grinned, clutching her hand in his all the same as he turned her down the narrow lane. "Now I can get to the purpose of why I brought you here."

They may as well have been strolling in St. James's Park. He seemed as much part of this world as that one.

"You probably already know this, but in England— in the view of most of my well-to-do contemporaries— poverty is a regrettable but necessary state of affairs. The poor must labor to fuel the machinery of society."

"It is no different anywhere."

"Indeed. And while the working poor are essential to a country, their work and their lives are not considered honorable. Even from the pulpits we hear it declaimed that there is some flaw in their characters that has made and kept them poor. Their sins drive them to poverty and poverty requires them to perform the drudgery that supports the rest of us."

Jane held back her own opinion, for she doubted these were Nicholas's views.

"There are many distinguished members of our society who still believe that the classes into which we are born were established by God. It is a system established for the purpose of order. To have superiors, then, you must have inferiors. Some exist to serve and obey, while others are born to command."

"This is the thinking that allows such brutal repression in Ireland."

"And other places, as well." His blue eyes met hers. "And that is why I brought you here. I wanted you to see that the suffering is not limited just to Ireland. Right here in London"—he made a sweeping motion of the people around him—"one finds the poor and hungry. There is suffering right beneath our almighty noses, but our response is the same."

"Society *chooses* to not see them," Jane offered. "Those above consider these people only good for cleaning their houses and sweeping their streets, for plowing their lands, for digging out their quarries, and serving in their armies and in their ships."

"And that is only the honest work."

"And they wonder why those in slums like this riot. And they wonder why people like those in Ireland and in the colonies in America chafe under the heavy yoke."

"Yes." Nicholas's grasp tightened. "But not everyone is so ruthless. Not all of us are blind."

He returned the greeting of a crippled old man leaning against the bare planks of a house before turning his attention back to her. "I brought you here because I wanted to show you my cause, Jane. Doing something for these people, especially those who are young and homeless, has been my own way of alleviating my personal guilt. And though this is not as heroic as anything you have done in Ireland, it is a starting point for me."

She shook her head. "You can make a difference here. The mere immenseness of the poverty of cities makes any contribution much more heroic than anything I have done."

"But there is so much to do."

He looked into an alley so tangled that no light reached the ground. Jane could see movement at the end of the alley, but whether it was human or animal, she could not tell.

"I brought you here so you would know that no matter where you go or live or decide to spend the rest of your life, there are people who will need you. Everyone in this country is not a Musgrave. There is bad and good. There are those who want to dominate, and some who want to share the bounty. And then there is one who wants you at his side in life and in love . . . for eternity."

She was so affected by his last words that the noise and people around them had become a blur. All she could see was Nicholas. A tug on her skirt, though, drew her attention to a little girl who was looking up with huge brown eyes at the two of them.

"Beggin' yer pardon, Sir Nicholas, sir."

She dropped her hand from Jane's skirt when their attention turned to her. She was dressed in a filthy and torn print frock and a broken black chip bonnet. Jane saw the child was wearing no shoes. "Ye dunno me, sir, but I'm Bessie's sister."

"Bessie, you say?"

"Oy, sir. A whiles back I used to share a room—'twas jist a hole, sir, really. But Bessie an' me was livin' with my brother . . . off Drury Lane. And then the Irishman and his slut come an' tossed us, sir."

"This is quite a history for one so little, Miss . . . Miss . . ." Nicholas crouched down until he was more at eye level with the child. "Since you know me, then perhaps we should be properly introduced."

A soft blush crept up the dirty cheeks. "My name is Sally, sir." She gave a shy curtsy and pushed her long rusty hair under the bonnet as she looked up at Jane.

"Nice to meet you, Miss Sally. And this is Miss Purefoy."

"Good to meet you, Sally." At Jane's smile, the girl blushed deeper and rubbed the palm of her hand on her thin dress.

"Do I know your brother?" Nicholas asked.

She shook her head. "But ye might be knowing Bessie . . . or maybe not. She's two years older than I, an' last winter—after we got tossed by the mick—ye

found 'er an' took 'er to one o' yer houses . . . the one
by the market.''

"Why did you not come with her?"

She blushed again. "I was afraid, sir . . . I ran an' hid.
But I ain't afraid now. D'ye remember her?''

"I am sure I will remember her as soon as I see her.''

"Last summer, Bessie an' me used to go about the
streets sellin' watercreases.''

"Did you?'' Jane asked encouragingly.

"Aye, miss. We'd go, 'Four bunches a penny . . . watercreases!' Our mum learned us to needlework and knit
when we was little. I used to go to school, too. But I
wasn't there long. I've forgot all about it now. 'Twas
such a time ago.'' The girl's fingers twisted nervously
before her. "But my mum died a few winters back, an'
my brother took off last month, an' I had to move out
o' the place here . . .'' She pointed vaguely toward a
nearby alley.

"Where do you live now, Sally?'' Nicholas asked
gently.

She looked down at her bare feet. "I've been on the
streets for a whiles, sir. But I've not been goin' hungry.
I work . . . I goes to a woman's house till eleven o'clock
on Saturday nights. All I have to do is to snuff the candles and poke the fire. They is Jews, sir, and have their
Sunday on Saturday, an' they won't touch anything; so
they gives me my vittals an' a penny besides.'' The
child's feet shuffled on the dirt. "But winter's coming, I
know . . . an' I miss Bessie.''

"Then you shall move into the same house with
Bessie.''

Nicholas continued to talk to the young girl, but Jane
found herself concentrating on him while fighting her
own emotions. She had loved him before, but now—as
she watched his gentle and caring dealings with Sally—
her affection for him grew even greater.

When they worked their way back to the carriage and
climbed in, they took Sally with them. Whatever else
Nicholas had intended to show her, though, was put
aside. Bessie, it turned out, was not at the house "by
the market,'' and as a result Jane received a tour of

several of a group of houses that Nicholas, she learned, had created to shelter street children. It was almost noon before they found the sister and settled Sally in with people who would care for her.

When they finally returned to Nicholas's house on Leicester Square, it was early in the afternoon, and they were told that Frances was visiting her friend Elizabeth and should not be expected for dinner.

"Thank you for today," Jane said under the watchful gaze of the fierce-looking steward. There were messages waiting for Nicholas when they'd arrived.

"I have to see to a couple of correspondences in the library," Nicholas told her. "Why not try to rest and come down and meet me there later . . . whenever you are ready."

She nodded and went to her room. Once inside, though, resting was the last thing on her mind. This side of Nicholas—the philanthropic part of him—had opened her eyes to the rest of his character. For the first time, she thought, she could really see him. Understand him. Much the same as she did, Nicholas presented only one side of himself to society. His was an attitude of a confirmed rake—sporting, independent, careless, and self-centered. He was outspoken, arrogant, and openly disdainful of the system that mandated how he should live his life. But in private, he could pursue his own valuable interests without the pressure of society's constraints. His generosity was for the sake of people in need and not contingent on the fashionably fickle philanthropies of the *ton*.

She learned today, from the people she had met in their tour, that Nicholas had established so far nearly a dozen safe houses for children across London.

Standing before the window, she knew that she admired him and loved him for the man that he was and couldn't wait to tell him so.

An hour was all that she was able to stay away. Dressing in a soft yellow dress that she once again wondered how Fey had managed to have made for her, Jane cast a final look at herself in the mirror before going down. Of everything in the trunk, this was the least conservative of the garments, and as she descended the steps, Jane's stomach was already dancing with the memories of their lovemaking in Ireland.

There was no denying it. She loved him. She respected him. She desired him.

The visits yesterday seemed to have paid off. The letters he'd received this morning were very encouraging. Nicholas sealed the last of his responses and handed them to his waiting steward.

"Have them delivered this afternoon, Charles."

"I shall have it done, sir," the burly middle-aged man assured him. "And how was your ride with Miss Purefoy this morning?"

"It was fine," Nicholas answered, straightening the papers on his desk.

"I hope you ain't tired her too much."

"I did not."

"Jack tells me you missed more than a few of the famous visiting places in our fair city."

Nicholas lifted his gaze at the jocular tone of his steward. "Miss Purefoy had already seen all that rubbish before. And before you ask . . . yes, she appeared to have enjoyed our little excursion. And yes, you may report all of this to Mrs. Hannagan."

"She'll be pleased . . . though I'm guessing she already knows." The man grinned crookedly, showing a missing front tooth and managing to look only slightly less ferocious. "We're all thinking Miss Purefoy's a keeper, sir. We just thought you might need to be told."

"Thank you, Charles. Now did I mention that I wanted those letters to be delivered today?"

"Aye, sir." With a polite bow the steward left the room only to knock a moment later to announce Jane's wish to see him.

Nicholas immediately rose to his feet. He felt almost foolish, the way his heart swelled in his chest when he saw her face.

"Am I intruding?" she asked shyly when Charles closed the door on his way out.

"No. I am quite finished." He came around his desk. "How was your hour's respite? Recovered from our jaunt?"

"I was too restless to lie down." She glanced back toward the door and smiled. "I made the mistake of saying the same thing to Mrs. Hannagan, and the sweet woman was ready to call in a doctor to have me bled. I have to thank Charles for coming in and putting her mind at ease."

"They are quite the pair, those two. They have been with me for years and can be quite entertaining." He let his gaze wander appreciatively over the dress she was wearing. "Mrs. Hannagan is easily rattled, but Charles took far too many blows to his head in his youth to let anything affect him."

"Blows to the head?"

"He was a boxer. A very good one, too, until a sly fox blinded him in his left eye at Wetherby's on Drury Lane. After that, the poor devil took quite a beating on that side for several years."

"So you took him into your service."

"Had to. He would have been killed if he'd continued to fight."

She continued to stand by the door, so he approached her.

"But I don't want to talk about Charles right now."

Her dark gaze flashed with awareness. "What do you want to do, sir?"

He took both of her hands in his and placed kisses on the soft palms. "Where did we leave off our conversation this morning?"

Instead of answering, she freed her hands and slipped them around his neck. "I do not feel much like talking right now."

Desire surged in his loins. "Then what . . . what exactly do you want to do, miss?"

She raised herself on her toes and brushed her lips against his.

"This." She repeated the kiss—this time with much more heat.

Nicholas lost himself in the seductive play of their mouths as soon as she pressed her body against his. She was all woman and fire, and he couldn't get enough of her. His mouth slanted deeply over hers and his hands were possessive when they caressed her back, her

breasts, cupping her bottom, and pressing her hard
against him.

"I want you, Jane. By 'sblood, I have missed you."

"I have missed you, too."

Her hands moved beneath his jacket as he tasted the
skin of her neck. His hands began to loosen the laces
on the dress.

"We should go upstairs."

"No. Here." She pulled him toward the nearest chair.

He was too focused on the moment to object to anything. His jacket was tossed to the floor. The front of
his breeches were opened as he sat back on the chair.
Jane lifted her skirts, and he drew her onto his lap, im-
paling her with a single thrust as she straddled him.

Nicholas echoed her groan as her muscles closed
around his member in the tightest of fits.

"You are so exquisitely perfect," he murmured. He
pulled down on the neckline of her dress, freeing her
ivory breasts. He sensed her holding her breath as his
tongue started running in circles around one of her nipples. With her moan of pleasure, he greedily took her
fully into his mouth.

Jane dug her fingers into his hair and guided his
mouth to her other breast as her hips rose and moved
around him.

He struggled for a moment to keep her steady and try
to salvage some of his restraint. But when Jane's head
fell backward, she looked like a goddess riding him, and
he lost all control.

Their release was fast and joyous, and each clasped
the other in their arms as the fulfillment of their desires
bonded their bodies and their souls.

For a few moments each of them fought to catch their
breaths. Their bodies were still joined at the most intimate of places. Her dress was a shambles—half on, half
off her body. His own shirt was partially unbuttoned and
her cheek was pressed against his shoulder.

"Well, this was certainly a most pleasant surprise," he
whispered against her hair some time later, once he'd
found his voice. The soft laugh he heard made him smile.

"I cannot believe I seduced you," she whispered, sigh-
ing contentedly.

"So . . . trying to take all the credit, I see," he teased, sliding his hands beneath her skirts and along the smooth skin of her thigh. "Do you mean you refuse to recognize how strategically I planned all of this?"

Before she could respond, a soft knock on the door jerked Jane off his chest. She looked frantically at him before trying to back off his lap.

"One moment, Charles," he said, grinning in spite of himself. He pulled up his breeches while trying to help her adjust her dress. "The poor devil will be terribly shocked."

A second knock came, but before Nicholas could call out again, the door opened slightly, and Clara's face appeared.

Chapter 29

Shock had made her stare for a moment longer than she should have. Shame then made her stumble backward as she turned and ran frantically upstairs.

Clara needed a place to hide, but upon arriving at the top of the stairs, she looked wildly about her, not knowing where to go or which room was safe.

They had not officially arrived yet. Lady Spencer was still outside, chatting with some lady who had been passing in an open carriage on the street. Servants were running about, either outside seeing to the luggage or inside preparing to receive the guests. One of them had told her that Miss Purefoy was in that room—the library—so Clara had knocked. Hearing no answer, she had simply peeked in.

She brought a hand to her mouth. It was only obvious what they had been doing. Too . . . too obvious. Crazy thoughts of pretending the whole thing hadn't happened ran through her head. She would just go back outside with Lady Spencer, she thought, and wait to enter the house officially with her. Whirling to run back down the stairs, Clara didn't make it a step, for Jane was facing her on the top stair.

"We . . . it was raining endlessly . . . in Bath," Clara stuttered. "So we decided . . . to come back to London . . . sooner than expected."

"Come with me, Clara." There were tears in Jane's eyes when she took hold of Clara's arm and dragged her up another flight of stairs.

The young woman went along without a struggle. At

the top they entered a bedchamber that she realized was Jane's.

"A lovely room," Clara whispered. "Bright sun comes in through those . . ."

"Please do not do this to me."

Clara turned and watched her sister leaning against the closed door.

"Do not pretend that nothing has happened, or that you failed to see us downstairs." Jane pushed herself away from the door and took a step toward her. "Be honest with me, Clara. Let me bear the guilt and the blame. Release your anger, somehow, instead of holding it in."

"Jane, you are a grown woman. What you do with your life . . ."

"What I have done with *your* life is what we are discussing now," the older sister said brokenly. Her cheeks were flushed. "Clara, I know you asked me, pleaded with me to leave Nicholas alone. You said that you were interested in him. That you were somehow planning to convince him . . . to marry you."

"But you could not do it."

"No, I couldn't. The fact is . . . I . . . we . . . love each other. And though I know that there is no chance of us ever having . . . a future together . . . at the same time . . . if you really wanted him . . . if you loved him even close to how much I love him . . . if you knew the man that he is . . . then I would . . . I would stay away." Jane batted at the tears coursing down her face. "But he deserves more than a mere contract. He deserves someone who will truly care. And *you* deserve to find a man who can love you as well."

Clara sat on the edge of the bed and battled her own raw emotions in response to Jane's fierce sadness.

"It is the most astonishing thing to be in love, Clara. As desperate as my life might appear to you—despite the fact that I may never have a settled future—loving Nicholas and being loved by him has given me something I have never had before. He has given me something I never felt with Conor."

Henry's face was so clearly etched in her mind's eye that Clara had no difficulty conjuring his image now. She did indeed know what it was to love . . . and to feel its pain. "But we are not all born to be strong. We cannot all simply go after what we want and succeed in getting it."

"But you were born strong." Jane crouched before her. "You and I are sisters—we are made of the same stock. While I have led my life as a rebel, you have striven to conform and to obey, to be the perfect daughter to our parents. In the process, though, you have caged up your own spirit." Jane's hands cupped Clara's. "You cannot continue to shoulder blame for me, to be the ever-compliant peacemaker in our parents' home. You cannot go on forever saying and doing what pleases everyone else and forgetting about yourself."

A memory long buried forced tears to Clara's eyes. She looked down at their joined hands.

"Blame belongs to those who have sinned, Clara. My past is my own doing. The life I have led has been led by my own choosing. Our parents' differences are as old as time, and there might never be a way to resolve it. But that is their life, not yours." Jane's voice dropped low, her tone filled with conviction. "Break the shell, Clara. Let me see my own sister. I thought I was seeing a glimpse of it that morning when you asked me to leave Woodfield House and Nicholas's life. But I know now that wasn't really you. Your reaction to what you witnessed a few moments ago confirmed it. You do not care for him enough even to fight."

"It is true. I don't love Nicholas. I told you that. I don't think I ever shall," Clara whispered. "And I am not angry with you for any of it."

"But I am angry with myself," Jane answered. "And it is not because of any regret over what Nicholas and I have shared, but for the years that I have allowed you to hide within your shell."

She reached out and lifted Clara's chin until their tearful gazes locked. "Tell me how you feel. Help *me*, and let me help *you*. Clara, it is time you pushed aside this facade of indifference."

"Sometimes I fear there is nothing inside of that shell." A choked cry escaped the younger sister's throat and she looked away. "It hurts too much to change."

"Why? As I see it now, it is hurting you more to stay the same." Jane again drew her sister's face around. "You are so sad, Clara. And I am not talking about today. You have been so sad for so long . . . and I cannot remember when it was that you changed."

"I know when it was that I changed." The words bubbled up inside of her. She had reached her limit, and there was no stopping the long-hidden truth. "My life changed forever when I walked into that village nine years ago and saw my sister keening over the corpse of her lover. I changed the day I saw you curse everyone who was responsible for Conor's death . . . even though you didn't know enough to curse me. I chose to keep a secret and hide my own sin."

Jane's face was bloodless when Clara looked up.

"It was my fault that Conor was arrested that week. It was my failure to do what you asked me. If I had delivered your message to him, he would not have come that morning. He would not have been captured . . . or killed." Clara sobbed wretchedly. "I was too afraid of doing anything against Father's wishes even then, so I lied to you and said that I had delivered your message. And then I saw what my lie did. It cost Conor his life. And with it, I destroyed your very future."

Clara buried her face in her hands and wept. "I am so sorry, Jane. I never knew . . . never thought how horrible the consequences could be. And for all these years . . . this thing has been sitting in my heart . . . and . . . and then I was so ruthless to you again . . . asking you to leave Nicholas when I really didn't want to marry him. I was so confused after Henry had proposed to me . . . before I ran away and ruined everything again. I just . . . I am the most hateful person . . . and you never see it. I have been ruined from the inside, as if some horrible worm has eaten through my soul . . . leaving me hollow. Yes, hollow . . . with only the shell for the world to see. Instead of trying to help me, you should hate me."

The mattress shifted. A moment later, Clara felt Jane's hands gather her tightly against her.

"I will *never* hate you. Do you hear me? Never. You were a mere child when I made you take that message.

Father had me locked away, but it was very wrong of me to put that weight on you." Her words were soothing. "And knowing Conor, he would never have changed his plans, no matter what message I sent or what danger awaited him. He was resolved for us to go through with it. His decision had been made."

Jane gently caressed Clara's hair as she spoke. "You see . . . the fault was with me for getting you involved at all . . . and with our father . . . and with this country . . . and also with Conor and me for being so unprepared and so blind." She brushed the wetness from Clara's cheek. "But one thing I have recently learned . . . the time comes when we all must part with the past. No matter who is to blame, I have finally decided to live what is left of my life. It is time to give over the pain of what went wrong. And Clara, you need to try to do the same. Life is too precious. *You* are too important to me. We must change the way things are." She placed a kiss on the younger sister's brow.

"But for so long . . . I have just been the same miserable pretender. I don't know how to change."

"Oh, yes. You do." Jane smiled gently. "And with some intensive tutoring from me, you can still earn the title of the second wicked Purefoy girl."

Clara felt a sense of giddiness rising inside of her. She hugged Jane fiercely and let the sadness ease its way out of her body.

"Thank you. Thank you for always being there for me. And thank you . . . for your offer of making me wicked." She pulled back and wiped the tears off her face. "I truly need it."

"Very well." Jane clutched her hand. "But before we start our first lesson, what was it that you said about Henry Adams proposing? I didn't think it was my imagination that there was something peculiar about you two."

"What on earth did you tell her? She didn't look at me crossly once during the dinner. In fact, I should say Clara seemed unusually cheerful this evening."

No sooner had everyone retired for the night than

Nicholas had been at her door. He had been genuinely concerned over what had happened this afternoon, and he and Jane hadn't been able to share a private word all night.

But simply talking had proven too difficult for them both.

"Do you really expect me to reveal a confidential conversation between two sisters?" she teased, rolling Nicholas on his back and stretching her body on top of his. She kissed his neck—tasted the hollow of his throat. "Do you know this was the first time we made love in a real bed?"

"You are changing the subject." His muscular arms wrapped around Jane, impeding her movements. "What did you tell Clara about us, Jane?"

"I told her that I love you."

The change in his face was stunning. The intensity of his blue eyes scorched her. She realized that this was the first time she had actually declared her own feelings.

"And did you speak them only for her sake?"

She shook her head. "I love you, Nicholas."

Jane heard the short breath that escaped his lungs, and she thrilled to his kiss. His manhood was hard once again, and she felt the molten pools forming within her, as well. But before their bodies could join again, he gently cupped her face and pulled back.

"What else did you tell her?"

"I told her you love me, too."

"What else?"

She shook her head in confusion. He rolled them on the bed again until he was covering her.

"Didn't you tell her that I have asked you to be my wife?"

She hadn't, but there was no need for an answer as he seemed to read her silence.

"Jane, I know I am undeserving of you, but . . ."

"It is the exact opposite . . . and you know it." She wrapped her arms around him and met his gaze. "I love you, Nicholas, and I am willing to spend the rest of my life with you . . . but not in marriage."

"Why not?" His temper flared.

"I have said it before, but you don't seem to want to hear any of it." She sighed. "There is scandal in my past. I never wish to taint your family name with . . ."

"Bloody hell." He pushed himself up, looming over her. "To be sure, you are the most stubborn woman ever born. Why can you not get it in your head that nothing of your past will have the slightest effect on our marriage—or in the way people treat you in the future?"

"And you are the most stubborn man," she retorted. "What is wrong with the two of us continuing on as we are? I might even consider leaving Ireland and coming to live in London. I could become your paramour . . . or concubine . . . or whatever it is they call those women these days. Mistress . . . that's it."

"I cannot believe you can offend me so casually!" He lifted his weight off of her and sat up. He ran a weary hand through his long loose hair.

Jane touched his back, sat up, and placed a kiss on his shoulder. "I was not trying to offend you. On the contrary, I am being helpful."

"Then don't be," he snapped, glaring at her.

A pang of vulnerability pierced her heart. Her face must have shown it, for he reached out gently and touched her face.

"I love you, Jane. Do you understand? I love you. I want to spend the rest of my life with you as husband and wife." His hand moved down and rested on her flat stomach. "Do you realize, after what we've shared, you might already be carrying our child?" He didn't wait for an answer. "But whether we have our own, or care for all the waifs who wander the streets without home or family, would it not be wonderful to work together to make a difference in the world?"

"I do." She drew her knees against her chest and set her chin on them. "But it is so complicated. I must do the right thing for you . . ."

"But how about us?" he prodded, wrapping an arm around her shoulder and pulling her against him. "Like it or not, it is already us, Jane, and we can do the right thing together."

He kissed her again, and she felt all of his passion and frustration in it. She could easily lose herself in the warmth of his mouth, in the caress of his hands. But he pulled away. Stretching her out on the bed, he pulled the bedclothes up and tucked them around her body.

"You are not staying?"

He shook his head.

"You need time to think . . . to sort things out in your mind. And I need time to cool my blood." His fingers twirled a strand of her hair. "I want you too much, Jane, and I am afraid I might be scaring you with so much pressure."

She opened her mouth in denial, but he placed a finger on her lips.

"Please . . . tonight . . . just think of us."

Chapter 30

Jane was pleasantly surprised when Mrs. Hannagan announced Lady Stanmore's arrival the next afternoon. She was even more delighted by the warmth of the greeting she received from Rebecca.

"I am so sorry that no one else is here this afternoon but me." Jane accompanied the other woman back to the drawing room and where she had been brooding and sketching for most of the afternoon. "Lady Spencer took my sister and Miss Frances out to visit some friends, and I haven't seen Sir Nicholas all day."

"Well, there is no need for an apology, for I came over just to see you." Rebecca glanced at the unfinished sketch on the end table before taking a seat. "I see Nicholas is not boasting about you without grounds. You are *very* good."

Jane was embarrassed about leaving her work out in the open. The exposed drawing was an attempt at capturing Nicholas's face, but no matter how many times she'd worked the sketch, she still couldn't take the expression of hurt out of his eyes.

"I . . . I have had very little formal training, and I fear it shows dreadfully."

She took a seat next to Rebecca as Mrs. Hannagan arrived, ushering a servant carrying a tray of tea and biscuits into the room. While the tea was being poured, Jane watched the two women chat pleasantly about the trials of new motherhood. A moment later, the housekeeper and serving girl left the two of them alone, closing the door on their way out.

"Do you know, this is the first time I've been separated from Samuel since he was born?" Rebecca turned her attention back to Jane. "Stanmore likes to tease me endlessly about my attachment to our sons."

"They seem like such happy boys."

"That is true so long as they have my undivided attention. Of course, there is no one to blame for that but myself." She smiled. "I suppose this is one of the trials of late motherhood. You have more experience in life, but at the same time you are less willing to take a chance."

Jane sipped her tea. Nicholas had told her that Rebecca was only three years older than she was.

"But I am sure you are wondering what I am doing here."

"Perhaps a little. But whatever the reason, I am glad for it."

"I am, too," Rebecca answered heartily, picking up her own cup. "It has been over a year since Stanmore and I were married. But despite all of the socializing that goes with my husband serving in Lords, there are very few women in London whom I would consider good friends."

She declined the offer of biscuits.

"Not that I have any great problem with that. My life is so full, and—this may strike you as odd—my husband and I have become best friends to each other. But still, when fate directs me to someone special like you— someone caring and intelligent and independent, someone who does not quite match society's expectations for women—I cannot help but want to pursue that friendship."

If those words had come from anyone else, if they had been spoken in any other way than the way Rebecca said them, Jane might have taken umbrage. As it was, though, she found herself completely at ease with the mixture of frankness and gentleness in the woman.

"You have a gift of making people feel quite special." Jane smiled. "Your happiness is enviable."

"I must admit to you that I wasn't always as happy." Rebecca took a sip of her tea and put the cup and saucer on the table. "I did my best with James for the ten years we lived in Philadelphia together, but there were as many hard times as there were good times. For those ten years, fears of my past, mixed with the uncertainties of the future, always preyed on my mind."

From the first moment they'd met, Jane had realized there was much more to this woman than met the eye.

"And even when I returned to England," Rebecca started again, "and after Stanmore and I became . . . intimate . . . I still had strong doubts of ever finding lasting happiness. You see . . . Stanmore wanted permanency . . . marriage . . . stability, but I thought myself unworthy of his attention . . . of his name."

"But Nicholas told me you are a half-sister to Lord North."

"Neither Stanmore nor I knew that then, and even if I did, it wouldn't have made any difference to me." She glanced in the direction of the closed door before turning to Jane again. "I had fled from London ten years earlier because I was certain I'd killed a man—in defense of my virtue—but I had killed all the same. But despite my refusal, Stanmore was not willing to give up our future. He threatened to abandon his life in England and return with me to the colonies. And since I refused to let him, I was sure he would go to the King if he must, to secure a pardon and have me stay."

"What happened?"

"Stanmore's lawyer *and* Nicholas discovered the truth about the alleged murdered man. As I was told later by them, I had only managed to wound the monster. A few years later he was killed by an angry husband."

Jane tried to stop the trembling of her hand as she placed the cup and saucer on the table. Though their backgrounds were very different, the similarity in how they felt—of not wanting to injure the man they loved— was so startling.

"Despite the connection to Lord North, the announcement of Stanmore's and my marriage was not without gossip and insinuation. But we managed to survive it very well, I think." She smiled proudly. "Knowing what I do now, having faced the elite in the course of dozens and dozens of social occasions, I can tell you that what they say means nothing when a marriage is strong."

Rebecca touched Jane gently on the knee. "I know you may think it is easy for me to say these things, since all of this is behind me. But if I could offer you a little advice . . . just listen to your heart and fear nothing about what others might think."

"Did Nicholas ask you to come and speak with me today?"

"No, he didn't. But seeing you at our home two nights ago brought to my mind memories of myself." Her gaze was direct yet tender. "Anyone watching you two can see that he is so helplessly in love with you . . . and that you are so deathly afraid."

Jane closed her eyes for an instant and then let out a long breath. "My fear is not of him. I love him more than I can ever put into words."

"And that is why you are trying to do what is right for him." She completed her thoughts.

Jane's head swam with all the difficulties ahead of them, but she also dared herself to imagine all the possibilities. The second far surpassed the first. It was a while before she turned her attention back to Rebecca.

"I appreciate what you are trying to do for me . . . for us."

She squeezed Jane's hand gently. "I did not come here for any answers, only as a woman paying a visit to a new friend." Rebecca smiled, rising to her feet. "But I had better get back before testing the patience of little Samuel's nurse."

"When are you going down to Solgrave?" Jane asked as she followed the other woman to the door.

"Tomorrow morning. And the invitation stands. Please come and see us."

"I shall try." Jane returned Rebecca's affectionate hug. "And thank you."

Mrs. Hannagan joined them by the open front entrance and wished Lady Stanmore good-bye, as well. When the countess's carriage had pulled away, Jane walked back inside with the housekeeper.

"I do not intend to be intrusive, Mrs. Hannagan, but do you know by any chance when Sir Nicholas is expected back today?"

Mrs. Hannagan gave Jane a warm smile. "Of course

I do, miss. He returned only a few minutes ago, but I told him that you and Lady Stanmore were having a private talk, so he went up to change for dinner rather than break in on you ladies."

Nicholas had just taken off his jacket and his cravat and was ready to take off his shirt when there was a knock on the door. Assuming it was his tardy valet, he called for the man to enter. He was surprised and delighted to see Jane's face peer around his door.

"May I come in?"

"Please do." He took a step toward her, but then stopped. It had been a struggle last night to walk away from her and to leave this morning before she woke up. It was far too easy for both of them to give in to their passions every time they came together. But that was not the way he wanted to share his life with her. There was so much more between them than just the physical fulfillment of their bodily desires. He was resolved to keep his distance and give her time to make a decision.

Jane entered the room and closed the door, leaning her back against it. He was still powerless when it came to resisting her, so he moved to the far side of the room to pick up a clean shirt. "I heard that you and Rebecca were visiting downstairs."

"We were."

He quickly shed his shirt and began pulling on the new one. "And how was your visit?"

"Yes."

His fingers paused. Nicholas struggled to keep his voice steady. "What did you say?"

Jane pushed herself away from the door and started toward him with measured steps. "I said 'yes.' "

"Yes . . . meaning . . . you had a pleasant visit?"

She shook her head, and then smiled and nodded. "We did have a very pleasant visit."

She came to a stop right before him. Her hands were clasped behind her back. Her chin lifted, her dark gaze charged with emotion.

"But I am really saying 'yes' to your proposal . . . 'yes' to spending the rest of my life with you."

Nicholas didn't give her a chance to take another

breath before he lifted her into his arms and whirled her around in a burst of excitement. "My God, I love you, Jane. You have made me the happiest man alive."

"And you have made me the happiest of women." They both came to a stop. She cupped his face in her hands and stared into his eyes. "There is still a great deal that we have to work out."

"We will . . . together."

"And it might take some time before I can sort everything out in Ireland."

"Then we shall sort everything out together, for I am not letting you too far out of my reach."

"There will be many who will be shocked by the news of our marriage."

"But there are others who will be delighted." He kissed her lips. "But none of them matters, anyway."

Jane hugged him tightly, feeling on her cheek the strong beat of his heart. She wouldn't let the doubts cloud her mind. She was through guessing how it was possible for everything to resolve itself.

For the first time in her life, she was daring to live beyond her dreams.

Chapter 31

When Jane arrived back in Ireland a week or so earlier than they'd planned, she found that nothing had changed and yet everything had changed.

Only Frances, already registered in a girls school in London, had stayed behind while Nicholas and Lady Spencer had traveled with her and Clara back to Woodfield House.

Although Jane felt no connection with her father—and certainly didn't care to seek his approval for this marriage—she had decided to abide for once by the etiquette of polite society. She had even encouraged Nicholas to withhold any announcement of their upcoming union until they'd had a chance to inform her parents. Of course, Nicholas's lawyers had carried a letter to the Purefoys ahead of time with directions to draw up the necessary papers, and the Spencers were told, as were the Stanmores, and a small but select number of Nicholas's closest friends. By the time the official announcement was published in the papers, Jane hoped, all of it would be nothing but very old news.

Despite the excitement of Nicholas's immediate circle of family and friends in England, Jane was completely unprepared for the warmth of the welcome that they received upon their return to Woodfield House. Everyone behaved as if there were nothing unusual about the baronet proposing to Jane. It was almost as if there had never been scandal associated with her name at all. Her mother was utterly jubilant, and her father more cordial than at any time Jane had seen him in her life.

"The proper announcements shall be sent out no later

than tomorrow morning," Lady Purefoy announced joy-fully to the women who had left Sir Thomas and Nicho-las in the dining room the night they arrived. Jane had never seen Nicholas more enthusiastic about talking to her father alone than tonight. "If you can help me, Lady Spencer, with the names and addresses of those you wish to notify, we can have them all go out tomorrow."

"I shall be delighted to be of any help that I can," the other woman offered.

"And I'd say this wedding absolutely demands two elaborate receptions—one here following the wedding service, and one in London." Catherine beamed at the prospect. "Perhaps we can arrange them so they will be only a month apart."

"Indeed, and the sooner the better," Alexandra agreed. "Before leaving London, I warned Mrs. Hanna-gan—she is Nicholas's housekeeper—to start . . ."

The two women continued to chat like the best of friends planning the most important event of their lives. Jane quietly moved away from the conversation and joined Clara by the window.

"I thought he would be coming here tonight," Clara whispered to her sister. Her gaze never left the road winding up through the valley toward Woodfield House's stables.

"I thought so, too." Jane stared in the same direction. "I sent a message to him, myself, as soon as we arrived. Mother does not seem very much concerned about the gossip that will surround Henry concerning what he said on my behalf the night of the ball. But it is important that he hear about my engagement to Nicholas from us, rather than being caught off his guard by someone else."

"The lawyers have been here nearly a week already." Clara's gaze seemed troubled when she turned to meet Jane's. "Perhaps he already knows . . . and he is upset . . . even jealous . . . and . . ."

"There is little chance of that jealousy business, little sister. Before I accepted Nicholas's proposal, I had to let go of my uncertainties and fears. You must do the same." Jane placed a comforting hand on her sister's arm. "Knowing Henry, he is probably busy right now with some act of charity, or some emergency."

"Then we may not see him tonight at all." Clara hugged her middle and looked longingly out the window again. "By heaven, I have missed him. And there is so much that I want to tell him. You . . . you have let out a monster in me. Now that I know what I want . . . and I have decided how to go about getting it . . . waiting patiently has become torture."

Jane smiled at the love and enthusiasm that had transformed her sister. Once they'd talked and Clara had explained about Henry's first proposal and her refusal, everything made sense. Thinking back, she could clearly recall all the signs that should have given her sister away.

"If I could escape, I would walk all the way to Ballyclough . . . barefooted, if I had to," Clara whispered impatiently. "This wait may kill me, Jane."

"You do not need to go on foot." She gave her sister a knowing look.

Clara cast a quick look at their mother. Lady Purefoy was still deep in conversation with Alexandra about the wedding arrangements. "Will you help me?"

"Of course, but only if you promise to ask Paul to arrange for a carriage and a couple of strong and trustworthy grooms."

"I will." Clara excitedly squeezed Jane's hand. "Thank you."

Clara slipped quietly toward the door, but Lady Purefoy's sharp eyes immediately noticed her daughter's movement. "Where are you going, Clara?"

"We are going for a walk in the garden." Jane immediately joined her sister. "You are doing such a fine job with your planning that we thought—if you don't mind— we would go outside and enjoy a little of this beautiful autumn night."

"Of course, we don't mind." Catherine smiled pleasantly. "But wear a wrap or something, you two. I do not want either of you catching a cold before the coming celebrations. And have Fey send out a servant with a torch for you. And . . ."

Side by side, the two young women left the room. Once outside, a fit of giggling took hold of Clara. "I cannot believe how much fun it is . . . to sneak out like this."

Jane was *certain* she had created a monster. "I think I will walk down to the stables with you, just to make sure that you do not do what you threatened just now—walk to Ballyclough, I mean."

At that precise moment, a distraught-looking Fey appeared from the servants' hall. Taking hold of Jane's arm, she begged for a moment's time with her . . . alone. Too excited to wait, Clara whispered her promise again to Jane and ran for the stables.

Jane turned to the housekeeper, who was obviously wracking her brain for the right words. But no choice of words could lessen the impact of the news she needed to share.

Egan was one of the last to arrive at the Shanavests' urgent gathering.

The number of men and women who had turned out was surprisingly large. But as Jenny told her the moment she crouched beside her, the purpose of the meeting had nothing to do with the terrible news Fey had conveyed. She shook her head at Egan's questioning look and motioned for her to join Liam, who was standing at one end of the dilapidated barn.

From Fey, Egan already knew that the magistrate had arrested the families—wives and children—of both Patrick and Liam early that morning, only a few short hours before the two men's return from Kildare.

The news was devastating, and as Egan made her way through the group, her mind cast about for different solutions. None, however, was comforting.

Liam was speaking to someone standing in the shadow of a rough-hewn post, while Patrick was crouched before a small peat fire not far away. His face showed the depths of his torment, and he did not look up when she touched his stooped shoulder as she passed.

At Egan's approach, Liam ceased his conversation with the stranger beyond.

"I am so sorry." She placed a hand on Liam's arm. Too many regrets were running through her. It was because of her that Patrick had been forced to go. If she had stayed behind instead of going to England . . .

Shaking herself, she forced back the guilt and tried to

focus on the present and how she could be of any use. "I came as soon as I heard the news."

The leader's expression showed how grateful he was to see her. "We'd better get started."

She nodded and took a step to the side. Glancing at the man standing beside her in the shadows, she realized it was Finn. She wasn't surprised that he was here or that he was wearing a mask and staying to the shadows. He was more of an outsider than she was . . . and she could hardly begrudge a man for trying to protect himself. After all, someone had identified Liam and Patrick.

The gathering hushed as Liam spoke a few words in greeting and then began explaining what had occurred at the meeting in Kildare.

"Every part of Ireland was represented. Indeed, not all of them go by the name of Shanavest, and there was some grumbling about that, to begin. But the grievances are all the same. Evictions, ill treatment of tenants by landlords and their dogfaced agents, land grabbing, the increasing brutality of the king's troops . . ."

Egan couldn't help but be impressed that, in spite of the distress of his own family, Liam was able to relay so clearly what he'd seen and heard.

"Although it was enlightening to see such a fine show of Irish fighting this tyranny in every part of this country for the same cause—'twas distressing to me and to Patrick that—"

"What of Ronan?" someone interrupted. "Ye seem to have lost him along the way."

"Good job getting rid of him." A few laughed.

"I didn't know that Ronan was going with them," Egan said quietly to Finn.

"Once you left for England, he couldn't keep his drinking or his tongue under control. The bloody fool was just too much trouble to keep around. It was my suggestion that Liam take him along. Sure enough, after meeting some of the groups from the north, he decided to take his leave and head north where the fight is more to his liking." The words, spoken in English rather than Gaelic, turned Egan's head sharply toward the man standing beside her.

"Henry?" she murmured.

"Finn, if you please." He squeezed her hand affectionately. "You are not the only person in Ireland who happens to be someone else as well."

"I . . . for so long now . . . you didn't tell me! Why now?"

"Listen to what Liam has to say. Not much matters after tomorrow night."

Confused, Egan turned her attention back to the meeting.

". . . far north and around Dublin itself, violence is becoming part of their everyday life. Killings, house burning, maiming of livestock has replaced filling in ditches and tearing down hedges and walls." Liam spoke with conviction. " 'Tis a vicious circle that is being created. They believe it works. But for us . . . the simple peace-loving people that we are . . . working together for the . . . the peace that we want for our . . . families . . ."

Her heart ached as Liam's voice faltered. He had to take a moment to gather himself before he could speak again.

"What Liam is trying to say"—Patrick rose to his feet—"is that 'twas clear to us that the Shanavests are going a different way from what we have always wanted. They seek blood . . . we have only shed it when we thought it necessary. We say that this group . . . our group . . . of Shanavests should disband . . . at least, for now. Despite everything that these people to the north and east are doing, there is no proof that any of it is working."

"If anything," Liam started again, "there is more retaliation against the tenants and cottagers in those areas."

"If we *were* to disband," Jenny called out from her corner, "and if we were to spread the word that we are doing it as a peace offering, do ye think the magistrate will let go of yer families?"

The question set a rumble of other questions and comments going in the assembled throng. Everyone knew about the two men's families.

"I don't know," Liam said softly. "But Patrick and I decided to tell you this long before we heard about our . . . our . . ."

" 'Tis worth trying," someone called, his comment seconded by others.

"I'm too old to be doing any more fighting," an older man announced to the cheers of some others.

"I've not lost the stomach for it," a young woman said.

"Nor I," added several others.

"We have nothing to lose," Jenny announced after realizing Liam was not confident enough to give an answer. "And we can always form our ranks again."

Silence fell over the barn until Patrick's brother-in-law spoke up. "But what of the deadline? Are we just going to stand by and watch our women and children hang?"

"Aye! The deadline is in two days."

Patrick's words sharpened Egan's attention. She knew nothing of this deadline or what the conditions were.

Jenny faced the crowd. "We'll spread word of our intentions. Send a message to the magistrate even. We shall talk as tough as that bloodless bastard Musgrave. We shall tell them that we want those women and children freed. He cannot hang innocents under such conditions."

Many voiced their agreement.

Egan turned to Finn. "What is this about a deadline?"

"The magistrate is looking to repeat the show of strength his predecessor employed nine years ago," he replied. "If certain leaders of the Whiteboys fail to turn themselves over to the dragoons at Buttevant by a certain time, he will hang their families."

Jane felt her blood run cold. "He wants Liam, Patrick, and me."

"He also wants Finn," the masked rebel responded. "All of us are to hand ourselves over to Captain Wallis before dawn, the day after tomorrow, or those women and children will die."

"He cannot."

"You know he can . . . and he will."

Egan let out an unsteady breath. "Jenny's recommendation will not work. Besides, Musgrave knows that he has us. We *will* hand ourselves over to save these families."

Finn nodded solemnly. "Yes, I know. That was why I said before . . . not much matters after tomorrow night."

One last meeting. One last midnight ride. One last night to be with him.

How quickly things change, she thought. Finally, violently, irrevocably. Shadowed by a cloud of doom, Jane took her time riding back to Woodfield House.

After everyone else had gone, the four rebel leaders had remained behind and talked. Finn had already tried to find out where exactly the two families had been taken, but he'd had no luck. Liam and Patrick, both distraught over the news, had not been any more successful. The only thing they had been able to discover was that during their absence, the dragoons seemed to have been doing an extensive search for any who were missing from the area. As luck would have it, somehow attention had been drawn to them.

Egan had had nothing to offer tonight. Suddenly the reason for her happiness had dissipated. Indeed, everything she and Nicholas had planned *was* as insubstantial as air.

The four had agreed tonight that there would be no substitutes. They all had been willing to meet again tomorrow night after midnight and go through with the exchange.

The only complications lay with arranging for a safe place for Liam's and Patrick's families to be taken to once they were released. With the two men as good as dead once they were in Musgrave's hands, Liam and Patrick wanted to know their loved ones would be safe.

Jane guessed it was already well past midnight when she returned Mab to her stall. The house on the hill was dark and quiet, but she knew that Nicholas would be awake and waiting for her. Moving in the darkness of the stable, she made her way toward the hidden passage leading from the tack room. She'd had no chance to tell him where she was going tonight, or when she'd be back. And now that she knew the truth, Jane also knew that she could not say a word to him about what was to come.

"Clear moon. Good night for riding."

Jane's heart leaped in her chest. Her hand was on the dagger at her waist before she recognized the voice as that of Sir Thomas. Shocked by the realization, she turned to find her father stepping out of the shadows of the tack room.

"Indeed," she answered simply. The fact that he was seeing her dressed in breeches, instead of a skirt—that she was out riding alone long after everyone else had been settled for the night—or that he might guess at some of her secret activities—no longer bothered her. She had nothing left to lose.

"It was very quiet around here without you going out and coming back in all hours of the night."

She bit back her surprise.

"But it was also very rewarding to know that for as many days as you were away in London, you were safe." He clasped his hands behind his back and glanced out a small window toward the house. "Nicholas and I had an extensive talk. Actually, 'battle' might be a better way of describing it."

With every sentence, he was managing to confuse her more, and Jane had difficulty keeping up her pretense of indifference.

"He wants none of your fortune."

She didn't know she had any.

"He insists on taking no land, no money, no dowry settlement of any kind. And he *is* pig-headed, by thunder."

Emotions rose up in Jane, even though she already knew how unselfish Nicholas's love for her was. It was the loss of it that made a tear slip down her face.

"But I can be as pig-headed as he is, devil take him. You are my oldest daughter. Rightfully, most of what your mother and I have should go to you and your future children." He actually chuckled. "But have no fear. We successfully settled our differences, but not before I forced him to become more flexible. This old soldier is not so easily beaten."

Jane cleared her throat, making sure she had a voice.

"I cannot understand the trouble you are putting yourself through. He already knows how my family perceives me. Nothing you say or do will make a difference in his opinion."

"Do not mistake me. I like him. But I don't give a damn about his opinion. It is you that . . ."

"Why?" The question wrenched itself from her breast. "What is all this about? Suddenly you act as if you care!"

"I have *always* cared about you, Jane." He took a step toward her.

"That's a lie."

"Do not speak to me in . . ." Sir Thomas forced himself to stop, and he ran a weary hand down his face. "Jane . . . I admit . . . I know I made a horrible mistake nine years ago. I knew you . . . I should have known that my action . . . in ordering that boy to hang . . . would not return my daughter to me. Ah, Jane! From the time you were a wee child you were different. You loved, you cared . . . you became a part of the people around you. Your mother and I came to Ireland when you were barely four years old, and not a year later you were running barefoot in those hills looking no different than the hungry Irish tenant brats."

She told herself she had no time to hear any of this. But her feet had become permanently rooted to the floor.

"When you were eight years old, you became deathly sick. Do you remember? All because one of the tenants had sold off his youngest daughter to the tinkers to pay a physician's fee when fever struck down the rest of the family." He came still closer. "Catherine and I thought we were going to lose you."

Jane looked down at her boots, fighting back tears.

"You brought her back," she said. Her father had a heart then.

"It was unfortunate that the girl died the year after when the fever came back to the valley. You mourned her as if you had lost your own sister." His voice was gentle, understanding. "I know you have been involved for years with these Whiteboys. You might think . . . that boy . . . Conor was the reason . . . or perhaps it was me and your will to go against anything I do or say. But even without us, you were . . . you are a person that had to be involved. You see injustice and you need to react."

"If you knew hanging those men was an injustice, then why didn't *you* do anything about it? Why don't you do something for the Irish now?"

"By the time my eyes were opened, a great deal of damage had already been done. I did the only thing that I could. I resigned my post."

"How convenient." She didn't bother to hide any of her hostility when their gazes locked. "But I have no time left to set blame or to try to reform . . . or educate you on how much there is left that can be corrected."

"Who would be better than Egan to offer vision to a blind man?"

His words stopped her from walking away.

"I knew about your activities with your blasted Shanavests, but I never knew you were Egan, the fearless leader of these people, until the morning of the ball." His gaze was actually admiring. "I should have known that you could not go down any road halfway. It has always been everything or nothing with you."

He was confusing her more than he had any right to do.

"Sir Nicholas tells me that you two plan to divide your time between England and Ireland. I am not asking any questions about what is to become of Egan, but I do ask you to make time to show me . . . to educate me . . . to make me understand where a change might still make a difference."

Why now? she thought. *Why must he be so late?*

"Believe me when I tell you that my motivation is not to set a trap for the others . . . or . . ."

Her gaze narrowed. "But the trap has already been set," she blurted out bitterly. "Even on the eve of the Shanavests' disbanding."

"What trap?"

She shook her head, walking away.

"You are too late, Sir Thomas. You are far, far too late."

Chapter 32

Finn had just closed the stall gate in the parsonage's stable when a woman carrying a small lamp approached the doorway. Thinking quickly, he tucked the hat and the mask under an old saddle blanket lying on the ground.

"Is that you, Henry?"

"Clara?" He straightened up, surprised. It took him a long minute, though, before he found the rest of his words. Like a beggar starved for sustenance, his eyes hungrily took in all of her. "What are you doing here at this late hour?"

"Waiting for you." She put the lamp down outside the stable and entered. "I arrived just as Mrs. Brown was going to bed. We had a cup of tea before I sent her up, and then I waited in your parlor for a while. After that I spent some time in your study . . . then back to the parlor . . . then I came out and waited in your garden."

She stopped a breath away from him. Her gaze took in his rough, homespun woolen clothing, his high boots.

"You still haven't told me why you are here."

Her white teeth flashed prettily as she smiled in the darkness. "Mr. Adams, you look more like a highwayman than a respectable minister."

"I do not know what you are about tonight, but I clearly need to find a way to get you home." He took her by the arm and started to lead her out of the stables, but she planted her feet.

"I have been away for more than a fortnight."

"I know."

"Then you should also know this is no way to greet someone whom you have been missing terribly."

He met her challenging and playful glare. "When did I say . . ."

She silenced his question by sliding easily into his arms and capturing his mouth in a kiss.

A throaty groan escaped Henry and before he could stop himself, he had deepened the kiss. His hands were greedily pressing every curve of her body against his. She moaned softly into his mouth when his palm cupped her breast through the dress.

He abruptly ended the kiss, pulling his hands away from her as if burned.

"No! This is wrong." He tried to take a step back, but Clara followed him, her hands reaching out to him.

"Do not dare to deny that you feel nothing for me, Henry Adams. And do not lie about not wanting me. False denials and lies are wrong, too. More wrong!"

She clutched at the lapels of his jacket, and as he backed against the gate of the stall, her body trapped him.

"I was young . . . stupid . . . impressionable in the most naïve way, but I loved you even then. I made a horrible mistake in believing that my parents knew what was best for me. But I was wrong!" She raised herself on her toes and looked into his eyes. "I told you before, and I am repeating it again. I love *you.* I want to marry *you.* No one else. And I don't give a rush if I must wear the same dress for the next twenty years . . . or if we have to live in a one-room hovel for the rest of our lives. So long as I am near you, then I shall be happy. And I shall make you happy, too."

She brushed another kiss across his lips and then let her hands drop. "And I am not giving up. I shall stay after you, Henry. I shall pester you, remain a thorn in your side, until you are ready to face the truth." She walked away then, but turned by the door to the stables. "Now, you of all people, a man who constantly preaches forgiveness, might consider practicing a little of that yourself."

"Clara . . . I . . ."

"I'll be back."

* * *

The sharp knock on the magistrate's door brought the man's head up.

"Bloody hell. What now?" Musgrave muttered before calling irritably, "Come in."

As the door opened, Sir Robert hastily covered the correspondence he'd been reading again and again for the past three days. He was not surprised at all to find Sir Thomas Purefoy accompanying Captain Wallis.

"How delightful to find you here at such an early hour of the morning, sir," Musgrave said, rising to his feet. "I was planning to stop at Woodfield House later today to give my regards to Miss Jane. I hear she is back from England."

"She is." Sir Thomas refused the offer of a chair.

"And did she have a pleasant stay?"

"Very. Thank you."

"You can leave us now, Captain," Musgrave said, dismissing the man.

"I hope you have no objections, Sir Robert, but I asked Wallis here to stay. This is not a social visit."

Musgrave nodded curtly and sat back in his chair behind his ornate desk. "What can we help you with today, Sir Thomas?"

The ex-magistrate took a folded quarto sheet of cheap, unmarked broadside from his pocket. Opening it, he flung it on Sir Robert's desk.

"These are circulating all over Munster. This one was found on the desk of the director of the new Butter Exchange in Cork City. Are you aware of it?"

"Yes, I am." Musgrave disdainfully brushed the paper aside. "I find nothing of value in it. None of the printers in Cork admit to having printed it. I think it is not worth the paper it is printed on."

Sir Thomas snatched up the paper, summarizing its contents as if Musgrave were not capable of comprehending it by himself. "It is a call for peace by the Whiteboys. By thunder, these notices say that the Shanavests are disbanding."

"I know what it says, Sir Thomas." He leaned back in his chair. "But as I said before, I find no value in it at all."

"And why is that, sir?"

"Because I shall accomplish the same thing without any noble peace offerings from them."

"And how is that?"

"By arresting and hanging them one by one . . . starting with their leaders." Musgrave smiled proudly. "This trash you hold shows that they are beaten. And now I shall crush them. With no leaders, there will be no band of ruffians. No band of ruffians, and there is no resistance. The lessons you have taught me have been invaluable, Sir Thomas. I am finally learning."

"You tried to take them before, but had no success."

"This time is different. I have bait, you see, and they shall come to me."

"What are you using as bait? Or should I ask . . . whom?"

"I am afraid I must refrain from answering."

"You do not trust me, Sir Robert?"

"It is not a matter of trust, sir, but the sensitiveness of the subject." Tired of the other man looming over him, Musgrave rose to his feet and faced the older man across the desk. "When you hanged those five Whiteboys nine years ago, you all but crushed the resistance in this area for years. Before dawn tomorrow, I shall hang four of the most active of the rebel leaders and start my campaign to eradicate the Whiteboys entirely."

"But there was no offer of peace back then. I would not have ordered the killing if there had been an option."

"You say that now, but I think not." Musgrave shrugged. "We all want to leave a legacy behind. I should like to be remembered as the one who hanged the cursed Liam . . . and Patrick . . . and Finn . . . and Egan. Yes, I should like it much better than being remembered as the foolish magistrate who agreed to let them disperse . . . for as long as it suited them."

Sir Thomas leaned menacingly over the desk. "We are discussing human lives. You kill those people now, and you stir up rebellion in others. Vengeance drives people to do mad things, Musgrave. The course you are choosing will bring unnecessary dangers to our own people's lives."

"How different a tune I hear now, Sir Thomas, from the one you were whistling scarcely a month ago."

"Speak plainly, Musgrave."

"Excuse me, Sir Thomas, but we are all entitled to make our own mistakes before we learn from them." He motioned to Wallis to open the door. "Now if you will excuse me, I have a great deal of work left to do before the arrests and the executions tomorrow morning."

Purefoy's face was fiery with rage when he stormed from the room ahead of Captain Wallis, but Musgrave didn't care a whit. He dug out the familiar letter from beneath the other sheets of paper.

The official correspondence in his hand had come from the Lord Lieutenant of Ireland three days ago. Musgrave had been called back to England. He was relieved of his duties . . . immediately.

He was no fool. He knew Nicholas Spencer was responsible for this. The insolent dog had been the only one who had ever threatened his authority, and Spencer had been completely charmed by the beautiful slut, Jane Purefoy. He must have acted quickly when he'd gotten to England.

The magistrate threw the correspondence back on his desk. Well, the Lord Lieutenant would have to wait, for he was going nowhere until he had finished with his plans. Indeed, Sir Nicholas's interest in the Purefoys would make her hanging all that much more satisfying.

Yes, some had to die—most especially Egan—before Musgrave obeyed any order inveigled by some cocky London rogue.

And yes, despite the former magistrate's illustrious past, Sir Robert didn't trust Sir Thomas Purefoy further than the length of his own sword.

Nicholas's arms tightened instinctively around Jane as she tried to slide from the bed. She turned and found him sound asleep. A tighter knot grew in her throat, strangling her, but she again fought back the tears. She forced herself to lift his hand slowly off her stomach as she slipped from under it.

Jane knew she was on the verge of falling apart, so she hastily pulled on her clothes. At the door, she looked one last time at his muscular arm spread over the side of the bed where she'd been pretending to sleep only minutes ago.

She had refused to get involved with announcements and wedding plans today. This day had belonged to only the two of them. Their lovemaking tonight had been hungry. She had touched him and kissed him and given herself to him as if there were no tomorrow.

And indeed, there would be no tomorrow.

He had wanted to talk of the future, but she could not bear it. She had wanted only rapture, the pure and simple joy of drowning in the moment, in the night, in each other.

She gave him one last look and a smile. Then she slipped out of his chamber, finally letting the tears fall, marking their final farewell.

Jane had to stop at her room and change into the clothing that signified that she was Egan. Although by dawn there would be no question that the two were one and the same, she refused to give Musgrave the satisfaction of arresting Jane Purefoy. No, it would be Egan that he hanged . . . Jane Purefoy would remain in the heart of the man she'd just left.

The ritual of carefully putting her hat on and pulling it low over her eyes, of sliding the dagger into its sheath, of tucking her pistol into her belt, was performed slowly, thoughtfully. Each movement brought back to her fully the purpose behind the cause she'd been fighting for. Each movement, completed one last time, fortified her spirit that she was dying that others would live.

She used the secret passageway to make her way to the stables. It was already past midnight, and the familiar sounds and smells of the old dark structure struck her fully tonight. These were things she wanted embedded in her memory, as well. She moved silently toward Mab's stall.

Aside from losing a life with Nicholas, she had one

great regret. Musgrave. The man would probably be li-
onized in the Houses of Parliament for his attention to
duty, cheered in the offices of the Lord Lieutenant,
toasted in the homes of English landowners.

But he had no empathy for the Irish. He would never
feel remorse for his brutality. Egan had a hard time believing he would go through with his promise to free the
families of Liam and Patrick in an exchange. She had
said so last night. But the other three men had been
willing to trust in Musgrave's honor.

She had the sickening feeling that *everyone* was to
suffer tonight.

Egan frowned when she looked into Mab's empty
stall. Confused, she looked for her saddle and found that
missing, too. Hoping that Paul had been alerted to when
she would need the mare, she walked out to the paddock, where the stable master might possibly be waiting
with her horse.

It was all quiet there, too. No horse, no Paul, no
anyone.

Beginning to feel a little rattled—for time was running
short—she moved hurriedly into another stall and saddled one of her father's horses instead. In all these years
nothing like this had ever happened. Paul knew that
Mab was not to be moved or ridden by anyone else.
Everyone knew.

A few minutes later, she left Woodfield House behind
and galloped through the night. The more she thought
of it as she rode, though, Egan was actually relieved that
Queen Mab, at least, would not fall into Musgrave's
hands.

The sharp knock on the door brought the startled
magistrate straight up in his bed. His mind and his eyes
needed a moment to adjust to the suddenness of the
disturbance. A soldier's urgent call outside his door
made him push the covers aside and rush to the door.
His unhappy manservant stood holding a candle behind
a young dragoon.

"What?" he screamed at the young man, who stood
ready to knock again on the door.

"'Tis Captain Wallis, sir." The soldier took a step backward. "He . . . he has . . . left the barracks. I rode here directly to let you know."

"Left to go where?" Musgrave snapped.

"To Cuchulainn's Seat."

The confusion and question must have shown in Musgrave's face as the young man quickly explained again.

"The captain and two dozen of his personal guard took all the prisoners for the exchange with the rebels. The captain told Corporal Evans that the meeting place and time had changed, and . . . and that you were already aware of it."

"What?" Musgrave's roar sent both soldier and servant back another step.

"We . . . had . . . no way . . . of knowing . . . sir . . . until . . . Sergeant Powers came back on duty . . . and he said . . . if you didn't go with them . . . then you didn't know. Begging your par—"

"When did they leave?" Musgrave shouted as he rushed about his room, dressing in haste.

"Just over an hour ago, sir . . ."

"Wake up whoever is left in the barracks." As the man leaped to go and do as he was told, a forbidding thought occurred to the magistrate. *"Wait!"*

Thinking a moment, he then gave the dragoon specific instructions of whom he should fetch . . . including his own man Sergeant Powers.

Captain Wallis had far more influence with these soldiers than he'd been able to achieve himself. And if the treacherous dragoon officer had decided to garner a few laurels for himself, then Musgrave doubted he would be able to get all of Wallis's men to fight against him.

But there were always a select few who stayed loyal to a cause.

Yes, this select few would be all that Musgrave needed to snuff out this untimely show of independence.

Chapter 33

The light from the torches on the ruined walls of the castle could be seen easily from the distance. As Musgrave and his men drew near, two dragoons appeared, riding toward them. The magistrate didn't order his own troop to stop until the oncoming riders had reached them.

"Where is Captain Wallis? What is the meaning of this?"

"He is waiting for you at Cuchulainn's Seat, sir," one of the men replied. "The exchange has been made."

Musgrave stifled his angry outburst. "He has the rebels?"

"Aye, sir," the second soldier responded.

Cursing openly, the magistrate spurred his horse ahead of the others. Halfway up the hill, another half-dozen dragoons were guarding a number of horses. He paused by the group momentarily. Jane's high-spirited mare pranced among the rest.

"Whose horse was that?" he asked brusquely.

"The rebel Egan's. She is in shackles up there with the other three."

His temper somewhat controlled, Musgrave ordered his own men to take positions along the road up the hill with the rest of the dragoons. Now that he had the rebels, there would be no taking them away. This might be a salvageable situation, after all.

Captain Wallis saluted smartly but was obviously avoiding looking at him directly as the magistrate remained atop his horse.

"There was no waiting, Sir Robert. The blackguards sent the message that they did not trust us to release their women and children in Buttevant. They wanted to make the exchange here. That was easily accomplished. We sent their women and children down that hill, one by one, as the leaders came up the same road." Wallis motioned for a soldier to take the bridle of the magistrate's horse as he finally dismounted. "This is the kind of action you have been encouraging for some time, sir. I know how much the arrest of these people means to you. I did not want to lose the—"

"Take me to them," Musgrave snapped at the man.

Of course, the Irish bastards were right. He had no plans of freeing those families. How much more dramatic the final execution would be with the wives and children watching and weeping. How much fiercer his reputation would be when he then marched the families directly to the docks and onto a ship bound for Australia!

He fell in step with Wallis. Of course, one of the disgraced families would remain. What a stir that would make in the Lord Lieutenant's office! They could do nothing to him, the hero who had ferreted out the very daughter of the great Sir Thomas Purefoy.

"There they are, sir." The captain gestured toward what must have been at one time the keep's great hall. A gaping hole showed that the floor was only slightly above the castle courtyard.

Looking through the crumbled stone walls, he could see the four people crouched down with their hands behind their backs, tied to each other in a circle. Musgrave pushed Wallis aside and climbed the half-dozen steps to the entryway.

They all were wearing black. No white shirts for them today, he noted. A woolen hood had been pulled over each prisoner's head. Musgrave roughly yanked the hood off the first. The man's head jerked back, and Sir Robert studied the rebel's calm expression. He showed no fear, in spite of the noose that was awaiting him.

"This one calls himself Patrick," Wallis quickly offered from the doorway.

Musgrave kicked the second man before pulling the hood off his head. This one's face showed his hatred, and he growled something in Gaelic.

"Liam," the captain said.

Musgrave gave the rebel another solid kick and moved on. He was about to pull the hood off the next one when something occurred to him. Of the two that were left, one had to be Egan. Wallis had met and seen Jane Purefoy on a number of occasions over the past few years. Why, he wondered, hadn't the captain mentioned the taking of the former magistrate's daughter?

From the long legs and size of the boots, Musgrave could tell the next rebel was a man. He stepped past him and stood over the last hooded figure.

From beneath the shapeless woolen sack, he could see tendrils of dark hair showing.

"Am I correct to assume this one is Egan?"

"She is, sir. You cannot imagine our surprise in finding that we knew her."

His elation returned, and he yanked the bag off her head. As the woman's dark eyes snapped up to his, Musgrave stared for only an instant before drawing the dagger from his boot.

"There shall be no hanging for this one."

Stepping beside her, he quickly put the knife to her throat.

"Drop it now . . . or you shall die." With the point of the knife pressed against the woman's throat, Musgrave looked up in surprise at the pistol pointed at him. Rage boiled up inside him when he met Sir Thomas's cold gaze.

"What do you care if she dies?"

"If one drop of her blood is drawn, you are a dead man."

"Very clever of you to hide your daughter and switch this one in her place." Musgrave's hand didn't waver. "But regardless of whatever you think you are doing, as magistrate I can do as I please."

"You were formally relieved of the duties and authority of magistrate nearly a week ago."

"That's a lie." Musgrave cast a quick look at the number of dragoons who had gathered behind Wallis. "Arrest this man. He is interfering with—"

"Both Captain Wallis and I received copies of the letter sent to you by the Lord Lieutenant. We had our own additional orders attached to it."

"This is a trick." He looked angrily at the watching soldiers. "You just want to execute these four yourself. You then can keep your slut of a daughter and still add to your glory!"

"As I tried to make you understand yesterday, with the Whiteboys offering to disband, our best course is to let them. Our own landowners and the tradesmen in Cork City are tired of the injustices Parliament is afflicting us all with. Our own people are crying out for change."

"You mean your daughter."

Sir Thomas ignored the comment and spoke clearly and methodically. "Killing these people will only stir the cauldron of violence. Hang them and it could be another dozen years before we have a chance of bringing any real peace to this region. Now drop that knife."

Musgrave's attention shifted to the man entering the hall from a side chamber with one of Wallis's dragoons behind him. Spencer.

"You . . . !"

The former magistrate saw the look in Musgrave's face change. As the man yanked back the woman's head to make the lethal cut, Sir Thomas fired his pistol. Musgrave's body jerked with the bullet's impact, and as his dagger fell harmlessly in the woman's lap, he dropped like a stone to the ground.

Pandemonium immediately erupted in the castle and down the hill. Shouts and orders rang out from Captain Wallis.

Nicholas tucked his own pistol back into his belt, hardly glancing at Musgrave as he stepped over the dead body. Sir Thomas was checking the neck of the woman as Nicholas pulled the hood off the last rebel's head. Paul's grinning face was the one that looked up at him.

"That bullet came a wee bit close, I'm thinking?" he said with a chuckle.

"Closer than you know," Nicholas replied with a nod toward Sir Thomas. Quickly Nicholas freed the man's hands and cut the ropes holding the others.

Acting on Sir Thomas's and Captain Wallis's orders, the stable master had arranged for himself and the other three servants to substitute themselves for the rebels. The Lord Lieutenant's directions were clear. The two were to assess Musgrave's response to being relieved before acting to forcibly remove him. No one knew, though, how far he would go.

"You need to catch up to them," Sir Thomas ordered Nicholas. "Before they walk through those barrack gates in Buttevant."

"Are you coming along? You were the one who made this work. I think they should know it."

Sir Thomas shook his head. "Until the Lord Lieutenant sends another magistrate I must act for the Crown." He lowered his voice. "The devil take me, I have no wish to be in a position of identifying any of these rebels if this madman's replacement should ask me."

Nicholas knew that Sir Thomas might retain the position of acting magistrate for years . . . if the Crown's bureaucracy functioned with its usual lack of efficiency. But the man was correct; it would be better for him not to see the faces of the rebels. And one rebel, in particular.

As Nicholas turned to leave, Sir Thomas stopped him. "But . . ." The old warrior's face softened slightly. "But tell Jane I'm trying."

There were still two hours left till dawn when the four rebels approached the last hill. Beyond it, they knew, lay the River Awbeg and the village of Buttevant.

The moon, still high in the sky, illuminated the solitary rider waiting for them on the crest of the hill. Jane immediately recognized him. She would know him anywhere.

"I did not tell him," she said quickly, seeing Henry's sharp look. "I told no one."

Not waiting for a response from the others, she spurred her horse toward Nicholas. He, too, having recognized them, rode in her direction. She couldn't be angry with him for being here. But seeing him this last time only added to the piercing pain of losing him.

The tears were already dancing on her face when she reached him. "What are you doing here?"

"Tell them to go back," he urged, nodding toward the three men who had reined in their horses. "There is no longer any need for an exchange."

"Nicholas, we *must* go or innocent people will die."

"Their families were freed tonight. But these men must turn back before one of Musgrave's men sees them and decides to finish something that his leader could not."

"I do not understand."

"Then come with me so I can explain it to them, as well."

Feeling somewhat stunned, Jane watched Nicholas nudge his horse toward the other riders. Pausing for a second to make sure she was indeed awake and that this wasn't a dream, she started after him.

None of them had bothered with masks tonight, and Nicholas simply stared for a moment when he came face-to-face with Henry Adams.

Jane addressed Liam and Patrick. "Sir Nicholas says that your wives and children have been freed."

Nicholas went on to explain that Musgrave had been killed tonight and the new, temporary magistrate strongly believed that he should reciprocate the offer of peace by the Shanavests.

Patrick and Liam looked at each other in disbelief.

"But as I was telling Jane, for the next few hours and until the change of command is completed, we do not want you anywhere near Buttevant."

Clearly neither Patrick nor Liam seemed to be able to fathom what he was hearing, and they looked at Henry in confusion.

"Sir Nicholas is not one to lie," the parson assured them quietly and confidently.

The burst of excitement from the two men was instantaneous. Patrick leaned over his horse and took Jane in an affectionate hug.

"Well, Egan . . . er, Miss Jane. Why not bring this

one around, sometime? Some o' these English can grow on ye."

"I thought you were disbanding," Nicholas said, apprehension creasing his brow.

"Patrick is talking about raising a cup or two, if I'm not mistaken," Liam said.

"Aye. Come around anytime. My wife brews the best ale from here to Limerick."

"I am not doing anything right now."

"Oh, yes, you are." Jane put a hand out and took hold of the bridle of Nicholas's horse, eliciting teasing comments and catcalls from the two men.

With a few parting words, Patrick and Liam rode off in the same direction they had all come. Henry, though, stayed and faced Nicholas's open amusement.

"Then you must be . . ."

"Finn," Henry said quietly.

"But why?" Nicholas questioned, his face growing serious. "What did Sir Thomas say? 'What would a respectable English churchman be doing fighting for a handful of discontented papist peasants?' "

"The answer is not so easy. I may have begun fighting for them because I witnessed great injustice . . . or because I believe compassion belongs to no single religion." Henry gave a short laugh. "Or maybe because, as the second son of an English naval hero, I have too much fight in my blood."

"I didn't even know that Henry was Finn until two nights ago," Jane admitted.

"Even though Liam and Jenny have known it for some time, I would have continued to keep that little secret if circumstances had allowed it."

With their horses standing side by side, Nicholas and Jane had at some point clasped hands. Henry's gaze now fell on their entwined fingers. "Mrs. Brown tells me there are marriage plans in the works."

Jane turned and smiled at Nicholas. "Now there are."

"Would you do us the honor of wedding us in your chapel?" Nicholas asked Henry.

"The honor will be mine," the parson replied pleasantly. "Of course, that is if I fail to convince Clara that she should marry me on the same day." He rubbed his chin thoughtfully and met Nicholas's astonished gaze. "You see, I am nothing more than a poor parish minister and it only makes sense for you to pay for the two sisters' wedding feast."

"I will be happy to pay for a honeymoon on the Continent for you and your bride, Parson Adams, so long as this wedding takes place in less than a month."

The two men grinned and shook hands on it, and Jane couldn't remember a happier moment in her life.

Henry rode away, leaving Jane misty-eyed and overwhelmed by this sudden turn of events. She looked into Nicholas's eyes. "You knew I was going away last night. Thank you for not trying to stop me."

He brought her hand to his lips. "You were Egan long before I met you. Your dedication and honor were on the line tonight. I knew you would not have me until you felt your duty had been done."

"You helped me . . . helped us. You saved our lives."

"But I cannot take credit for the events of tonight."

"I recall Stanmore mentioning some correspondence regarding Musgrave when we were in London."

"That was just a preliminary step," he admitted, smiling crookedly. "Through some people I know, I was able to persuade the Lord Lieutenant of Ireland that Musgrave was teetering on madness. Sir Robert was issued an order and called back to England, but when we arrived here, I found out that the cur was ignoring the order."

They nudged their horses down the hill and away from Buttevant.

"Someone else was far more influential in what happened tonight."

Her mind raced, trying to think of whom he could mean, to no avail.

"Sir Thomas," he said.

As the name sank in, a hundred feelings washed through Jane. Shame mixed with pride. Relief mixed with disbelief. Gratitude mixed with hope. She looked blankly ahead and they rode along in silence.

"He saved my life," she finally blurted out. "He saved

the lives of these men and their families. And yet, I . . .
I cannot bring myself to face him . . . to thank him."

"I think he knew as much. He asked me only to tell
you that he is trying."

She stabbed away at a runaway tear. "It was so much
easier to hate him—to ignore the possibility that he had
some compassion left in him."

"I do not believe he expects you to forgive and to
forget overnight. At the same time, I believe that he is
trying to be a different man. Perhaps you should simply
let it rest at that." Nicholas's hand reached for hers
again. He pressed her fingers again to his lips. "I believe
the sun is about to rise for us."

Jane looked up to the sky lightening in the east. A
new day beginning. She let out a ragged breath and tried
to cleanse her mind and heart of everything that was
past. She met Nicholas's loving gaze and thought of their
own new beginning—of their marriage.

"Us! I love that word," he teased.

"Us," she repeated, and then smiled. "I must say you
were pretty easily gulled into paying for my sister's
honeymoon."

He laughed. "I would pay for a honeymoon for everyone from Cork City to—where did Patrick say?"

"Limerick."

"I would pay that and more for that smile on your
face."

She leaned toward him. "I should have asked for
more."

"Anything, my love," he said, pressing his lips to hers.

She drew away, but for only a moment.

"Well . . ." she whispered, smiling happily. "This is
all I shall ever want. Just 'us.' "

Epilogue

London, Christmas Eve

She could have been murdered on the Cheapside. She could have been drowned in the Thames. She could have been kidnapped in Westminster.

Nicholas stormed in the front door, stomping the snow off his boots. He'd been to Stanmore's . . . and to his mother's new house. No one had seen any sign of her.

He threw off his cloak and hat as Charles appeared. "We've been scouring the neighborhoods, Sir Nicholas. Nothing. Mrs. Hannagan's about to have a stroke for worry, sir, and the guests are arriving in an hour."

"Damn the guests." He turned to one of the grooms. "Did you check again with Mrs. Cawardine?"

"Aye, sir. The painter lady was certain that her ladyship had promised to come by for luncheon with Sir Joshua Reynolds himself, sir, but she never arrived."

Nicholas glanced at his pocket watch. It was already past six. Queasiness had gripped his stomach an hour ago when she should have been home, and it still had him. She hadn't looked very well this morning. He should have been more forceful in asking her to stay at home.

If anything had happened to her, he'd just . . .

"The carriage, Sir Nicholas!" the footman shouted in the front door. "Just coming up the Square, sir!"

Nicholas strode out the door, pushing past the man and frowning up at the worried-looking driver reining in the team before the house. As the carriage lurched to a stop, Nicholas yanked open the door, only to see his beautiful wife's smiling face greeting him. She was shivering in her gray wool dress. No cloak. No hat and gloves, and God knew what else was missing. At least she had a blanket around her.

"You gave them away again to some poor beggar on the street, didn't you? By 'sblood, Jane, how many times must I tell you that if you catch your death in this cold . . ."

"Now, Nicholas . . . there is no need to frighten these two friends of mine." She pulled down the blanket covering her lap and the filthy faces of two street urchins peered out from either side of her.

He immediately climbed into the carriage and closed the door to keep out some of the cold. "Who are these two? And where did you find them?"

"They haven't told me their names, yet." She hugged each of them to her side. "But I think proper introductions can only be made after they get a warm meal in their bellies and a warmer bath."

Nicholas sighed in resignation. "And would you like Mrs. Hannagan and Charles to entertain the guests while we take these two to Angel Court?"

"No! It is Christmas Eve, Nicholas." She gave him a pleading look. "Can't they stay with us . . . for a while, anyway?"

It was impossible for Nicholas to refuse his wife anything. He wrapped his coat around her and motioned through the window of the carriage for Charles to approach.

The children were wrapped in the blanket and hurried into the house, but Jane put a hand on his knee, holding him for a moment.

"Nick, it is all right, isn't it?"

He put his arms around her, grateful that she was home and safe.

"The poor, dear creatures were so lost . . . and alone . . . and hungry. Everyone I asked on the street said they'd just been sleeping in an alley and begging there for weeks." Her eyes shone with her tears. "You don't mind me bringing them here, do you?"

He shook his head and pulled her tightly against his chest. "I don't mind at all, my love."

She held tightly to his hand. "But you've already told me it is generally better for these children to move into one of the houses . . . since there may be other children there that they know . . . and . . ."

"It is very well to bring them here, too," he assured her, kissing the wetness off her cheeks.

"And we can raise the three of them together. We can take—"

"Three?" he asked, looking around the carriage.

When she took his hand and guided it to her belly, his words caught in his throat. He stared at his own fingers spreading possessively over the life that was growing inside her.

"Jane . . ."

She nodded once. "One more wee one won't be too much trouble?"

There was no fighting his emotions.

"Not at all, my love." He drew her tightly against him again and let his own joyful tear fall. "Not at all."

Author's Note

Since the twelfth century, England's heavy hand has gripped Ireland's heart.

Peaceful settlers. Conquerors. Colonizers. The English have been a part of Irish history for nearly a millennium. Since almost the beginning, they have tried to dominate and plunder this land of artists, scholars, and saints.

In the early eighteenth century, the governments under the first Hanover kings began instituting "Penal Laws" that were intended to strip the Irish of all land and all civil rights. The brutal and repressive policies imposed on the Irish at the time have been described as no less than cultural genocide. By the mid to late 1700s, however, the English landowners and merchants who had been long settled in Ireland were also chafing under the repressive colonial policies. Many saw the essential unfairness of the situation for the Irish, too, and petitioned for changes. They were, however, largely without a voice in Parliament. The situation for the Irish was truly desperate, and they began to organize themselves into resistance movements from Tipperary to Ulster.

The Whiteboys that you have just read about were a real part of that resistance. All over Ireland, these groups sprang up. The Ribbonmen. The Defenders. The Oakboys. The Rightboys. Every part of Ireland had its own bone of contention, and every resistance movement had an organized response to it.

When we introduced Sir Nicholas Spencer in *The Promise*, we knew—long before we ever finished Rebecca and Stanmore's story—that he was a man who needed a very special heroine. Jane Purefoy and her volatile and dangerous world in Ireland seemed to offer us just that. We hope you enjoyed the story.

Finally, we'd like to thank Timothy O'Sullivan for his help with Gaelic. We'd also like to thank Miriam O'Sullivan—friend, expert on Ireland, and travel agent extraordinaire—and her husband, Greg O'Sullivan, who not only helped us with our research but also helped to keep us safe from "bears" taking up residence in our garage! Thank you.

As always, we love to hear from our readers. Email us at mcgoldmay@aol.com. Or visit us at www.May McGoldrick.com.

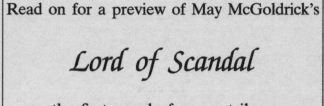

Read on for a preview of May McGoldrick's

Lord of Scandal

the first novel of a new trilogy

London
January 1772

"We are going in the wrong direction!"

Instead of turning and passing under the ancient Temple Bar, the carriage had turned east on Fleet Street, and the driver was now whipping his team through the busy traffic going into the City. The lawyer raised the head of his cane to the roof of the carriage to get the attention of the driver, but the touch of Millicent Wentworth's gloved hand on his sleeve made him stop.

"He is going where he was directed, Sir Oliver. There is an urgent matter I need to see to at the wharves."

"At the wharves? But . . . but we are already somewhat pressed for time for your appointment, m'lady."

"This shall not take very long."

He sank back against the seat, somewhat relieved. "Since we have a little time then, perhaps I could ask you a few more questions about the secretive nature of this meeting we have been summoned to attend this morning."

"Please, Sir Oliver," Millicent pleaded quietly. "Can your questions wait until after my business at the wharves? I am afraid my mind is rather distracted right now."

All his questions withered on the man's tongue as

Lady Wentworth turned her face to the window and the passing street scene. A short time later the carriage passed by St. Paul's Cathedral and began wending its way through a rough and odorous area in the direction of the Thames. By the time they crossed Fish Street, with its derelict sheds and warehouses, the lawyer could not restrain himself any longer.

"Would you at least tell me the nature of this business at the wharves, m'lady?"

"We are going to an auction."

Oliver Birch looked out the window at the milling crowds of workmen and pickpockets and whores.

"M'lady, I hope you intend to stay in the carriage and that you will allow me to instruct one of the footmen to obtain what you are looking for."

"I am sorry, sir, but it is essential that I see to this myself."

The lawyer grasped the side of the rocking carriage as the driver turned into the courtyard of a tumbledown wreck of a building on Brooke's Wharf. Outside the window, an odd mix of well-dressed gentlemen and shabby merchants and seamen stood in attendance on an auction that was already well under way, from the looks of things.

"At least give me the details of what you intend to do here, Lady Wentworth." Birch climbed out of the carriage first. Despite the biting wind off the Thames, the smells of the place—combined with the stink of the river—were appalling.

"I read about the auction in the *Gazette* this morning. This is the estate of a financially ruined physician by the name of Dombey who moved back from Jamaica last fall." She pulled the hood up on her woolen cloak and accepted his hand as she stepped out. "Instead of going to debtor's prison, Mr. Dombey last week took his own life."

Birch had to hurry to keep up with Millicent as she pushed her way through the crowd to the front row. "And what, may I ask, in Mr. Dombey's estate is of interest to you?"

She didn't answer immediately, and the lawyer found

his client's gray eyes searching anxiously among the few piles of personal articles that were left on a makeshift platform.

"I hope I am not too late."

The lawyer did not ask any more questions as Millicent's attention turned sharply on the set of wide doors that led into the building. The bailiff was dragging out a frail-looking black woman wrapped in a tattered blanket. A crate was placed on the platform, and the old woman—her neck and hands and feet in shackles—was pushed roughly onto it.

Birch closed his eyes for a moment to control his disgust at this evidence of the barbaric and dishonorable trade that continued to curse the nation.

"Lookee, gennelmen. This here hag was Dr. Dombey's personal maid," the auctioneer shouted. "She's the only Negro the medical bloke carried back with him from Jamaica. Aye, sure, she's a rum thing with her wrinkled black face. And she's of an age to rival Methuselah. But gennelmen, she's said to be a weritable African queen, she is, and bright as crystal, they tell me. So e'en though she's worth a good thirty pounds, what say we start the bidding at . . . at a pound."

There was loud jeering and laughter from the group.

"Look now, gennelmen. 'Ow about ten shillings then?" the auctioneer announced over the roar of the crowd. "She's good teeth, she has." He roughly pulled open the woman's mouth. There were crusts of blood on the chapped lips. "Ten shillings? Who'll start the bidding at ten shillings?"

"What bloody good is she?" somebody shouted.

"Five, gennelmen. Who'll start us at five?"

"The woman is nothing more than a refuse slave," another responded. "If we were in Port Royal, she'd be left to die on the wharf."

Birch glanced worriedly at Millicent and found a look of pain etched on her face. There were tears glimmering on the edges of her eyelids.

"This is no place for you to be, m'lady," he whispered quietly. "It is not right for you to be witnessing this. Whatever you came for must be already gone."

"The advertisement said she was a fine African lass."

A middle-aged clerk, sneering from his place at the edge of the platform, threw a crumpled *Gazette* up at the old woman. "Why, she's too old to even be good for—"

"Five pounds," Millicent called out.

Every eye in the place turned to her, and silence gripped the throng. Even the auctioneer seemed lost for words for a moment. Birch saw the woman's wrinkled eyelids open a fraction and stare at Millicent.

"Aye, yer ladyship. Yer bid is in fer—"

"Six pounds." A second bid from someone deep in the crowd silenced the auctioneer again. All heads in unison turned to the back of the auction yard.

"Seven," Millicent responded.

"Eight."

On the platform the man's face broke out into a grin as the crowds parted and a well-dressed gentleman stepped to the front. "Why, Sir Jasper, 'tis a pleasure, sir."

"Ten pounds," Millicent said with great vehemence.

Birch turned to study the man who had lately positioned himself as Lady Wentworth's chief nemesis. Sir Jasper Hyde, a large plantation owner in the Caribbean and supposedly a good friend to the late Squire Wentworth, had been pressuring Millicent on many occasions for the past six months.

"Twenty."

"Thirty."

The lawyer turned to Millicent.

"He is playing with you, m'lady," he said quietly. "I don't believe it would be wise—"

"Fifty pounds." From his tone Sir Jasper might as well have been requesting his gloves and hat from a doorman.

There was a loud gasp of disbelief.

"I can't let him do this," she explained quietly while giving a nod to the auctioneer for a raise in the amount to seventy pounds. "Dr. Dombey and this woman spent some time on Wentworth's plantations in Jamaica. From the stories I've heard from Jonah and some of the others at Melbury Hall, she is a person of great importance to them."

"One hundred pounds." Jasper Hyde's bid made the crowd shift uncomfortably.

"He only wants her in order to punish me," Millicent whispered, turning away from the stage. "This is retribution for not agreeing to his terms and selling Wentworth's plantations to him. He will hurt her . . . kill her, perhaps . . . and then be sure that I learn of every ugly detail of it." Her hands fisted. "I owe this to my people after everything Wentworth made them suffer."

"That it, yer ladyship?" the auctioneer asked. "Yer giving in?"

"One hundred ten," she relied, her voice quavering.

"You cannot afford this, m'lady," Birch put in firmly but quietly. "Think of the promissory notes Hyde already holds from your husband. You've extended the date of repayment once. But they will all come due next month, and you are personally liable . . . to the extent of every last thing you own. And this includes Melbury Hall . . . and even the Africans on the plantation in Jamaica. You just cannot add more fuel to his fire."

"One hundred twenty," Jasper Hyde put in casually.

The rumbling in the crowd became more pronounced. There were even some comments to the effect that he should let the woman have the slave.

"One thirty, milady?" the man on the platform asked with an excited grin.

"You cannot save every one of them, Millicent," Birch whispered sharply. When first asked by the Earl and the Countess of Stanmore to represent Lady Wentworth in her legal affairs a year ago, he'd also been informed of the woman's great compassion for the Africans that her late husband had held as slaves. But no warning came close to the truth that he'd witnessed since knowing her.

Wiping a tear from her face, Millicent started pushing her way out and toward the carriage through the crowds. Halfway out of the yard, though, she swung around and raised a hand.

"One hundred thirty."

A round of exclamations erupted from the crowd. Gradually, people parted until she was facing Sir Jasper across the mud and dirt of the yard. The man's high beaver skin hat and his jacket were of the latest fashion and impeccably clean. His boots shone despite the muck everyone else had to step through. His cold and almost translucent blue eyes regarded her for a moment before he waved a cane dismissively at the auctioneer. "I would just as soon allow Lady Wentworth to have her Negro at the price of a hundred thirty pounds."

There was no noise from the circle of men as he started toward Millicent. Two bruisers stepped out of the crowd and took their places on each side of their master, escorting him.

Birch stepped forward to shield his client. "Why not wait in the carriage, m'lady? I will take care of the details here."

"I am not afraid of him, Sir Oliver." She moved beside him.

Millicent Gregory Wentworth could not be considered a great beauty, nor could her sense of style be called au courant by the standards of London's *ton*. But what she lacked in those items—and in the false pride so fashionable of late—she made up in dignity and humanity. And all of this despite a lifetime of oppression and bad luck.

"Lady Wentworth, what a delight to run into you on such a dreary day." Hyde gave a polite bow and stopped a short distance away. "My apologies for not realizing you had arrived in London, or I would have paid you a visit. How long are you planning to stay?"

"If you will forgive me, sir, I have neither the time nor the patience at present for pointless conversation, so good day." She nodded her head before turning away.

"Hardly pointless, considering that as the creditor to Dr. Dombey's estate, it is my natural curiosity to know when and how you intend to pay for your purchase."

Millicent somehow managed to hide her astonishment. But Birch was not too successful. For the first time in years, he found himself ready to strike a man. And he noticed that more than a few in the crowd shared his sentiments, as several shifted and murmured menacing comments.

"You took advantage of me, sir," Lady Wentworth finally managed to say, eliciting a few loud words of agreement from the onlookers. "You drove up the price purposely."

Hyde's men stared down the few complaining souls around them.

"Now, I don't know why you would say something like that. But back to the settlement arrangements. I am afraid, considering the large number of promissory notes I hold from you, that—"

"You mean, from Squire Wentworth."

He waved her off. "Still, my good lady, you have no credit available with me, and I cannot hand over the slave until payment has been made."

Millicent reddened. Her gloved hands were shaking, and Birch saw her tuck them into the folds of her cloak. "You shall be paid, sir."

"I'm afraid I must demand payment by this afternoon or—"

"Send your agent to my office in the Middle Temple at two o'clock, and your money will be waiting," the lawyer cut in. "And make sure the woman is delivered at the said time."

"I *can* afford to pay for her, Sir Oliver," Millicent asserted as soon as they were back in the carriage.

"I know you can, m'lady. But I didn't think you cared to continue that hostile public confrontation any longer."

"No, I didn't. Thank you," she said quietly, looking out the small window of the carriage. The slave woman had already been removed from the stage. Millicent couldn't help but worry about how much more pain these horrible people were going to inflict on her before she was brought to the lawyer's office this afternoon.

As they rode along in silence through the city, she thought of the money she'd just spent. A hundred thirty pounds was equivalent to seven months' worth of salaries of all twenty servants she employed at Melbury Hall. It was true that this purchase would cut deeply into her quickly shrinking funds. And she wasn't even considering the money that she needed to pay Sir Jasper next month. Millicent rubbed her fingers over a dull ache in her temple and tried to think only of how much good it would do bringing this woman back to Hertfordshire.

"Lady Wentworth," the lawyer said finally, breaking the silence as they drew near their destination, "we cannot put off discussing your appointment with the Dowager Countess Aytoun any longer. I am still completely in the dark concerning why we are going there."

"That makes two of us, Sir Oliver," she replied tiredly. "Her note summoning . . . inviting me . . . to meet with her arrived yesterday afternoon, and her servant stayed until I sent her an answer. I was to arrive at the Earl of Aytoun's Hanover Square town house today at eleven a.m. with my attorney. Nothing more was said."

"This sounds very abrupt. Do you know the countess? Have you ever met?"

Millicent shook her head. "I don't. But at the same time, I didn't know Jasper Hyde, either. Nor the half-dozen creditors before him who have endeavored to come after me from every quarter since Wentworth's death." She pulled the cloak tighter around herself. "One thing I've learned this past year and a half is that there is no hiding away from those to whom my husband owed money. I have to face them—one by one—and try to make some kind of feasible arrangement to pay them back."

"You know that I admire you greatly in your efforts, but we both know you are encumbered almost beyond the point of recovery already." He paused. "But you have some very generous friends, Lady Wentworth. If you would allow me to reveal to them just a hint of your hardship . . ."

"No, sir," she said sharply. "I find no shame in being poor. But I find great dishonor in begging. Please, I don't care to hear any more of this."

"As you wish, m'lady."

Millicent nodded gratefully at her lawyer. Sir Oliver had already served her well, and she trusted that he would honor her request.

"To set your mind a little at ease, though," he continued, "you should know that the Dowager Countess Aytoun is socially situated far differently than Sir Jasper . . . or your late husband. She is a woman of great wealth, but she is rumored to be exceedingly . . . well, *careful* with her money. Some say she is so tightfisted that her own servants must struggle to receive their wages. In short, I cannot see her lending any money to Squire Wentworth."

"I am relieved to hear that. I should have known that with your attention to detail we would not be walking into this meeting totally unprepared. What else have you learned about her, Sir Oliver?"

"She is Lady Archibald Pennington, Countess of Aytoun. Her given name is Beatrice. She's been a widow for more than five years. She is Scottish by birth, with blood of Highlanders in her veins. She comes from an ancient family, and married well besides. The countess led a very quiet life until the scandal that tore her family apart this past summer."

"She has children?"

Sir Oliver nodded. "Three sons. All men. Lyon Pennington, the fourth Earl of Aytoun. Pierce Pennington, who moved to the American colonies after the incident. And David Pennington, a soldier in the service of the king."

"You said there was a scandal."

"Indeed, m'lady. It involved a young lady named Emma Douglas. I understand all three brothers were incredibly fond of her. She ended up marrying the oldest brother and became the countess of Aytoun this past year."

Millicent had no chance to ask any more questions as their carriage rolled to a stop in front of an elegant mansion on Hanover Square. A servant in gold-trimmed livery greeted them as he opened the door of the carriage. Another servant escorted them up the wide marble steps to the front door.

Inside, the mansion was even more magnificent. As Millicent glanced around, they were informed by the steward that the dowager was waiting to receive them.

"What *was* the nature of the scandal?" she managed to whisper as she followed the steward and another servant up the sweeping circular stairs to a drawing room.

"Just rumors, m'lady," Birch whispered, "to the effect that the earl murdered his bride."

"But that is . . ."

The door to the drawing room was opened and they

were announced. Trying to contain her shock and curiosity, Millicent entered.

There were four people in the cozy, well-appointed room. The dowager countess, a pale gentleman standing by a desk that had a ledger book open on it, and two ladies' maids.

Lady Aytoun was an older woman, obviously in ill health. She was sitting on a sofa with pillows propped behind her and a blanket on her lap. Dark eyes studied the visitors from behind a pair of spectacles.

Millicent gave a small curtsy. "Our apologies, my lady, for being delayed."

"Did you win the auction?" The dowager's abrupt question caused Millicent to look over in surprise at Sir Oliver. He appeared as baffled as she was. "The African woman. Did you win the auction?"

"I . . . I did," she somehow managed to get out. "But how did you know about it?"

"How much?"

Millicent bristled at the inquiry, but at the same time she felt no shame for what she'd done. "One hundred thirty pounds. Though I must tell you I don't know what business it is of—"

"Add it to the tally, Sir Richard." The dowager waved a hand at the gentleman still standing by the desk. "A worthy cause!"

Millicent's lawyer stepped forward. "May I say, m'lady—"

"Come and sit. Both of you. And pray, save the idle prattle, young man."

Sir Oliver, who probably hadn't been addressed as "young man" in decades, stared openmouthed for a moment. Then, as he and Millicent did as they were instructed, the countess dismissed the servants with a wave of her hand.

"Very well. I know both of you, and you know me. This pasty-faced bag of bones is my lawyer, Sir Richard Maitland." The old woman arched an eyebrow in the direction of her attorney, who bowed stiffly and sat. "And now . . . the reason why I invited you here."

Millicent could not even hazard a guess as to what was coming next.

"People acting on my behalf have been reporting to me about you for some time now, Lady Wentworth. You have surpassed my expectations." Lady Aytoun removed her spectacles. "No reason for dallying. You are here because I have a business proposition."

"A business proposition?" Millicent murmured.

"Indeed. I want you to marry my son, the Earl of Aytoun. By a special license. Today."

ONYX

MAY McGOLDRICK

Three sisters each hold a clue to their family's treasure—and the key to the hearts of three Highland warriors....

THE DREAMER
0-451-19718-6

THE FIREBRAND
0-451-40942-6

THE ENCHANTRESS
0-451-19719-4

"May McGoldrick brings history to life."
—Patricia Gaffney

"Richly romantic." —Nora Roberts

To order call: 1-800-788-6262

"Brimming over with Passion and Excitement."
—Romantic Times

LAUREN ROYAL

AMETHYST   199510

A talented jeweler who's engaged to a man she does not love, Amethyst Goldsmith loses everything when the devastating fire of 1666 sweeps through London. But in the aftermath of disaster, she lands in the arms of the dashing, unattainable Earl of Graystone.

EMERALD   201426

Second in the dazzling *Jewel* trilogy, Royal presents the passionate adventure of Jason Chase, the Marquess of Cainewood...

AMBER   203917

The final novel in the acclaimed *Jewel* trilogy. When Kendra's brothers catch her with a mysterious highwayman, they demand that she marry him. But this dangerous, complex man may not be at all who he seems...

To order call: 1-800-788-6262